THE SHADOW REVOLUTION

By Clay Griffith and Susan Griffith

CROWN & KEY TRILOGY
The Shadow Revolution

VAMPIRE EMPIRE TRILOGY
The Greyfriar
The Rift Walker
The Kingmakers

THE SHADOW REVOLUTION

Crown & Key

Clay Griffith
and Susan Griffith

DEL REY • NEW YORK

The Shadow Revolution is a work of fiction. Names, characters, places, and incidents either are the product of imagination or are used fictitiously. Any resemblance to actual persons, living or dead, events, or locales is entirely coincidental.

A Del Rey Mass Market Original

Copyright © 2015 by Random House LLC
Excerpt from *The Undying Legion* by Clay Griffith and Susan Griffith copyright © 2015 by Random House LLC

Published in the United States by Del Rey, an imprint of Random House, a division of Random House LLC, a Penguin Random House Company, New York.

DEL REY and the HOUSE colophon are registered trademarks of Random House LLC.

This book contains an excerpt from the forthcoming book *The Undying Legion* by Clay Griffith and Susan Griffith. This excerpt has been set for this edition only and may not reflect the final content of the forthcoming edition.

ISBN 978-0-345-53950-2
eBook ISBN 978-0-345-53951-9

Printed in the United States of America

www.delreybooks.com

9 8 7 6 5 4 3 2 1

Del Rey mass market edition: June 2015

To our editors at Del Rey including Sarah and Tricia,
who have let us follow in the footsteps
of some of the people who inspired each of us.

Thanks to Stan, Jack, Steve, and John,
plus Ray and Forry. You guys are responsible.

To the fires of my forge—Joss Whedon,
Walter B. Gibson (or Maxwell Grant as he was known
to the world), hours of D&D, Elizabeth Peters,
Bernard Cornwell, Chris Claremont,
and Edgar Rice Burroughs.

THE SHADOW REVOLUTION

Chapter One

A BOLD MOON HUNG OVER THE DARK LONDON cityscape. A shroud of fog obscured the ever-present grime as yellow smudges of gas lamps created black silhouettes of the skyline. London showed its hidden nature only at night. People moved like wraiths, appearing out of nowhere, shades made suddenly solid.

The misty moonlight gave the city an otherworldly aspect in which Simon Archer reveled. He nodded amiably to passersby, but his senses were tuned to the indistinguishable world around him, listening, feeling for a shred of anything out of place.

"Do you know where you're going, Simon?" Nick Barker grumbled. "We do have important business we could see to. Or we could head to the pub for a pint."

Simon twirled a gold key on a chain attached to his waistcoat. "You didn't have to come."

"Of course I did. What kind of a friend and mentor would I be if I went drinking without you?"

"What kind, indeed. Her note sounded urgent, but don't worry, we won't be away from the hunt for long." Simon then intoned in a stage profundo, "Something hungry moves in the shadows of our fair city. We've heard it whispered in and out of every tavern. And we are the men to put an end to it."

Simon arched an amused eyebrow. His dark hair, just slightly longer than was permissible in polite society, fell rakishly over his high forehead but did not cover his piercing green eyes. Sideburns slipped down to just above his jawline toward the curve of his lips, giving him a permanent sardonic expression. He wore simple tweed trousers with a somewhat threadbare coat, not his normal attire but one that would allow him to blend in among the locals of St. Giles Parish. Even so, he looked more fashionable than the shorter, stockier man walking beside him.

"So who's this old friend of yours we're meeting?" Nick asked. "Do I know her?" The man possessed the build of a common brawler and the sartorial tastes of one. Likely once a very handsome young man, Nick had creases born of time and experience as well as unshaven stubble, which made him appear somewhere over forty years old. His brown hair was short and ruffled, kept without care. Nick struggled to keep up with Simon's purposeful long strides as they threaded their way into the wretched Rookery.

"She was from before I met you. Just after my mother died—God rest her soul—when I first came to London." Simon couldn't help the flicker of pain that crossed his sharp angular features even after so long. "Marie d'Angouleme was a . . . an actress of some repute back then." He sighed at the memory.

"Marie d'Angouleme." Nick whistled in appreciation. "You knew her? I saw her once at a party. Good Lord, why would you stray from that woman?"

"I didn't. She left me."

"She left you? But you're Simon Archer, London's greatest gentleman of leisure!" Nick grasped his chest in mock surprise.

Simon flashed a grin that blazed in the darkness. "I wasn't London's great gentleman then. I was a boy from Bedfordshire with no great place or purpose."

"And now suddenly she wants to meet with you again?"

Nick gave a suspicious frown. "In this parish? After how many years?"

"Six or seven. I owe her a bit of my time. She was kind to a chap new to the city."

"She was kind because you paid her way. You, my friend, have never been able to tell the difference between genuine kindness and deception."

Simon tsked. "Sincerity can't be faked, only deceit."

The two men ventured deep into the wretched Rookery. They passed blocks of condemned structures pressed together and rows of tenements in such disrepair that planks of wood were used to hold up their dilapidated sides. Glassless windows were boarded up or stuffed with rags and newspapers. The streets were full of garbage and human offal. The stench was strong. The air was pitch-black in the narrow confines. This area enjoyed its shadows.

Among the ruins stood a female figure.

Enough faint light filtered from shaded windows and closed doors to illuminate her. She looked smaller and so much older than Simon remembered, and it struck him hard. Years ago she had been adorned with grand jewels and opulent fabrics, and yet even those had barely been able to hold in her audacious and flamboyant manner. Now her garments were gaudy rags of torn lace and soiled silk. When her pale eyes alighted on his form, she must have seen the shock in his expression because she pulled her shabby cloak tighter, concealing her embarrassing attire.

"Beatrice." Simon smiled at her.

A frail laugh slipped from garishly painted lips. "You remembered."

"Of course."

"You're the only man who ever called me by my real name." Despite her gratitude, she glanced nervously at the darkness surrounding them.

Simon laid a gentle kiss on her pockmarked cheek, which had once been porcelain. He gestured to the man behind him. "May I introduce Nick Barker, a good friend. Nick, this is Marie d'Angouleme, grand duchess of the theater, queen of the West End, and thief of my heart."

Her features relaxed in friendly greeting, but there was unease in her eyes, the mark of a woman betrayed too often by sweet words and hasty promises. Her hand plucked at Simon's sleeve. It lingered on the material with practiced intent. "This doesn't seem your usual attire. Dressing for the neighborhood?"

"You might say that." He studied the even more shabby condition of the former demimondaine. It seemed incredible, as if she were dressed for a part in a play. "What happened, Beatrice? How did you come to this? You had everything."

"Yes, I did once," she said wistfully, regarding his tall frame. "But a wrong turn here, a twist of fate there."

"What about your magic?" Simon asked. He noticed her worried gaze dart to Nick, but he gave her a reassuring nod. "You were quite skilled."

Beatrice shrugged with a wan smile before stepping back into the shadows once more. "As with all things in my life, I made missteps there too."

"You should have come to me earlier." He reached into his coat. "How much do you need?"

"Jesus God, Simon." She glared at him in anger. "I'm not asking you for money."

Annoyed, Nick demanded, "What is it you want if not that?"

Ignoring the accusatory barb, her hand alighted on Simon's chest, her finger tracing a strange symbol on his shirt. She actually shivered although Simon didn't think it had anything to do with the cold. Her skin turned abruptly pale beneath the cheap rouge. "I have a . . . customer. An aristocrat named Lord Oakham. Do you know him?"

"I've heard the name," Simon replied.

"He isn't a regular, but not a stranger either. I was with him last night and, afterward, I saw him fall into an argument with another man on the street not far from here. About what I do not know. But I saw . . ." Beatrice faltered, fear overwhelming her countenance. Her shuddering grew worse, her voice lowering.

Simon brushed a soothing hand across her forearm. "What is it, Beatrice? I will help you if I can."

She steeled herself with the same determination that Simon had seen her use before stepping out alone onto the stage. "I saw him transform into a beast and slaughter that man."

"You saw Lord Oakham murder a man?"

Beatrice shook her head violently. "No. Just what I said. One moment, he was a lord and the next he wasn't. He changed his shape, Simon. He became a monster." Her eyes rose to meet his. "Do you believe me? I wasn't drunk. Nor am I now."

"Have you seen him since?"

"No, but it's worse," Beatrice stammered. "Lord Oakham saw me witness the event."

"Are you sure?"

"Yes."

Simon struck a cavalier pose. "Well, let's simply shift you away from here. I would take it a kindness if you would stay at my home at Gaunt Lane for as long as you need."

Beatrice paused, looking at his face for signs of hesitation, but there were none. Even so, she shook her head. "Dear Simon, I don't fear for my own life. But someone should know. Someone who I hoped could do something. I thought of you."

Without warning, a huge shape fell among them, bearing Beatrice hard to the ground and batting Simon and Nick roughly to the side. A massive animal snapped its long jaws and clamped onto Beatrice. Her terrified scream lay heavy in the fog. Simon scrambled to his feet, but he wasn't fast enough to stop the great beast as it twisted its head and ripped through the woman's shoulder.

"No!" Simon screamed.

A menacing growl rolled loud, hammering the men's ears as a pair of red eyes punctured the black veil of night. The creature rose on canine hind legs, tall and loose-limbed, to a height of eight feet. Its snout was almost the length of Simon's forearm. Saliva and blood dripped through the long sharp teeth in its open jaws. The stench of blood mingled with the distinctive musk of wet fur. The hair on Simon's arms rose as his breathing deepened and energy flooded his body.

"Damnation," muttered Nick. Then he snapped his fingers. A flicker of flame sprouted from his fingertips, lighting the gloom. "Don't rush in. Don't be stupid."

"It killed her!" Simon yelled.

"It'll kill us too unless we keep our wits." Nick pulled his friend a step away. "That's a werewolf, in case you didn't know."

Simon shrugged off the man's hand. Where sensible men would have run, Simon strode toward the menacing shape. His leather shoes squished with each step in the garbage-strewn lane. He uttered a single word that was not English and brought his hands together, stiff-armed, in a sharp clap. Thunder crashed. The hulking beast was blasted back, slamming into the bricks behind it. The force left a deep crater in the wall.

With bricks clattering around it, the thing gathered its long limbs and stood, growling. The rank stench of rotting flesh washed over Simon, but he didn't hesitate, moving closer to the shadowy beast.

Nick came up on the left, forcing the werewolf to choose between them. The older man slapped his palm onto a nearby wall and the flames on his hand transferred to the spot on the bricks where it stayed, offering light in the dark alley.

"Steady," Nick breathed, casually placing his hands in his pockets.

Simon had already selected the spells he needed to cast.

The werewolf's head swiveled as if debating which to strike first. Its frustration erupted in a violent roar that flecked spittle across the alley, striking both men. Neither flinched. The creature turned to Simon and stepped forward.

"Now," Simon shouted, as the werewolf drew close.

Nick's hands flew from his pockets and balls of fire shot from his palms. Two flaming orbs splashed against the werewolf's massive chest. It howled in pain; its fur and flesh were seared in a wash of fire.

The enraged werewolf lunged. The snap of teeth came within a hairsbreadth of Simon's face as he flung himself back. He kicked out, connecting with the snapping jaw, striking it to the side, spraying blood.

"Again!" Simon commanded, scrambling to his feet.

Nick let loose another barrage of fireballs, while Simon grabbed a thick wooden beam from the side of a building and smashed it over the head of the beast. Its howl of pain became a shout of fury.

It leapt and landed beside Simon. He swung the beam again and it splintered across the werewolf's smoldering arm and chest, shattering into wood pulp. The creature towered over him, its arm lifted for a killing blow.

Nick grabbed the werewolf's throat and his hand burst into blue-hot fire. With an agonized howl, a hairy arm swung wildly and slammed Nick's shoulder, sending his limp body flying amidst the debris. Then the creature lunged after him.

Simon seized the beast's hind leg and his fingers dug deep into the bristly fur. When he whispered a druidic phrase, the huge werewolf jerked to a halt. It glanced furiously over its shoulder, so Simon heaved it off its clawed feet and threw it to the side as if it were a spent rag. It crashed into a heap ten feet away.

The massive wolf head swiveled toward Simon for a moment but then opted for easier prey, turning again for Nick. Simon slapped his hands together. The deafening crack filled the alley and sent the beast careening into a spin. It dropped to all fours and clawed for purchase, leaving deep gouges in the cobblestones. Simon knelt and slammed his hand to the ground. A whispered word sent a wave of power shaking through his arm, as if it would snap the bones, before it passed into the earth. He wrenched his hand from the powerful grip of the ground, cutting off the power.

A cascading shock wave rumbled toward the werewolf. The monster tried to leap away but lost its footing and fell. The wave tore past and hit the side of a building. Bricks cracked and groaned. Then with a shudder, as the great beast was rising, the wall collapsed on top of it in a shower of stone and dust.

For a moment, Simon thought the fight over and moved toward Nick, but the sound of shifting rubble made Simon turn. The werewolf rose from the mound of stone, its fur a smear of blood and dust. It sprang with horrifying speed at Simon, knocking him down. The back of the man's head struck something hard. He heard Nick shouting. The foul breath of the beast gagged him. He was inches from the salivating jaws.

A shadowy figure fell from the heavens. There was a whistle of steel and the werewolf reared up with a shriek. Simon caught a glimpse of a man clad in black, wielding a long claymore one-handed. The beast clutched its side, blood spewing between gnarled fingers. It cowered from the new figure, showing fear for the first time. Then it leapt away into the darkness.

"That's right, you cur!" The man in black fired a

weapon that sounded like a cannon at the creature's flee-ing form. The firearm was a heavy pistol with four bar-rels. Amazingly, it let out a whisper of steam as the smoking barrel rotated away from the breech and a fresh one clicked into place. "You know me now, don't you?"

Simon came to his feet, shaking the last of his vertigo aside with the determination of a bear. His coat was in ruins, but he was largely unscathed. He felt a slight tremble in his legs; the magic had left him weak, but he felt a rush of relief at being alive. He clapped a grateful hand onto the newcomer's shoulder. "You came in the nick of time, sir."

"Shut it!" snapped the sharp retort in a thick Scottish brogue, and the man brushed Simon's friendly gesture aside. "You came to a werewolf fight without silver. I've been tracking that beast for days. I won't have you two mucking things up with your petty sorcery. That beas-tie belongs to me, and me alone!" Then he was gone, racing on the trail of the bleeding beast.

Simon stared after the Scotsman for a brief moment, but then he turned and ran for Beatrice, shouting to Nick as he passed, "Are you all right?"

"Right as rain." Nick rolled his shoulder with a wince of pain.

Simon fell to his knees in the blood. Beatrice's brutal-ized body was splayed on the cobblestones amidst the refuse, twisted like copper wire, clothes shredded. He slid his hands under her. She coughed weakly and her eyes opened. Simon shouted, "Nick! Quickly."

The other man was at his side already. He squatted and put a hand on Beatrice's forehead. "She's nearly gone."

"Then stop talking," Simon cried, "and help her."

Nick concentrated on the woman's face. He breathed heavily and closed his eyes. Beatrice jerked and cried out in pain. She reached up a red hand and took hold of Nick's wrist, trying to wrench it from her head.

"Stop," she whispered.

"No, Beatrice," Simon soothed. "Nick has some vivimancy. He can help you."

"Don't." She looked up at Simon. "Don't."

"Yes." Simon tried to pull her hand from Nick's arm.

"She's right, Simon," Nick said. "I can't do her any good."

"What do you mean?" Simon asked sharply. "You've got the power. Use it."

Beatrice touched Simon's cheek. "Aether is killing me. I abused it for so long. I'll die soon anyway. You can't save me. Just let me go."

"No," Simon argued. "Just let Nick get you balanced. Then you'll come to my home and I'll care for you. I can come up with something."

"Simon, please." She smiled with bloody teeth. "There's nothing you can do."

"She's right, old boy." Nick took his hands away from her. "You're overstimulated by your own aether, but try to see it straight."

"No!" Simon shouted, glaring angrily at Nick.

Beatrice murmured, "I'm glad I saw you again, Simon. You're exactly the same as you were." A strange look of sadness and disappointment passed over her face, then all emotion departed, leaving only waxy flesh. She went limp under his hands.

Simon squeezed her cool hand. "Damn it."

"She was eaten up, Simon. The aether was in every part of her. She should've been dead months ago." Nick stood. "But at least she gave us Lord Oakham. If we can find him again."

Simon's voice was brittle. "I know where we can find him. We'll see to Beatrice first." He placed her hands gently on her chest.

Chapter Two

THE NEXT DAY, SIMON MADE HIS USUAL ROUNDS to the clubs, but he couldn't find a reason to go inside. He met a few acquaintances on the street, but their gossipy chatter held little appeal. He stopped for coffee in a shop he never frequented to ensure he didn't have to meet any of his normally amusing companions. He felt no desire to be amused.

Finally, Simon started toward the place he wanted to avoid. In the Rookery, he discovered through a liberal spread of coins among streetwalkers that Beatrice kept a small room near Dyott Street. He also found that many of the older women disdained her for thinking she was better than the others, having come from the world of a society courtesan as she did. The younger girls, however, found Beatrice to be kind and sharing, often allowing them to stay in her room when they had nowhere to go.

The building on Dyott was in vigorous disrepair. Simon could smell every aspect of human life. The floors were cracked and sticky. Cold air blasted through smashed windows. With suspicious eyes following him, he climbed the creaking stairs. His stylish suit marked him as an outsider, a man in search of a tradeswoman. It was a surprise to no one when he stopped at Beatrice's door. He couldn't be sure if the news of her death had reached her home yet. In such a community people commonly moved, disappeared, or died without fanfare.

The door was locked, but it was an easy matter for Simon to force it with a white-gloved hand. He stepped inside the cold cubicle, a tiny flat with a cracked window, a thin mattress, and a single chair.

His hand lifted to cover his dismay. Beatrice had once lived in a suite of rooms near Leicester Square with a maid and a cook. It had been warm and bright, full of art and furniture from Paris. Her bed had been larger than this entire flat.

"Why didn't you contact me?" he muttered. "My God, why let this happen?"

Simon's mind cast back to their final weeks together. Their separation had been amiable enough. Simon had imagined he loved her; she had been passionate, comforting, and encouraging in all ways. He remembered the warmth and gentle softness of her body. But he knew now that was the passion of a young man in his first love affair among the avenues of a great city. He had loved her, but had been *in love* with the places she took him and the people she showed him. And he understood that she had greater opportunities than a young gentleman with money but no family pedigree. She was always courted by lords and officials. He had taken comfort in the confidence she had given him, assuming that he could move forward and thrive, which he had.

Simon gazed over the meager possessions in the room. A makeshift open closet along one wall held several threadbare dresses. There was a small clutch of badly used makeup as if they had been taken from the trash. In another corner were several large stacks of newspapers, some yellowed with age. A pair of scissors sat atop one stack. On the far interior wall was a curtain although there shouldn't have been a window there.

Simon stepped to the drape and pulled it back. He twisted his head curiously at what was behind it. Newspaper clippings were pinned to the wall. Dozens, if not hundreds of them.

He leaned close to see a society report of a party at Lord Cutshaw's home. Simon recalled that party and, in fact, saw his name in the item. Next to that was an article describing a spring horse race in Wiltshire. Simon had been there too, and his name appeared among the guests. The opening of the Pyramid Theater in Covent Garden. His name was there. And in the next. And the next.

Every fluttering scrap of newsprint held a mention of some event or gathering where Simon had been present. It was a wall charting his social activities over the last seven years. The time since he and Beatrice had parted.

However, below the phalanx of society notices were three small clippings. One was a story of how Lord Cutshaw had exposed fraudulent mediums preying on unfortunates around his country estate. In fact, Simon had rooted out those cheats who had victimized Lord Cutshaw himself. A second item told of reports of a monstrous glowing panther in Salisbury. Simon had investigated that too, while spending a delightful week at the local derby with Lady Dunston. And there was a final clip about the Pyramid Theater closing for renovations, while rumors persisted that the management had been forced to shut down by a vengeful spirit. The tone of the piece was mocking, but Simon knew the theater had been haunted by bloody ghosts because he had been the one to silence them.

He stood back, stunned. Here was his life in London. Parties. Galas. Derbys. Operas. And a handful of pathetic mystical interventions more suited to a sleight-of-hand huckster than a man who laid claim to being the last scribe on Earth, the only man alive who could own and command the aether through spell and word.

Beatrice had always had a little interest in mysticism. She had been an accomplished enchantress, but one with a clear ceiling on her skills. Still, she had always claimed the only limit to Simon's occult abilities was Simon himself. And now he saw that she had been watching him from afar and documenting his progress.

Simon took in the vast swathe of society items and few notices relating to the occult. He would have liked to make the excuse that his magical activities were secret and by definition would not be in the press. This was true. His identity as a magician was known to few; only Nick knew the full extent of it because Nick had been a teacher of sorts. However, Simon knew he could have written a detailed account of his true occult exploits using paper not much greater than the few clips under his eyes.

He would have liked to make the excuse that the previous years had been consumed learning his craft, studying arcane texts, and practicing inscriptions. And this too was true. His skills had become extraordinary, but of late there were far too few evenings that he gave over to study when a night out called. He could claim to have added little value to anyone's life using his unique skills.

Simon stood shivering in the freezing flat of a woman who he believed had left him behind. She had dedicated herself to him, and he hadn't even known it. And he certainly hadn't deserved it. He lowered his head under the petty weight of the voluminous chronicle of his achievements rustling in the wind before him.

"My God, I am exactly the same. Just as you said."

Simon felt warm tears sliding down his cheeks and he hoped they were for Beatrice.

IT WAS DUSK WHEN SIMON ENTERED THE FRONT door of his Gaunt Lane town house to hear Nick shout from the drawing room, "Where have you been all day?" Simon tossed his hat carelessly on a small table and draped his coat over an already overcrowded hook.

He entered the sitting room to see Nick lounging on the sofa with shoes kicked off and shirt collar open. The room, as always, was comfortable, in a bachelor sense. It was a veritable disaster of unshelved books and piles of newspapers, as well as old plates, cups, and saucers. But a warm coal fire glowed in the hearth. Simon set his walking stick on a table and poured a glass of whiskey before refilling Nick's proffered tumbler.

Nick stared at Simon, clearly seeing the emotion on his face but saying nothing.

Simon lifted a newspaper from a table and noted it was several months old. "I had errands to run. Did you become petrified on the sofa and need help turning over?" He then saw a scowling yellow cat sitting in the doorway. "Did you feed the cat?"

Nick craned his neck to stare at the little beast. "Have we ever fed the cat?"

"I thought you did. And he looks hungry. Or angry." Simon took his pipe from the bookshelf and began to fill it with tobacco.

Nick stretched and crossed his feet. "While you were out buying a new stick, I was working. I went by Lord Oakham's club."

Simon spun quickly. "And?"

"He wasn't there. The servants wouldn't tell me his whereabouts."

Simon perched on the edge of an overstuffed chair. "You didn't go looking like that, did you?"

"Like what?"

"Like you." The younger magician touched a rune inscribed on the bowl of his pipe and whispered a quiet word. He felt heat and the tobacco began to burn.

Nick scowled. "Give me a bit of credit, will you? I used a glamour spell. They thought I was a proper gent, such as yourself. For all the good it did."

Simon stared off into the distance with his pipe clenched between his teeth. "Oakham is expected at Viscount Gillingham's ball tonight. Along with half of London's better set."

"How do you know that?"

"Because I know things. In any case, we'll attend too. We'll latch on to his lordship if he shows and follow him. Do you think you can manage a shave and a suit of proper clothes?"

"No. I'll just use a glamour spell again. I still have a bit of the potion." Nick sipped whiskey. "That Scotsman seemed as if he knew what he was about. You don't want to leave the wolf hunting to him?"

"I do not." Smoke drifted up from Simon's pipe. His eyes were focused somewhere between the clock on the mantel and the planet Jupiter.

Nick regarded his friend for a moment. "You haven't said much about last night."

Simon grunted. "Not much to say."

"I thought she was—"

"Leave it," Simon snapped with a quick stare at the older man.

"No." Nick spun around on the old sofa and sat up. "I don't think I will leave it. I thought she was a friend of yours."

Simon glared a silent challenge at Nick to be met with

the unblinking eyes of his friend. Finally he said, "You don't want to hear it."

"Not without another splash, no." Nick stood and poured more whiskey. "Now I do."

Simon sat back and stretched out his legs. "Do you remember what she said to me before she died?"

"That she was glad she saw you."

"The other bit. That I was still the same."

Nick regarded him with mock seriousness. "You're a handsome fellow, no doubt. And you've held up well."

"Thank you, but that's not what she meant." Simon stared into the red glow of his pipe. He listened to the coal fire hissing from the hearth. He reached into his jacket pocket and pulled out a thick pile of clippings from the newspapers. From his other pocket, he drew out more. He tossed them on a nearby desk. "I went by her rooms this morning. She had cut every item from the newspapers where I had been mentioned in the years since we parted."

Nick raised surprised eyebrows at the tattered stack of newsprint. "She did? I thought she left you."

"She did."

"Well, she seemed to have nursed a rather vigorous obsession."

From his waistcoat, Simon pulled a slim collection of news items and held them up. "That gigantic mound of clippings deal with my various appearances at parties and galas, or rumors of affairs and indiscretions to which I've been attached."

"Impressive."

"These few here are reports of uncanny little stories that Beatrice correctly presumed I was involved in as a magician." Simon laid the paltry few occult clippings next to the mountain of society stories. "That is the sum total of my life."

Nick smiled. "You certainly do attend a lot of parties."

Simon stared glumly into the distance.

"Simon, you couldn't know she carried a torch for you," Nick said with sympathy. "She never tried to contact you until yesterday. How could you—"

"That's not the point." Simon's voice was exasperated.

"Oh. What is the point then?"

"What am I doing?"

Nick shook his head, confused.

Simon continued, "What am I doing with my life? I came to London to become a scribe."

Nick grew frosty. "You are a scribe, and an excellent one. Better than you realize apparently. Magic isn't like playing the piano. A few lessons don't suffice."

"A few lessons? I've been studying since I was a boy from my father's notes. And we've been working together for over three years. And yet, we couldn't deal with that werewolf last night."

"That thing was a monster and it was powerful. We weren't prepared for a lycanthrope. It took us by surprise. Threw us off balance a bit, but we recovered and could've taken it eventually."

"I don't think so. If that Scotsman hadn't shown up, we'd be dead." Simon sighed. "We knew there had been killings around town. We were hunting something. For six months, we've been talking about how London seems different, as if something dark is out there. But it was just a game. As with everything we do, we weren't serious, and we weren't prepared."

Nick looked angry. "So you're saying that you haven't become an accomplished scribe because I haven't trained you properly?"

"No." Simon paused and let the damning silence drag out before conceding, "I had already become a complete wastrel when I met you. All I cared about was women and . . . well, and nothing. Women. And whatever magic could gain me. Then, for the first year we were together, we worked hard. I learned a great deal. But the last year or so, we've lost our momentum." He glanced at the pile of news clippings.

"It takes time," Nick repeated.

"That's not good enough." Simon sat up. "Why am I even studying to be a scribe? What's the purpose? Just to live in a cave and accumulate knowledge?"

This time Nick stayed silent, his eyes half-closed with contemplation or annoyance.

Simon asked, "What's the use of power in this world?"

"No, no. Greater magicians than you have started down that road over the centuries. If you involve yourself in the normal world, it will make you pay. There's a reason magicians stay in the shadows. We are feared, Simon. I don't care how powerful you may grow as a scribe, a knife or a musket ball will kill you as easily as it will anyone else. If you want to change the world, learn a trade like blacksmithing."

"I'm not talking about trying to change the world, Nick. But I couldn't even save Beatrice."

"We'll find Oakham, don't worry. We'll make him pay. And we should be able to even up those stacks a bit. Is that what you want?"

"It's a start." Simon smiled at his friend's genuinely solicitous question. He had grown weary of his own gothic brooding, so he rose and took up his new walking stick.

"That's a handsome new stick," Nick said, obviously grateful that the tone was shifting. "Is it appreciably better than your two hundred others?"

"Yes, it is. I had Penny Carter make it." Simon drew out a glittering blade and said with excitement, "Speaking of Lord Oakham, guess what I saw at Miss Carter's shop today?"

Nick furrowed his brow. "Lord Oakham?"

"No. A four-barreled pistol called a Lancaster."

"Like the Scotsman carried?"

"Just like it. Its exact twin actually. Miss Carter made the brace for him. I asked her to send for me the next time she expected him in. I'd like to chat with him."

"He didn't seem keen on a chat last night."

"I wasn't at my best last night, but I'm sure I can charm him. I want to know more about him and his activities, particularly if he's active in London." Simon swiped the blade through the air. "Lucky to have this in time for tonight."

"Doesn't look like silver."

"It isn't. Quite the finest steel I've seen though. A Japanese swordmaster couldn't have done better. That woman is a wonder." Simon cleared a work surface by shoving books off the desk onto the floor. He produced a sheet of paper from his coat pocket and laid it out. It had precise runic sketches grouped in a narrow column down the center.

Nick joined him with whiskey in hand, watching intensely as Simon set the sword on the desktop and placed the sheet of paper over it so the row of runes were positioned over the blade. "A little inscription, eh?"

Simon reached into a drawer and drew out an empty glass inkwell, which he set within easy reach. He glanced at the crackling fire, then at Nick. "A bit of heat, if you please."

The older magician smirked and snapped his fingers. Flame engulfed his entire hand. Simon indicated he should apply the fire to the paper. Nick waved his glowing hand near the sheet. Immediately the thin paper smoldered and crinkled, then vanished in a puff of white smoke. Both men stared at the sword. The runes were now transferred onto the blade in ashy black.

Simon settled himself in a chair before the desk. He

produced a carved ivory case that contained a beautiful pen that, in place of the nib, held a thin needle. He took up the inkwell and ran his finger over the glass, feeling the etched rune on it. He said a strange word rarely spoken aloud. Green wisps suddenly appeared inside the bottle like smoky snakes. Simon could feel the power as its proximity resonated; all his senses awakened to its seductive call.

He dipped the needle-tipped pen into the green aether. He hunched over the blade and carefully began to apply the glowing instrument to the blackened runes. If he got even one slight inscription wrong, it would be a waste of time and the ruin of a perfectly good stick sword.

After only a few strokes onto the steel, he went back to the inkwell and it was clear again. Once more, he spoke aether into the bottle, dipped the pen, and returned to his scribing. He continued this procedure as he worked his way down the thin blade. He must have been perspiring for suddenly a cloth patted his forehead and he paused to smile gratefully at Nick. He flexed his hand to ease the cramping. He took in his art and he smiled. The sword was incised beautifully, making the new blade appear eons old. Then he bent to complete the final strokes, and the moment he did, the blade flared a brilliant hue of emerald. Simon touched the blade and whispered, and the glow altered to a watery blue.

"Well done, old boy." Nick stepped back with an exclamation but quickly came forward again when the glow faded and the blade lay dormant upon the table. "What does it do other than glow?"

Simon announced with a smile, "Think of it as thaumaturgical galvanism. When active, it will be like holding the heat of a bolt of lightning."

"That seems safe enough."

Simon accepted the cloth and wiped his face. He

stretched out his tight shoulders and laughed. "And it didn't take nearly as long as I suspected."

Nick pointed to the mantel clock. "Three hours."

Simon thought his friend was playing a joke, so he checked it against his pocket watch. In fact, it had been more than three hours since he sat down before the sword to inscribe it. "Well. I suppose I should get dressed for the party. Wouldn't want a nasty comment in the papers tomorrow." He jumped up but had to put out a hand to steady himself as the room tilted.

"Easy." Nick took his elbow in a firm grip. "You've a touch of aether euphoria."

"Nonsense, I'm as fresh as a baby," Simon exclaimed before taking a few staggering steps with knees that felt far too unsteady. "I'll just have a seat."

"Wise." Nick guided him back to the chair. "You used a lot of aether for that sword. I'm surprised you're even coherent."

Simon shook his head to clear it. "When will I stop being impacted by aether this way?"

The older magician said, "I've seen a few who always have it. It's just the way it is for them. Others, like me, never have even a touch of aether drunkenness. We burn out of aether temporarily if we use too much, but we don't get falling-down stupid and start laughing like an imbecile. You're too eager. You burn through aether too fast. You'll probably get past it."

Simon sat back and closed his eyes. He had to admit, he actually enjoyed the sensation of aether euphoria, but he knew it had a price. It limited the length of time he could practice magic, and it could be a risk if he was overcome by it during a dangerous struggle, as with the werewolf in the Rookery.

Nick pulled his overcoat off the arm of a chair and plunged a hand into the pocket. He came out with a small crystal vial. He shook it to determine if there was still clear liquid inside. He thumbed off the cork and drank. Nick scowled at the taste but then made a few peculiar motions with his hands. The unshaven, slovenly man shimmered and was replaced by a finely dressed young aristocrat. He was a handsome, almost pretty, young man with wavy blond hair and shapely lips that might have been rouged in the old style. Nick turned to survey himself in a wall mirror that was largely covered by coats.

"I'm ready for the party." Nick's gravelly voice issued from the lovely young man's mouth. "Sir Thomas Wolfolk won't mind if I'm him tonight."

"You go on ahead." Simon replaced the blade in its wooden sheath. "You'll forgive me if I shave and put on actual dinner clothes." He began to unbutton his waistcoat.

"Do you have time?"

Simon gave the man a cold stare. "You're not suggesting I arrive early at a party, are you?"

"God forbid even a lycanthrope deny Simon Archer a fashionable entrance."

Simon eased himself back to his feet, grateful the euphoria was waning. He saluted with the walking stick and kicked off his shoes into the hallway. He hurried upstairs to dress, beginning to enjoy the anticipation over the coming evening.

Chapter Three

SIMON STRODE UP THE GRAND PORTICO STEPS
of the mansion, a Georgian pile north of Great Russell
Street. His stick tapped sharply on the stonework, the
only outward sign of his agitated state. Inside the but-
tressed vestibule, the stiff-limbed butler stared at him in
surprise, clearly doubting that Simon belonged at this
ball. Simon smiled and produced the invitation from his
jacket pocket. The servant studied it for a long moment
but then nodded and handed what he believed was an
expensive engraved invitation back to Simon. In fact, it
was a piece of blank cardstock with a few runes inscribed
on it. Simon tossed his crisp white gloves into his hat and
handed them over with his overcoat but kept his stick.
The servant's face remained impassive as he turned ele-
gantly on his heel. He announced to those already gathered at the late hour the arrival of Mr. Simon Archer.

All heads turned to stare.

Secret whispers circulated openly around the vast entry
hall as Simon confidently swept in with a commanding
and unrepentant stature. He extended a gracious greeting to his host, the Right Honorable and Extremely Surprised Viscount Gillingham, who bowed and introduced
his rather homely wife, who stood with mouth agape.

Next to the host couple stood the round and ruddy

Prime Minister Charles North, and his extraordinarily beautiful spouse, Grace. The prime minister greeted Simon with admirable civility and presented his wife. While Simon had certainly heard of Mrs. North, he had never met her. She outshone her husband in every respect, and unlike the prime minister, she was beloved by the lowly and the powerful alike. Her angelic air and calm pastel gown didn't fool Simon as he noticed her covetous gaze when she acknowledged him.

She offered a demure smile, and said, "A distinct pleasure, Mr. Archer."

Simon kissed her hand, his lips lingering just a second too long. "One that is all mine, madam."

Her glittering smile was hypnotic though her eyes were full of constant scrutiny, taking the measure of him in a way that would have cowed a lesser man. Simon held her very direct stare and stepped back, with a bow aimed at Mrs. North. That deed done, he plunged deeper into the crowd seeking out Lord Oakham; his scrutiny penetrated every corner of the room but to no avail. His thoughts turned dark against his wishes despite the fact that many young gentlemen of leisure lifted hands in jolly greeting, doubtless relieved by his arrival as it meant the dull gathering might be infused with new exhilaration. Most of his random encounters were pleasant, but sometimes eyes went wide with surprise at seeing him here. Simon did make eye contact with a young woman who was unfamiliar to him. Likely new to the London scene. She was perhaps eighteen and quite lovely. To his amusement, a large woman in a vast hoop skirt snatched the girl by the arm and pulled her to safety. Simon continued on, expanding his search into more distant parts of the rambling mansion.

"Mr. Archer?" came a feminine voice from behind a half-closed door.

He cautiously pushed the door back a few inches. A

shapely figure stood outlined in the pale light of the window.

"Would you step inside, please," she asked, "and close the door?"

When he did, the woman stepped into the glow of a lamp. Grace North. Her smile was both winsome and alluring; the interpretation was left up to the viewer, as were the consequences of a misstep based on that interpretation.

"Mrs. North. May I help you?" Simon bowed. He chose to assume she had only broken away from the receiving line for some specific and practical errand.

"I have a question for you."

He nodded for her to proceed.

"How did you come to be here?" she asked.

"You beckoned me in."

"I believe you take my meaning, sir. I mean here at this party." Grace looked him in the eye with the quiet steel of an experienced politician. "I personally reviewed the guest list. Your name was not on it."

Simon took a step closer. "I was a late addition to the field, like the Derby."

"There were none."

"I am a dear friend of the viscount's."

"You are not."

Simon displayed surprise. "You are impossibly well informed. I am stunned you even recall my name from meeting me at the door."

"Please, Mr. Archer. You are a gentleman of some repute."

"You give an odd accent to *gentleman*."

"I use it politely. You are widely considered a scoundrel and bounder."

"Am I?" Simon now feigned melodramatic insult. "I thought I was well liked."

"As are most scoundrels. So, tell me, why are you here?"

"I am flattered that such a talented, powerful, and beautiful woman is so engrossed with me." Simon moved close enough to smell the delicate lavender scent in her flaxen hair. When she moved her head slightly, the shadows slid over her glass-smooth features, creating an odd hardness that quickly faded like a strange glimpse from the corner of the eye. She showed no fear or hesitation. Clearly, he would not overwhelm her with physicality.

"My husband is the prime minister. I prefer that he remain prime minister. Therefore, I am compelled to distance him from scandal or from characters of ill repute. If I believe you to be a threat to his reputation, you cannot be allowed near him."

"Madam, I haven't the slightest desire for intercourse with your husband."

She stared at him evenly. "I have no reason to trust you. I don't know you, and you are a man of questionable family."

Simon felt a jolt of true coldness, and his false, smoldering gaze vanished. "Mrs. North, I should not like to think a woman of your refinement is impugning the honor of my mother."

"Do you deny your own mysterious pedigree, Mr. Archer?"

"No." Simon looked down at her with a cruel smile. "I am a bastard."

"What is your business here tonight?" Grace repeated, unconcerned with his anger.

He considered walking out. And he considered cursing her, then walking out. That, however, seemed unworthy to him, and even in his bitter state, he still couldn't waste the potential value of a connection to the prime minister's wife just for a momentary satisfaction. He took on the attitude of a roué no longer pretending that his charm or rage was legitimate.

"Why else would I be here?" he said with a sly narrowing of his eyes. "Beating the bushes. Trying to flush a quail or two for a cold winter night."

A slight smile touched Grace's lips and her eyes slid quickly over his tall frame. "I'm not sure I believe you."

Simon shrugged without comment. She seemed perceptive and capable of smelling out his rakish burlesque. Still, she tilted her head with nominal acceptance. Then a peculiar softening of her eyes betrayed an interest in Simon beyond her political interrogation. At least, that was one interpretation. She held out her hand. Instinctively, he took it.

"Good shooting to you, Mr. Archer." Her warm fingers closed gently around his. "Would you mind leaving the room now?"

Simon kissed her hand with as much conviction as he could muster to play the gentleman who sensed a chance at unusually rare game. "I hope I will see you again."

Grace North stared into his green eyes with an enigmatic invitation. Her voice took on a slight huskiness. "Who can say what the future holds?"

He let her fingers slide from his and stepped back with a satisfied purse of his lips. He went to the door and left her standing in the gloom. Once out in the hall, he dropped the foolish smirk. He was annoyed by the diversion from his task at hand and angered by the comments that reflected on his mother. He was not unused to snide chatter about his illegitimacy, but coming from such an angelic face, it seemed even more savage. Grace North had put Simon badly off his game. Under normal circumstances, he already would have been acquainted with her corset. Now, all he could do was eye the crowd for Lord Oakham.

In lieu of finding his quarry, Simon sought out Nick's dandified alter ego, Sir Thomas Wolfolk. And he was likely in one spot. He strolled through the ballroom, where he signaled to a waiter carrying a tray of champagne. Glass in hand, he threaded his way to another room, where a savage cribbage game was being waged. He greeted the players and joined the table.

Sir Thomas Wolfolk leaned around a lovely young lady to acknowledge him with a broad smirk. Simon merely raised his eyebrow and brushed his well-tied white silk cravat. A new game was played and Simon consulted his cards.

Sir Thomas grinned. "I saw you scoring points with the wife of the prime minister. Was she probing you as to your opinion on the Reform Act?"

"Please don't diminish Mrs. North with your scandalous taint," muttered an amiable voice from across the table. Henry Clatterburgh was technically the third Earl Moorhaven, but never advertised it. He was a longtime fixture at the Home Office who ignored Simon's awkward social standing because he apparently enjoyed losing at cards.

Without looking at his hand, Simon displaced one of his cards, announcing the total to be twenty-eight. The assembled players groaned and folded their cards, while the observing crowd laughed and applauded.

Sir Thomas's mouth fell into a minor scowl. "I had hoped the champagne would have rattled your mathematical abilities."

"Yes rather, I have more than six cards left," grumbled Henry Clatterburgh. Then his head shot up from his cards, gaze riveted across the room. "Oh my!" His features fell with disappointment. "Oh. It's just Kate Anstruther."

The entire table turned to see a woman paused in the doorway. She was extraordinary. Not only was she tall, but unlike the other women in the room who wore their hair tight against their heads or tossed into ringlets, she let her lustrous auburn hair, full of waves, fall on either side of her face before gathering upon her straight but slender shoulders. Her high cheekbones accentuated emerald eyes that flashed in all directions. She wore a long gown of red so dark it was all but black. It was drawn tight at the waist and flowed over the hips. The sleeves were full, but not to the wild extreme of others in the room. Her shoulders were bare and the curve of her throat was accentuated by a simple pearl choker.

There was a sureness about her, and her mouth displayed a disregard for her surroundings. She understood the potency of the crowd but didn't care. She wasn't trying to garner attention, but she did nonetheless. It gave her a power so strong it almost had a scent. Beatrice, in her heyday, had drawn the eye with equal power but in a completely different way. Beatrice had done it through astounding displays of personality and pure sexuality. It now struck Simon as having been a bit desperate as he watched the profoundly self-contained Kate Anstruther.

Simon turned back to his cards with an ache in his chest and managed a mildly interested, "Hm."

"That's all you have to say?" Sir Thomas stared at him. "You're not in any way affected by her? Were we looking at the same woman?"

"We were." Simon shifted a few cards in his hand. He turned to see Kate's form vanish into a jungle of black tails and opulent gowns. "She's very pretty."

"She's very pretty," the blond man repeated in a bland monotone. He shook his head in dismay. "Have you died?"

Simon didn't reply. He removed and fingered the gold key he always carried and waited for the man with the next play.

"Just as well, Simon." Henry scowled with disappointment. "She is a beauty, but I hear she's a reader." He spoke the word as if it had been *radical*. "I'm surprised she's here tonight. Since her father disappeared a few years back while exploring some damnable dark jungle, she flitters on the edge of society but never quite lights on a branch."

Sir Thomas laid a card on the table with his eyes fixed on Simon. "Sixteen."

Henry hooted in triumph and discarded also. "Twenty-six!"

Simon slowly placed a four of clubs. "Thirty."

"Bah," Henry grumbled, then spouted, "Unbeliev-able luck!"

Simon calmly collected his winnings. "You dealt me a grand hand, Henry. You have no one to blame but your-self." He scooped up a pile of gold sovereigns, declaring that he had grown bored with the game.

"You're not leaving so soon, Archer?" declared Henry. "You have my year's allowance in your hand."

"You'll find me at Lord Remberton's garden party in a fortnight, Henry. Make sure to skim enough money from your ministry coffers to attract me." Henry snorted good-humouredly at Simon's droll statement. "Gentle-men, I and my creditors bid you a good evening. Sir Thomas, a word with you?"

Simon wandered down a corridor past a large library with the winsome blond man at his side. "Have you seen Lord Oakham about?"

"No. I was here easily an hour before you, but he hasn't made an appearance."

"Did you have any problem coming in?"

"No. Sir Thomas Wolfolk is always welcome," Nick said with a laugh, "even when he's actually in Jamaica for the year."

Simon shook his head in exasperation when a noise from the library caught his attention. It was a woman's firm but alarmed voice along with a man's forceful com-mand.

"Excuse me," Simon said.

"Oh leave it be. It's just a lover's quarrel. We have other interests."

"I won't have a woman fighting off a drunken bully when there are gentlemen about."

"As you please. I'm back to the tables. If you need me, Sir Galahad, do call."

Simon kept his scowl of disappointment from showing as he entered the library.

Chapter Four

"REMOVE YOUR HAND, SIR WILLIAM!" CAME KATE Anstruther's agitated but resolute voice.

"Don't be so shy, my dove." Sir William Titchmarsh had the woman pressed against a large Grecian amphora partially hidden by a spray of fronds.

"If you do not move your hand," she said through gritted teeth, "I will be forced to do something very impolite."

"I do love a bit of fire." Sir William laughed, becoming more aggressive, his fingers roving lower.

Kate's eyes narrowed to slits. She reached into her beaded bag and her hand emerged clutching a small bulb of stiff rubber with a narrow silver spout. She raised it to Sir William's face and squeezed the bulb. An oddly sparkling dust shot out. He froze almost instantly and proceeded to launch into a series of violent sneezes that nearly toppled him to the floor. Kate slipped from the corner and left him to stumble against the wall.

"Sir William, I do hope you're not coming down with some horrible pestilence." She knew very well he was only mildly indisposed since the dust was her own concoction.

The man's beady eyes were already red and he vigorously rubbed his hand under his nose, trying to catch his breath. He managed to regain a semblance of a lurid smile. "Merely momentarily assailed by your heady feminine fragrance."

"How odd. I am not wearing perfume. Perhaps you smell your own cologne water. It is reminiscent of the stench of puddles one would leap over in the street."

He grabbed her arm. She was about to put a knee to his unprotected privates when someone tall and dark seized Sir William's shoulder and hauled him back with barely restrained fury.

"That, sir, is enough!" The voice of the stranger rang loudly even over the distant music of the quartet and the hum of party chatter. The rondo missed a beat and faces appeared in the doorway.

Kate straightened and stared in astonishment at the figure she recognized as the notorious Simon Archer. From the dark hair to the sharp cut of his jaw, he was the model of masculine strength and good looks. Kate's cheeks actually colored.

Sir William Titchmarsh spun around. "How dare you, sir!" His expression faltered when he saw who had laid callused hands on him. Then he brought his bluster to bear once more in the form of a flailing right fist.

Simon easily dodged the blow and promptly riposted with a lightning-fast jab of his own. Sir William slammed into the amphora. Kate's hand darted out quickly, righting the teetering vase but allowing Sir William to drop to the floor.

Kate's dark eyes flashed at Simon as the gaping silence of the rest of the room was noticeable. "What is wrong with you? I was in no danger, I assure you."

From his place on the floor, Sir William countered in a nasal drone, "The lady was thoroughly enjoying my repartee."

Kate let out her breath slowly and said to Simon, who leaned upon his walking stick as his gaze swept over her, "Sir, I appreciate the exhibition of your manly virtues; however, I am perfectly capable of deflecting his *repartee*. But, by all means, continue with your pummeling if you feel the need."

Surprised, Simon's jaw snapped shut. There was only a moment's pause before he said, "I profusely apologize for coming to your rescue."

"I accept your apology, sir. And I thank you for making me the center of attention."

"Most women find that appealing."

"I'm not most women."

"Clearly."

Sir William reached up for help. Both Kate and Simon saw the hand but ignored it. The fallen man struggled to his feet. Thanks to her dusting, his crimson face was swollen as if stung by a hive of bees. His eyes were nearly crusted shut. Kate tried not to smile as he brushed his tailcoat with a huff.

"Of course you must realize," he mumbled, "that this rather endangers the remainder of our evening together."

"Oh!" Kate lifted a hand to her cheek. "I had hoped we would have several hours more of your amateurish groping to look forward to."

"You are an insufferable harridan, Miss Anstruther," the man sputtered through puffy lips. "It is no wonder eligible men flee at your approach."

Kate sneered back at the blotchy prig. "I advise you to do the same, Sir William, while you still can."

She whirled away and stalked from the library, parting the amused and tittering watchers. As she emerged onto the ballroom floor and turned around, she nearly bumped into Simon Archer, who had followed her.

"Miss Anstruther, I apologize again for my behavior."

She searched his face for a sign of sarcasm, but it wasn't there. "No need, Mr. Archer."

"I'm most grateful." Simon stepped back and regarded her with his piercing eyes. Perhaps this was the
time-tested gaze of the playboy, no doubt guaranteed to
bring the most hesitant London maiden to her knees.

Kate steeled herself for his approach. It always happened. Whether skillful or blunt, like Sir William, she
had suffered this same scene endless times in countless
ballrooms.

Simon bowed. "I bid you good evening." And with
that, he turned and strode away.

Kate stared after him with a blank face. *Extraordinary.* Unlike every other man, Simon Archer did not
press the battle when the field was clearly lost. She realized that much of her stern response toward him was
her embarrassment at being careless enough to fall into
such a ludicrous situation with a pathetic fop such as Sir
William Titchmarsh. He was only reacting as a chival-
rous gentleman was trained; he had no way of knowing
she didn't need rescuing. Kate watched Simon Archer's
tall form, and despite her best efforts to remain stern,
the corners of her mouth quirked upward.

She boldly watched him a few moments more when
he was arrested by another man who spoke to him. Kate
started. He seemed to be conversing with a rumpled figure who looked like a tramp off the street, but when she
blinked, in fact, she saw that his companion was a pop-
injay dressed in overly colorful formal wear. How odd.

Kate wanted nothing more than to be done with this
London cattle yard and return to Hartley Hall in Surrey
so she could settle back into her alchemical laboratory.
She only wanted to work on formulas that promised
results from mathematical precision and careful atten-
dance to detail. However, that was impossible at the
moment. Her sister was still traipsing about the prem-
ises with her escort for the evening.

She scanned the room. Amazingly, her eyes fell again

on Simon Archer. He was standing with a crowd near the string quartet, watching the violinists with great interest. His eyes flicked up to her, and she looked away. She felt an unwise urge to speak with him again and started toward him when suddenly the exquisite figure of Grace North slipped into Simon Archer's circle.

Kate exhaled and slouched back against a pillar as Simon reserved his considerable attention for Mrs. North. The prime minister's wife laughed and laid a bold hand on his arm. It was surprising and annoying how disappointed Kate felt watching the scene. With relief, she spied her wayward sister and made her way over.

"Good evening, Kate." Imogen stood smugly pursing her lips. The younger Anstruther was attractive, if still a little girlish, with a desirable cherubic appearance versus Kate's sharp, angular features. Imogen favored their mother, while Kate resembled their father. Imogen's brunette hair was delicately curled and she was dressed to attract attention, with a very tight waist and very low bodice of golden silk taffeta. Even Kate's eyes were unwittingly drawn to her sister's surging chest, and she heard the disapproving mutterings of the surrounding women, including the notable use of the terms "inappropriate" and "bosom."

Imogen fluttered her gilded fan. "That was quite a performance with Sir William."

"Are you ready to leave, Imogen?"

"Leave? It's still early. Although I can see how you might wish to depart. Ah, here's Boylan."

A tall, sandy-haired man appeared before them. He had the slightly inelegant tread of someone trying to obscure heavy drinking. Colonel Boylan Hibbert, late of the Eleventh Bengal Lancers, had latched on to Imogen like a lamprey some months ago. He smiled drowsily and turned to Kate, bending at the waist. His glance slid too indolently along her body as it worked up to her eyes. He was handsome certainly, but in a peculiarly meaningless way. He was pale, without the usual burnt-in sun of a tropical officer, with a thin moustache and fading blond hair. There was a hard, disdainful air behind the smirk that he wore like a badge of superiority.

"Miss Anstruther. How lovely you look."

"Colonel Hibbert," Kate replied, overwhelmed by the impression of a precocious nasty boy playing at being a man.

He glanced pointedly at her bosom before turning to Imogen's much more ample one. "I will fetch punch, my sweet."

Imogen watched him stalk across the room, saying, "He is such an attentive lamb. He would move the ground under my feet to save my walking if he could."

"What a shame for you he lacks that power."

"He has other powers," Imogen said in a loud stage whisper for the benefit of gawkers nearby. "He is a . . . magician."

"Is that some sort of metaphor? If so, I pray you do not go on."

Imogen laughed. "No. He is a true magician. He is a master of the dark arts of the East. He learned such things while serving in India."

Kate was unimpressed. "Would you keep your voice down, please? You've already made a spectacle of yourself in that gown."

Imogen squared her shoulders and raised the mounds of her bosom. "You're jealous."

"Imogen, do you want to be branded a trollop?"

"It's preferable to being a hag." Imogen smiled like the sweetest girl possible.

Kate took several breaths, willing her shock to subside so she could maintain the façade of polite conversation. Her sister was not behaving rationally. She was a mockery of her true self, seeking only to antagonize her elder sister, at which she was doing a marvelous job. "You have no idea what a slip now will mean for your future. You will be shunned by the society you crave, and your marriage prospects will be severely curtailed."

"Thank you, *Mother,* but I have no need of prospects. I will marry Colonel Hibbert, and we will live in London, and perhaps on his vast tea plantation near Calcutta."

"Colonel Hibbert is a cad of the worst caliber. He has no tea plantation near Calcutta or anywhere else. He has an interest in you only because you are an Anstruther."

"How can you be so cruel? Is it because you are alone and no one will ever love you the way Colonel Hibbert loves me?" Imogen turned aside, clapping her hands in delight as Colonel Hibbert returned, bearing a crystal cup of red punch. She fawned at her escort with an extravagant gesture, revealing several large gold rings, one with a huge ruby that their father had brought from India. Imogen liked to pretend that the stone had been pried from the forehead of a pagan idol. And it certainly could have been true, given their father. "Oh, thank you, Boylan. That is so kind of you. I'm parched."

Kate added with alarm, "Yes, thank God you arrived when you did. I feared she might collapse from thirst."

Imogen slurped the punch and giggled. "Oh, it tickles my nose!"

Hibbert laughed uproariously, but his eyes lingered on Kate. She was considering various ways to gouge them out when he said, "Tell me, Miss Anstruther, do you share your father's well-known interest in the mysterious and occult knowledge of the world?"

"Why do you ask?"

"Are you familiar with tantric practice?" Hibbert laid fingers on Imogen's bare shoulder.

Kate felt her face go scarlet and her eyes harden into

ice. She knew to what he referred. To Westerners, tantric magic implied uninhibited sexual intercourse under the guise of spiritual exploration. She was unsurprised that this was the extent of Colonel Hibbert's appreciation of the *dark arts*.

Kate leaned into Hibbert with a social smile pasted on her face, her gaze sweeping the room as she spoke. "Sir, if I were a man, I would demand satisfaction for your crude behavior. As it is, this will be the last time I see you. I forbid you from again blighting my family with evidence of your existence."

"You can't control me, Kate," Imogen said, a bit loudly. "Boylan, I have a ghastly headache."

Hibbert looked confused. "You wish to leave?"

"Finally," Kate said. "Let's go, Imogen."

"I prefer to be alone," Imogen said with melodramatic exasperation. "I will take the carriage. You can find your way back, can't you? Good. Thank you so much for ruining my evening." She fled to the door.

Hibbert watched his companion disappear, then growled at Kate, "If you think you can keep us apart, you are mistaken. She is of age."

Kate rounded on the man. "I don't care if she is Madame Methuselah herself. If you trouble my sister again, I will bury you in a hole so deep, you will never be found. Am I clear, Colonel?"

Hibbert sneered and pushed past Kate with the effrontery to actually jostle her. It was all Kate could do not to seize the man's arm and wrench it behind his back. He was wiry enough that she had no doubt she could do him considerable damage before any of the shocked gentlemen could pull her off. Still, she restrained herself. She nodded openly to several gawkers, forcing them to turn back into their gossipy clutches with furtive glances at the famed harpy. Another successful evening out for Kate Anstruther.

Kate saw Colonel Hibbert across the room pausing in discussion with Lord Oakham. As mildly as she was impressed that he had any associates in high places, her opinion of Lord Oakham suddenly plummeted. Still she was curious. After they had parted, she decided to have a chat with Lord Oakham alone. She needed information about Hibbert if she was to put an end to his depredations.

Chapter Five

LORD OAKHAM WEAVED THROUGH THE THRONGS,
dressed impeccably with a high cravat and long waistcoat. Simon set down his champagne without taking his
eyes off the man, an image of Beatrice's torn body filling his vision. His mouth drew into a thin, hard line.

Simon stepped behind the string quartet and asked a
nearby servant for a pen and ink. Looking around, he
could not spot Nick in the crowd. He hid his frustration
at finding one man but losing the other. When the servant brought what he had asked, Simon penned a quick
note and laid it on a passing serving tray. It wasn't long
before it was picked up. The note was addressed to Lord
Oakham, and Simon watched as it was delivered. The
man read it, excused himself from his present company,
and departed the ballroom.

Simon waited a moment, then followed. He wanted
his lordship as far removed from the guests as possible
for a few polite questions to determine if he was indeed
their quarry. Sir Thomas emerged from the crowd to
fall into step beside Simon.

"Just in time," Simon said to his friend.

Sir Thomas grinned a broad, eager smile most unlike
the flaccid ones typically offered by his namesake. "I

wouldn't miss our entertainment for the evening. It beats a tired game of cribbage any day. Where is he heading?"

"He is meeting Sir Thomas Wolfolk in a private drawing room upstairs." Simon's attention remained riveted on the distant lord.

"That was intelligent of me," Sir Thomas said smugly.

The number of people thinned out as they went upstairs. The sound of the party grew muted and distant. They approached the drawing room. The door was ajar. The large room had a crackling fireplace on the far wall, and in the dimly lit interior, they could see the figure of Lord Oakham standing by an ornate Chinese mirror, checking out his reflection. He was a sizeable man, florid-faced and thick. Simon stayed outside the door, while Sir Thomas entered alone.

Lord Oakham turned expectantly. "Good evening, Sir Thomas. I had thought you were in Jamaica."

"I returned home," Sir Thomas replied politely. "It was ghastly hot. Had you any idea the tropics were so tropical?"

As the two men conversed, Simon studied their quarry, searching for some proof that the man in front of them was the werewolf from the Rookery. Beatrice could have been wrong, although he doubted it. Lycanthropy was fairly unmistakable. He ran the fight back through his mind, trying to determine where the beast had been struck. Oakham's neck had been burned black where Nick had grabbed him by the throat. That wound should still be healing in spite of a werewolf's fabled regenerative properties. Lord Oakham's high cravat prevented an easy inspection. Simon's eyes narrowed, trying to peer closer as Lord Oakham questioned Sir Thomas's etiquette.

"I hardly think this is the proper time to discuss Catholic emancipation." Lord Oakham scowled. "Though I would never favor such a thing. Beastly papists."

Lord Oakham caught a glimpse of the man at the

door, and Simon saw his nostrils flare slightly. Both Simon and Nick had been uncharacteristically liberal with their cologne to mask their scent, but they had no concept of a werewolf's olfactory powers. The lord took a step back suddenly, his eyes widening in confusion, glancing quickly between the two men. The shifting of the man's head revealed a hint of red scar tissue on his neck covered by the cravat. A glow began in Lord Oakham's pupils.

The flush of furious revenge swept through Simon. His jaw tightened, and his mouth went bone dry. He stepped out of the shadows. "Perhaps you would rather discuss the murder of Marie d'Angouleme."

Sir Thomas cursed unbecomingly at Simon's hotheadedness as a low growl emanated from inside Lord Oakham's chest. Incredibly, Oakham grabbed a towering life-size marble statue and thrust it at the two men. Simon and Sir Thomas threw themselves out of the way of the shattering chunks of marble.

The man in front of them transformed into a menacing, dark shape. His chest broadened to double the width and his clothes rent with an audible tear. Arms lengthened and treacherous claws grew out of his fingertips. His head grew larger, and with a loud cracking, the bones of his jaw displaced and extended. A creature stood large and hunched, snapping two luminous red eyes in their direction.

Simon rose to his feet and pulled the blade from his stick in a fierce jerk. The beast lunged forward with claws raised to strike. Simon parried the blow, twisted, and stepped in close, forcing the arm down and out. He leaned back and kicked the beast in the chest, staggering it onto its haunches. Pulling the blade back, Simon prepared to thrust, but the werewolf leapt to the side and the blade plunged through empty air.

The glamour spell dropped from Sir Thomas Wolfolk, and Nick Barker lifted his hands, both engulfed in flames. Twin fiery orbs crashed against the creature, eliciting a howl. Smoke curled around its furry head and long snout. Bony, clawed fingers clenched, then extended in pain as the beast staggered back.

A butler knocked and entered with a stern face, prepared to lecture the raucous guests. He stopped cold at what he saw. What was once Lord Oakham turned toward him.

"Run!" shouted Simon, hoping to distract the monstrosity as well as motivate the terrified servant.

With speed like a striking snake, the beast charged. It grabbed the elderly servant around the throat, lifting him like a rag doll into the air. The man's gurgling scream was stifled.

Simon ran forward with a hoarse growl, uttering a dead word, and the sword flared blue. He drove the glowing blade into the werewolf's side. The beast arched with a screech, throwing a powerful arm at Simon. He ducked, yanking out the blade as he did, and darted back as the creature turned toward him, dropping the servant. The werewolf attacked, but Simon's blade darted like lightning to parry the wicked blows. A long claw caught the blade flat and sent the weapon skittering across the floor.

Nick extended his arms out to his side, gathering a wind, and slammed his hands together to blast it toward the monster. The force of the gale hurled the beast against a glass-fronted cabinet.

Simon uttered another phrase and wrenched the ornate mirror off the wall. It weighed several hundred pounds at least, but he wielded it like it was merely a lady's vanity glass instead of something twice his height and breadth. He swung it about and slammed it against the hairy back of his opponent with an explosion of glass and dust. He hadn't expected it to do anything more than to stagger the werewolf momentarily, but to his surprise the creature screamed an unholy sound and flailed in agony. Simon looked at the smashed glittering remnants on the floor.

"The glass," Nick shouted, "must have a silver amalgam on it."

Simon snatched a large sliver of broken mirror like a dagger, slicing the werewolf. The beast snarled and clutched its chest, though the wound was a shallow one. Simon ran for his sword nearby as Nick tossed another fireball over Simon's shoulder and struck the beast in the face. Blinded by pain and flame, the werewolf spun and bounded out the open door into the hallway. Simon cursed and tore out after it.

A lone figure stood facing the beast. A slender figure. A woman. It was Kate Anstruther.

Dread filled his soul at the thought of another death he could not prevent. "Get the bloody hell out of here," Simon roared at her.

But she did not. Instead she strode forward, her hand reaching into her bag of all things. The idiot. The monstrous Lord Oakham was no Sir William Titchmarsh.

Kate's hand whipped out the bulb filled with the debilitating dust and squeezed it in the werewolf's face. The creature howled again, staggering backward, and sneezing violently. Instead of bowling through the determined woman toward the stairs, where a few onlookers stood in shock, it blindly fumbled across the hall, smashing through a closed door.

"Mad dog!" Kate shouted loudly, scattering the guests gathered behind her. They fled back down the way they had come.

Simon ran at the creature, tackling it. They tumbled into the room. He summoned his strength and grabbed hold of the muscular arms, jerking them back and trying to pin the beast into submission. But the werewolf could not be contained. It flexed and gave a mighty heave, throwing Simon into the path of the onrushing Kate and Nick. They all went down hard.

Indignant shouts revealed they were not alone in the room. Simon's blood went cold. He caught the heady aroma of burning opium. Four men and one woman were slumped over couches and high-backed chairs. Simon stumbled to his feet and lunged at the beast, but the werewolf was faster and leapt atop the mahogany billiard table in the center of the room, then among the languid revelers. They did nothing to protect themselves, merely staring at the horrific apparition in dumb fascination as if it were a product of the drug, as they went down under its fearsome claws and teeth. Simon grabbed the werewolf by the shoulders and flung it across the room.

Kate ran to one wall with a coat of arms crisscrossed by two swords. She yanked free a gleaming saber and took a stance between the wounded victims and the werewolf. Moans and screams filled the air along with the stench of blood. When Simon shoved her away, she shoved him back and stood her ground. The beast rose yet again to its feet. It was a mass of berserk fury. Simon thought her either foolhardy or bloody brave, but he wasn't about to let her test her mettle against such unbridled rage.

Nick charged while the werewolf's attention was on Simon and Kate. His hand sparked again into flame and he landed a grip on the beast's muzzle, sending a wash of fire across the creature. It screamed as its skin began to smoke. Kate darted in suddenly and made an expert thrust between the ribs. The werewolf lashed out and caught Nick, flinging him against the wall. Howling, it turned on Kate. She backed away.

Simon uttered another runic word. He grasped the heavy billiard table. He picked it up as he would a child's toy and swung it at the werewolf. The billiard table slammed into the creature, sending it careening into the opposite wall hard enough to bring down paintings and leave a large crater in the plaster.

The werewolf scattered the smashed portraits in its fury, bellowing and trying to rise again to its full height. Simon did not permit this. The mahogany table swung again and caught the monster full in the face, snapping its head around with a spurt of blood and dislodged canines. The beast licked the blood dripping down its snout and fixed fiery eyes on Simon.

Nick shoved himself to his hands and knees, speaking in a harsh guttural language that was nothing like the fluid and almost poetic words that had passed across Simon's lips. The air in the room flinched.

Simon glared at his partner, about to issue a warning, but it was too late. A sickly yellow-green smoke began to build around the beast. The werewolf swatted at it, fear beginning to show in its blazing eyes. The smoke engulfed it and the beast writhed. It staggered and fumbled weakly against an overturned divan.

"Now!" Nick rasped, collapsing to the floor.

Simon swung his massive weapon once more. The audible crunch of bones filled the room. Simon battered the helpless creature twice more at full force, smashing off chunks of the billiard table in the process. The beast went limp on the rug under the mahogany wreckage.

The werewolf was dead.

Simon staggered back and dropped what was left of the billiard table heavily to the floor. Kate lowered her dripping sword, breathing hard. He stared at her flushed face and victorious gleam.

"Mad dog?" he intoned with a bemused cock of his head.

Kate threw the sword to the side. "Well, shouting *werewolf* seemed pointless."

An inebriated laugh bubbled up from his chest as he leaned wearily upon the upturned gaming table turned weapon. She shook her head in confusion and turned to tend to the survivors. There were only two, a man and a woman. Thankfully the opium kept them calm, despite their grievous injuries. Kate tore strips from her tattered gown and set about binding their wounds.

Simon turned to Nick, who still sat on the ground. His tone was harsher than he intended, but he kept his voice to a whisper. "What did you use on him, Nick? It wasn't vivimancy. It was a curse, wasn't it?"

Nick faced Simon with a tired smile. "I needed something with a bit more power to weaken the bloody thing. Necromancy is the overmatched man's best friend."

"You said you'd stick to vivimancy. Necromantic spells have unforeseeable consequences."

"So does a werewolf trying to tear my head off. I didn't use it against the beast in the Rookery, and you griped about how we were almost killed and your whole life was wasted. Now I use it and you're griping too. Make up your damned mind. Vivimancy was worthless in these circumstances. And, even so, the two disciplines are reverse sides of the same coin." Nick kept his gaze purposefully away from the unmoving victims.

"It's never worth the price," Simon shot back.

"It's hard to philosophize with teeth at your throat." Nick walked over to where Kate tended to the two survivors. He put his hands on both of them. There was a slight greenish glow around him. Both victims twitched and took deeper, more comfortable breaths, while Nick slumped even more. "There, satisfied? They'll probably survive now."

Kate looked at Nick with confusion. "What just happened?"

Simon turned at the sound of alarmed voices coming

up the stairs. He motioned to the window. "Best not to be seen here."

Nick tipped his head to Kate and opened the window.

"You're just going to leave?" Kate was indignant. "How are we going to explain a werewolf?"

"What werewolf?" Simon asked.

She pointed at Lord Oakham and saw that he had already reverted back to a battered human form lying bloody on the rug. He was nude but for tatters of his once-lavish clothes, which were draped over him. "Oh."

"It's best none of us was seen here," he prompted, motioning her to the window. "A bit hard to explain."

"I'll stay. I doubt they will charge me for killing a man with a billiard table."

"Thank you for your timely assistance." Simon smiled, appraising the woman with new eyes. "You are most curious, Miss Anstruther."

"The same can be said for you, Mr. Archer."

He bowed, then darted out the window after Nick.

Chapter Six

IT WAS A LOVELY AUTUMN DAY IN LONDON, BUT Simon found it difficult to enjoy, still conflicted and sore from the fracas of the night before. A leisurely coffee at the Lich Gate, his favorite shop near Soho Square, was an attempt to create a sense of calm. He had first come here with Beatrice years ago, and the familiar sounds and smells gave him a discomforting sense of melancholy.

The gossip among the patrons enlightened him as to the versions of the horrific events at the home of Viscount Gillingham that circulated in the city this morning. The overwhelmingly accepted account of the story was the sudden and unfortunate onset of mental ague by an aristocrat who had a history of unusual behavior and oddly radical politics. There was a whisper of the word "monster," but it was said either with a smirk or a serious tone, which would be discounted by any but the insane or the few truly informed. Simon would have to attend the various rumors that would certainly circulate later. But rumors were rumors; they meant little.

He mourned his failure to prevent further loss of life but took some comfort in the fact that it could have been so much worse. Had the werewolf found its way to the main floor of the party, the bloodshed would have been catastrophic. The nation might have been facing the death of the prime minister and his beloved wife, as well as many notable members of Parliament and the court.

Then an odd smile played over Simon's lips as he thought of Kate Anstruther standing toe-to-toe with the hulking creature with nothing more than a bulb of noxious perfume to defend herself. Remarkable.

Simon watched leaves drift down the street and consulted his watch. He had received a message from Penny Carter to come to her shop in the early afternoon. Apparently the Scottish werewolf hunter was due to pick up his repaired weapon. With a smug smile, Simon could not help but admit he looked forward to relating the demise of the hunter's kill. It was a matter of pride after all. Werewolves were rare beasts in Britain.

Carter's Wonder Repository was busy at this time of the day though none of the browsers seemed the occult sort, just everyday customers attracted by the wonders on display in the window. One man was in need of a watch repair, while an elderly woman was looking for a gift for her niece and was fascinated by an intricate music box that had two articulated figures that danced and pirouetted to a lively tune. Penny worked behind the counter efficiently, though clearly she was uncomfortable undertaking the public job her brother usually performed.

Simon lifted his hat. "Good afternoon, Penny. Where is Charles this fine day?"

"Hello, Mr. Archer," the young woman greeted. The smile directed at him was genuine. "Visiting relatives in the east."

"Am I in time?" he asked.

She nodded. "I expect him within the hour."

"Excellent." Simon smiled. "I'll just have a seat."

"He's not punctual, but my textbooks might help pass

the time. You're a man who appreciates a wide range of learning." Before Penny could say more, a customer distracted her.

The shop boasted a pleasant alcove by the front window filled with books, most of them on engineering and steam theory. Simon had a smoke, watching the crowd ebb until he was alone in the shop.

It was more than an hour later when the doorbell tinkled and in walked the dark Scotsman. The man was tall and rugged and draped in a black woolen, double-breasted greatcoat. His long hair was pulled back tight and tied up in twine. His face was harsh and lean in the stark light, though he was probably no more than thirty years of age.

Simon raised an eyebrow as he set aside a mechanical sparrow. "We meet again."

The Scotsman stared at Simon as if trying to place him. Then recognition seeped in. "Ach, it's you." He leaned against the counter, placing the thundering great pistol with four odd barrels onto it. There was a leather harness under the man's greatcoat that held twin holsters and at least one dagger.

Penny's head poked out from the back and she waved a hand. "Be right with you, Malcolm."

First-name basis, Simon noted. The Scotsman came here a great deal then, and it wasn't for the fanciful toys either.

"Glad to see you well," Simon said. "I have news about our friend from the other night."

"Have you?" came the clipped retort.

"Yes. If you've lost the trail, don't dismay."

The Scotsman practically growled. "What do you mean by that, sir?"

"He won't trouble us again. As of last night, he is no more."

The man's eyes bored into Simon. "I doubt that. I had sign of it along the river all night."

"Then I must question your tracking skills." Simon's lips held a light smile.

The Scotsman wasn't amused. "Maybe you merely think you killed the beastie. And in fact merely dispatched a stray dog in the dark."

Simon chuckled at the man's strained wit but shook his head. "Stray dogs don't have canines as long as my hand, nor need to be beaten to death with a billiard table."

Malcolm frowned, about to make a retort, when Penny emerged from the back. She picked up the four-barreled Lancaster pistol, which promptly fell into several pieces. She turned red with anger. "Bloody hell! Do you know how long it took me to craft this beauty? This is a precision firearm, not a club! If you don't treat it properly, it won't save your life when you need it!"

"I'm not hunting pheasant," Malcolm retorted. "It gets a bit rough. If my other pistol is ready, I'll take that one and I'll keep the spare you gave me for a while longer."

Penny grumbled but then grinned dangerously back at Malcolm and Simon. "My two best customers. Have you been introduced?"

Simon thrust out a hand toward the Scotsman. "Simon Archer of Warden Abbey."

Malcolm took Simon's outstretched hand. "Malcolm MacFarlane of Rowardennan."

At the mention of the name, however, Simon's eyes went suddenly dark. Malcolm pulled his hand back instantly.

"Rowardennan?" Simon asked slowly. "Did you know a John MacFarlane who hailed from that area? Twenty years or so your senior."

"I did." Malcolm stiffened. "My father's name was John MacFarlane. What business is that of—"

Malcolm never finished the sentence. Simon slammed him against the wall with shocking force.

"My father," Simon spat coldly, "was Edward Cavendish. Your father killed him."

Malcolm's fist crashed into Simon's cheek and rocked his head back. Simon countered with a backhand across the Scotsman's temple. Simon's chest exploded as Malcolm drove an elbow into his breastbone and his breath rushed out of his lungs so fast it drew spots in his vision. He went to his hands and knees, dizzy as hell and disoriented. He noticed a leg beside him. He grabbed it and yanked, bringing Malcolm down to the ground.

The Scotsman's thick hands fell on Simon's shoulders and tried to gain leverage over him. Simon rolled and brought Malcolm with him, slamming into the table and chair and scattering books. Twisting quickly, Simon jerked aside and scrambled to his feet.

"Here now. Not in my shop!" Penny was shouting, but when Simon stood and turned, he met the meaty fist of the Scotsman. It snapped his head to the side, a spray of blood erupting from his split lip. He stumbled but managed to keep his feet. He spun around and drove a punch into the man's unprotected middle. It doubled Malcolm over, just so he could meet the knee that Simon brought up with ferocious force.

The Scotsman went flying back. Simon staggered forward, leaning on the counter and trying to catch his breath. Malcolm stepped into his field of vision. Hard, angry, and wiping blood from the corner of his eye.

"Your father was a gutless bastard," Simon snarled.

Malcolm slammed Simon's stomach, growling, "That may be, but I'm the only one that gets to call him that."

Rage boiled inside Simon. His bloody face looked up as he leaned back against the counter to brace himself. He lifted both feet, crashing his heels into Malcolm's exposed midsection. The Scotsman flew backward. Simon staggered forward to grab Malcolm's upraised arm. The look of surprise on the Scotsman's face made Simon smile despite the split lip. Simon's fist smashed into Malcolm and the man went down like a sack of potatoes.

Simon turned back to Penny, whose face was slowly recovering from her shock and turning a livid red. He coughed wetly, feeling a sense of gratification sweep over him. "Family matter."

"Are you blokes mad? This is a business not a brawling ring."

Simon's small victory was short-lived. Malcolm leapt on him and they crashed against the counter. A heavy weight bashed Simon's face into the wood. He struggled to right himself, but the muscles in his arms felt like lead weights.

Simon flashed on his mother crying as she told him of the night his father died. The anger flared bright once more. He shoved Malcolm off; it wasn't clear how. He didn't think he used magic, although he couldn't swear to it.

The Scotsman stumbled to his feet again like a dark wraith, seizing some strange metallic contraption off a bookshelf and brandishing it. Simon heard Penny shout in alarm, although it was more out of alarm for her work than a warning to Simon. His strong arm blocked Malcolm's blow, and with a wild shout, slammed his forehead into the other man's head. Simon roundhoused Malcolm in the jaw. The Scotsman crumpled in a flurry of arms and legs. The startled expression on his face spoke clearly that he hadn't expected to lose this fight.

Too bad.

To his hardheaded credit, Malcolm tried to push himself up yet again, but from the looks of it, he wasn't sure of his surroundings. The Scotsman shook his head, unsure why he was still on the floor.

"Your services are no longer needed here," Simon snapped. "You're to leave London as soon as you pick your sorry carcass up from the floor."

Malcolm spat blood and drew the back of his hand across his mouth. "I'll leave when I'm ready, and not before. Not for you nor any man."

A splash of cold water hit both men in a drenching wave, bringing them to a sputtering silence.

"Out! Both of you!" Penny roared, holding an empty bucket.

"Bloody hell, woman!" the dark Scotsman bellowed, wiping at his dripping face. "The fight was already over!"

Penny's fist balled on her hip. "Good thing, then, or I would have shot the both of you."

"What about my pistols?" muttered Malcolm.

"Come back for 'em when you regain your senses." Penny shook her head. "That's the last time I try to introduce friends."

Simon stiffened and extracted his damp wallet, laying a considerable amount of currency on the counter. "My apologies, Miss Carter."

Under the engineer's stern glare, the two drenched men slogged from the shop much to the curiosity of those on the street. They retreated into an alley around the corner and faced one another.

"You're wrong, Archer," Malcolm muttered through clenched teeth, meeting Simon's haunted eyes. "On my honor, you are."

"Your honor," Simon hissed, but something in the Scotsman's forlorn acceptance made him let go of his rage. Maybe it was the pain in Malcolm's eyes that matched his own. With a face like stone, he held the man's gaze, debating what he should do.

Malcolm's hand rested again on his blade. His body was tense with muscles coiled. "Let's get this over with if you demand it."

"Still ready to defend your father's name then?" Simon retorted icily.

"I've long since stopped trying."

"Tell me why I should believe John MacFarlane didn't kill my father when I've always known he did."

"I know the story of that night, and it's nothing to be proud of for my part. My father was ordered to kill a man named Edward Cavendish, but he drank so much he wouldn't have been able to stab a dead goat. He couldn't go through with it."

"How do you know this?"

"He told me."

"Why should I believe that?"

Malcolm's eyes flared angrily. "The MacFarlanes aren't adverse to killing, as is well-known. My father would have admitted to the deed if he had done it. It would be better to be a killer than a coward."

Simon's body was rigid. "So then, who murdered my father that night in Scotland?"

Malcolm's shoulders slumped in sympathy. "I don't know. My father never knew. My father never rose above the bottle again. He died in a puddle of his own making."

Simon studied the Scotsman, watching every twitch of his muscles, every turn of his lips. This man, regardless of what his father had or had not done, believed that his father was innocent of this one crime at least.

Malcolm's face struggled not to reveal any emotion. "If I had the answer, Archer, I'd give it to you."

"Lucky for you, Mr. MacFarlane," Simon said with a sad smile. "I won't hold the son responsible for the sins of the father." He clasped his hands behind his rigid back and walked away, leaving the hunter standing alone.

Chapter Seven

THE INTERIOR OF ST. GILES WAS FLICKERING IN the candlelight. Drafts made the flames shudder, creating a disturbing pattern of moving shadows around the space. Two thick candles in heavy stands were posted on both ends of the casket.

Simon sat in the front pew. He leaned forward, his hands resting on the handle of his walking stick. His mother's gold key dangled from his fingers like a rosary. He watched the coffin in which the body of Beatrice rested.

He could recall spring afternoons when he had been boyishly content that he would spend his life with her. The pinpricks of light reflecting in her eyes the first night she blew out the lamp in her bedchamber. Her gentle touch warming his neck. He remembered the smoothness of her thighs under his palms. She laughed constantly. She loved poetry and would often cry when reading aloud. He had taught her the proper pronunciation of runic spells.

Simon heard the sound of a man clearing his throat and shuffling his feet. He glanced up to see the sexton in the darkness near the altar. The man bobbed from foot to foot, eager to be on his way but still respectfully silent.

Simon took a breath and rose. He laid a hand on the rough wooden top of Beatrice's coffin. He lifted the lid a few inches and slipped a few clippings of newsprint inside. The articles she had saved as evidence of his *advancement* in the mystic arts. He closed the casket, unwilling to look at her in the winding sheet. He preferred to remember her from that spring night long ago. The sexton came forward with a credible look of sorrow and comfort. The man raised a finger to his forehead in deference.

Simon reached into his pocket and pulled half a crown. "I'd take it as a great kindness if you'd see her settled well."

The sexton's unshaven visage locked on the coin. "Well, sir, I don't know if the vicar will have it." He looked up in alarm. "Given what she . . . who she was, sir. You understand, it's not my thoughts, sir."

Simon pulled a second coin and held both of them out. "I'd take it as a great kindness."

The man took the money with a comforting nod. "Very good, sir. I'll do well by her. You may trust me."

"Thank you. And I will provide a grave marker. You'll help me place it when the time comes?"

"Yes, sir. I will. God bless you, sir. She must've meant something to you."

Simon regarded the sexton. Then he touched the casket again before turning and striding from the otherwise empty church.

ST. GILES WAS NO MORE THAN A TEN-MINUTE walk from Simon's town house in fading fashionable Mayfair, but he had no wish to return home. He preferred to stay in the shadows tonight, so he made his way to the Devil's Loom. A drinking establishment had existed on this spot since the reign of Edward III. It was nearby the Resurrection Gate, where condemned prisoners were given a last pint before being hustled to the scaffold at Tyburn.

Simon found a spot in a nearly hidden corner of the pub. He slouched in a seat with his long legs up in a chair and stared through the thinning crowd into the far wall. He tapped the gold key idly on the tabletop. His jacket was gone and his white shirt was wrinkled and open at the collar, hanging loose at the cuffs. He threw back a gin and set the glass down, no longer calling for another. Another came just the same, as the previous ten had come.

Beatrice would be in the ground by now. His father had been in the ground for nearly thirty years. Simon had seen to Beatrice's killer. However, John MacFarlane hadn't killed his father. It was as if he had buried one and exhumed another.

He scrubbed at his face, trying to keep his thoughts coherent. He didn't want to give up any of his long-cherished beliefs passed on by his mother, including the tale of his father's murder. There was only one problem—he believed Malcolm MacFarlane. The sooty eyes of the Scotsman were true like steel. Hard and unmovable. Malcolm was what he said and nothing more.

Malcolm MacFarlane was an honest man.

Over the years, Simon had come to terms with the fact that his father had been murdered. There was nothing Simon could do about it. He had honored his father by continuing in his role as a scribe. He studied magic. When his mother died eight years ago, Simon had come to London to live. His intention was to immerse himself in his magical studies and become a scribe.

However, he found city society beguiling and distracting. Despite the fact that his questionable parentage would always set him apart from complete propriety, he still navigated it with ease. Simon came to perfect his own roguish personality, which put him inside the drawing rooms and even boudoirs of London. Everyone knew he was the son of Elizabeth Archer and an unknown father. The persona of a charming rake was a necessary construct to make himself appealing at all levels of society, because otherwise, he was just a rich bastard.

"Well, well," came a voice, "so this is where all the gin has gone."

Simon looked up with fierce annoyance to see Nick standing at the table. He slumped deeper into his seat.

"Oh, thank you," Nick said, pulling a chair from under Simon's feet. "Don't mind a drink myself."

Simon growled. "Damn it, Nick. I want to be alone if you don't mind."

Nick signaled for a pint. "You nearly are alone, old boy. The place should've shut hours ago and you look very drunk."

The barman brought the pint grudgingly, and said with emphasis, "Time, gentlemen."

Simon finished his gin and held up the empty glass. "Another, please!"

"You're not getting another." Nick hooked an arm over the chair. "Let's head off home, shall we?"

"You go if you're tired." Simon studied his watch, holding it upside down. He scowled at it. "It isn't late at all. If they won't serve me here, I'll go to the club."

"The club? Which club would that be? You'll find no doors open to you at this hour except your own."

"I can drink at home in the morning. I've got to celebrate tonight."

"What are you celebrating?"

"I have acquired a new outlook on life."

"Have you? What became of your old outlook?"

"It has been rudely torn away." Simon waved a hand and leaned over to pat Nick on the chest. "But no matter. You will have a role to play in it because you are my friend."

"Gratified to hear it. Would you care to share, or is it a secret?"

"Everything's a secret to someone." Simon put a finger to his lips. "The Order of the Oak killed my father."

"What?" Nick stared hard at his friend. "Your father? You've never mentioned your father before. What the hell are you talking about?"

Simon held the empty glass to his mouth and drained the final drops of alcohol. "My father was a member of the old Order of the Oak in the days when it was a true guild of magicians, before the collapse during the French Revolution and the purges. The new Order decided that his loyalties to the previous management were annoying, so they dispatched a man named John MacFarlane."

Nick flinched with surprise. "How do you know this? The Order was nothing if not secretive."

"My mother. The night my father was killed, he knew MacFarlane was coming, so he sent my mother away for her safety. At the time, she was with child." Simon touched his chest. "My mother never saw my father alive again."

"I'm sorry, Simon." Nick swirled beer in his glass, staring deeply into the amber liquid. "When did your father die?"

"He was murdered late in 1802, and I was born early the next year. He never saw me, nor I him."

"What was his name?"

"Edward Cavendish. He was a scribe, as I am. Did you ever meet him in your travels and wide circles of acquaintances?"

Nick shook his head. "No."

"He was Byron Pendragon's right hand during the

last days of the Order, in the days when they were a wall between humanity and darkness."

"Pendragon?" Nick now looked doubtful. "Your father was Byron Pendragon's right hand? Did your mother tell you this too?"

"Yes!" Simon sat forward with eyes alight. "After Pendragon was betrayed and killed by one or both of his compatriots, Ash and Gaios, they also killed my father for defying them."

Nick drained his pint and set it down. "Aside from the fact that you have no idea who really killed Byron Pendragon, you're telling me that your father knew Pendragon, Ash, and Gaios?"

Simon glared at the doubt in his friend's voice. "Perhaps I shouldn't have told you anything if you're merely going to mock me."

"You have to credit my doubts, Simon. You're talking about the three nearly mythological figures who founded the Order of the Oak centuries past. Now you tell me your father knew them, and was killed for it. It's a bit like saying you're family friends with Robin Hood and King Arthur."

Simon stood unsteadily, flushing with anger, remembering the tears his mother shed telling him the story of the night his father died. "You don't have to believe me."

"Wait, wait." Nick smiled and urged his friend to resume his seat. "I never said I didn't believe you. I'm just trying to understand what you're telling me."

"Then allow me to spell it out for you. Since I was a boy, I believed that my father was murdered by John MacFarlane on the instructions of someone high in the Order of the Oak. I now know that to be wrong."

"How do you know that?"

"That man we met the night Beatrice died, the Scotsman, his name is Malcolm MacFarlane. He is John

MacFarlane's son. And he told me that his father did not commit that crime."

Nick sat waiting, then when he realized that was the end of the story, he shook his head in disbelief. "He *said* his father didn't do it? That's it? Why would you believe him? Of course he would lie about it. And don't you think it's a bit convenient that you happened to run into him out of the blue?"

Simon tightened his hands on the glass. "Yes, it is convenient because now I know the truth."

"But how do you know?"

"I know it!" Simon shouted. "I don't know how. Or why. But I believe him. Damn him. And so I must search for the man who killed my father. I must say good-bye to you."

Nick slammed his glass down. "You drunken idiot! What about everything you talked about the other night about the purpose of your power? You're just coming into your own. You're finally a half-decent scribe now."

Simon put a hand to his forehead. "Plans change."

"Oh shut it. You sicken me. That courtesan was right about you. You'll never stick to anything. You're petty."

Simon snarled through gritted teeth. "How dare you speak to me in that way."

"I'm the only one who will. Before you wander off into some misguided personal vendetta, you had best listen to me for a moment. I've lived a long time, Simon, a very long time. I've had my share of quests for vengeance. And I wasted an enormous amount of life doing it."

"Are you telling me to forget my father?" Simon's voice was slurred with gin.

"If you'd shut up and listen to me, you'll hear what I'm telling you. The trail for his murderer is long cold. Don't forget it, surely, but don't let it consume you. Move forward with your life. Learn to be a scribe. Use your abilities to help those like your Beatrice. Let that be your tribute to him. To her. That is a better way to remember them both."

Simon gazed again into his empty glass. "A man should do something if his father is killed."

"You're doing something. Look, Simon, the years after Pendragon were chaos. A lot of scores were settled in the shadows. And most of the good members of the Order played it smart and kept their heads down. If you wander off into that darkness now, you'll never find the path again. You will be acting for the benefit of no one but yourself."

Simon slowly shook his head in confusion.

Nick continued, "You said yourself that something is growing in the dark. If you leave now, who will stand in its way? Your father waited this long for vengeance. He knows what you're about, and I'm sure he approves."

Simon sat still for a long moment. "I'll do you the courtesy of considering what you've said. However, to do so I need another drink, but this place has obviously dried up." He stood and reached for a jacket that wasn't there. He tugged on his unfastened shirt cuffs. He did a credible job walking, only bumping into two tables and three chairs on the path to the door, where he paused. "I bid you good evening, Mr. Barker."

"That isn't your hat."

"Good." Simon replaced a soft hat on the rack. "I was distraught at my taste when I thought it was."

The two men stumbled together out into the cold and stood underneath the pub's sign, which featured a cloven-hooved goat man weaving what appeared to be a human shape on a fantastical loom. Simon immediately went to turn up his nonexistent coat collar. He tried several times before acting as if he was suddenly warmer. He studied the street in one direction, then the other.

"Now," Simon said, "would you direct me to the Pall Mall Club? Or the Mayfair."

Nick settled against the brick wall. "You're unfit."

Simon glowered. "Do you mind showing some good manners? Is the Cagliostro Club in this neighborhood?"

"It moves. I believe it's in Greenwich for the winter."

"Excellent. I'll find it." Simon staggered off to the north, not toward Greenwich at all.

Nick caught Simon by the arm and steered him in a homeward direction. The pair walked in silence for a while, with Simon leaning heavily on Nick.

"I've decided you're right, Nick," the scribe said suddenly. "I trust you."

"Do you now?" Nick nodded silently as he shifted Simon's weight to get a better grip on the drunk magician. Simon could barely manage a grin between his pounding head and his bone-weary exhaustion. With Nick supporting him, his feet slapped down one after another as they lurched along the sidewalk.

Simon started to chuckle. "Stay on the path now, my good man."

Nick grunted, and the two men staggered toward home through the dark and cold, leaning on each other.

Chapter Eight

KATE ANSTRUTHER STRODE UP THE FRONT STEPS of Hartley Hall bathed in stark, cold morning sunlight, her cheeks ruddy and her hair unkempt. Beside her padded the long, graceful form of an Irish wolfhound. Laying a hand on his massive head, she gave him leave to continue patrolling the grounds. The hound bounded away.

As soon as Kate entered the house a footman came forward to wrestle off her mud-caked black boots as she leaned against the doorframe. She also surrendered her heavy leather coat and padded off in stocking feet, taking the stack of newspapers from the butler. A maid trailed behind carrying clean shoes and a change of clothes. Kate took the shoes but waved off the clothes, feeling the maid was overstating the condition of her mud-specked breeches and heavy cotton blouse.

She entered the morning room, where a fire had been laid and breakfast prepared on the sideboard. She took a cup of coffee and flipped through the first newspaper until she found the story she sought: the report of Lord Oakham's death at Viscount Gillingham's party. Apparently, according to knowledgeable sources, poor Lord Oakham succumbed to a violent fit. The prime minister and wife were on hand to comfort his lordship in his last moments. Funeral arrangements were pending.

She opened a second paper that was known to be a bit less friendly to the regime and found a small item that the noted Tory, Lord Oakham, had perished at a party of Whigs attended by the Whiggish prime minister and his beloved wife. There was no attribution of cause of death, but there was a hint that his lordship might have died in a violent way, perhaps in a duel, perhaps linked to Lord Oakham's radical politics.

Kate shook her head. So that was it. Neat and tidy. The other deaths hushed up. She paced before the window, staring out at the late-autumn gardens. She saw the two men she had just left continuing their circuit of the grounds. One of them was the head gamekeeper, and he carried a wide-bore shotgun. She had set a guard around the house to intercept Colonel Hibbert should he attempt to contact Imogen. Kate felt assured by her defenses, but now she needed to go on the offensive.

She had already spent a day lingering at home since that horrific night at Viscount Gillingham's. After leaving the party in the wee hours of Saturday morning, she had recovered Imogen from a cousin's home where they were staying the weekend and come straight from London, reaching Hartley Hall at dawn. Imogen had stomped angrily to her room, from which she had yet to emerge. Kate had collapsed into the fitful sleep of exhaustion, only to rise a few hours later and seek refuge with her alchemy. But every image of beakers and tubes of bubbling liquid was torn apart by visions of that horrible beast that had been Lord Oakham.

A werewolf. Hibbert. Imogen. What—if any—were the connections?

Did Hibbert know that Lord Oakham was a werewolf? Was he one himself? Before the party, everything seemed clear. Kate had had no doubt she could ward off a simpleton suitor. Now, however, new plans had to be made.

In frustration, she had made for the study, where her

father had kept his notebooks and journals. Late into Sunday night, she pored through the many volumes devoted to his world travels, including his frequent observations on the strange and occult. She searched for information on lycanthropy, and she found some. Her father had encountered tales of were-beasts, and made a record of them. However, there was certainly no credible mention of lycanthropy in Britain.

Her father would have been in as good a position to know as any. He was Sir Roland Anstruther, a great explorer and perhaps the most widely traveled man of his day. If a hierarchy of English manhood of the last century were created, Sir Roland would rest under a bare few—Nelson, Wellington, Cook. He was a deity of the Empire. Yet, to Kate, he was her father. She could hear his deep, wild laugh and feel his rough hand around hers. He had the warmest blue eyes. There was no bird's warble he could not identify nor animal track he couldn't sort out. He had taught her French and German and sent her overseas to make use of them. He had made certain she could sit a horse like a lady and fight like no gentleman. He was a master mathematician and an engineer, and Kate always admired his analytical, practical nature.

She also valued his attachment to mysticism, and very few besides her knew how significant it was to him. As a child, it was a way to spend time with him when he was at home and as an adult it was sheer curiosity. Kate had devoted much of her time to a scholarly pursuit of magic and its history. She had pursued the discipline of alchemy, perhaps because it combined the reproducible specificity of science and the misty spirit of the occult.

Again her thoughts drifted to the mysterious Simon Archer, as they had many times over the last day. Handsome and confident, with the wry sensibility of a gentleman of means. Kate had sensed something strange in him, as if he wore a mask. Something dark that he either tried to hide or didn't recognize himself. Plus, he clearly performed acts a normal man couldn't. He lifted a mahogany billiard table that must have weighed hundreds of pounds. He wrestled with the monstrous were-wolf as Kate would with her beloved hound, Aethelred.

And then there was his companion who, one moment, appeared to be a languid fop, and the next, an unshaven street vendor. Very odd. To say nothing of the fact that the fellow produced fire from his bare hands.

Kate wondered what manner of men these two were, but now, as the sun was rising on a chilly Monday, she needed to set plans in motion. She stood before the fire when she heard the door open.

"Hogarth," Kate greeted warmly, "I was just going to send for you."

He was a tall man, well over six feet, and his livery hid the fact that he was stunningly muscular. Kate had taken many a boxing lesson from him, secretly so as not to scandalize the other servants, and knew that he was as well-knit as any man she had seen in an undershirt, which, admittedly, was few. He was not handsome but striking in a grim fashion. He had dark and quiet eyes. She had never seen him discomfited.

"I will be going into London tomorrow." Kate found an appetite now that she was finished waiting and had a plan of action. She reached for a plate, shooed Hogarth away from serving her, and began to pile on eggs and sausage.

"Yes, Miss Kate. Shall I accompany you?"

"I would like you along." She sat and began to eat voraciously. "It's time to deal with Colonel Hibbert. I want to find out more about him. What few inquiries I made since he latched on to Imogen left me unsatisfied. I intend to run him to ground."

"But you say he is associated with Lord Oakham, who is a lycanthrope," Hogarth reminded her matter-of-factly. "Was a lycanthrope. He must be dealt with outside normal channels. Your father asked me to take care of you and your sister. Leave it to me."

Kate stared into his dark eyes. He betrayed no more emotion than if he had offered to pour her another cup of coffee, which he did. "I don't intend to murder the man."

"No?"

She laughed as she cut a sausage. "No, Hogarth. At least not until I know exactly what we are dealing with. I will do everything I can, legally, to expose and ruin this wretch, if he is indeed just a mere wretch. If I can drive him from the country, I'll do that. But I have no idea of his connection to Lord Oakham. It could have been mere coincidence. That is the kind of thing I need to find out before I take any action."

Hogarth posed by the window with his hands behind his back. "I see."

There was a knock at the door and Mrs. Tolbert, the white-haired housekeeper, came in. She seemed quite distraught. Kate straightened, expecting the news that Hibbert had appeared on the estate.

"Miss Kate." The housekeeper recovered a bit of her posture. "I've just been told some alarming news by Miss Imogen's maid."

"What is it, Mrs. Tolbert?" Kate struggled to keep her voice steady.

"Miss Imogen is gone."

"Gone? Gone where?" Kate rose from the chair.

"I don't know, miss. One of her travel bags is gone, and some of her clothes are missing."

Kate felt Hogarth moving to her shoulder as she slammed her hand onto the teak table. "Damn it!"

Mrs. Tolbert said, "One of Miss Imogen's horses is absent from the stables. The maid is blameless, I'm sure, miss."

Kate waved her hand. "I don't care who helped her at the moment. Thank you, Mrs. Tolbert. Have a change of clothes laid out for me." The housekeeper withdrew and Kate turned to Hogarth, taking some solace in his steady visage. "Hogarth, we're going to London now. I'm sure she's gone to Colonel Hibbert. Have the post chaise ready."

"Yes, miss. However, given that the matter of the werewolf is still a concern, I suggest we acquire additional help. You mentioned two gentlemen from the party. Perhaps they might be able to assist you in this matter."

Kate shook her head doubtfully. "I have no knowledge of these two. One was using some sort of disguise to appear as Sir Thomas Wolfolk. The other man was Simon Archer."

That took Hogarth by surprise. "Simon Archer?" He repeated the name as if it held some recognition.

Kate regarded her manservant. "You know him?"

"I know of him," he clarified. "He is a gentleman of a particular sort."

Kate couldn't tell whether Hogarth referred to the man's social standing or something else. She shook her head. "This is a family matter."

"Miss, you know that Colonel Hibbert is a man of dark purpose, and he may have dark resources. I suggest you consult with Mr. Archer on the matter."

Kate couldn't deny she had thought of the same thing, though perhaps for another, more personal, curiosity. Simon Archer had wielded considerable power, as had his friend. These appeared to be the first true magicians she had come across, other than in journals or letters penned by her father. If Archer was a trustworthy figure, it would be useful to have him on her side. She noted the quiet assuredness on Hogarth's face. "Very well. It's worth the effort to contact him."

"Yes, miss. An excellent idea."

Kate's lips held a peculiar smile as she went for the door.

Chapter Nine

A WELL-DRESSED WOMAN SHOULD NOT HAVE been walking unescorted on the edge of the Devil's Acre in Westminster so late at night unless she had business. This woman did, but not the usual kind. She appeared gigantic, easily over six feet tall, with flowing blond hair. Her face was set with eyes like glaciers. She wore a cloak that rippled around her and hid her true shape, allowing imaginations to provide her with any manner of body. It did nothing to diminish her imposing stature, and her stride made her seem even grander; it was long and measured like a soldier's. She was a Valkyrie come to life, a handsome woman, no doubt, but her size and power outshone her striking features.

She paused at a crowded corner to get her bearings. All these hovels looked alike to her. A group of ragged men huddled around a nearby fire. They stared at the statuesque woman in amazement.

"Lost, my dear?" one of them asked, eliciting some laughter from his friends.

Without looking, the woman replied, "I am looking for the Boulware Club."

The man strolled to her side with a gap-toothed smile, emboldened by the gibes of his companions. "It's just around the corner there. On your way to meet someone there?"

She started off, but the man scrambled in front of her. "Here now. What's the rush?" The top of his oily head came to her chin as he backed up to keep pace. "My my, you're quite a tall one."

A few of his lads moved away from the fire, closing behind her. The woman's eyes shifted slightly, but she kept walking. The lead man reached out and touched her arm.

"Here now, why so rude? I'm just offering you a bit of business before you get to the Boulware."

Her cloak fluttered. There was an audible sound of bones cracking. The man screamed and staggered away from her, his arm bent at an unnatural angle.

One of the men trailing her darted forward and the woman spun to face him. He realized none of his friends had come along and stopped. The woman's hand darted out like a viper. Strong fingers collected his threadbare coat at the collar. She lifted the man off the ground and swung him against a lamppost. The man's breath whooshed out so he couldn't scream.

The woman slammed him against the iron post a second time. He struggled in her grip. The man's head clanged against the lamp twice, then again. His fellows backed away, gaping with disbelief as the woman battered their friend bloody. Finally she lifted him with one hand over her head and threw him to the pavement. He grunted and rolled into a ball, a pool of blood spreading from his head. She whirled back to her original course, unmindful now of the amazed crowd who watched her from the street and from many windows. None tried to stop her.

Around the corner, as promised, was the Boulware Club. It was a sagging old Restoration edifice that perhaps had been grand in its day but was quickly suc-

cumbing to the blight of the area. She stepped onto the
crumbling porch and pushed open the front door.

There was no doorman outside to question her. There
was no butler inside to meet her. There was only a grimy
foyer and a staircase up to the next floor. She noted a
sitting room off the entryway where several sets of eyes
turned lazily toward her, then opened wide at the sight.
She made for the door of the sitting room, sparking
even wider eyes.

She surveyed the parlor with its flickering lamps, drooping wallpaper, badly used furniture, and men just as
badly used. They were typically old men in worn clothes
that were a decade out of date. It might have been the
Regency to this roomful of society detritus.

She announced, "I want Colonel Boylan Hibbert."

The men lowered their newspapers and worked pipes
in their wet mouths. The woman tired quickly of their
confused stares so she regarded the man nearest her.
He sat in a patched armchair next to the fireplace. He
was dressed for dinner but wore slippers with the big
toes worn through. His white hair was thinning and he
clearly had neglected to shave for several days.

She asked him, "Do you know Colonel Hibbert?
Where are his rooms?"

The old man twisted his head in thought or senility.
He removed his pipe. "He resides in seven-B, which is
up the stairs and third door along on the right. However," he added when the woman started away, "he has
a guest at the moment, I believe. I would be happy to go
up and tell him you are calling."

The woman glanced over her shoulder at the man with
a disdainful smirk. When she turned back to the stairs,
she heard him mutter, "Irregular. We must tighten the
membership regulations."

The woman climbed the creaking stairs. Voices rose
in argument or passion. She heard laughter and crying.

Tobacco smoke mixed with coal gas, and even a hint of opium. That last sweet smell grew stronger as she reached the door and pounded the wood with her fist.

The door swung back to reveal Colonel Hibbert in a tattered smoking jacket, a colorful dhoti, or Indian cloth, wrapped around his waist, and bare feet. A long-stemmed pipe was clenched in his teeth. His eyes were red-rimmed and half-closed.

The Valkyrie pushed past him into the room, followed by Hibbert's drugged leer. The room was overwhelmingly grey, the floors, the walls, and the linens. One feeble lamp cast vibrating shadows. Hibbert closed the door slowly and leaned against it. He gave a smile that once might have been charming.

"Gretta." Hibbert bowed clumsily. "Welcome to my home. I've just put on the kettle. Would you care for refreshments?"

She glanced around the wretched place and sniffed. "You've fallen far, Hibbert."

The man snorted with amusement. "I find the finer clubs no longer welcome more worldly men. Anatomize a few worthless doxies in Calcutta and suddenly a gentleman is no longer in fashion."

Gretta grunted with lack of interest in his personal plight. "Is she here?"

"She came when I whistled." The colonel pointed to another door with the stem of his pipe and grinned lasciviously. "She is abed."

"And have you done as instructed?"

"She has been given a dose of the elixir. And I believe I am owed something. Though I would have gladly done this service for free." The man's expectation flared through the opium haze.

Gretta produced a blue bottle from inside her cloak and tossed it to Hibbert.

He stared at the glass vial with a mixture of relief and

desire. "I can assure you, Gretta, the lovely Miss Anstruther will do anything I ask, and she has." Hibbert
glanced at the tall blonde in false modesty. "Oh, I'm
sorry, my sweet, for my impolite masculine bluntness."
Then he chuckled. "Although, why should I fear? We
are both men of the world, eh, Herr Aldfather?" He
grinned at his jest, particularly given the annoyed glare
she gave him. He collapsed into a chair, nestling his
bottle. "Opium. You never turn your back on a gentleman."

"Colonel Hibbert, neither your childish humor nor
your assistance are needed any longer."

From his filthy armchair, Hibbert drew on his pipe,
taking a drowsy interest in what the woman was saying. "Oh? That's too bad. I was rather enjoying her. But
no matter. What shall I do next?"

"Nothing."

"Well then, I should like better quarters. There's no
privacy here for a man to engage in . . . certain practices."

Gretta studied the lanky wretch of a man. "No."

"No what?"

"There will be no *better quarters* for you. There will
be no *certain practices* for you."

"Look here, old hound, I'm giving that Anstruther
chippie to you. She's primed and ready. I deserve something, don't I?"

"You deserve to be killed and eaten."

Hibbert stared into the bowl of his sputtering pipe
with a disapproving sneer. His voice was slurred from
narcotics. "Here, I won't have talk of eating me in my
own home."

The woman came toward his chair and reached for
him. A horrific screech filled the room. Shades of bright
yellow sprang from the floor, terrifying figures of translucent vapor with fingers and skeletal faces twisted in

anguish. The shades coalesced around the woman, who showed surprise for the first time. She swung her strong arms as the sickly, spectral things ripped at her. Her head was slapped from side to side, raising scarlet welts on her cheeks. Her blond hair flew around her face, long strands torn from her scalp. With a shout of anger, she scrambled quickly to the door, keeping an arm up to cover her face. The yellow spirits did not pursue her. They hovered around Hibbert, giving off a weird, cackling noise. Then they thinned like morning mist at dawn and disappeared into the floor.

Gretta crouched, breathing hard and collecting herself. Her blue eyes penetrated the thin man who had made her crawl. She stood slowly and brushed her clothes. Now she saw that Hibbert's chair sat in the middle of a magic circle chalked onto the wood. She glanced at the bedroom door.

"Oh, it's the same in there." The man smirked with unctuous superiority. "Miss Anstruther is reclining in the middle of another circle. Approach her, and my nasty familiars will rend the skin from your body. Which will only serve to make you more masculine than you already are." He chuckled at his witticism.

"What's your game, Hibbert?" Gretta's voice cracked with restrained anger.

"It's no game. I want what's owed me. I don't have to give Miss Anstruther to you. I can just enjoy her a few more days, then use pieces of her in my conjuring. It would slacken my taste nicely for revenge against the Anstruthers."

Gretta went rigid. Her veins bulged and tendons in her neck grew taut. She began to shiver.

The man squirmed in his chair but kept his voice even. "Your act doesn't frighten me, Gretta. I've the upper hand here. You are toying with a conjurer who

learned his art in the Dark East. What do you have to
match that?"

The woman's pale skin suddenly went dark. Her back
hunched and the cloak bulged with powerful muscles
pushing from inside. Her fingers twisted and gnarled,
growing black with claws growing from the tips. Gretta's head grew larger and her blond hair turned the
color of coal and seemed to blend with a thick coat of
heavy fur that rose from her entire body. Her mouth
widened and the white teeth grew ever larger. Clawed
feet tore free of shoes.

She shrugged off her heavy cloak and shook herself.
The remnants of clothing slid from her gigantic frame.
A massive werewolf stood with dripping jaws. She
dropped heavily onto her hands and dug her claws into
the floor. Blackened lips rippled with a growl.

The man drew his feet up into the chair, staring
wildly at the creature. He pointed the stem of his pipe at
her. "Here now, Gretta. Stop that noise. You can't pen-
etrate my circle, even in that form."

"No?" she rumbled and exploded at him.

Hibbert shrieked, dropping the bottle of opium, which
shattered on the floor. The yellow shades appeared immediately, enveloping the great beast. Her back bowed
as if she had hit a wall. However, she muscled forward
with her hands, gouging curls of wood from the floor.
The yellow, misty horrors wailed and tore at her head
and back. Their hands, trailing steam, ripped bloody
rows in her hairy flesh. Still, Gretta drove closer to the
little man in the chair. The shades roared as if in hellish
pain, continuing to swirl about her, raking her. Despite
the brutal damage they dealt, they lost ground with
each crunching step she made.

Gretta's ferocious glare never wavered from the terrified Hibbert. Her snout strained to within a foot of the
man and she bared her teeth. The tip of her huge tongue

lolled from her mouth and licked his face. The man screamed and bolted. The instant he broke the circle, the shades vanished and Gretta toppled against the empty chair.

Hibbert took three steps before a huge claw fell on his back. He hardly had time to shout when his back opened in a flood of gore. One shoulder with the arm attached fell to the floor, while the rest of the man staggered drunkenly for a few steps, teetering backward, and spun to the ground.

Gretta slapped at the motionless body. She sniffed it closely and only smelled death. She grunted a bestial laugh.

With two long strides, she reached the bedroom door and pulled it open. She peered into the bedroom. Filthy curtains floated in the cold wind.

"Damn him!" Gretta cursed.

The huge werewolf stepped to an empty bed with an open window next to it. There was a second chalk circle on the floor, but with Hibbert dead, it had no power. The bedclothes were rumpled and Gretta could smell a recent occupant. A female. The scent went from the bed to the window and out.

The Anstruther girl was gone.

Gretta gathered her cloak and inspected the nasty, steaming wounds on her arms, legs, and torso. Painful, but they would heal. She went to the bedroom window and took a deep huff of the air. Out there among the smoke-shrouded rooftops and alley warrens black with shadow, there was a slight scent of the girl.

With a fluttering of her cloak, Gretta leapt out into the cold night.

Chapter Ten

THE ANSTRUTHER FOUR-HORSE POST CHAISE rocked to a stop on the Strand. Simon parted the window shade and glanced out. He nodded with satisfaction to Kate Anstruther, seated across from him. She threw up the shade and stared out with open disdain at the white marble Italianate edifice with its row of flickering gas lamps.

"Imogen is in there?" she asked, her voice grinding.

"This was Hibbert's last given address, so it is likely. It is a good thing your manservant directed you to me. The Mercury Club is not overly friendly to women." Simon sounded apologetic. "I'm certainly no choirboy, but these chaps are quite despicable in many ways that cannot be spoken of in polite company. I know members in passing."

"In passing?" she repeated in a questioning tone.

"In passing," he said, letting it go. "They cultivate a façade of mystery. Like to pretend they are magicians. In reality, they are adult boys with too much time on their manicured hands."

Kate snorted with agreement. Her mood had deteriorated since she had met with Simon at Soho Square an hour ago to explain her situation. Now she was more a caged animal spoiling for a fight. The way she held herself, there was a studied aggression to her, an economy of motion and nervous energy he had seen in athletes.

Just as interesting to Simon was the Anstruther's manservant, Hogarth, who rode outside with the driver. He was an odd character who hardly spoke, barely moved, and exuded a strange power and authority. Simon found him a bit disturbing.

Despite her virulent mood, Simon was glad Kate had come to him. He had intended to contact her because he couldn't let the events at Viscount Gillingham's go unexplored. She had handled herself with such mastery.

Simon said, "If you'd care to wait, I will go in and make inquiries."

Kate threw open the carriage door. He quickly followed her out onto the Strand with a look of mild dismay. She cleared a path through the late-afternoon crowds until a liveried doorman of the Mercury blocked her from the dark wooden door. Simon quickly darted in front.

"Good afternoon." He smiled broadly to the doorman.

The doorman relaxed at seeing a gentleman with the lady. "Good day to you, sir. Is this your party?"

"It is."

"Was the Circle alerted that you were coming today?"

Simon cleared his throat and deposited a gold sovereign into the doorman's gloved hand. "You haven't seen Colonel Boylan Hibbert in the last day, have you?"

The doorman gazed back without emotion as if the cash exchange hadn't occurred. "You'll need to speak to Lord Argyle, sir, with such inquiries."

"Is he in?"

"He is, sir." The doorman stood aside. "You will, of course, stand for your guest, sir."

Simon gave the doorman a quick salute of silver-handled stick on hat brim, then ushered Kate and Ho-

garth into the hushed, dignified cool of the Mercury Club.
A magnificent chandelier glittered over their heads and a
grand staircase curved up to the second floor. Doorways
opened into lavish parlors and libraries and smoking
rooms. There was no sound save the footsteps of a valet
who approached across the checkerboard-tile foyer.
Simon placed a calling card on the man's gold salver.

"I should like to see the Archdruid, if you please."

Kate scoffed, which caused the valet to divert his
attention to her before turning silently and departing.

Simon chided Kate. "Do try not to mock, Miss Anstruther. This is a serious conglomeration of very serious men. And Lord Argyle is the most serious of them
all."

"I shouldn't expect anything less of an Archdruid?"
Her eyebrow arched with bemusement. "Is he a real
Archdruid? In that case, I apologize."

"He's a git with a magic fetish. But the Archdruid, or
Lord Argyle as mere mortals know him, is a man of
influence, and if you challenge his fantasy, he'll never
tell us anything."

Kate clasped her hands behind her back, rocking on
her heels. "Wouldn't want to embarrass the Archdruid."

"Archer!" A man descended the carpeted grand staircase, waving his arm enthusiastically. He was short and
fat with wisps of white hair flying from his mottled
dome. He wore a long, broad-sleeved silk robe embroidered with moons and stars. In his pudgy fingers, he
clutched a crooked tree branch as a wand of some sort.
The man trundled up and shook Simon's hand with a
sweaty grip and a jovial greeting. He eyed Kate with
approval. "Splendid to see you again, Archer. I see you
finally decided to take us up on our offer of membership. And you brought a guest!" He poked Simon like a
naughty schoolboy.

Simon cast a baleful warning eye on Kate. "This is

Miss Kate Anstruther. Miss Anstruther, I have the honor
to present the Archdruid, Lord Master of the Mercury."

Kate nodded politely though her impatience showed
in the way her mouth tightened.

"I bid you welcome." The Archdruid flourished his
diminutive twig at her, causing Kate to suddenly peer
over at the intricate woodwork around the door as if
her life depended on it. The plump Lord Master looked
a bit put off, but he regarded Simon. "Did you say *Anstruther*?"

"I did. Miss Anstruther is the eldest daughter of Sir
Roland."

"Ah!" the Archdruid exclaimed, bending slightly at
the waist. "You do us honor."

Simon gave Kate a surreptitious shake of his head to
warn her off any argument.

The Archdruid took Simon's arm. "When your membership is finally settled, we would even consider including you in the Inner Circle. Come now, Archer, you're
our kind of people." He winked toward the woman.
"Obviously."

"I fear, your lordship, that my time is not my own
these days. I will give it serious consideration, however.
For now, I would like to ask a question of you."

The Archdruid's pleased expression faded but still
remained courteous. "Of course, Archer. Shall we go
into the Golden Grove?" He pointed his jagged branch
toward what appeared to be a normal sitting room.
"Your servant can wait outside, and we can have your
guest taken to a room upstairs, where she can prepare
herself."

"Prepare myself?" Kate burst out, hands balled on
her hips.

Simon coughed. "Now, my dear, your needs will be
attended to presently."

Kate shot him an angry glance. A very angry glance.

The Archdruid looked her up and down quite shamelessly, and Simon took the opportunity to shoot the woman another silent plea, begging her restraint.

The fat druid elbowed Simon. "Fiery. I should think you'll be in for it later."

"I make the same prediction. But if we could briefly speak here. I am trying to find Colonel Boylan Hibbert, late of the East India Company."

"You are? That gentleman is no longer a member here."

Kate stiffened in alarm. "Since when?"

The Archdruid glared at the woman for speaking out of turn, and said to Simon, "A year perhaps. If I may trust you with a confidence, he was a bit too free with his behaviors. We have high standards here. Colonel Hibbert was beyond the pale, so to speak. We can't have ourselves held up to scorn or scandal."

Simon felt a cold dread seeping into him. If Hibbert was too peculiar for the Mercury Club, it spoke volumes about his potential danger. "You wouldn't happen to know his current place of residence, would you? I'd take it a great kindness if you did."

"He did recently ask for a room here. I refused him lodgings, of course. At that time, he reported that he could be contacted at the Boulware, room seven-B, if we changed our mind. We have not, and we have seen no more of him."

"When was this?"

"Perhaps two weeks ago. He had a young woman on his arm. Blond. Rather stupid, but attractive and well dressed. Colonel Hibbert obviously would rather make his address the Mercury for a wealthy piece such as her."

Simon couldn't react fact enough to stop Kate. She stepped forward and unleashed a thunderbolt right cross to the Archdruid's jowl. He spun helplessly and collapsed to the tiled floor.

Hogarth hadn't shifted an inch, but there was a strange, slight smile on his lips. Simon blinked and glanced down calmly at the drooling, semiconscious Lord Argyle, tangled in his druidic robes.

Kate rubbed the fingers of her right hand while staring at the man on the tiles. "If I find out my sister was here, and anyone touched her, I will return and rip you into pieces."

Simon extended his arm toward the door. "Miss Anstruther, it appears this interview is concluded."

Hogarth held the door. As Simon passed the manservant, he said, "Quite a punch your mistress has."

"Miss Kate is quite an effective puncher with either fist." Hogarth dispassionately regarded the fat man on the floor. "She didn't seem to require her left hand for this one, however."

"No, she didn't." Simon laughed loudly. He pressed another gold sovereign into the doorman's glove. "Thank you for everything. A very satisfying visit."

Simon joined the woman as she climbed into the carriage.

THE POST CHAISE MADE ITS WAY WEST ON THE Strand, fought through a snarl at Charing Cross, and inched along Whitehall toward Westminster. Soon the towers of Westminster Abbey rose through the gloom on their left and the sprawling Halls of Parliament grew visible in the distance. The dim, medieval warrens north of the grand Abbey created a gloom inside the carriage.

Simon tugged on his cuffs. "We're heading for a rather sketchy area. It's known as the Devil's Acre, for good reason. I suggest you stay in the coach."

"No," Kate stated plainly.

He didn't think such a ploy would work but as a gentleman he had to make the attempt. His fingers tapped lightly on his knee. "You say Colonel Hibbert had some interest in magic, but did he ever exhibit any signs of being a practitioner?"

Kate drew in a deep, calming breath. "I never saw Colonel Hibbert evidence any skills of any sort, short of a loathsome ability to enchant Imogen. She often claimed he meddled in the dark arts, but she is a silly-hearted romantic."

"He's a poseur in all likelihood. Though the fact that he interacted with Lord Oakham, however briefly, makes me wary." Simon tapped his walking stick idly on the floor. "Mind though, our singular goal is to remove your sister from the situation. Hibbert can be dealt with, if needed, in the future, at a time and place more to our advantage." He peered out the carriage window. The cobblestone lanes were narrowing.

The coach rocked to a halt and the door flew open. Hogarth stood outside, a large shadow in the dark. The buildings beyond him were dilapidated and miserable. The Boulware Club was a club in name only.

Simon swung out and helped Kate from the coach. "Miss Anstruther, bloody knuckles to a minimum, please." He strode forward into the gloom.

The front door squeaked when they entered. A few bored fellows who sat reading newspapers or playing cards or smoking away their lives turned to look at the passing visitors. However, none of them were interested enough to speak.

Simon whispered, "Hogarth, take a position in the rear yard in case our quarry manages to slip us."

The manservant checked with Kate for approval, and she nodded. Hogarth padded out.

Simon led the way upstairs, each step creaking under their feet, his hand grasping his walking stick. The banister was loose and felt oily from generations of un-washed hands. The ceiling had once been artistic plaster tiling, but it was water-stained and crumbling now. The stink of humanity was barely masked by the cloying haze of coal smoke.

Simon said quietly, "He brought a woman of breeding here? What power does he have over her?"

"His only power is that he isn't me," Kate replied bitterly. "He offers Imogen the freedom that apparently I don't."

They moved along the hall and stopped at a flaking door where there was a number. He pointed at it and put a finger to his lips. There was a metallic undertone to the stench in the building and his boots felt tacky as he moved them. He looked down to see he was standing in a dark stain that had seeped a few inches from under the door.

Blood.

He lifted one foot and it parted from the floor with a sticky pull. It was relatively fresh.

Kate stiffened in alarm. "Imogen!"

Simon whispered a word and smashed open the heavy door with a swift punch. Inside, the walls were stained with blood. A crumpled body lay in the middle of the room. Simon drew his stick sword and the blade flashed blue in the dim.

When Kate tried to rush past him into the room, she slammed against his arm like it was an iron pole. She was breathing wildly.

Simon stepped inside, his shoes squelching in the blood. He surveyed the sitting room, where blood covered nearly every inch of the floor like a repulsive carpet. Everything else seemed in place. Furniture upright. He noted a kettle burned black on a grate over the now-cold fire. There was a second door, but it was closed. He took another careful step, listening. He heard doors out in the hallway opening and voices raised in anger or curiosity.

The body in the center of the room had one of its arms ripped off. The clothes were peculiar for central London, a colorful dhoti wrapped around his waist and what was left of a smoking jacket. A pipe lay in the blood, and Simon smelled the faint hint of opium. The grey face had a moustache and very surprised eyes.

He turned back and shook his head to Kate. She seemed slightly relieved that the cadaver wasn't her sister, but then she rushed for the closed door. Simon stopped her and she started to shove him aside with, "My sister is in there."

"Miss Anstruther," he hissed quietly. "Please stay here. We have no idea what may be inside that room."

With a steady hand on the chipped-glass doorknob, Simon listened again, trying to block out the buzz of curiosity from outside. The sounds of the city reverberated louder behind the closed door.

He knelt quickly and ran his hand through the blood. With a dripping index finger, he began to scrawl runes on the door. After he completed several symbols, he drew a bloody circle around them. He whispered and the circle shimmered translucent and became a window into a bedroom. The bed was unmade but not tossed. Vases and lamps were sitting upright on tables.

Simon saw no bodies nor any great washes of blood. However, the rear window was open. Not broken, merely open. The dingy curtains danced in the wind. A wisp of silk snagged on the soft wood, splintered by time. Perhaps Imogen had time to flee.

"She is not here," Simon reported. His attention was drawn back to the dead body on the floor. It lay within a circle of magic and Simon caught the faint whiff of brimstone. There was something about the man's face.

Simon stepped carefully through the blood and knelt next to the cadaver without putting his knee down. He used the tip of his walking stick to move the head from side to side, examining the features. "I know this man."

"What?" Kate exclaimed with anger. "Why didn't you say before that you knew Colonel Hibbert?"

"I didn't know him as Colonel Hibbert. I encountered him years ago at a party. His name was Sunderland, and he was a doctor."

Her voice rose an octave in distress. "He wasn't an officer in the East India Company?"

"He was. He was a brilliant surgeon in their ranks, but deeply disturbed." Simon rose and stepped carefully from the blood. "He was drummed out of the East India service for practices they would not even commit to a private report. It was said that he murdered numerous Indian women for his own amusement."

Kate put a trembling hand to her cheek and stared at Simon in disbelief.

"And more," he continued, "I assume you're not aware that your father encountered Dr. Sunderland . . . Colonel Hibbert here, in India, and was instrumental in having him broken from the service and ruined in acceptable society."

"Oh my God," Kate whispered. "What has he done to Imogen?"

Simon crossed back to the rear door and threw it open. He saw a hint of blood on the floor leading toward the open window. Bloody footprints. They were close and regularly spaced. Walking, not running. They were the footprints of a huge hound.

A werewolf.

Chapter Eleven

THE HACKNEY CAB CLATTERED EAST ALONG OX-
ford Street. Kate huddled under a blanket in the evening
chill. She was silent and grim, and had been since they
left the Boulware. She said for the tenth time, "Why
can't we go back to the Mercury Club and inquire after
Hibbert's other contacts?"

"Tomorrow," Simon confirmed easily. "Hogarth has
returned to Hartley Hall should she return there. I've
put the word out. If someone has seen something of
your sister, we'll hear of it soon."

"The lamplighter you spoke to?"

"Yes, they're very helpful lads. There is no more
we can do tonight." He shouted up, "Cabbie, south on
Crown."

"Right, sir. Where're we headed?"

"Gaunt Lane."

There was a pause as gas lamps flashed by. "I don't
know any Gaunt Lane, sir."

"Drive on. I'll point it out."

The hackney turned right onto Crown Road. Simon
could hear the cabbie muttering about there being no
Gaunt Lane, and he'd wager his rig on it. After a few
minutes, Simon tapped the edge of the roof and pointed
with his cane. The driver swore.

On their right was a narrow gated lane and an aged bronze plate reading GAUNT LANE.

"I never," the driver breathed, shaking his head. He accepted Simon's generous tip. "Thankee, sir. I'd have sworn there was no such street. Ever. You and the lady have a pleasant evening, sir."

"My cousin," Simon said. "Up from Surrey."

"You have a lovely family, then, sir."

Simon waved pleasantly as the cab rolled away, and Kate said, "I'm surprised he had never seen this lane."

"He's already forgotten it. The street plate is runed." Simon ushered her past lamps that glowed strangely toward a home on the short dead-end lane. It was a most unremarkable residence, almost bleak. He noticed Kate staring at one of the odd gaslights. "Don't get too close. Lit by brownies; they're quite vicious."

"Brownies? Please, Mr. Archer. I appreciate your attempts at levity, but there is no need."

Simon shrugged. "Still, don't get too close to them if you value your fingers."

Kate scoffed again, but then squinted close at the flickering lights. Little figures moved behind the pebbled glass.

"You realize," Simon said at the door, "that it may not be completely respectable for a lady to be staying the night with a gentleman."

"I want to stay in London to be near the search. I'll risk the blow to my reputation." Kate glanced at Simon. "I'm not inconveniencing you, am I?"

"My house is yours for as long as you wish," Simon announced graciously. There was no door handle, but when Simon brushed a brass plate, the door opened. Once inside the narrow foyer, he took her wrap. "Would you care for a bite to eat? Or a cup of tea?"

"I wouldn't want to trouble your servants at this late hour."

"You won't. I have none." He tapped the opaque glass of a lamp and clicked his tongue as if summoning a pet. The light rose obediently. "No need for a cook, as Nick and I dine out. But I'd like to think I'm a skilled chef, at least skilled enough if you're hungry."

Kate watched as he tossed her topcoat casually onto a chair. "I wouldn't say no to a cup of tea. I don't think I can sleep just yet."

"I'll put the kettle on."

"Might I freshen up first?"

"Take the room at the top of the stair, second on the left. There are suitable nightclothes in the closet, and you should be able to find a change that will serve for tomorrow. Or I can arrange to have your clothes laundered. If it's too dark in your room, simply tell the lamp to burn. If it balks, tell it you're speaking for me."

Kate gave him a curious glance and went up. Simon stuck his head into the sitting room; it was empty. He padded upstairs and knocked on Nick's door. There was no answer; his friend was likely drinking at the Devil's Loom. He returned to the ground floor and made his way to the back, removing his coat before shuffling around the kitchen to gather things for tea.

A sound at the door alerted him to the arrival of Kate with her eyes half-closed and distant. She had shed her jacket and wore an embroidered plain-weave cotton dress with gigot sleeves. The long skirt brushed the floor.

He said, "If you'd care to settle in the sitting room, I'll be right in."

Kate studied the frosted glass of a lamp. "Would you mind if we just sat in the kitchen? Some comfortable domesticity would be calming."

"Excellent idea. It's a terrible disaster in there. My housemate is quite a slob. Gather around the table. Did you find everything you needed?"

"Yes, thank you."

"And did the lamps cooperate?"

"Eventually, although I had to play a simple game of Simon Says," Kate remarked wryly. "And your closetful of ladies' nightclothes and outfits of varying sizes shows remarkable taste. They are for . . . ?"

Simon set the kettle on the cold stove, trying to appear nonchalant. "Guests."

Kate shifted the sugar and cream from the counter to the simple oak table, regarding him with a side glance. "Should I inquire further?"

He gave a slight smile. "Only if you wish to know more."

She remained silent on the matter and continued to set the table. Finally, after moments of quiet punctuated by only the clatter of dishes, she said, "What do you think happened to my sister, Mr. Archer?"

"I don't know." Simon watched her. The reserve of power she dredged up so she could attend tasks even in the face of such emotional burdens was extraordinary. "The fact that Imogen did not share Hibbert's fate at the Boulware is heartening."

"Perhaps the killer simply carried her away," Kate muttered.

"I don't think so. Werewolves don't do that sort of thing." He took a stubby grease pencil from the stovetop and began to write symbols on the steel kettle. The runes glowed faint green and the sound of water boiling rose almost immediately. "If it had killed her, she would have been there, dead."

"Do you believe that lycanthropy is transmissible?"

"No, I do not. Everything I've heard about werewolfism says it's something a person is born with. There's never been credible evidence of one werewolf creating another. There's never been an epidemic of any sort. I wouldn't fear that Imogen has been transformed in any way."

"Oh, where is she, Mr. Archer?" Her eyes followed his movements even as they betrayed exhaustion.

"I don't know, Miss Anstruther, but we shall find out. I pledge that to you."

"Thank you." Her voice was growing ragged with fatigue.

"What troubles me most is that there appears to be another werewolf. The creatures are rare enough, but to have two in one location is damnably unusual. As is the fact that Hibbert wasn't consumed. It's a bit odd."

"A *bit* odd?"

"Werewolves are animals, Miss Anstruther. They kill for the same reasons animals kill. For protection and for food. And the man was merely killed and mutilated but not eaten. Biscuit?"

"You make it appetizing, but no, thank you." Kate grimaced.

Simon crunched into a small cookie as steam began to hiss from the kettle. "Do you shoot? I can arrange for you to have a pistol loaded with silver."

"I do. So you hold to the legends about silver?"

"To an extent," he said cautiously as if she would dispute it and expose the fact that his lycanthrope knowledge was hardly encyclopedic. He poured boiling water into a small porcelain teapot with a simple flower painted on it. "Certainly anything will harm them, but they are ungodly tough. Silver seems to make the wounds more grievous and gives us a chance at taking them down."

"And is magic a substantial weapon against them? Your style of magic seems particularly effective."

Simon hesitated, pouring cream into her cup to buy time. He recalled all the warnings that his mother had impressed on him about maintaining secrecy, as well as Nick's constant demands to stay in the shadows. Still, he looked at the troubled expression, which shifted beneath the assured pretense on Kate's face. She had already seen so much it seemed ludicrous to pretend any further. He was eager to take Kate into his confidence, so he said with offhand casualness, "Yes, magic is very effective."

She seemed to visibly relax as he poured tea into their cups. "You've a very dainty teapot for a man."

"It was my mother's." Simon adjusted the teapot slightly and tapped it lovingly with a finger.

"Was she a magician too?"

"No, she was better than that. She was a saint with no interest in magic, only in magicians."

"Well, in my family, I had some exposure to mysticism, but I must admit I've never experienced magic used with such everyday facility."

"Parlor tricks. A criminal waste of skill, given what the greatest of us are reportedly capable of. Like using a cannonball to send a love note."

"If you don't mind me asking, what school of magic do you practice?"

He sipped tea. "I am a magician of the type often called a scribe."

Kate's tired eyes widened. "I've read about scribes, but even the most trusted magical tomes hold them to be as rare as rocs and likely extinct in our time."

"Well, I'm not quite ready for a museum display, but there are very few of us. In fact, I might be the last. Much of the knowledge related to the discipline is lost."

"But not gone entirely."

"No. I've a rather large library dedicated to the art, and Nick has a useful store of knowledge. He's been something of a mentor for a number of years, helping me to perfect my use of runes to cast spells."

"Your friend is a scribe as well?"

"Nick?" Simon laughed. "No. He's something of a

jack-of-all-magical-trades. There's no classical way to describe him. There is little in the way of practical magic that he can't muster in some fashion."

Kate set her cup down with an exhausted stare. "Believe me when I say I would love nothing more than to discuss this topic at length, but I hope you won't think me rude if I go to bed. The day is catching up with me. The tea was delicious. Thank you for it and the company. And for everything you've done."

"You are most welcome." Simon stood. "Sleep well. If you need anything during the night, my room is at the end of the hall."

The woman shuffled from the kitchen. Simon leaned back in his chair, listening to the sounds of her footsteps on the stairs and her bedroom door closing. There was much to contemplate about the turn of events and it required another biscuit. Kate was ever more fascinating; she had more than average knowledge of the occult, just like Beatrice. But she was wildly different, as he had noted at Viscount Gillingham's home. She was an extraordinary blend of unbendable and uncontrollable. Simon couldn't imagine what horrifying emotions were embroiling Kate, but she was holding up far better than he would've suspected. The woman's strength was remarkable. He hoped something good would come out of this affair for her, but it was hard to imagine it could.

Chapter Twelve

KATE ROSE AFTER A RESTLESS NIGHT, SHIFTING and sighing in the dark. A peculiar wall clock that appeared to have a glow told her it was after eight o'clock. Scandalously late to rise. She quickly found suitable clothes from the many outfits in the closet, all complete with dressmaker tags. She felt a little better that she wasn't just the next in a line of occupants of these fashionable outfits.

Coming downstairs, Kate smelled coffee and porridge and turned into the kitchen. "Good morning, Mr. Archer. Oh." Kate looked at a short, stocky man who was stirring a pot on the stove. She had seen him at Viscount Gillingham's fighting alongside Simon but never spoken to him. "I'm sorry. I thought you were Mr. Archer."

The man gave her an arched eyebrow. He seemed completely unfazed by the sight of a woman coming downstairs in the morning. Obviously he had spoken with Simon about the situation. Hopefully.

"Did you sleep well?" he asked. "I took the liberty of starting a bit of breakfast. My name is Nick Barker. I am Simon's . . . colleague."

"Have you seen Mr. Archer? Is he up?"

Nick tossed her a fine bone china cup. "He went out."

"Without me?" She cursed under her breath, catching the cup easily.

Nick chuckled at some private thought. "He seemed anxious." He jutted his chin at the coffeepot on the stove and continued stirring.

She poured a cup for herself. "So you cook as well?"

"As well?" Nick laughed, but without much humor. "Simon likes to trot out his old *I'm a chef* tale."

Kate grinned uncomfortably as Nick continued to chortle.

"His concept of cooking is cultivating an extensive knowledge of the chefs in the finer clubs of London. Left to himself, Simon couldn't toast a herring."

Kate collected things to set the table. She noted Nick's gruff glance as he watched her move easily around his kitchen.

"Make yourself at home," he muttered.

"I'm sorry, Mr. Barker. Are you the type of bachelor who is offended by feminine assistance?"

"I'm not much offended by anything." His tone was resistant nonetheless.

Just then, Kate heard the sound of the front door. She went quickly to find Simon tossing his hat onto a table.

"What did you find?" Kate exclaimed, her interest in his discoveries outweighing her annoyance at being excluded.

"I went to the Mercury and the Boulware again. I spoke to several servants and residents in hopes of further information on Colonel Hibbert or to find someone who had seen Imogen recently. There was one man at the Boulware who saw a rather large blond woman. He describes her almost like a man. Afterward he heard a disturbance in the colonel's room."

"A woman killed Hibbert?" Kate surmised. "A jealous quarrel? What about the werewolf?"

"The witness was drunk. His reliability is quite lacking."

"What shall we do now?"

"Let's go into the sitting room and discuss it." Simon directed her into a sun-dappled room of very masculine style. The homey scent of leather and wood. Suitably disheveled. Books everywhere. Used dishes stacked in various spots. Small piles of burnt tobacco on corners of tables and desks where they were knocked from pipes and left.

"I apologize for the state of the house. I'll bring coffee." Simon stepped to the door of the parlor. "Nick! Coffee!"

A muffled rude word wafted from the back.

Simon began to tidy the room halfheartedly, taking small stacks of books and making large stacks of books, sweeping pipe ash from the desk onto the floor.

Kate parted the sheer curtains to peer out. She jumped when she saw a wiry orange cat sitting on the brick sill staring strangely back at her. "Mr. Archer, please. Cleaning seems pointless now. What is our next step?"

"Quite." He dropped the stack of books he was carrying and brushed his hands on his trousers. "Something we should be aware of. It's possible that the police may question us about Colonel Hibbert's death."

Kate whirled from the window. "Why? How do the police know we were there?"

"They don't, or they shouldn't. And I suspect they won't spend much effort on a man such as he. However, if they manage to connect Hibbert to Imogen Anstruther, it would lead them to you."

She nodded, vexed she hadn't considered that possibility before now. "What will we tell them?"

"The truth, of course."

"The truth?" She looked doubtful, her arms folded across her chest.

"Not the *entire* truth." Simon laughed as he moved next to Kate. "The entire truth is rarely necessary, which is precisely why I smudged out the werewolf tracks at the death scene. No sense in giving the boys at Scotland Yard a more difficult riddle than they can solve. I will also want the shoes you were wearing last night so I can destroy them. Bloodstains and all." He opened the window and the cat leapt inside. "Don't worry, we'll work out a logical story before we need it."

"You don't strike me as a cat fancier." Kate watched the animal patter off down the hall.

"Well, he's the former owner of this house," Simon said cryptically. "And he refuses to leave."

There was a rap at the front door and Simon started. "A visitor. That's unusual. In fact, nearly impossible."

"Is it the police?" Kate's eyes widened. "You said the house was warded."

Simon went to the hallway, where Nick appeared too. Both men seemed disturbingly unnerved. "Are you expecting anyone?"

"No. You?"

The two men walked slowly to the front door. Nick stood to one side and his hand began to sparkle with faint flickers of flame. Simon pulled his walking stick from a wicker cobra basket and drew out the sword.

Kate heard a slight crack and realized it was her fists tightening.

Simon touched a panel on the door and it shimmered into transparency. He reared back in surprise. Nick noticed his reaction and leaned over to look out.

"Who the devil?" Nick asked.

"I can't fathom how he found us." Simon lowered the sword and triggered the door to swing open. "Good morning, Hogarth."

"Sir." The Anstruthers' massive manservant stood

calmly on the stoop, eyeing the narrow blade in Simon's hand. "Is Miss Anstruther here?"

"Hogarth!" Kate raced forward before Simon could answer. "What is it? Have you heard from Imogen?" Her questions were desperate.

"Miss Imogen has been located, ma'am."

Kate didn't like the way he had phrased that response, nor his guarded tone. "Where is she?"

ACROSS THE THAMES RIVER FROM WESTMINSTER was Lambeth, where stood a rambling Georgian palace known as Bethlehem Hospital, often called Bethlem for short. It was perhaps the most well-known medical facility in the entire city, and the most feared. The polite citizens would cluck their tongues and pay proper homage to the progressive concept of Christian kindness and scientific treatment for the patients there. But more often than not, they suppressed a shudder of horror at the thought of the wild-eyed lunatics screaming in the cold shadowy dungeons of "Bedlam" asylum. And they prayed it would never be them.

Kate knew she was dreadfully pale as she followed a white-clad orderly through the spacious main hall. The comforting footsteps of Simon and Hogarth were close behind. Gratefully, no drooling, gibbering patients wandered about. The smell was a noxious blend of sweat and faint chemical. Attendants and doctors in their long coats, well dressed and serious, nodded sympathetically.

The orderly opened a door and stepped aside. "Dr. White will see you."

They entered a vast front office and Kate saw an older man behind a distant desk. He was shrouded by bright light from a sweep of windows behind him. He rose quickly and came forward, buttoning his jacket politely.

He was white-haired but moved with vigor. A man of great concentration, he focused on Kate as he used both massive hands to take hers.

"Miss Anstruther, thank you for coming so promptly." His voice was deep and comforting.

"How is my sister?"

"Please, won't you sit?" Dr. White directed her to a plush leather chair, one of several in the corner of his office.

"Thank you. Doctor, may I present my friend, Mr. Simon Archer."

Dr. White shook Simon's hand. "Mr. Archer, we've met briefly."

"I recall. Three years ago at the Royal Society's ball honoring the memory of Sir Joseph Banks."

"You have a prodigious memory, sir. I believe you were favoring the recently widowed Lady Houseworth that night. Most kind of you to provide her with support in her time of grief."

Kate glanced at Simon, and save for a tightness in his jaw, he offered no reaction to the comment.

Dr. White consulted the gold watch hanging on a sparkling chain from his waistcoat. He gathered a brown folder from his desk and sat down opposite Kate. "I know you're anxious, Miss Anstruther. Most understandable. So let me tell you all I know."

The doctor drew eyeglasses from his pocket and propped them on his nose. He opened the folder and consulted several sheets of closely written notes. "Let's see. Your sister was seen wandering the streets in Westminster two nights ago in a state of extreme agitation and mental confusion. While that is not an unusual condition for some, it was clear to observers that your sister was a woman of status, not a tramp down in her cups. She was approached by a constable who determined that she was unable to make a satisfactory accounting of herself and displayed a paranoia that was aggressive and dangerous. As it didn't appear to be the obvious result of alcohol or narcotic, the constable had her brought here.

"She was admitted and questioned by one of our doctors. During a brief moment of lucidity, she claimed to be the daughter of Sir Roland Anstruther. At which point, I was called to consult, having seen both of his daughters in the past at various functions, and I confirmed that she was Sir Roland's youngest." He put aside the papers. "I then sent a message to Hartley Hall, and here you are."

"What is wrong with her?" Kate asked.

"I don't know, to be frank. But let me caution you, the disorders of the mind are not so simple as mere physical maladies. That said, I haven't had the opportunity to do more than make the briefest of observations. And she has been under enormous sedation to stifle her deranged behaviors."

"Did she mention a man named Hibbert?" Kate said.

Dr. White consulted his notes for a few moments. "No. Is he someone of importance to her?"

"He was."

The doctor's gaze flicked uncomfortably to Simon. "May I speak quite frankly, Miss Anstruther?"

"Yes," Kate replied. "You may say anything in front of anyone here."

His voice lowered. "A physical examination of your sister gives me ample reason to believe she may have been ill-used by a man. I'm very sorry to tell you that."

Kate gripped the arms of the chair, threatening to rip them off. "Could that violation explain her extreme condition?"

Dr. White removed his eyeglasses and held them thoughtfully. "I don't know. Despite our desire to categorize all forms of life, the human mind resists the most cunning tactics of science. Every person is an individual with unique reactions to emotional disturbances. Miss Anstruther, would you characterize your sister as a sensible young woman normally?"

Kate looked down and back up with solid conviction. "Yes. Normally."

"I see." Dr. White paused to adjust his tie. "I am going to recommend that you take your sister home."

Kate relaxed visibly. "Thank you, Doctor. So you think she will be fine once we bring her home?"

"I won't tell you that, but I strongly suggest you keep her at home for the foreseeable future. The normality of that environment can do nothing but help her. And quite frankly, a woman of her stature and family shouldn't be here. I've managed to keep the knowledge of her identity confined to a few here to decrease the possibility that the public will learn that the daughter of Sir Roland Anstruther was a resident, even for a short while. I wish to minimize the potential for scandal at all costs. I have pulled all the papers that were filled out at her admission. As of now, she was never here."

"Thank you, Dr. White."

"I will provide you with a strong tincture of opiates that will assist you in keeping her calm. I fear I cannot give you much hope for her future, but I do not wish to dissuade you from hoping."

Kate exclaimed, "Isn't that a bit extreme?"

"I understand your consternation, but remember, you haven't seen her. I don't know how she acted prior, but I can only assume she wasn't in her current state." He gave Kate a pointed stare. "You weren't keeping her confined, were you?"

"No, of course not."

Dr. White replaced his glasses and gave an odd, inappropriate smile. "Well, you will now."

Chapter Thirteen

HARTLEY HALL SEEMED TO ERUPT FROM THE SE-
rene Surrey countryside. Originally it had been a mod-
est Tudor-era country house, but Sir Roland Anstruther
had enlarged it over his years of residence until that
quaint old relic had long ago been subsumed by a sprawling grey stone structure partially hidden in scarlet-
leafed ivy. It was a half-mad but magnificent structure
inextricably mixed with the landscape by way of con-
servatories, loggias, pergolas, and large French windows. To some it might appear overwrought, but there
was a chaotic charm to it. The large turrets gracing
some of the corners made it appear as if it were a stalwart protector of its five-thousand-acre estate and could
hold back any encroaching army.

Hogarth carefully took the insensible and lethargic
Imogen in his thick, muscular arms and carried her inside without a word from his mistress. Kate ushered
Simon and Nick in, where she spoke a few calming
words to the butler and housekeeper, who stood with
wide eyes, staring at Imogen being carried past. She dispatched the two servants to see to the guests and followed Hogarth upstairs.

Simon and Nick were invited into the library, where
maids appeared with tea and coffee. The room was large

enough to host a meeting of both Houses of Parliament. Drapes were pushed aside to let in the fading sunlight and a fire was laid in the hearth. Afterward, the two servants who had met Kate at the door introduced themselves as Barnaby the butler and Mrs. Tolbert the housekeeper. He was quite rotund and had an emotionless face; she was aging and likely in her final years at the famous estate, with all the authority that a woman in her position had gathered in that time. Barnaby unlocked the liquor cabinet with a set of keys and offered drinks. Simon graciously declined, and when the servants realized he was not going to let slip any information about Imogen, they excused themselves.

Simon carried a cup and saucer as he strolled deeper into the library. Everywhere his eye lit, there was some sort of strange and wonderful object. Artifacts. Constructions. Relics. Maps. Books.

He encountered a huge portrait of Sir Roland that dominated the vast room. The man was handsome, with his hair pulled back in a queue. He was dressed in clothes from the reign of George III. He stood with his right hand on his hip and his left hand extended and open. An acorn rested in the palm of his hand. The background was a tropical sea scene with a British frigate in full sail. The expression of the man was odd, however, for a formal portrait. He had a slight smile on his face as if he found the prospect of fame amusing, as if the very act of sitting for a portrait, of being immortalized, was laughable.

"So young." Simon eyed the ship in the painting. "HMS *Resolution*. This would have been around the age when he traveled with Cook to Hawaii. Seems like a pleasant fellow, given his later reputation as a stern taskmaster in his own expeditions."

"Hawaii is where the natives beat Cook to death. A lot of Englishmen will end up that way in hot places around the globe if we keep pushing ourselves out there. Hello, have a look at this."

Simon saw Nick hold up what appeared to be a chunk of rock about the size and shape of a fist. He had seen a similar object before in Paris, buried in a warded trunk beneath the tiles of Notre Dame. It was a gargoyle heart. He couldn't help but be awed. Even Nick gave an impressed shake of his head and tossed the lump of stone organ back on a shelf.

There was a machine on a table that appeared to be manufactured of pure transparent crystal. It was only a foot square. The interior was clear and the inner workings were visible with intricate gears and levers apparently crafted from delicate crystal. Light sparkled against the facets and rainbowed across the room. It was an extraordinarily beautiful piece of work but had no obvious function.

Simon's attention was immediately diverted by a large reptilian skull on another bookshelf. "What do you think of this beast, Nick? It appears to be an enormous crocodile but of a type I've never seen."

The older man glanced briefly. "It's a dragon."

Simon tilted his head. "You say that rather matter-of-factly."

"That's because it is a matter of fact. It's a dragon skull. I saw one in Persia."

"Is it useful for anything?"

"Holding a dragon's brain."

Simon ran a finger along the spiked eye socket and suddenly realized he heard an odd noise. "Do you hear a buzzing sound?"

Simon and Nick looked at each other and started searching for the source of a metallic vibration. They noticed a small square hole in the wall near the ceiling. Something moved inside the dark space. Simon spoke a rune to life, feeling new strength. An object spurted out into the room and hovered in the air with a hum. It was about the size of a billiard ball with a weird blur around it.

Simon and Nick tensed, moving to the center of the library. The thing hovered over a lamp sconce on the wall. It settled onto the brass with nearly invisible, springlike legs and the blur stopped to reveal that it had wings like a bee. Then a narrow snout extended from the orb and dipped into the lamp. With a flick of a small flame, the lamp was lit. The wings began to vibrate again, and the ball rose into the air, drifting toward the next lamp. Once the lamps were lit, the weird little insect zipped up to the ceiling and crawled back into the wall on tiny legs, and was gone.

"What in the hell?" Nick muttered.

Simon went to the door and leaned out into the corridor. There was another of the metal bugs fluttering at a lamp in the hall. He then noted a number of the square holes high up in the wainscoting throughout the house.

A servant paused. "Sir? May I help you?"

"No, thank you. Just noting the, um, lamplighters."

"Oh yes. The lampflies." The young man looked around as if he no longer even noticed the little automata flying about. "They'll all be back in their hives soon."

"I hear hissing. Are those lamps gas?"

The servant continued to show politeness. "Of a sort, sir. Sir Roland again."

"Amazing." Simon returned to the library.

Nick stood by the French windows and threw them open. "Going for a walk to check out the grounds. I'll be back in a while and we can start for London."

"Be careful where you step and have a look for lycanthrope signs, will you." If a werewolf had killed Hibbert, it wouldn't be implausible that it might be stalking Imogen. Simon had never heard of the beasts being so methodical; still, it was better to err on the side of caution.

He heard footsteps approaching the door. Kate entered slowly, her body bearing the weight of the last couple of days. To Simon, she looked lovely and charged with determination despite her unruly hair and the dark shadows under her eyes.

"How is your sister?" Simon asked, pouring coffee for her.

"Confused." Kate drank gratefully. "Seems to have no sense of what has occurred the last few days. Perhaps that is for the best. And she's very anxious. Walking around the house. She went into Father's private study and started looking at everything as if she'd never seen it before."

"That's not surprising, I suppose."

"I gave her the dose from Dr. White, and she is resting now."

"It will ease the trauma of what happened to her in Hibbert's company." Simon shook his head sadly. "When did your sister's odd gentleman caller begin courting her?"

"Late summer."

Around the time the werewolf killings began in London, thought Simon grimly.

Kate took a small cloth and laid it over the crystalline machine, dousing the fractured light that sparkled through the room. She noted Simon's look of curiosity, and said, "Sometimes I can't bear the reflections."

"May I ask what that machine does?"

"I have no idea." She shrugged with a bemused smile. "My father built it."

"Amazing. Did he build those mechanical insects as well?"

"The lampflies? Yes, one of his favorites. You'll see many things around Hartley Hall that he crafted,

Mr. Archer. He was an engineer of extraordinary talent. But his mind could run swiftly. He would sometimes build and abandon." Kate looked around the library. "Where's Mr. Barker?"

"He's taking a stroll in the gardens."

"Oh." She said with a tinge of alarm. "That may not be safe."

A man's shout came from outside. A figure appeared through the glass, running headlong toward the house with something large loping behind him.

Kate rushed to the French windows and threw them open. The man raced gratefully past her into the library, while Kate faced outward and threw her arms wide. A gigantic shaggy grey beast bounded at her, all legs and teeth. Simon started for her side.

"Aethelred!" she shouted. "No!"

A huge wolfhound crashed against her, wide paws on her chest, its massive head above her shoulders. She wrapped herself around the lumbering dog, straining to hold him. He crashed back to the ground, nearly taking Kate with him. The dog went placid instantly, slapping the doorframe with his gigantic tail. Kate took a deep breath of relief and pounded the beast's shoulder lovingly. She stepped back into the library, with the dog pressing her to one side.

Simon let out a breath and looked askance at Nick. "It's just a great puppy. No doubt quite harmless."

"Oh no," Kate said. "He's extraordinarily harmful."

"He didn't even bark," Nick sputtered. "Luckily, I turned and saw him charging."

"He never barks before he attacks."

Nick slid from the shelter of Simon, muttering, "I don't know why you feel the need of attack horses."

Kate laughed as she muscled Aethelred back outside and closed the door. The dog stood breathing mist onto the glass, following his mistress's every move. "Don't let Aethelred's rudeness overshadow my gratitude for your efforts. I want to thank you for everything you've done for Imogen, and for me."

"You're quite welcome." Simon leaned against the keyboard of an aging pianoforte. Out of habit, Simon took the key from his waistcoat and began to twirl it idly between his fingers.

Kate's eyes locked onto the key and she came quickly from the window. Simon tightened his grip out of instinct as she reached for it, saying, "Where did you get that?" She took hold and stared intently at the bow of the key, where the filigree flared into a symbol, a stylized compass.

Simon exchanged a curious look with Nick. "It belonged to my mother. Why do you ask?"

"Wherever did your mother get it? May I see it, please?" She tugged on the key, which he had yet to relinquish. She gave Simon an exasperating frown. "I'm not going to steal it."

"Well, the way you charged at me was a bit unnerving. Did you learn that lunge from Aethelred?" He released the key and let Kate lift it closer to her eye. "Why do you ask?"

She didn't reply but started for the door. Simon leapt to his feet.

"Here!" he called after her. "You said you wouldn't steal it."

"Oh, just come with me." Kate called over her shoulder and rushed from the library, followed by Simon and Nick. She strode down the main hall to the impressive grand staircase. Without breaking stride she swept up. Servants parted, some trying to ask questions, but were quickly left in her wake. Hogarth caught sight of her and followed silently.

Kate led the small phalanx of the curious toward the rear of the house, down a corridor where the lamps were set low. She paused before a door and reached into her pocket to remove a ring of keys. She unlocked the door.

The room beyond was a sizeable study filled with books and papers and more curios. In any other country house, this would have been an admirable library in and of itself. Simon followed Kate inside, then realized that most of the books on the shelves were, in fact, bound journals with written symbols on the spines.

Kate went to the far wall and began to pull books from the shelves, stare behind them, then slip them back into place. She shoved skulls aside and even shushed a dangling shrunken head before relocating it to a tabletop. Finally, she shifted a glass bell jar containing a small skeleton of a creature that resembled a bird with three heads.

"Aha!" She held the key out in front of her, comparing it to the wall behind the weird bird. "I knew it!"

Nick muttered, "I'm a bit frightened."

Kate stepped aside and pointed at the wall. "Look here, Mr. Archer. Don't just stand there. Look."

"Careful," Nick warned softly, which caused a crease of annoyance to appear in Kate's brow.

Undaunted, Simon joined her at the shelf and peered at the wall. There was a strange mark in the plaster. It appeared to be a scorch mark. It was the same compass design that was on the top of the key.

"Odd," he said.

"Odd?" Kate actually swatted him on the arm. "Your understatement staggers me. That symbol has been incised on this wall for years. I can't remember exactly the first time I saw it. And here it is on this key. My father's key."

Simon started. "Your father's key? I beg to differ. It was my mother's, and I received it when she died. She had had it for years."

Kate huffed in annoyance and began to scan the journals around her. "I'll show you." She ran her finger along the spines and read labels. "Eighteen eleven. Seventeen ninety-seven. Paris. The talking hound of Silesia. Just wait, I'll find it."

Simon looked at Hogarth, but the servant didn't betray any uneasiness or curiosity about his mistress's behavior. Nick leaned against a desk with arms crossed, looking confused.

She continued to lay hands on journals. "Where the hell is it? Automatrixes. Feasibility of an Arctic Canal. Damn it!"

Simon said, "We could help you look if you'd tell us what you are looking for."

"If I knew that, I'd have it by now. Why don't you stay the evening, gentlemen? It's far too late now to leave for London regardless."

Nick hesitated. "I think we should get back."

Simon contemplated Kate's request, then shrugged at Nick. "There's nothing we can do tonight. Tomorrow is soon enough. Miss Anstruther, we would be honored to dine in Hartley Hall."

Hogarth coughed lightly. "Shall I prepare rooms, miss?"

"Yes, thank you." Kate waved a distracted hand. "Show them to their rooms and we'll reconvene at dinner. I'll have it by then."

"Would you mind if I had my key, please?" Simon inquired quietly.

"Your key?" She scowled and thrust it back at him. "Here, if you must."

Simon raised a bemused eyebrow at her frustration. The woman was a panther when vexed.

Hogarth bowed slightly and extended an arm toward the door. "Gentlemen, follow me, please."

As they departed, Simon glanced back over his shoulder to see Kate scrambling on top of a desk to peer at journals on higher shelves. She cursed loudly.

Nick muttered, "Maybe we should've left both of the Anstruther girls in Bedlam."

Simon laughed and twirled the key. "I think this is turning into an enjoyable jaunt in the country."

Chapter Fourteen

SIMON AND NICK WERE PROVIDED DINNER clothes so perfect they might have been tailored for them. As they both descended to the dining room, they noticed a lampfly zip past.

Simon laughed. "Remarkable place."

Nick shook his head. "How hard is it to have someone light lamps?"

"Saves on servants," Simon said. "I haven't seen nearly as many as a house this size should have. I'm sure there are tremendous labor-saving devices all over the estate."

They continued down with Nick muttering about pointlessness. He had balked at shaving, which scored him disappointed glances from the butler in the dining room. Both men were surprised to see Imogen present. She wore a fashionable flowered gown of muslin with balloon sleeves. She curtsied, seeming only slightly disconcerted, and stared at Nick with hard eyes, but she said nothing. Then she appraised Simon with an approving smile and clutched the back of the chair where she was to sit next to him, as if someone would move it out of the room.

The dining table was long but set with only four places at one end. Tasteful flowers accented the array of

glasses for water and wines and the arsenal of silverware next to each of the fine china plates. Menus rested
in each spot. Simon perused his and was much impressed, particularly given they'd only had a few hours.

A side door opened. Simon glanced up from the menu
and his eyes widened. Kate entered in a gown of dark
velvet that clung to her narrow waist and expressive
hips. The pale skin of her strong bare shoulders shone
beautifully above the rise of her breasts. Her auburn
hair was twisted in a fetchingly wild tangle on top of
her head, framing the strong cut of her cheekbones. Her
green eyes covered the room, lingering a moment on
Simon as he bowed, sweeping past Nick to settle with
concern on Imogen. Kate approached the table, and
only then did Simon see one of her father's journals in
her hand.

"Please, everyone sit," she said graciously, her attention focused on Imogen's pale features. "There's no for-
mality among us, despite the setting. It's merely been a
long time since we've had visitors at Hartley Hall."

Kate sat at the head of the table, with Imogen settled
at Simon's right and Nick on her left. Legs were barely
under the table when oysters were placed before everyone. Simon lifted his small glass of white wine and
stood.

"If I may offer a toast to our hostess, Miss Anstruther,
and to her lovely sister, Miss Imogen. We thank you for
your hospitality. It is a great honor to pass an evening at
Hartley Hall."

Kate nodded and sipped, and before Simon could sit,
she had opened the journal, her face alight with the excitement of discovery. "Here. Look."

Simon made a show of setting down his oyster fork
with an indulgent smile. The yellowed pages of the journal were covered in scrawls, some legible, some not.
Some words. Numbers and formulas. Symbols he had

no familiarity with. He did see several detailed drawings of what appeared to be the very key nestled in his waistcoat. He removed the key to compare. The drawings were clearly the very thing.

"When was this written?" Simon asked.

"The journal is dated seventeen ninety-nine, but there are loose sheets of papers stuffed in there that I believe are from even earlier."

"Thirty years ago. Curious." Simon handed the journal to Nick, who was more interested in the oysters. "I suppose it's possible that your father knew my mother and gave her the key as a gift. She certainly never mentioned having the acquaintance of Sir Roland Anstruther."

Kate said, "I don't think that likely."

"Why?"

"From what I can read of my father's notes, the key isn't just a keepsake that he would hand off. Unlike many of his creations, he was quite focused on this one."

"I don't see anything particularly extraordinary about this key."

"Good God," Nick breathed. He was holding a ragged sheet of parchment he had pulled from between pages. His eyes were wide. He turned the sheet and held it up.

Simon recognized runic scribing on the page. Magical symbols, similar to those he used. In fact, disturbingly similar.

He snatched the sheet from Nick's hand and stared at it. His breath grew short. More sheets were held out to him. He took them from Nick and laid them on the table, stymieing the servants who sought to remove the oyster course and bring the soup. Simon went from sheet to sheet, running his fingers along the symbols, comparing them. Even in his intense concentration, he noted the faint scent of Kate's perfume as she came to his shoulder.

"Those are magical runes," she said.

"They're more than that."

"In what way?"

"I am almost certain they were written by my father."

"Your father?" Kate exhaled in shock. "Your father was a magician?"

"He was a scribe. Like myself. I recognize his style from notes of his that I have." Simon looked at Nick with a slowly spreading grin. "These are spells written by my father."

Kate asked, "Why would my father have them?"

"I have no idea, Miss Anstruther. I have no idea at all. But it's damnably exciting, isn't it?"

She laughed honestly for the first time since he'd known her and put a hand to her breast. "Can you tell me what sort of spell is written there?"

"No, not yet. It's beautiful though. His hand was so elegant."

Kate returned to her chair and took a long drink of wine. "I can tell you that from what I've read in the journal, the key you are holding is an object of extraordinary power."

Simon and Nick and Imogen all looked at the key. It caught the golden light of the candles.

"What sort of power?" Simon asked.

Kate sat forward dramatically, resting on her elbows. "I have no idea."

Simon waited for a better answer, then realized she was done. "What?"

"My father was a man of secrets too. He didn't just write a simple note about the thing."

Simon held up the key in front of his face. "Then how do we know it does anything?"

Kate sipped wine. "Would two such men work together on a mere piece of jewelry?"

"Well, I see clear evidence," Simon said, "that they

knew each other and that your father has some of my father's runic scribbling. But that they actually worked together on this key? We can't say that for sure."

Nick then grunted and held up one final sheet. It was a rough sketch of the key with runic symbols drawn on it.

"On the other hand," Simon added.

IT WAS A LONG DINNER OF ANIMATED DISCUS-sion that provided no further clues to their parents' association. Kate and Simon went through the journal page by page, continually exclaiming at notes and facets of Sir Roland's work. She did notice that whenever the conversation went to Simon's father and his life, particularly those years when he might have worked with Sir Roland, Simon would divert to another topic. It was deftly done, but Kate knew equivocation when she saw it. Clearly, he wanted to maintain secrecy about his father. At the end of it all, there was no consensus on what the key was or was not.

Finally, after many hours and candles nearly burnt to the silver sticks, Kate received word that Mrs. Tolbert needed to discuss certain issues. Kate suggested that Imogen should go to bed, given the stressful events of the day, but her request was ignored. The young woman seemed unaware of any stress and continued to hang on Simon's every word with tired, drooping eyes. Simon recommended with a knowing wink that Kate attend her business, and he would entertain Imogen.

Kate rose from the table as port was poured for the two gentlemen. She found Mrs. Tolbert waiting patiently in the Blue Room. "We could go over ledgers later, Mrs. Tolbert."

"It isn't ledgers, miss. I need to know about Miss Imogen's condition, so I can know how best to help her and you. You told me precious little when you brought her home."

Kate felt the truth in the woman's statement. "Of course, you're right. This is not to go any further." The housekeeper nodded. "Imogen has had a difficult time. It is likely that she has been ill-used by Colonel Hibbert."

Mrs. Tolbert grew hard, eyes narrowing with anger. "If you'll pardon my saying, your father would have something done about the man."

"Something has been done. Colonel Hibbert is dead."

The housekeeper regarded Kate with a look of respect but didn't say more, merely waited.

Kate continued, "Our goal is to keep Imogen comfortable and calm. I have a special draught to relax her when needed. Treat her as you always would, but alert the staff that her behavior may be a bit odd."

"Yes, miss. We'll do everything needed for the poor angel."

"I know you will, Mrs. Tolbert. Hartley Hall is likely to be a bit upside down for the immediate future. I appreciate all your efforts."

"No matter, miss." The housekeeper pushed her hands into her apron pockets. "It isn't as if Hartley Hall hasn't seen its share of upside-down days before."

Kate watched the solid old woman trundle from the Blue Room and she felt as if the house was once again set right, as much as it could be. She returned to the dining room with a somewhat lighter heart and opened the door to an unexpected scene.

Simon stood in front of Imogen, who perched on her chair in complete concentration. He held a top hat upside down by the brim and waved his right hand over the open hat. He held it low enough that Imogen could peer inside. Beyond him, Nick leaned back in his chair, draining a large glass of port, with one foot against the table. Two serving maids, along with Barnaby the but-ler, stood behind Imogen's chair, watching Simon with the attention of a hawk.

"Completely empty?" Simon waited for Imogen to peer deeply into the hat and nod in agreement. He smiled mysteriously and placed the hat on his head. He swept his hand along the brim and tapped the crown. His eyes flicked quickly to Kate, and he said, "And since a lady has arrived, a gentleman always tips his hat."

Simon removed the top hat and something moved in his hair. He gave a shallow bow toward Imogen, who squealed with delight, while the servants laughed and clapped their hands.

"What is it?" Simon cried with mock alarm. "Is there a beast on me?"

Imogen laughed and hesitatingly reached out to him. Simon moved a step closer in invitation. She scooped a hedgehog off Simon's head and cradled it in her hands. She held it up to show the other girls.

Kate laughed at the ridiculous scene. "What exactly is happening here?"

"Look," Imogen said. "Mr. Archer produced a hedge-hog out of thin air. It's a miracle."

"Yes," Kate agreed, giving Simon a pleasant smirk. "He's quite the wonderworker."

The maids returned to their duties and Nick pulled his foot from the table under Kate's quick baleful glare.

Simon bowed fully to Imogen. "I regret you must say good evening now, Miss Imogen. I look forward to see-ing you tomorrow."

The young woman seemed confused at first but then rose and curtsied, following his lead. She extended the hedgehog back to Simon.

"Oh no," he said. "You may keep him."

"No," Imogen replied simply. "He won't be safe with me."

Kate felt a hot pang of sadness as her sister placed the tiny, helpless bundle in the man's hands. Simon glanced at Kate with concern, but Imogen seemed completely untroubled. She kissed Kate on the cheek and went out of the dining room with a maid at her heels.

"I'm sorry, Miss Anstruther," Simon said. "I hope I didn't overstep myself."

"Not at all, Mr. Archer. It was wonderful to hear her laugh, if only for a moment." Kate stroked the hedgehog with her finger, smiling at the prickly little thing. "Now that you've revealed the great mysteries of your occult sciences, if you and Mr. Barker will come with me, I'll reveal a bit of mine."

She led Simon and Nick into the corridor and toward the rear of the sprawling country house. After much walking, she reached up into her hair and pulled out a hairpin with a small key attached.

"Gentlemen," she said, "you are the first outsiders to whom I have shown this room."

"We are practically family, after all," Simon quipped.

"Not quite." Kate unlocked the heavy door. "I have told you I am a scholar of the occult, but there's more." There was a flush of excitement on her cheeks as she opened the way to her sanctum.

She lit oil lamps on wall sconces to reveal the room that used to be a parlor but now hosted several worktables covered in laboratory glassware. There were many beakers with colored liquid or bright granules. Apothecary cabinets lined one wall holding endless small bottles of herbs and chemicals and unidentified objects. The other walls were covered by crowded bookshelves, with more books resting in stacks on every flat surface.

Kate announced unnecessarily, "I have an affinity for alchemy."

Nick whistled. "An affinity? I'd say you have a fixation."

"I should have guessed by the effectiveness of your discombobulating snuff." Simon tilted his head, reading the spines of books, making grunts of recognition. He jerked up in surprise and seized a heavy volume from a sideboard. He drew a finger along the embossed lettering on the cover. "Al Hashiri's *Miracles and Wonders*."

Kate regarded him with a look of mild doubt. "You've read it?"

"I have." He opened the book and stared in shock. "Oh. This is in Arabic."

"Yes. Didn't you say you had read it?"

Nick laughed as Simon handed her the book a trifle sheepishly. "I read the Latin translation."

Kate slid the book onto one of the shelves. "No shame. The Latin version is quite serviceable."

Simon shook his head with an impressed smile.

"What is that thing?" Nick asked from across the room. He was staring at a very large glass jar filled with greenish liquid in which was suspended an object of some sort.

"An old experiment," Kate replied. "I've put it aside for now."

Simon joined his friend at the jar. "Good Lord. Is that a thorn?"

"Yes. From a rose."

"It's two feet long."

"That was the largest I could manage and still have a rose in any meaningful way."

"Where's the flower?" Nick asked in awe. "Did you have to build a separate shed for it?"

"I haven't any. Everything broke apart. I only managed to save that thorn in a suspension."

"This is extraordinary," Simon said.

Nick commented, "You must really like flowers."

"Yes, Mr. Barker," she responded coolly. "I turned all my scientific knowledge to the singular feminine goal of making pretty flowers." She turned back toward Simon, who covered his amusement with a gentle cough. "I wanted to apply the process to increase crop size to feed more people. Alas, the plants were too fragile and fell to dust. And the fragrance of the rose was dreadfully poisonous. I lost several songbirds unfortunately."

A horrid inhuman squeal broke the night, followed by a terrible howl.

"Aethelred!" Kate sprinted for the French windows at the rear of the room.

The doors were hardly open when Simon took her upper arm in a rough hand. "Stay here."

As soon as he released her and started into the dark, she was on his heels. "Aethelred!" Her shout elicited an annoyed glance from Simon.

He gave Nick a few quick hand signals, and the shorter man took off in another direction through the shadowy garden.

"Is it too much to hope that Aethelred turned up a badger?" Kate asked without conviction.

"It didn't sound like a badger to me." Simon pulled a small pistol from his jacket and handed it to Kate. "That weapon is loaded and primed, so be careful."

She welcomed the heft of wood and iron in her hand. "Nor did it sound like a werewolf."

"Stay close to me."

They started off along the path between high shrubs. Faint starlight cast the garden in deep shadows and dappled the weird landscape. Kate's heart pounded and she listened hopefully for the sound of her dog's panting or thudding paws approaching. A frigid breeze rustled the branches around them. Their feet squished on the worn grass path. Simon kept his left hand back, maintaining contact with Kate's arm. Despite herself, she found the gesture comforting and welcome.

They reached a break in the high topiary and Kate

heard a soft whine. She slipped through the gap into a grassy court. A large, dark shape lay before her.

"Aethelred." She ran and knelt beside the dog. The hound tried to lift his head and his heavy tail thumped once on the ground. She lowered her hand toward his furry neck.

"No!" Simon pulled her hand away. "Don't touch him."

Kate angrily jerked free. "He's hurt. He needs help."

"I know." Simon dropped to one knee next to her with a solicitous move toward the dog. "But you will need help yourself if you aren't careful. Look here."

He indicated the hound's shoulder and, in the dark, Kate saw that the fur was matted wet. She didn't smell blood, but there was a strong musty, loamy stench. Then she spotted a long thread-thin spine sticking out of the dog's neck, wavering with each heaving pant. She squinted at it. "What is that?"

"A quill of some sort."

"A porcupine? Here?"

"Nothing so blasé, I fear."

Kate had to restrain herself again from touching her beloved dog. "He won't die, will he?"

"I hope not."

"Simon! Look out!"

Kate barely had time to flinch at Nick's alarm before she saw a shape charge into the starlight from the shadow of a nearby yew. It was vaguely human, but hunched, pale white, and glistening. It ran with a strange, gangly motion, and Kate had the sense of great bulbous eyes that twisted in many directions and finally settled on her. Its flesh twitched. She reached to pull back the hammer on the pistol, but Simon bore her to the damp ground under his weight.

Nick yelled as he ran past, "You all right, old boy?"

"I am," Simon shouted, eyes locked on Kate. "Miss Anstruther, are you hit?"

"Hit?"

Simon grabbed her and bent her forward, touching the back of her neck and pushing roughly through her hair. His actions startled her. He ran his hands over Kate's shoulders and torso.

"Mr. Archer!" Kate pulled away. "I would've thought you knew my policy on that."

"Be still! I'm checking for quills."

"I can check my own chest for quills, thank you."

"We should return to the house now. I don't know what that thing was."

"What about Aethelred?"

"There is little we can do for Aethelred at the moment. I prefer to move you to safety."

She was surprised by his coldness. "Will you not help your friend then?"

"Miss Anstruther, that creature was the source of the quills which struck your dog."

"How can you be sure?"

"Because I have two of them in my back." He twisted to show a pair of filamentous spines quivering in his formal jacket. "And I fear I will be quite paralyzed in a few minutes and completely unable to help you. Shall we move inside?"

Galvanized now, Kate pulled Simon to his feet, and he pressed heavily against her as they staggered back to the garden path. He was stiff-legged by the time they entered the laboratory. As soon as they were inside, he fell sideways onto a leather sofa and lay motionless, eyes open, chest rising and falling shallowly.

As quickly as she could, Kate unfastened his white shirt collar and removed the stays from his shirtfront. When she pulled the material back, she saw a muscular chest covered with intricate tattoos. Scores of runic script ran in various lines and curved around his torso just under the neck bones and across his pectoral muscles, the ink an ebony black against his skin. The writing was only vaguely familiar but she couldn't read a word of it. Suddenly he seemed less like a gentleman and even more a man of mystery.

Kate wrestled him from his shirt and tails, careful not to touch the quills that came away with his coat. She stared at the tattoos covering even the hard contours of his arm. The runic symbols intertwined in a vaguely disturbing fashion and seemed to move as his hand dropped limply to his side.

She hovered nervously. "Mr. Archer, can you hear me?"

His wide eyes didn't shift.

There was a knock at the door and a muffled voice. "Miss Kate, is there a problem?"

She rushed to the door and opened it to reveal Hogarth. "There is an intruder on the grounds. Please attend Imogen and have all the doors and windows locked."

"I will put more armed men around the grounds."

"No. The intruder is very dangerous and our people aren't prepared. Just see to the security of the house."

"Very well, miss." Hogarth noticed Simon on the sofa. "Is Mr. Archer injured? Shall I send for Dr. Nothergill?"

"No. I'll look after him." Kate closed the door and spun around to see a figure leaning over Simon. She shouted and Nick turned in annoyance. He held the two quills in his hand with a handkerchief. His pant legs were wet from the knees down.

Kate asked, "Did you find the thing?"

"No. How's Simon?"

"He's been poisoned. His breathing is slowing."

Nick's eyes filled with fear. Kate turned away from his pained expression and began to search the laboratory, hoping for inspiration. Something must spark an idea. Some formula. Some concoction. An antidote.

She turned to see the rigid Simon gasping for air.

"He's dying!" Nick shouted.

"Wait." An idea pierced Kate's mind. "There is an elixir that Norsemen of the Dark Ages used to increase their vitality in battle. It might allow Simon to counteract the deadly effects of the poison. I don't know. It's not a sure option."

"Why are you still talking to me? Do it."

"Perhaps if you stop blustering and help me. Open that cabinet and fetch the stinging nettle and the bottle labeled ox heart." She went hurriedly to a shelf and pulled a book. Flipping vellum pages, she scanned the Latin inscriptions. She didn't have all the proper materials, but hopefully she could find usable substitutes. She unlocked a chest and removed a flask of green liquid.

Nick set bottles on the worktable. "You know what you're about, don't you?"

Kate didn't look up. She measured with practiced fingers doses of crumbled herbs, sections of twigs, small piles of rare earths. Once she had the proper amounts, she scooped them into a mortar and crushed them together. When she had a suitable blend, she took up the flask of green and a chemical dropper.

Kate held the open flask over the mortar and tipped it. She pulled several drops into the pipette. This substance was not part of the original medieval recipe, so she was estimating the amount needed. A mistake could well have dreadful consequences, perhaps even worse than simple death. She squeezed the green liquid into the mortar and sniffed. A metallic tinge went deep into her nose. It was active. She worked the substance into a heavy paste.

"Traditionally," she said, "Norsemen used it as a poultice. We don't have time for that. I am going to apply it directly to his gums."

Nick reached for the mortar, but Kate pushed past him and went to Simon, who lay gasping on the sofa. His eyes were rolled up in his head as she knelt next to him and took a dollop of the greenish paste onto her finger. She spread Simon's lips and began to slide her finger along the wet surface of his upper gums. After an inspection of the work, she repeated the action across the lower. She wiped her hands, feeling a minor tingling on her fingers.

Nick was at her shoulder. "Is that all? Is that all you're doing?"

"Mr. Barker, be still, I beg you." Kate was suddenly very aware of the loud metallic ticking clock on the mantel.

Nick exhaled anxiously, cracking his knuckles. He muttered threats under his breath, or perhaps a prayer.

Simon's breath turned wetter, as if he was strangling. Then his gurgling croaks stopped.

Nick froze and gave a sick moan. "No."

Kate held up her hand to silence him, willing Simon to breathe, staring at the stark stillness of his chest. It should work. Her theory was sound.

Suddenly, Simon took an explosive gasp and rose nearly off the sofa. Kate was there to grab his arms, holding him steady. His eyes sprang open. His hands clutched the upholstery like claws, nearly tearing the leather. His muscles were rigid cords. She eased him back down. He lay still, exhaling harshly through his nose. His mouth clamped shut.

"Simon, try to relax." Kate pressed the palm of her hand against his chest, covering a dark rune. She could feel the wild pumping of his heart. It nearly matched her own. "Don't panic. Try to control your breathing as best you can."

Simon's eyes locked on hers. She could see under-standing and gratitude beneath the wildness. His trem-bling hand fumbled over hers.

Kate gasped with relief. It had worked. She had saved him. Her fingers curled tight around his, offering him her resolve and reassurance, her head bowed, offering a prayer of gratitude. Nick brought a blanket and to-gether they draped it over the shivering man. She looked into the mortar and saw a bit of the green paste remain-ing. "Mr. Barker, I am going to save Aethelred."

"It's dangerous out there." Nick had a hand on Si-mon's damp forehead. "That thing is still about."

"I don't care." She lifted Simon's pistol. "Mr. Archer is out of immediate danger, or at least beyond what I can do for him."

Nick stomped to the French windows. "Fine. I'll come with you then if you're so damned set on it." As Kate slipped past him onto the terrace, he added quietly, "Thank you."

She glanced back and saw abject relief on the man's face. "You're welcome, Mr. Barker." Kate started back into the dark and suddenly foreboding garden without hesitation.

Chapter Fifteen

A BEAKER BUBBLED OVER A FLICKERING FLAME as Kate observed a final experiment before closing up the laboratory. She was examining Imogen's blood to determine if she could see any foreign bodies or strange additives that might explain her sister's continuing dissociated state. Kate felt compelled to try to aid her sister, although she was unsure what she could do.

Simon waited with her as she dallied with the complex apparatus. He watched her, obviously fascinated by her work, all the while tapping his foot and flexing his fingers, keeping time with some internal concerto.

When he glanced away, Kate looked up from her work to observe him. His face was still a trifle pale and the skin around his eyes dark as if from lack of sleep, but he had a contented expression like a husband at the fireside.

Aethelred lifted his head from where he was curled awkwardly in the corner. Kate pursed her lips at the dog; he appeared to be recovering well enough from the poisoning. He thumped his tail twice, then went back to sleep.

Simon removed a small blue vial from his pocket and uncorked it. He took a sip. "This concoction of yours is amazing."

"Don't become dependent on it."

"No, no. Once this dose is gone, I'll need no more. It's quite bracing though. This is how you saved me from the poison?"

"Not exactly. What you have there is an *elixir vitae* that restores stamina. It's an ancient Norse recipe. It's a relatively simple solution; even I use it occasionally to work longer." Kate stirred uncomfortably. "I suppose I must make a confession to you, Mr. Archer. What I did two nights ago when you were poisoned was to start with that elixir but then alter it. I fully admit that it was a shot in the dark."

Simon regarded her curiously but with no anger or accusation.

She continued, "I used a bit of the solution from the gigantic rose. There was no time. I had to fire your blood. It was a risk but a calculated one."

He raised his hands in acceptance. "Well done. It worked." But then he shot her a melodramatic glare. "Am I in danger of my heart crumbling like your rose?"

"No." Kate smirked but then grew thoughtful, and said with less force, "No."

Simon rose and moved to the coal grate next to the wolfhound's bed.

"Are you feeling ill?" Kate asked quickly.

"Have no fear. Just a bit stiff. It seems the cold affects me like an old woman."

She returned to writing her notes, being exaggeratedly prim. "I can have Hogarth fetch a shawl for you."

Simon stared at her as if gazing at a painting. "I thank you, but I will content myself with the warming glow of your wit."

Kate smiled without looking up. "Mr. Archer, may I ask you a personal question?"

"I'd say you've earned the right."

Kate realized her eyes were locked on his chest. She

quickly glanced at her table but slowly eased back to him. He furrowed his brow in amusement as she began, "When you were unconscious, I removed your shirt."

"That's personal but not a question."

She cleared her throat. "I saw your . . . those . . ."

Simon stared at her, shaking his head, playing cheerfully obtuse.

"Your tattoos," Kate huffed. "You know damn well what I mean. You're completely covered in tattoos."

"Well, obviously you preserved a shred of my dignity the other night or you'd know that I'm not *completely* covered in them. But yes, I have tattoos, and you wish to know why."

"It's really none of my concern, I know. It's just that you said you were a scribe, and they are masters of inscription, of written magic."

Simon held up his hand. "I am a carver."

Kate leaned back. "A what?"

"A carver. It's a vulgar term for a scribe who practices inscription using his own body as the tablet." As he talked, Simon unfastened his shirt cuff and began to roll up his sleeve. The dark runic lines wrapped around his muscular forearm. "These are spells. They allow me to perform alterations to myself or to the immediate sphere around me. It would be the same as writing the spell, but obviously it's much faster since here it is already. I merely speak a focusing word or phrase, and the spell comes active."

Kate gazed at his inscribed arm. "That's how you perform feats of incredible strength?"

"It is."

"Does it hurt? The tattoos I mean."

"Not now. It was painful to receive them."

"Did you do it yourself?"

"No. That would take more skill and willpower than I possess. I had them done by a couple of mystics who can perform such tasks. Rare fellows indeed. The first was on the Barbary Coast, and the second was in Norway. But it's been over five years since my last tattoo; they may both be dead by now. I suspect what I have here is what I will always have." Simon came toward her. "Would you care to examine them?"

"No, I've examined them." Kate jerked with embarrassment. "I mean I had to when I removed your clothes. I mean . . ."

"Step out into the dark for a moment." Simon laughed and crooked his finger at her. He opened the French window and went onto the brick terrace. He blew into his cupped hands for warmth. Then he rolled his sleeve up over his biceps and whispered a word.

Against the night, a bright green pinpoint appeared on his forearm. In the blink of an eye, the light moved along his arm as if writing one of the tattoos anew. The entire arcane pattern glowed and Simon waved his arm, creating a weird blur of emerald in the night.

"Amazing," Kate breathed.

"Shall I show you some demonstration?"

"No need. I've seen you do extraordinary things. And I'd rather you not tire yourself needlessly."

"As you wish." Simon passed by her into the laboratory. She followed quietly and closed the door. He returned to his place by the warm fire, taking his time rolling down his sleeve and fastening the cuff.

"I've never seen anything like you, Mr. Archer."

"And you likely never will. I am the only one of my kind, after all."

"Are there limits to your power?"

"Certainly. I'm a human being. Just flesh and blood and bone. These tattoos allow me to funnel aether through my body, but I can't physically or mentally manage unlimited amounts nor sustain endless forces tearing through me. If you ram too much powder into a cannon, it will blow apart."

"How much is too much?"

Simon gave her a sly wink. "That's the whole trick, isn't it? I don't know."

Her voice was hushed with awe, "It's true magic, isn't it?"

"Well, it's not quite pulling a hedgehog out of a hat, but it's something, yes." Simon came to the edge of her table and placed his hand down on the surface with a metallic clatter. When he pulled back, the gold key rested before her. "I want you to keep this."

Kate looked up at him. "But it was your mother's."

"In a way, yes, but I'm sure that it was your father's before that. More than that, you have the skills and the resources to study it."

"You have no interest?"

"I have an enormous interest and hope to work with you on it. However, there's no reason you can't start to work. Your scholarship and intellectual grasp of the subject is far superior to mine. I am jealous of how you studied, while I attended parties and drank."

Kate was warmed by his consideration for her intelligence and by his willingness to surrender an object that obviously meant a great deal to him. She lifted the key and gripped it in her hand. "Thank you. Why don't you take the pages with your father's runes and attempt to decipher those?"

Simon was quiet a moment, then bowed his head graciously to her, his emerald eyes narrowing to points beneath his dark brow. "I shall."

Kate coughed. "As soon as you can, I'd like you to spend several weeks here at Hartley Hall, and we can work together on this. As our fathers did."

Simon hesitated. "I feel as if I'm abandoning you

going back to London with that intruder still about. I wish Nick hadn't gone yesterday while I was laid up."

"He waited until you were out of danger."

"I suppose the old fellow can only wring his hands for so long."

"He did a great deal," Kate said. "But you needn't worry about me. I have men around including Hogarth. And I'm capable myself."

"Indeed you are."

"I will feel better with you following leads in London."

"And it's certainly possible they will intersect with yours at some point. We have to assume the thing we saw is part of the situation with Colonel Hibbert, and he is tied in with my werewolves. It's far too coincidental that we would experience this sudden downpour of the occult."

"Agreed." Kate tapped one of the journals on the table with the key. "The thing that poisoned you is a homunculus. Clearly, it had been human once. He was altered either mechanically or alchemically. Or both."

"I've seen homunculi before, but never exactly like that. It moved well, and the poisonous spines were a clever introduction, half muscle and half metal. Whoever forged it is an extraordinary craftsman." Simon wandered idly about the room, studying the walls and surfaces. "It would be fascinating if we could trap it."

"I say kill it." Kate's eyes sparked with fire.

"If necessary, but it would be preferable to study it."

"It's preferable to me that it not be here at all."

"That's understandable, but don't you want to find out why it is here? Isn't it always better to know than not? You're a scholar."

"When something threatens my family, scholarship be damned." Her steel gaze met his.

There was a knock at the door, causing them both to

jump, and Kate called out to enter. Hogarth stepped inside, and said in a quiet voice, "Pardon me, but Miss Imogen is talking to herself."

Kate could see that the servant was distressed. "She's had opium. That's not too unusual."

"I glanced inside and saw Miss Imogen standing by an open window. I coaxed her back to bed, then lingered outside her door. She was soon talking again."

"I'll check on her." Kate started for the door with a glance at Simon that brought him to her side. Hogarth and Aethelred followed. "And then perhaps we should have a look around outside."

Simon retrieved his walking stick from beside the door. "Hogarth, would you be good enough to bring a heavy cloak."

The servant veered off as Kate, Simon, and the wolf-hound took the stairs. They hurried down the hallway, and Kate took a deep breath, putting her ear to a door. Her eyes tightened. She heard the sound of Imogen's voice quite plainly, although she couldn't make out the words. Then, in the silence left when Imogen stopped talking came a strange whooshing sound that could have been the wind.

Aethelred whined suddenly and pressed against his mistress with his tail drooping behind him.

Simon pulled the sword from his cane. "He senses something."

"The homunculus?" Kate straightened in alarm.

"I hope it is. We can settle it once and for all."

Kate reached for the doorknob, but Simon seized her wrist. He shook his head and signaled for her to wait. Hogarth jogged toward them carrying an oiled-canvas rain cloak. Simon took it and motioned Kate away from the door. Aethelred hunched low, muscles tensing, hackles stiff on his neck. The dog glared at the door.

Simon mouthed the words, "Keep him out here."

"You think it's in there with her?" Kate's heart pounded in her throat at the intensity in his eyes. She fought the urge to rush inside as Hogarth took Aethelred by the collar, pulling him back lest the dog give them away.

Simon immediately turned the knob and pushed the door open. Shadows in the bedroom all seemed to move on their own accord. The orange glow from the fireplace flickered in the draft. Imogen stood in front of a large wardrobe across the room. She turned at the sound of the door.

Simon inched into the room. His head swiveled from side to side, searching the black corners. Kate slipped behind Simon, who held the canvas cloak up in front of him, with the sword still in one hand and the empty stick in the other. The window was open and Kate could see her breath in the damp air.

"Why are you in my room?" Imogen's voice was full of familiar haughtiness, but there was something blank in her eyes. She wasn't truly looking at Simon. She was staring into the distance beyond him.

"Are you alone, Miss Imogen?" he asked.

"Just leave."

"Would you step away from that wardrobe, please?"

"Imogen," Kate coaxed anxiously, "come to me."

Imogen stood rooted in place. The wind blew her nightgown and the pale moonlight from the window illuminated her shape beneath the billowing fabric. Kate started around Simon, inching toward Imogen. The young woman reached up and put her hand on the door of the wardrobe. Simon tensed.

There was the sound of a struggle from the hallway. Kate turned in alarm to see a huge shape rushing in and past her. Simon shouted and grabbed her by the arm, pulling her behind the cloak, which he swung like a bullfighter, particularly since he had his stick sword in his hand. A grey furry hulk pushed through the canvas and loped toward Imogen.

When Aethelred reached the young woman, the dog thrust his body between her and the wardrobe and pushed her back a few steps. Imogen grinned and threw her arms around the great dog's neck with a childlike laugh.

Kate ran forward and grabbed Imogen's arm. She reached for Aethelred's collar but found it gone. She then saw Hogarth standing inside the doorway with the broken leather strap in his hand.

"Come, come," Kate commanded both her sister and the dog, tugging them away. "Hogarth, take Imogen and Aethelred to my room. And stay there with them."

"Yes, miss." The manservant took the hound firmly by the scruff and put an arm around Imogen's shoulders. He escorted the pair from the chilled room. Their footsteps faded.

When Kate turned back to Simon, her eye caught a shade sliding along the wall. As the shape moved, it went from dark to bright pale white. "Behind you!"

Simon moved so quickly, Kate barely saw him. The stiff cloak snapped like a kite in the wind, and it fell heavily on the homunculus, which appeared suddenly pale in the darkness. Simon spoke in a quiet whisper and seized the draped form in a bear hug. It flailed, fighting to extract itself from the tangled cloak and Simon's immensely strong grip. It thrashed like a wild animal, slamming him against the heavy wooden bedpost. Simon staggered and the sword cane dropped from his grip. He attempted to regain his footing to prevent the thing from taking him to the floor. The frenzied creature took advantage of its unsteady assailant and wrenched itself free.

"Kate! Get back!" Simon shouted as it darted for the open door.

Quills barely missed her as she launched herself aside.

Still tangled in the cloak, the creature scrambled out of the room, seeking escape. Simon lit out after it.

The sword glinted on the floor and Kate snatched it up. She tore out into the corridor to see the homunculus with one arm free from the folds of the cloak. Quills rose along its white skin. Kate hissed a warning. In the shallow light, Simon barreled into it with a broad shoulder and drove it down the hall toward the stairs.

The impact sent the creature over the banister into the air. The cloak fluttered free. The homunculus plummeted to the tile floor twenty feet below, where it fell hard on its back. Simon leapt the rail and dropped to the foyer with the sinewy grace of a panther. The thing was already on its feet and pounding away through the wide doors of the library in a desperate attempt to escape. Simon snatched up a large chair, single-handedly, and bolted after it.

Kate bounded down the stairs, hardly touching them, wildly falling forward. She hit the floor and raced for the library in time to see the chair smash into the back of the homunculus, sending it sprawling. It gathered its ungainly legs under it again and rose quickly, angry and confused. It spun to face Simon and Kate.

From beyond the sweep of windows, a vigorous moon illuminated their foe for the first time. Its face was humanesque in proportion, but its eyes were large and bulbous, like a chameleon's. The nose was nothing but two slits and the mouth was a wide gash with snapping sharp teeth. The body was nearly translucent white and it crouched upon long arms, misshapen and bent twice as if it had multiple elbows. The hunched shoulders bristled with threadlike quills that rippled like a field of grain in the wind. It appeared to be naked; Kate noted the contours of thigh muscles and the bulges of bones at its knees, plus long, splayed toes pressed against the wood floor.

"Dear God," Kate breathed. The horrible distinction between the thing's human characteristics and its unnatural anatomy left her ill. She was torn between a fierce curiosity about its unusual nature and a desire to see it destroyed. She reached back and closed the library door, locking it, trapping them inside the moonlit room with the creature.

With a hiss, it twisted to show its back. Simon snatched a heavy table and raised it in front of Kate and him like a knight's shield. There were multiple, rapid plunking sounds against the wood as thin but deadly quills impacted like crossbow bolts. Simon rushed the creature, slamming it into the wall and pinning it there with the thick table.

Tubular pliant fingers crept around the wood near Simon's face. A bony arm reached for him. Kate swiped at the arm with Simon's sword, slicing it deep. The creature shrieked and thrashed, shoving the heavy wooden table aside in its pain.

"Get back!" Simon shouted at Kate as he leapt onto the white creature. His bare hands seized it by the throat. The homunculus thrashed, but Simon held firm.

Something seemed odd. Simon wasn't moving, but neither was he quivering in near paralysis. He was rigid like a statue with his fingers dug deep into the creature's flesh. What Kate could see of Simon's skin appeared pale and lifeless, but perhaps that was the sheen of the moon. The flailing homunculus was dragging Simon awkwardly after him. Spines shot, clicking off the walls and the chair Kate scrambled behind.

The thing crashed through the French windows, sending shards of glass twinkling in the moonlight. It slipped in the wreckage and collapsed to the walkway under Simon's immobile form. He was grasping the creature with so much strength the thing wriggled like a fish in a vise, but the magician had yet to even flinch, as if frozen in place. The homunculus's chest was heaving. Pale hands dropped away from Simon's back to splay out beside it. Like a trapped animal that had exhausted itself and succumbed to debilitating terror at being confined, it fell into stillness. Somehow, Simon was choking it to death.

Kate rose carefully, noting numerous quills sticking out of the chintz fabric of the chair. Foot by foot, she drew closer. The homunculus panted in a hoarse gasp like a baby with the croup. The creature's bulbous eyes shifted to her and she froze. It didn't move further, except to close and open its mouth. Kate reached Simon's feet. There was something odd about the way his clothes fell over his unmoving frame. It was like cloth draped on stone rather than a man. There was no rise and fall to Simon's chest. His eyes were open, but glassy. She pointed his stick sword toward the creature.

"Simon?" Kate murmured, and the creature's eyes slid to her again. She pressed the point of the blade against the thing's chest, but again, it only moved its gaping mouth. "Are you alive?"

Simon flinched and drew in a gasping breath like a man breaking the water after a long time submerged. The white creature flicked its attention to him and quills rose along the thing's shoulders.

"Kill it," Simon wheezed.

Kate instantly plunged the blade deep into the soft white flesh where she knew a human's heart would be. It was disturbingly easy to stab the thing. The homunculus gave a sharp hiss. Simon whispered a word and the blade of the sword glowed blue and hot. Kate felt a strange vibration through the silver handle and almost let go of it. The creature gurgled and fell still.

Simon gasped in pain and wrenched his fingers from the creature's neck.

"Were you struck?" Kate placed one hand on his

back, which felt stiff and corded, but she maintained an eye on the homunculus.

"No." His voice was deep and strained. His arm drew back with aching slowness and he put his hand flat against the ground. He began to hoist himself up off the homunculus as if a crane lifted him. He fell over and lay supine, nearly motionless, beside the white creature. Kate shouted in alarm. Simon raised an arm and it sounded like twigs snapping. His eyes caught hers and, impossibly, his mouth curved into a slow smile. "I will be fine in a moment. Would you mind checking to ensure it's dead?"

Kate looked at the motionless thing. The thin sword, now plain steel, still protruded from its rib cage. Then it fell over with a metallic clang. Kate jumped back, fearful that the creature was stirring. Rather, the thing's chest was collapsing into a sizzling crater. The tips of its fingers and toes began to bubble into whitish liquid. The eyes popped and its face caved in.

Simon's head turned with a grating rumble. He scowled at the dissolving thing.

Kate grabbed Simon under the arms and dragged him away from the pool of ghastly ooze that drained from the white creature's boiling remains. In less than a minute, it went from a body to viscous mush interspersed with odd metallic lumps.

"Well," groaned Simon, "that's unfortunate."

Suddenly the pool of ichor stirred with a muffled, clicking sound. Short metallic rods lifted from the morass as if alive. They pivoted and jammed their ends into the large bulbous object that had been the creature's skull. Metal rods extended and lifted the dripping skull from the ground.

Kate scrabbled for the sword. She leapt to her feet and slashed at the horrific, insectlike object. The tip of the sword rang off the skull. Kate found it disconcerting that

the eye sockets were staring back at her as the thing scuttled through broken glass and raced away. With spindly
metal legs, it veered one way, and Kate turned, but then
it made a quick swerve, nearly causing her to lose her
footing trying to follow. It accelerated onto the lawn and
slipped into a row of sculpted hedges. There was a brief
rustle of leaves, then silence. Kate stopped and tried to
listen for the sound of clicks over her own breathing.

It was impossible. She made one last scan of the area
and returned to the library. Simon was still lying on the
floor where she had left him. His eyes were a bit glazed
and his lips had the oddest smirk.

Kate settled next to him with the sword still in her
grasp. "I can't believe what I just saw."

"It was a bit unexpected." Simon rolled his shoulders,
regaining some flexibility, although his arm flopped
wildly as if it was numb.

"What did you do to yourself?"

"It's a spell that hardens my flesh. The benefit is that
it renders me invulnerable to nearly anything. The dif-
ficulty is that I am unable to move or breathe. When I
begin to black out, the spell wears off. And I become
supremely vulnerable." Simon worked his jaw up and
down, accompanied by crunching sounds. He laughed
painfully. "Magic has its ups and downs."

Kate slumped to the bricks and put a hand to her face
with a hiccuping laugh that heralded the exhilaration of
survival. She heard the footsteps of servants pounding
toward them and watched steam rise from the disgusting puddle that used to be a living creature. "Is this
normal activity for you, Mr. Archer?"

"I wouldn't say it's an everyday thing, no." Simon
took her hand with his peculiarly cold and hard fingers.
"And by the way, thank you for saving my life again."

Kate was disturbed by how inhuman his touch felt.

Chapter Sixteen

IT WAS DARK AND COLD INSIDE THE VAST ARCHED cellar. Men and women shuffled through the chamber, yet they were not the common breed of London homeless who searched the tenement streets for stoops or basements to shelter in. Some wore fine garb, although days of hiding had taken their toll.

One man held court in a corner, growling out a rage to any who would listen. "Who is she to tell us? I was born in Wessex. What of her? She's from far away."

"Lincolnshire?"

"No," he snapped back. "Denmark or Norway or some damn place no one comes from. What can she do that we can't do for ourselves? What can she give us that we can't take?"

A woman spoke up. "She has the wulfsyl."

The man glared and pulled his threadbare coat tighter. "We can get our own. She must get it from somewhere. Why can't we do the same?"

More in the crowd turned toward him, exchanging glances and nods.

The man flexed his arms. He was large, muscular, and fierce. His long, unkempt beard was flecked with spittle and his eyes glowed. "I don't care what the rest of Gretta's little packs are doing. Aren't you sick of hiding in the dark, waiting for the pathetic meals she brings? Lord Oakham stood up to her. He didn't hide in the dirt just because she said to."

There was a ripple of dismay, and someone said, "And now Lord Oakham is dead."

"He was alone. We are together."

A girl, perhaps age thirteen, who wore a dirty pink frock and had tangled blond hair, said, "Aren't we all the same kind? I never knew there were so many. I thought I was alone. Now I think we should protect one another. Why should we fight her?"

The man sneered. "That's all well and good, girl. But I don't like taking charity. I was made to take what I need!" He spread his hands over the crowd. "And where is she now? Is she here in the cold with us? No! She is somewhere warm and soft, while she leashes us here like her slaves. I am no one's slave!"

A silence from the far side of the chamber collided with the aggressive rumble the man had created. The quiet touched his followers, who looked to see its source. The wanderers in the cellar parted for a woman who approached.

Gretta Aldfather stooped for comfort in the low ceiling of the cellar. Her tall frame moved with quiet precision and her vast cloak barely moved. Her face had the cold dispassion of the Arctic. The statuesque woman stopped a few feet from the man who had been pontificating. To his credit, he didn't shrink but stared evenly up at her.

"Samuel," she asked quietly, "what is this about?"

"I'm surprised to see you here, Gretta. Aren't you afraid you might dirty yourself?"

Gretta stood motionless. The crowd began to shuffle, some toward the vociferous Samuel but most away.

He took her silence for hesitation. "We've had enough of you, Gretta. We don't need you here."

Gretta smiled slowly in understanding. "You're an idiot. Like Oakham."

"You killed him."

"I didn't, but he deserved it all the same. All of my other lieutenants followed my rules. But he broke my curfews. Brought attention to us. His foolishness brought a hunter to London."

"I'm not afraid of hunters," Samuel replied haughtily.

"Then you're a fool," Gretta said. "MacFarlane is about, and if he gets your trail, you'll be dead, just like Oakham."

Samuel waved dismissively. "MacFarlane is nothing to me. If you're afraid of him, perhaps you'd best go home."

"I'm offering a new age for our kind, but you're too much a beast to see it."

"A new age?" the man scoffed. "We kill. That is what we do."

"I agree." Gretta threw back her cloak to reveal that she wore her antique leather cuirass over her bare ivory skin. She reached behind her and pulled a large, double-edged battle-axe, which would've taken the strongest of men to wield.

Samuel showed trepidation for the first time, but it was brief. Physical violence was his currency, as it was for most everyone gathered there. He flexed his fingers and grinned. "Do you hope to cow me with that toy?"

"I have no interest in cowing you." Gretta's voice remained deathly quiet.

Samuel laughed, throwing his arms to encompass his friends. "You think you can kill all of us?"

"Yes." Gretta tightened her hands on the haft of the axe with a leathery squeak.

Samuel stepped back into the group of ten supporters, his body starting to shake.

Gretta surged forward with axe swinging. Before it

could reach its intended target, it struck one man and cleaved him near in half before continuing to gouge deep into another. She tried to pull her weapon free, but it was caught in the rib cage of the second victim. Gretta growled and yanked, producing a shower of bone and blood. She spun in an arc of steel as other figures closed on her. Screams and snarls vibrated the cellar.

Samuel had doubled over as a man but straightened as a beast. His horrible sneer grew grotesquely wide, splitting his face open. Then his nose and chin length-ened into a snarling canine snout with rows of terrible teeth. His large hands grew dark with scimitar claws. As muscular as he had been, his bulk increased. Shoul-ders hunched and brawny. Arms long and powerful. His clothing tore, revealing matted black fur sprouting beneath. He shook himself violently and sprang for the blond woman.

With amazing speed, Gretta brought the axe straight out in front of her, bracing her powerful legs as the large werewolf slammed into her. The impact drove her back, but the beast was held away from her by the length of the weapon so his clawed swipes fell short. With a tremendous shout, Gretta surged forward and pushed him off his feet, slamming him down onto the floor. She pressed the eye of the axe into his chest with all her considerable might, causing him to snarl with pain.

The sounds of growls, stretching flesh, and cracking bone that accompanied the lycanthrope change came from all parts of the room. Figures writhed in the ec-static torment of transformation.

In the time it took Gretta to raise a foot and stamp on one of Samuel's arms, she changed too. In the unbe-lievable blink of an eye, she went from Valkyrie to a huge wolf on her hind legs, still draped in a cloak, with her powerful torso straining against her leather armor.

Samuel struck at her with his free arm and snapped pointlessly with his jaws. Gretta curled back her lips and gave a sound that might have been a laugh. Then she pressed down onto the haft of the axe creating a cry of pain from Samuel and the echo of snapping bones beneath the blunt crown of the blade.

She went to one knee, clutching a clawed hand over Samuel's neck. Before he could even reach for her arm, she came away with his throat. He quivered. She stood and, in an instant, drove the axe blade through his chest so deeply it pinned him to the floor.

Gretta turned and slashed at other figures. She moved like a reaping machine, putting claws through victims and crushing others with her teeth. Bodies fell around her. A few larger werewolves leapt for her, clambering onto her back, biting her neck and shoulders.

She whirled, pulling attackers off like fleas and smashing them to the ground. She crushed them with her heavy tread. She gored them with her murderous hands. Her lithe form climbed over bodies, grabbing for more of them, killing any who came near her.

Werewolves struggled to move back, fighting to get away from her savagery in the narrow confines, to be far from her berserker rage. Hairy bodies crouched and scuttled, pressing against the brick walls, falling on their knees and backs, praying their submissive postures might save them.

It didn't. Gretta continued to kill, even those who offered no resistance, who whined and begged.

"Gretta! Stop!" The young girl ran forward, a little human among the writhing mass of monsters. She planted her tiny feet in a pool of red and held up her small pink hands to the bloody heaving monster. "Stop! Please!"

The towering creature raised clawed hands, and blinked. Gretta's snarl calmed and she stood with heaving chest, looking down at the young girl. The beast let out a final rumbling growl and lowered a massive, bloodstained hand on top of the girl's head. The child flinched ever so slightly at the touch. More of the cowering pack, now transformed back to mere humans, scraped forward, cringing on the ground.

Ignoring them, Gretta kicked into the mound of dead, and reached down to wrench her battle-axe free from Samuel the traitor. Gretta was a woman again, bloodied and flecked with gore. She fastened the axe on her back and adjusted her tattered cloak. She pointed at several of the survivors. "You and you. Bury them under the floor. Then you will all come with me. I have a place where I am gathering everyone."

One of the miserable wretches crawled forward. "We are with you, Gretta. We didn't fight."

"No, you didn't." Gretta sneered at the supplicant. "At least they did."

The Valkyrie waited by the door as holes were dug for the dead. With some interest she watched the girl who had confronted her. The girl helped dig, with an occasional glance over her shoulder at Gretta. The little thing was bold, and Gretta briefly wondered if she should be killed.

After the dead were hidden in shallow graves, the survivors gathered their meager belongings and trudged out behind their leader. The ramshackle door slammed shut on the cellar, leaving behind the stench of blood and waste.

After a few minutes, a shadow stirred in a deep corner. A figure rose from behind a pile of detritus. He smelled of urine and dirt because he had covered himself in those substances before secreting himself in the cellar when the beasts had gone out yesterday. Filthy scents had covered his normal human smell from the gathered lycanthropes.

Malcolm had gone from trailing what he thought was

a single rogue werewolf to finding a den of the creatures in the heart of London. That was horrific enough, but then *she* appeared.

Gretta Aldfather. Close enough to touch. The multitudes that she had slaughtered in her long life were unknown. Clearly, she was preparing to raise her totals.

Malcolm stepped around the mounds of freshly turned earth and made his way out of the bloodstained cellar. He needed to find a way to wash this filth from him. And then he needed help.

Chapter Seventeen

SIMON KICKED HIS WAY THROUGH DENSE, WET brush. His heavy boots were caked with mud and his trousers were wet up to the knees. His breath misted before him. Still, his strength was back and he felt invigorated to be out on a crisp fall morning. He also felt the inebriating filaments of aether winding through him, lightening his mood.

He slapped a sodden branch aside and found himself on a narrow path in the forest. It was a useful track toward Hartley Hall. If he were approaching the house, this would be a natural path to use.

Simon took a heavy clay tablet from under his arm. It was about the width of a dinner plate and several inches thick. One side was inscribed with reversed runes that he had incised into the wet clay last night before baking it hard overnight. He set the tablet on the ground, rune side down, and knelt in the mud. He pressed a hand onto the circle and began to recite. As he spoke, the clay grew warm and glowed green. He spat out the final phrase and felt aether rush from him to the tablet and into the earth. With red raw fingers, he pried up the clay piece to see faint green runes glowing in the wet dirt.

Something huge slammed into his back. He was hurled into the brush. The scent of wet fur and the sound of ragged breathing surrounded him. He saw teeth and a huge pink tongue.

Aethelred licked his face. The wolfhound threw back his massive head and released a long, deep howl. Simon laughed and tossed an arm around the jovial dog's neck.

"A bit of warning next time, eh?"

"Mr. Archer!" Kate's voice cut through the forest.

"Here, Miss Anstruther."

Kate waded through low-hanging branches and pushed onto the path. She wore a long, thick coat and heavy boots. Her hair, as usual, was wild around her face. She looked down curiously at the man and dog. "It's a bit damp to be frolicking on the ground, isn't it?"

"Is it?" Thoroughly soaked, Simon climbed to his feet with Aethelred pressing against him, panting happily.

Kate snapped her fingers and the dog came dutifully to her side. "I knew Aethelred would find you."

Simon retrieved the clay tablet from the undergrowth, cleaning wet weeds from it. "His penchant for silent stalking is as amusing as ever."

Kate eyed the tablet with interest. "Is it working?"

"Well, I assume. I've set ten wards around the grounds. I'd like to put at least ten more to be sure."

She walked to where the faint imprint of the circle lay in the mud. "I don't see anything."

"Good. We don't want a glowing beacon to warn intruders."

"And you're sure it's safe for the staff? The gamekeepers walk these paths frequently."

Simon smiled mysteriously, wiping his perspiring brow. "It will only be triggered by some being of unnatural composition, such as a homunculus or werewolf. Every type of occult being has aether traces on it of a peculiar type. Obviously I can't know all those mystic signatures, but I can manage enough to encompass the creatures we've already run across. Hopefully none of your gamekeepers are homunculi or were-wolves."

"No." Kate slowly slid her foot over the circle in the dirt. "I can't vouch for Hogarth, though. What happens when a homunculus comes near it?"

"He will explode." Simon laughed loudly.

She eyed him critically. "You seem a tad tipsy this morning."

"Your scotch is safe! I promise." Simon placed a hand over his heart dramatically, but at seeing her mood was less inclined, he made an effort at sobriety. "What you see is an annoying consequence of excessive aether drain. It will pass. Unfortunately, these wards are only temporary. This rough clay tablet is not the best tool, but I haven't time for proper inscription to protect an estate of such size. However, I can renew them as needed."

Kate patted the wolfhound. "Thank you. If you can spare a moment, you are needed at the house."

Simon grew serious. "Something wrong with your sister?"

"No. Your friend, Mr. Barker, has returned unexpectedly. And he's brought someone with him."

Simon hurried with Kate along the path until sprawling Hartley Hall rose up before them. They walked side by side through the fading autumn garden, past hedgerows and statues. Groundskeepers with rakes watched them pass. Kate led the way to the rear of the house and a gracious room called the Blue Room. She opened the French doors and entered with Simon on her heels.

Nick sat near the fire, holding a cup. He grinned, regarding Simon's mud-covered clothes. "Well, there you are, squire. Sorry to intrude on your new bucolic way of life with my city problems."

"I apologize for not rushing back to London in the three days since I nearly lost my life. Oh, and by the way, we managed to kill that creature. What have you accomplished in the interim?"

Nick jerked his thumb to his right. "Found this."

Malcolm stood in the corner as quiet as a shadow and just as grim. "We have business."

"You seem to be everywhere." Simon's voice was cold. He noticed Kate's surprised glance between the two men. It wasn't difficult to detect the obvious, personal chill in the room. Simon felt his wet clothes now with miserable discomfort. The dour face of the Scotsman annoyed him with its simple assuredness. He ground out, "I owe you an apology, Mr. MacFarlane."

The Scotsman continued to stare without great expectation.

"Brace yourself," Simon said with grave importance. "It seems there is a second werewolf in London after all."

Malcolm raised a tired eyebrow, clearly unimpressed.

Simon feigned extreme distress. "I'm sorry. I didn't mean to put you to sleep with that news."

"Brace *yourself*. There is an *army* of werewolves in London. And they are under the command of one of the vilest monsters to ever walk our Earth: Gretta Aldfather."

Blood drained from Simon's face and cold seeped into his limbs. Even Kate gave a sharp gasp of recognition. He cleared his throat to recover his voice. "How do you know this?"

"I had been tracking one of the beasts in the Rookery and found a den where twenty or so of the creatures were holed up."

"Twenty!" Simon exclaimed. "Werewolves? Together? Are you sure?"

Malcolm ignored the incredulity in the man's voice. "I could tell many of them were fresh to their condition. Wulvers, they're called. They don't have firm control of their transformations, and they're not at full strength. Still, in a pack they're dangerous enough for all that, and I thought it alarming. Until I saw Gretta; then I knew it was so much worse. I saw her once in Russia years ago. It's her without question. The only positive about her being here is that she may kill off the other primes. I saw her kill one and a few of his allies. There can only be one leader, and she is it."

"Jesus God." Simon leaned on the hearth, seeking Nick's experienced gaze for support. "What do you think we should do?"

"Do?" Nick held out his hand to the fire. "Nothing. If we fight Gretta Aldfather, we're dead. Everyone else has been."

"That's hardly inspiring stuff."

"I'm only trying to inspire you to not fight her." A mix of anger and fear crossed Nick's features.

Kate clutched her hands together, standing alone in the middle of the room. "Is this the monster who was after Imogen?"

Simon straightened and forced the worry off his face. "Hibbert may have been stupidly involved with Gretta, and she killed him. We can hope that Imogen was just a bystander who was lucky enough to escape."

"But we don't know that," Kate pressed. "She could've been involved in something she didn't understand. After all, the homunculus was here for a reason. And it seemed to be Imogen. It could all come back to this Gretta Aldfather, yes?"

Simon took a deep breath. "Yes."

The sound of bones creaking was audible as Kate squeezed her hands together. Her face was drawn, her mouth a slit of terror. Simon regarded her with sympathy.

Nick glowered at Simon. "This is exactly the sort of idiocy I was trying to avoid. It's all well and good to wander around the city doing little magical chores. But we know the atmosphere has been growing more poisonous out there. We've been sensing it. There's dark magic everywhere. And here it is writ as large and dark as possible. This is Gretta Aldfather and a pack of werewolves like no one has seen before. There is absolutely no reason to be involved in this, Simon. I told you we should stay in the shadows. Hungry sharks swim these waters and we're bleeding like stuck fish out here! We've already done enough. This is far too big for us." He pointed at Kate. "Who are these people to us?"

Simon remained calm even though he had never seen Nick so furious. "On the contrary, this is exactly the sort of thing we should be dealing with. This is why we've learned magic. Nick, we can't turn our backs now. It isn't just Miss Anstruther. All of London is at risk." Simon offered his friend a questioning glance. "Once, I might have followed you into the shadows and left the work for others more capable. But not now. And that's partly owing to what I've learned from you."

"You never learned this sort of stupidity from me." Nick fumed silently for a few moments, then said, "You're not going to fight Gretta, are you?"

"Yes, I am," Simon replied.

Malcolm crossed his arms. "Good."

"WEREWOLVES ARE SAVAGELY TERRITORIAL." SIMON poured wine for Kate but looked at Malcolm, who sat at his right. The dining room was closed and the servants sent away. The meal was simple and the setting spartan. "How can they be together in such quantities?"

Malcolm ate like a starving man, seemingly disengaged from the conversation. He glanced up, chewing a chop. "From what I observed, Gretta has control of a sizeable store of wulfsyl." He began gnawing the bone.

Kate set down her silverware. "Is she an alchemist? Even the best authorities have only limited understanding of wulfsyl."

"I've no idea where she gets it, but I don't take her for having such knowledge." Malcolm tossed the bare bone onto his plate and scoured the serving trays for more food. The sleeves of his shirt were rolled up and his jacket was hung on the back of his chair as if this were a communal meal at a coaching inn.

Kate said, "So wulfsyl allows the lycanthrope to control their transformation?"

"Hard to say." Malcolm pointed for Nick to pass a plate of cheese. "I think they gain some control of their transformations as they age. I tend to believe they use wulfsyl to retain some sort of rational thought while they're in beast form."

Simon said, "That way they can remember what they did as an animal. What fun is slaughtering if you can't recall the slaughter?"

Malcolm shrugged in agreement while spearing a hunk of cheese with his large dagger. "That's why Gretta is so dangerous. She's hundreds of years old, and she handles her berserker rages better than any other. She's both brutal and rational."

Nick shook his head. "She's so hard to control that the Order of the Oak threw her in the Bastille a hundred years ago." He grunted a laugh. "Bloody peasants stormed the place not knowing they were destroying the magic wards on the prison."

Simon regarded Kate. "You are familiar with that story? Byron Pendragon, who was a scribe and one of the founders of the Order of the Oak, built the Bastille during the Middle Ages to be a sorcerous prison. It was intended to be the eternal home for the most dangerous magicians and creatures on Earth. When it finally fell, there were still a few remaining mystical prisoners there, including Gretta. We know some of the others. There was Ferghus O'Malley, the fire elemental who caused the Great Fire of London. Nephthys, the Egyptian demon mistress whose monstrous armies were so horrifying, Arabs and Crusaders united against her. The Baroness Conrad, half woman and half machine, who ruled huge swathes of India. There was a man, or a woman, with no real name who used alchemy to change his shape and his or her identity each time he wished to murder innocents. And, of course, Gaios the Mad, the earth elemental who reportedly caused Vesuvius to erupt. There were likely other things locked in that prison that we don't know about. However, we do know that all those monsters escaped into the chaos of the Revolution. In the aftermath of the escape, Byron Pendragon was killed and the Order fell."

She replied, "I knew some of it. But it's so terribly real now. Not a book or journal or scary story told by candlelight."

"This whole affair may be some echo of the old Order of the Oak," Simon said. "My father was a member, and a close associate of Pendragon's. I suspect Sir Roland was affiliated in some fashion as well."

Kate merely nodded in thought. "If this beast woman is looking to settle some old score through Imogen, she's picking the wrong fight. My father isn't even about. He disappeared years ago. Where is yours?"

Simon breathed out. "Shortly before my birth he was murdered by Pendragon's enemies."

Kate impulsively took Simon's hand. "That's horrible. I'm sorry you've had to live with that." Simon didn't move his hand out from under hers, and his eyes remained riveted on Malcolm. She sat back, and asked,

"Mr. MacFarlane, have you any connection to the Order of the Oak?"

The Scotsman pursed his lips. "It's a long story, Miss Anstruther." He merely sat back, staring at the candles. The silence dragged on with no evidence of his speaking further.

Simon gave a smirk. "And you tell it so well."

Malcolm colored and his nose creased in anger. "What would you have, Archer? Shall I repeat the tale of my father's wasted days and besotted death? Would that make you feel better?"

"It might." Simon gripped his knife and glared in Malcolm's eyes.

"I leave it to you to tell it then so you may enjoy it all the more."

Kate slapped her hand on the table, rattling the dishes. "For God's sake! There are monsters at large. And my sister is in mortal danger every second we don't deal with it. I don't know what's between you two, but please engage in a match of smugness later."

"Right," Nick muttered, pouring more wine for himself. "Although there won't be a later for us."

Kate pointed at Simon. "I know you somewhat and trust you. And you vouch for your pessimistic friend there. But do you trust Mr. MacFarlane? Otherwise, we'll have him out and settle this affair ourselves."

The Scotsman rose from the table with indignation. "Here! Who are you to—"

"Shut up!" Kate jabbed her finger at him. "And sit down until I give you leave to go."

Malcolm fumed in silence but resumed his seat.

"Now"—Kate regained a professional demeanor—"Mr. Archer, what say you about Mr. MacFarlane?"

Simon nearly started to laugh. He studied Kate's commanding face in the candlelight. She had a refreshing way of coming directly to the point. He found her attitude very alluring. He glanced quickly at Nick, who rolled his eyes with clear recognition of Simon's interest in the woman.

"I trust him," Simon said without looking at the Scotsman.

Kate nodded with acceptance. "Very well. Mr. MacFarlane, what say you? Will you join us?"

The Scotsman sat contemplating various answers, stringing out his silence until Kate began to draw herself up in annoyance. He quickly said, "That's why I'm here."

Simon stood up immediately and regarded the company. "Now, with that foolishness settled thanks to Miss Anstruther, let's talk about wulfsyl because that is our Trojan horse to strike inside the enemy camp."

"Yes," Kate said vigorously. "If we can find their store and destroy it, might they go mad, and might they even turn on Gretta and rip her to pieces?"

"But then we would have lunatic werewolves running loose in London," Simon said. "I'm thinking of something a bit more surreptitious. It's common to poison vermin, I believe."

Malcolm grunted in dismissal. "Not possible. I once laced a cadaver with enough Prussian blue to kill every wolf in the Carpathians, and it did nothing to the werewolf that ate it."

Simon replied, "I suspect we can do a bit better than cyanide. We do have the finest alchemist in England." He turned to Kate.

She grinned with a dark eagerness.

KATE TOOK UP RESIDENCE IN HER LABORATORY. She had spent years cross-indexing her source material so she could lay hands on the proper sources, and she soon surrounded herself with books and journals that involved lycanthropy and wulfsyl. The alchemical masters rarely mentioned the fabled concoction, but she had developed the skill of working between sources, pulling one bit of information from one place and a different snippet from another.

Under her left hand was a text about lycanthropy in thirteenth-century French, and under her right an Italian source on mysterious alchemy. Both authors mentioned that werewolves often sought certain substances to enhance their bestiality or their humanity, depending on which source she chose to believe. The French authority claimed that the beasts scoured the forests for particular mushrooms under the full moon. The Italian, on the other hand, believed that werewolves imbibed some strange potion during certain seasons of the year or particular times of the month. However, it mentioned that one of the primary ingredients of the potion was a mysterious mushroom that was rare and precious. A helpful sketch of the most likely mushroom sent Kate to a massive Flemish source on *materia medica,* which led her to identify the ghostbloom mushroom. And then she pulled an old scroll from Denmark called *Plants of the Dead.* She found the Danish version of the ghostbloom, which assured her that the misshapen white fungus rose only on freshly turned graves under the light of the moon.

So much was mere speculation. Kate dropped her head in her hands with a heavy sigh. So much work to do. So much depended on her. Imogen was upstairs sleeping, innocent, apparently unaware of the dangers around her. Kate had to protect her sister; she had done such a poor job so far. Every time she thought of it, her chest constricted.

If only her father had been here.

But he wasn't. Would he be proud of her or would he be disappointed in the way she had handled the estate

THE SHADOW REVOLUTION 165

and the family? The effort of holding the weight of his legacy upon her shoulders was like a lodestone, but she had borne it willingly, an undying hope that the family would one day be whole again. Only everything was flying apart.

Kate heard a scuffling sound behind her. She straightened quickly, wiping the emotion from her face, and turned to see Simon in the doorway holding a serving tray. He seemed concerned, so she pushed back her shoulders, smiled, and raised a jaunty eyebrow.

He stepped forward. "Pardon my interruption, but you've been at it for hours. The staff were concerned that you ignored the call for dinner."

Kate glanced at the clock and noted with alarm that it was nearly 2:00 a.m.

"No doubt you were too distracted to eat," Simon continued smoothly. "I know all too well. I have a distinct habit of disappearing in my own library. Ask Nick."

Kate sat back stiffly in the leather chair and stretched her neck and arms. Simon settled the tray in front of her pointedly, whisking off the cover of a meal of chicken and figs. Kate was blind to all but one thing.

"Tea! Splendid!" She reached for the cup.

"I debated something stronger but settled on this."

"Stronger later. This now." She rubbed one of her shoulders and groaned.

Simon moved behind her. "If I may, a shaman showed me a miraculous method of relieving kinks in one's muscles."

Kate nodded cautiously. He took up a spot behind her and laid hands on her shoulders. She froze and her breath stilled as his fingers began to knead. Her eyes closed. His thumbs caressed up her spine, along her neck, to the back of her head. His hands were warm and soothing. She could feel their heat through her blouse and believed that if they touched her bare skin, they would sear her. "You say a shaman showed you this?"

His hands swept back to her shoulders and began to work their magic there. It was scandalous but felt like heaven. Kate's head dropped back limply and struck the hard muscles of his abdomen. Her breath escaped her. She suddenly sat up straight, reaching for the many tomes before her.

Kate coughed to clear her throat. "Um. I've run down a few leads on how wulfsyl is created."

"Good. Where does that take us?" Simon's voice rumbled in her ear like a jaguar prowling through the dark jungle. He stretched past her to remove the sugar bowl from her reach and she realized that she had spooned copious amounts of sugar into her tea.

She sipped the horribly sweet liquid, gathering her thoughts. "If I can determine how it's made, I can figure out a way to adulterate it."

Simon removed the hand that had lingered on her shoulder and came around to face her. His gaze was intense. "Miss Anstruther . . . Kate, this may be beyond my purview to say, but I'm bound to say it."

"Please do." All the relief brought by his brief massage fled in a new rush of tension.

Simon pondered for a moment. "People such as you and I live in a frightening world."

"I'm not afraid of this fight."

"No, it's quite clear you aren't. You may be a bit too unafraid, but that's neither here nor there. My point is that in our world, decisions over life and death are ours alone. Faced with threats to humanity like Gretta, the police or the courts or the Church can be no help to us. We must face the challenges, and that is our greatest risk."

"Yes?"

"However, there is also no one to judge us on our actions. And that is our greatest threat."

"Do you have doubts about what we're planning?"

"Not a bit." Simon continued to stare at her with green eyes that seemed to shine despite the shadowy room. "There is nothing we could do to these beasts that I would find too brutal. However, you must consider yourself too. There are certain lines that, once crossed, there is no going back."

"I don't understand you. What line could there be here? These things are monsters. We are required by decency to destroy them when we find them."

Simon held up his hand. "Yes, I agree with that. I'm merely offering you a final chance to reconsider. They are monsters, but they are also humans, of a sort. Plus, we are not striking the enemy in the heat of battle. We are slipping into their beds and dripping poison in their ears. There are some who might find that troubling."

"I'm not one of them. They're animals."

He nodded at her, apparently satisfied. His stern appearance lightened, and the issue was gone. Moral quandaries were vanquished. Kate couldn't draw her eyes away from him as he leaned forward and laid a warm hand on her chilled fingers, the contrast of which made her heart pound harder. He seemed on the verge of saying something, but then his face turned serious. He took a step back, sliding the plate in front of her.

Kate took a deep breath, faced with the juxtaposition of a simple meal sitting on top of journals filled with notes on lycanthropy. She leaned forward, resting her chin in her hand. "You amaze me, Mr. Archer. I knew you were a man of great conscience. Your sympathy extends even to those monsters you hunt."

"Eat." Simon stood there a moment more. "When was the last time you were in bed, Miss Anstruther?"

Kate opened her eyes wide at the boldness of his comment but then realized it was she who had misinterpreted a simple question. Or had she? "Do you ask because I look like hell?" She pushed a wayward lock of hair behind her ear.

"I wasn't commenting on your appearance. Although apparently exhaustion suits you. Still, a few hours spent between crisp sheets would do you a world of good."

Kate swallowed consciously, not sure what he had implied, but just the thought brought a round of chills. She picked up the utensils and cut into the meal in an effort to distract herself. But all the while, she followed his straight back to the door. Kate blamed her flush on the spices in the food. Then her hand absently reached up to touch her neck, which still pulsed with the heat of his touch.

Chapter Eighteen

KATE FELT BADLY OUT OF PLACE IN THE DEVIL'S Loom.

The close, musty scent of sweat and beer mixed with suspicious glances from the locals. Knowing eyes pinned her as a provincial swell with no attachment to the neighborhood. They also stared at Malcolm beside her, but with looks of concern, and even fear.

Simon stood at the bar chatting amiably with a group of rugged workingmen. They all laughed and slapped one another's shoulders, and Simon bought them ales, and the laughing and slapping commenced anew.

Kate sipped a glass of pedestrian sherry, wishing it were something stronger. "Mr. Archer seems to be getting on."

Malcolm grunted and shifted. She could hear the telltale rattle of his twin Lancaster pistols beneath his coat.

"It's remarkable," she continued. "Everyone likes him. From lords to longshoremen."

"Yes." Malcolm grunted again. "Everyone."

"It's almost unnatural."

The hunter downed his scotch with a grimace of whiskey criticism. "It's because the man has no soul."

"That's a terrible thing to say, Mr. MacFarlane." Kate twisted her head quickly, shocked.

"It's not meant as a criticism. He is exactly what he needs to be, whenever he needs it. But I can tell you, we've never seen the true man."

Kate regarded Simon, who continued to master his audience with a glib phrase and a direct, manly look in the eye. Perhaps the grim, uncomfortable Malcolm was merely jealous of Simon's easy nature.

The Scotsman murmured, "I wonder if he's ever seen it either."

"Mr. Archer learned how to survive in a society that cared little for him. No different than how you learned to live out in the wild, I imagine. Some may call you uncivilized and uncouth."

Malcolm shrugged, taking no offense.

"Doesn't make you any less of a man, does it?"

Malcolm grinned. "No, it doesn't."

Kate sat back. "Any more words of wisdom?"

"His friend, Nick Barker, is a coward."

"Why do you say that?" she asked with surprise. "Because he doesn't want to stand up to Gretta Aldfather?"

"Among other things. I abhor magicians who prefer the shadows instead of facing someone outright."

Kate recalled how, after the fight with Lord Oakham, she had seen Simon upbraiding Nick for some distasteful action to bring the battle to an end. And there was no denying Nick's reluctance to get involved with Imogen's problems. Still, he had done something to help the wounded and he was Simon's friend. She was coming to trust Simon's judgment. "Perhaps there is more to Mr. Barker than we know."

Malcolm snorted his skepticism. "I'd certainly wager that."

"Regardless, Simon Archer is one magician who does not stand in the shadows."

"Perhaps. We'll see who stands and fights when hell breaks loose."

"Do you have character assessments of me then?"

Malcolm slowly raised his eyes to her. His hunter's countenance sent chills along her spine. Gratefully, her attention was drawn to Simon as he shook hands all around his group of chums, signaled to the barman for another round for them, and came smiling back to the table. He sat opposite Kate and Malcolm, glancing curiously at Kate's penetrating expression.

He drummed his hands on the tabletop. "We're on for tonight at St. Andrews Holborn."

Kate leaned close. "Those men you were talking to are body snatchers?"

"Yes and please don't stare at them. They went on lookout yesterday at several funerals around town. They were going out to St. Andrews tonight."

Kate pulled her gaze away from the three men at the bar in their heavy twill trousers and cloth caps pulled down over sullen eyes. "But don't they want the body?"

"I paid them more to stay away than a body would fetch from the surgeons at St. Barts. In addition, tonight is nearly a full moon; they'd just as soon stay here and get drunk as try to open a grave under the bright eye of Selene."

Malcolm said quietly, "I'm surprised that men such as these vile resurrectionists are your friends."

"*Friends* is a bit strong. Although I don't begrudge a man a living wage in this day and age."

The Scotsman muttered, "Wonder if you'd feel the same if it was your carcass they were pulling from the grave?"

"Hopefully I won't find out for many years." Simon gave Kate a charming wink.

She raised her glass with relief and changed the subject. "You seem quite at ease. Please tell me you haven't had cause to sneak into a cemetery before?"

Simon leaned back with a mysterious smile.

* * *

"THREE O'CLOCK." SIMON SNAPPED HIS WATCH shut.

Kate rubbed her gloved hands together. The air was damp and cold, and a stiff wind swirled down Holborn Hill. The gaslights up on the rise flickered cheerfully, but the three companions loitered in the shadows at the base of the hill among ramshackle buildings. No one had passed them in nearly twenty minutes. Even the night cabs had disappeared. The nearly full moon hosted long, silver clouds racing over its face.

"It stinks down here," Kate pointed out.

"The Fleet ditch is hardly a garden spot. How long does it take the mushrooms to sprout? Do they need more moonlight?" Simon clapped his hands together to warm them, muffled by thick, fingerless gloves.

"They'll be up by now. We should go on. They won't stay long."

Simon pulled his heavy scarf up over his nose.

"That's not suspicious," Malcolm said. "You look like a highwayman."

"Shall we?" Simon extended his arm. Kate took it and he touched her fingers fleetingly before he led the way uphill. They turned off through the street through a jumble of buildings, where they found a narrow flight of rickety stairs. They climbed up and slipped into alleys, moving along brick walls and darkened doorways. They made several turns, dodging piles of trash and crawlers huddled in stoops. Simon blazed the trail with authority, banishing any apprehension Kate felt. His confidence was intoxicating. He dove into a narrow passageway that ended in a wrought-iron fence. Through the bars was St. Andrew's squarish steeple, moon-bathed in a yard full of gravestones and overgrown trees.

Simon bent with his hands laced together. "You first Malcolm, then—"

"Shh." The hunter held up a finger for silence. He sidled up to the fence, listening hard.

Kate heard nothing but the wind and the flapping of their own clothes. She could almost imagine the tombstones creaking as if they were growing from the earth. She caught Simon's eye and he shrugged.

Malcolm stepped back into the alley and motioned them to follow. He whispered, "There's someone in the churchyard. More than one person. Might be our quarry."

Kate breathed hard in anticipation, ready to put practice into action. She felt for her father's pistol in her belt and the short sword at her hip. She also had a leather bandolier over her shoulder. It was designed for large hunting shells, but it now contained vials of potentially useful potions. Her long dress was gone, replaced by a heavy skirt that fell midcalf. She wore boots and a leather jacket over a thick man's shirt. She felt rather rugged in a way. Excitement rather than dread coursed through her.

She heard a quiet snapping of impatient fingers. Malcolm was already crouching atop the spears of the iron fence, reaching down for her. She stretched up and he dragged her into the air and onto the precarious fence top. She barely kept herself from toppling headfirst to the grass of the churchyard. Simon came up beside her.

Malcolm dropped silent as a cat. He turned and took her as if she were weightless. Simon hit the ground with a grunt that brought a cautionary glance from the Scotsman. Malcolm signaled for them to be silent and follow him. He kept along the fence, moving in the shadows of the neighboring buildings, toward the northern yard, which was some twelve feet above the road outside, thanks in part to the natural roll of the land and in part to the centuries of dead, buried layer upon layer under the church's grounds. Gravestones stood everywhere, many crooked and colored black by time, scattered chaotically through the burying ground.

They crouched behind a stone sarcophagus. Kate heard noises now. Not voices, but shuffling steps and the light crunch of clothing. She crept upward, her fingers feeling the cold marble even through her gloves. Eyes topped the mossy vault and she saw three figures walking among the graves, all wearing long coats with hoods. They moved slowly and awkwardly toward a long, low mound of freshly turned earth, where she noticed several small shapes shining white in the dark dirt. Tall, high-capped mushrooms sprouted from the grave.

Simon whispered from the corner of the oblong tomb where he peered out. "Get down."

One of the figures turned in their direction and Kate saw a ghostly pale face. It was gruesome, flat, and misshapen, with large, bulbous eyes.

She gasped and dropped quickly. "It's a homunculus."

Simon hissed, "Did they see you?"

Kate raised an acerbic eyebrow. "Just after they heard you, yes."

Growling with annoyance, Malcolm pulled his pistols as he rose to his feet. A ropy white object flew at him with a solid wet thud. He was spun around hard, losing one of his pistols.

Simon grabbed the Scotsman to keep him from falling. "Malcolm, don't kill them."

"Don't kill *them*?" Malcolm exclaimed, wide-eyed, recovering his bearings.

"We have to follow the—" Simon's whisper was cut off by another tentacle whipping around his throat. His scarf began to smoke.

Kate drew her weapons and swung the broad-bladed sword, crushing the taut tendril against the marble. She heard the crunch of mechanicals and fluid spurted out, hissing over the lichen.

"Acid!" Simon shouted roughly, pushing Kate back. He took hold of the tentacle while whispering a word. He pulled once and snapped the appendage where Kate had cut it. The white creature stumbled back onto the ground several yards away.

Malcolm vaulted the tomb, while Simon frantically stripped off his sizzling gloves. The white man-thing fought to push itself up on the ends of one of its sleeves. Where its hands should have been there were white tendons that whipped along the ground like angry snakes. Malcolm stepped up to the creature and the other tentacle slapped around his ankle with a hiss. The Scotsman didn't react, but calmly placed the barrel of the pistol against the pale face.

Simon came around the vault, tossing his scarf aside. "Careful! He's full of acid."

Malcolm blasted the creature's head into pulp. "What did you say?" He turned, wiping chunks of brain matter from his face.

Kate saw a second homunculus staggering forward. She aimed and fired her pistol with a spark and a massive whoom. The homunculus flew off its feet and slammed to the grassy ground. It rolled from side to side, moaning in pain, scrabbling at the wound in its chest.

Simon looked back at her in surprise. "Nice shot."

Malcolm strode forward, aiming down for the coup de grace. He fired, but the white creature leapt up with the grace of an acrobat. The ball gouged the dirt. Cursing, the Scotsman spun away, pulling a long dagger. The thing brought a fist down on Malcolm's shoulder with an impact that could be heard across the churchyard. The blow pummeled the Scotsman to the ground. The white creature clamped a large, muscular hand around Malcolm's throat. The man gagged and rolled his eyes up in his head.

"It's going to break his neck." Simon seized the arms that held Malcolm. The white face turned slowly and regarded Simon with no emotion.

Kate saw Malcolm's other pistol on the ground near her. She hefted the weapon and rushed forward to where the two men struggled with the creature. She pushed the Lancaster pistol against the thing's gut and pulled the trigger. The blast wrenched Kate's arm and she thought her elbow was broken. The shot shook the creature, but it didn't lessen its hold on Malcolm. She heard the Scotsman gurgling. Kate pulled the trigger again and a second ball exploded into the thing, opening a huge, gaping wound in its stomach. Steaming black gore spilled out, glistening in the moonlight. At least this one's blood was not laced with acid.

Simon gave an odd throaty laugh and grunted with a great effort. He tore the thing's arm from its socket, sending a spray of liquid from the ragged shoulder. Malcolm tumbled to the ground. Simon lifted the creature by the neck and threw it nearly twenty feet, where it slammed with a crack against a tree. Malcolm continued to struggle with the disembodied arm whose fingers were embedded in his throat. His face was turning blue.

"Simon," Kate called. "It's still strangling him."

Simon spat out, "Kate, go for the third. Don't let it leave."

As Simon began to pry the rigored fingers from Malcolm's raw flesh, Kate ran for the last creature. The thing was standing up from the fresh grave with a cloth bag in its hand. The mushrooms were gone from the dirt. She reached for her bandolier, but her arm was almost numb from the shock of the pistol. She fumbled a vial out and hurled it. The glass container bounced in the grass without breaking. She cursed and scrabbled for another. The white creature looked at her, then loped toward a low wall, high above Holborn. Kate threw the next vial and it hit the thing squarely and shattered. A bluish mist spread, causing the figure to stagger and jerk spastically. It was no more than a tranquilizer, but she only needed to delay it for a moment. The thing knelt, gasping in the fumes. It began to slip free of its coat.

Kate ran up behind the thing, ready to grab the homunculus if necessary. The creature spun around on its knee and a mass of wormlike appendages burst out of its stomach. The glistening fingers slapped around Kate's head, sticking like paste. She was pulled down onto her knees and the sword flew from her hands. The wriggling tendrils dragged her forward, scratching as they slithered across her skin. Between the morass of colorless things sliding over her face, she saw a slit opening in the center of the pasty monster's stomach, stretching into a toothed maw. She struggled harder, wrenching her head back and to the side. The wriggling flagella slid off Kate's head, clutching instead her shoulders and upper arms. It allowed her a gasping breath. She fought against it, but the tendrils drew her toward the champing orifice. She kicked against its groin and shoved back.

"Well done, Kate!" Simon shouted. "Don't let it get away yet." He slapped his hand against the creature's back and whispered. There was a brief flare of light around his hand and the thing's white skin.

A mechanical clanking sound rang out and two stalks rose above the homunculus's shoulders. Then the stalks split as if on a hinge on the far end, and extended like a thin telescope to a length of nearly ten feet. Strange fibers began to drop from the long rods, spreading as if unseen spiders were spinning a web that flapped in the wind.

Kate felt Simon's fingers digging into her shoulders. His strength must have been failing him because she could still hear the wet sounds of the grotesque mouth getting closer. The magician was exhausted and barely standing. He locked eyes with her. He was both fearful and angry. With a last wrench he freed one of her arms.

The long, bony extensions from the creature's shoulders flapped with a thunderous push of wind. The silky drape thickened into an opaque, fibrous sheet.

"Wings!" Malcolm shouted, and Kate saw a flash of steel just beyond her nose as a blade sliced down into the mass of worms.

She managed to pull her head a few inches away from the slurping maw in the creature's abdomen, but that was as far as she got. Incredibly Malcolm's long knife was quickly obscured in squirming tendrils. The hunter tried to pull the weapon free, cursing in Gaelic.

Kate frantically dug into her jacket pocket and felt a hard glass vial. She pulled it out and fumbled with the cap, trying to struggle against the tendrils. The vial popped up out of her hand and she flailed quickly, catching it in midair. She thumbed out the stopper and stuck her hand with the vial into the pulsing fleshy hole in the creature's stomach. She quickly turned up the bottle and pulled her hand out, feeling a burning sensation even from that brief touch.

The homunculus jerked and made a gruesome noise. The colony of worms around Kate's shoulders pulled loose and withdrew. She breathed in a free, cold breath of relief. Suddenly a flood of green ichor roared from the pulsing gash. The warm goo washed over her face, leaving a metallic stench.

Kate fell back onto the ground, crying out in alarm.

Strong hands grabbed her and pulled her away. She felt thick cloths wiping her face and hair, and heard both Simon and Malcolm saying something over top of each other. It was probably meant to be calming, but it sounded like a cacophony of panic.

She realized she wasn't burning; nor was she in pain. She was merely covered in wet, disgusting ichor. She tried to shove away the men's frantic ministrations. She grabbed the cloths they were using to scrub her raw, and shouted, "I'm fine! Stop it!"

Both men stood over her, staring in alarm. Simon was without his coat, which she now held in her hands.

"I'm fine," she said a bit less frantically. "Where's the homunculus?"

Simon stood and looked around. The creature was nowhere to be seen.

"There." Malcolm pointed into the air.

Over the steeple-dotted skyline of London, a white shape with large wings labored through the moonlit air. It was a poor flier, but was already closing in on the Thames River.

Kate scrambled to her feet, trying to ignore the cold ooze that dribbled down her back. "We've lost it! All that effort, and we've lost it."

Simon laughed as he continued to stare at the flying thing. "Not at all. We'll find it soon enough."

"How?" she asked. "It's almost out of sight now. Why is this funny to you?"

Simon took his damp coat from her hand. He reached inside and withdrew a tube of paper. He unrolled it to reveal a three-foot sheet of vellum inscribed with a map of London and a weird variety of runic symbols around the border. He held up his left hand. "I transferred a rune to the homunculus. And I can now track that rune using this map. Here, Kate, you've got a little something just there." He reached over and used his index finger to scrape a dollop of ooze from her cheek. He flicked it onto the ground. "There. That's better."

"How could this be hilarious to you?" Kate couldn't understand the boyish glee that Simon had on his face. Was he truly that ignorant? Then she realized this must be the aether drunkenness that Simon talked about. It was peculiar and disturbing. She looked at Malcolm, and the dour Scotsman was staring at Simon with confusion as well.

"No," Simon replied lightly, but ran a rubbery hand over his face in an effort to wrest back control over his wits. He tossed his jacket aside. "Well, that's the end of that coat."

"I hope the next one regurgitates on you so I can have a bit of a laugh." Kate jutted her chin at the map. "Well, start tracking."

Simon chuckled to himself and spread the map out on the top of a tomb. He pressed his hands against the vellum and began to chant quietly. The lines of the map glowed a faint green, shifting around the streets of London as if it were a living thing. Then there was a green blip just over the river due south of their location at St. Andrews Holborn. Simon took a deep breath and lowered his head.

When he looked up at his companions, there was an emerald fire sparking in his eyes. He laughed again, but it was no longer giddy. It was a dark, brutal laugh.

Chapter Nineteen

BEDLAM SAT LIKE A SQUAT TOAD IN THE MIDST
of its walled grounds on Lambeth Road. The expansive
brick building consisted of a central block with a front
entrance boasting six Doric columns supporting a central pediment. Wings extended out either side to create
a massive structure almost six hundred feet in length.

"Bloody hell," muttered Malcolm.

"You have no idea." Simon rolled his map, which had
led them here, and stuck it in his waistcoat.

Kate's stomach plummeted at the sight of the hospital from which she had extracted her sister only a few
days before. The ramifications stared her suddenly in
the face. Why had Imogen really been brought here?
Was Dr. White involved, or was he ignorant of what
was happening in his hospital? Her jaw tightened in unbridled anger. What she had seen as a helping hand was
now suddenly a vicious lie.

Her eyes snapped to Simon, who was quietly regarding her. "How do we get inside?"

"A window would be the best," he said. "Preferably
an office."

"The windows are barred with iron," Malcolm pointed
out with a scowl, peering through the gates with their
brash rosette circles.

"A minor inconvenience."

Simon decided to enter through Dr. White's office, which was at the front and to the right of the outermost column. The doctor was most likely in his residence at this hour, which was at the back of the hospital. There shouldn't be many guards, or keepers as they were called, since most patients were locked in at night. That would give them a better opportunity to explore and find out where the mushrooms were being stored, or if the wulfsyl itself was here.

Street traffic was minimal, but they went down quieter Kennington Road before stealing over the thick wall. As they slipped across the deserted grounds, the dark windows showed little movement inside. The windows were set high so the patients could see nothing but the sky above.

"I hope you brought explosives or acid." Malcolm tested the thick iron bars covering the window. They were set firm in the casement without even chips of concrete to show weakness.

Simon's lips curved into an exasperating and knowing smile as he laid his hands on two bars. He whispered something that Kate vaguely recognized as ancient druidic.

"If you think praying will help, by all means," growled Malcolm, his annoyance sparking dangerously.

The muscles in Simon's shoulders bunched and his arms tightened. Kate noticed his chest bulging beneath his shirt. Suddenly the metal bars parted with a screech of bending iron. There was no way a slender man such as Simon Archer should have been able to do such a thing. He paused, listening for any reaction to the squeal of the bars. When he heard nothing, he breathed out heavily and regarded Malcolm.

"Then again maybe it will help," the Scotsman remarked with surprise. "There's more to you than meets the eye, sorcerer."

Simon reached in and wedged his fingers under the window. With a quick push, the sash went up. He climbed up between the space between the bars. Malcolm regarded him strangely as he helped Kate inside.

The office was illuminated only by the moonlight outside, but it was enough to show that the room was empty. Simon was already at the door, listening with an ear to the wood. Then he grabbed a bottle of India ink from a bookcase. Dipping a finger in the neck of the bottle, he began to draw a series of symbols on the door. Part of the wood went transparent to show a clear hallway outside.

Malcolm's eyes widened in amazement. "You're a scribe."

"Obviously." Simon shot back a grin before his mouth twisted with distaste. "A sorcerer. How provincial."

"I thought all your kind was dead."

"You would be wrong again." Simon smiled infuriatingly at the hunter.

"Gentlemen, let's concentrate on finding the ghostbloom." Kate lit a single candle and began to rifle through the papers on Dr. White's desk.

Simon came to her side and picked up a journal. He flipped pages, scanning the notes. Malcolm continued to observe the hallway. No keepers passed, and were hopefully ensconced in their rooms, cozy by a fire.

"Here." Kate brought a document closer to the candlelight. "There are rooms earmarked for special projects, and they're under White's lock and key."

Simon's expression was grim. "That's the women's criminal ward."

"That doesn't sound suspicious at all," Malcolm muttered.

"Worth a look." Simon set the open journal on the

table and tapped it with his finger. "There are also notes here about patients receiving unique treatments in the basement level."

"What sort of treatments?" Kate asked. Her stomach was a hard knot.

"Doesn't say. The criminal wards are closer. We'll look there first. If necessary, we'll venture below and see what the good doctor has been up to."

"Are we sure he's involved?" Malcolm glanced over.

"No, we're not sure, but the coincidences reek."

"He'd better pray he isn't involved." Kate's tone was ice-cold. It wasn't an empty threat and both men knew it.

"Someone's coming," Malcolm hissed.

Simon doused the candle with his hand and they fell silent. Through the shimmering portal in the door, they saw a distant figure carrying a dim lantern. The gaslight in the hall was set low so the lantern came toward them like a wavering specter.

"Can he see us through the door?" Kate whispered.

"No," Simon answered.

Malcolm shot them a cross look and put a finger to his lips.

Kate's muscles tensed for action as the watchman stopped in front of the office door. He came so close she could make out small details like a half-healed welt on his face, perhaps due to a wild blow from a crazed inmate or a drunken brawl after hours in a pub. His bored gaze swept over the door and stopped right at her, as if he could see her, but he didn't react. It was uncanny how Simon's transparency spell worked. However, it was also unnerving how exposed she felt. Even her breathing stilled as the keeper stared oddly at the door, his face twisting in a grimace. Then, gripping his lantern tighter, he walked toward the men's wing. His echoing footsteps faded, and for a moment, Kate imagined what it felt like to be an inmate here, fearful at such a sound.

Minutes passed before Simon moved to open the door to peer out. The hallway was empty. He rubbed out the script, smearing the ink before they headed left for the female wards. The front hall was carpeted with a threadbare rug up to a point. The closer they got to the east wing, simple amenities like side tables and plants vanished. Every several feet they passed under gas fixtures set high in the arched ceiling to prevent the inmates from tampering with them, and to keep the miniscule light focused above and not below.

Simon was in the lead, while Malcolm took up the rear. As they made a turn to the right and started down another long corridor, the atmosphere changed. Beneath the hissing of the gaslights and the clanking of metal upon metal, there were incessant moans and grunts and pitiful wails. The sounds echoed around the stone walls, rising and falling, until Kate was tempted to cover her ears with her hands to silence it.

Simon paused to slide back the narrow viewing slot in one of the doors. The piteous face that showed in the dim glow reared back in abject fear, crying out and scrambling as far as her chained foot would allow. Taken aback, Simon closed the slot and regarded his companions.

"I might've been the devil himself the way she reacted."

"The devil does walk these halls." Kate resettled her bandolier for reassurance.

"The keeper may swing back this way soon enough," Malcolm added.

THE CARPETING MUFFLED KATE'S FOOTFALLS BUT every few feet the sound changed oddly, as if she passed over something hollow then solid again. She pointed it out to Malcolm beside her. "What do you think it means?"

"Beams in the floor most likely," Malcolm stated, eager to be on their way, his eyes flashing from one dark corner to the next. He hurried her along after Simon.

An eerie sound that hadn't been there before penetrated the air. A faint scratching. Muffled and distant. It seemed to be following them, first loud then faint, then loud again.

"What is that noise?" Kate asked, her eyes tight with trepidation.

"Perhaps rats?" Simon offered, his mouth twisting with disgust.

Then something caught Kate's ankle and she was flung forward against Simon. She had the forethought to keep her cry of alarm in her throat. Only when she saw milky white fingers protruding from under the edge of the carpet did she gasp.

Simon quickly turned back, staring at the frantic hand slapping the floor. He seized the edge of the stained wool runner that covered the hall.

Malcolm placed a hand on his arm. "Are you daft?"

"Can't hurt to check under the rug." Simon waited until Malcolm moved his feet, which the hunter did grudgingly. "At worst we may find just how bad they clean."

"You're too glib by half, Archer."

Simon smirked, but it didn't linger. "I'm not leaving something behind that could attack our rear or call out an alarm."

Neither Kate nor Malcolm could argue that point.

"Stand ready," Simon told them.

Kate put her back to the wall and raised a vial in her hand while Malcolm aimed his pistol.

Simon flung up the rug with a great rolling wave that cleared ten yards down the center of the corridor. Down the length of the passage, a series of rectangular hatches were set in the floor. The hatch at their feet had a hole gouged out of it. The pale hand extended from the jagged gap, touching the floor around it, as if seeking the iron bar that locked the door into place.

Simon knelt and the ghostly hand slid back into the blackness. He peered into the hole with the candle, then reached for the bolt. Kate and Malcolm came even more alert. Simon pulled back the bar and lifted the hatch. Nothing leapt out at them save a horrid stench.

Kate leaned over to look. "Oh my God."

Under the hatch was a rusted grate of iron. Beneath that was a homunculus huddled inside a cramped space that was no more than four feet square and perhaps four feet deep. Its white head awkwardly tilted up. Inhuman black eyes were dull with pain.

"What in the name of hell?" Simon whispered. He looked along the row of hatches. "They keep them under the floors."

Kate covered her face. "We've been walking on them. How many are locked in like this?"

"For the love of God, close it." Malcolm slid the toe of his boot under the hatch and kicked it over shut. A faint mewling started from underneath. Malcolm thrust the bolt home with his foot and turned away, grim and pale. "There's nothing we can do for it. Let's move on."

Simon pulled the carpet back into place with a sad grunt of resignation. He put a hand on Kate's back and they started after the Scotsman. "I've never seen anything like this. I never wanted to."

Kate took a shuddering breath. "What horrors did Imogen experience in here?"

Simon didn't respond except to tighten a comforting hand on her arm.

They approached an iron gate that separated the galleries, the *curables* from the *criminals*. Kate saw Simon's lips move silently and he laid his hands on the bars. With another muscular pull, the bars creaked apart.

This time Malcolm didn't bat an eye but walked through quickly with his long blade out. Kate followed and Simon stepped through before bending the bars back into place.

A change in temperature made Kate shiver. The stark stone floor and ceiling of plate iron could account for it. There were no fireplaces or vents, and the cold seeped up from the floor. Her feet were like ice blocks in minutes.

The lighting became nonexistent. Simon's candle was a poor replacement for gas lamps, but Kate was grateful for anything to hold the shadows at bay. She kept a hand in her pocket, holding a vial. It gave her fortitude.

A moan abruptly intensified into a scream, then subsided into sobs. Shadows shifted against the walls as they went down the corridor past doors, some of which were open. Her eyes darted left and right, trying to focus on the movement. But the darkness beyond the candle's glow was too deep. Dust and debris she'd rather not name littered the corners. A stench that threatened to make her gag was building in her nose. Human waste and, God help her, the smell of rotting meat.

Her foot slipped on something and she looked down. She stared at the slick spot on the floor. Kneeling, she ran a finger over the substance. The hair on Kate's arms rose. "Simon," she hissed.

"What?"

Malcolm turned with him. They were already farther down the corridor than Kate. An expression of shock crossed his features as he looked up at the ceiling. His knife rose in a swift jerk.

Before Kate could utter another word, something heavy dropped on her. Cold, slime-covered appendages wrapped around her shoulders, pinning her arms and knocking her off balance. With amazing speed, she was dragged toward an open cell and pulled inside as if she were an escaped inmate.

Even though her upper arms were trapped, Kate had enough freedom to draw a small dagger from her belt. With a Herculean effort, she dug it deep into the thigh of the homunculus. It reared back and flailed uncontrollably. The homunculus released Kate but its eyestalks shifted left and right as Simon and Malcolm darted into the cell.

It ran at the men. The creature screamed as Malcolm's blade flashed and cut off an eyestalk. Its long arms struck at Malcolm, slamming him to the side as it vaulted up to the ceiling. Simon grabbed its leg and yanked it back down hard, smashing it onto the floor.

Kate scrambled out of the way, but then hands tangled in her hair and yanked her backward. The grating of rusting chains filled her ears as something dragged her off her feet. Simon took a step toward her, but the homunculus rolled to its feet and jumped on his back. He was borne to the ground roughly as the creature pounded his head and shoulders.

Malcolm ran past Simon and swung his long-bladed knife above Kate's head. There was a strangled shriek and the grip on her eased. Malcolm lifted her by the arm, pulling her back toward the door in the same motion. A chain snapped taut behind her and snarling followed.

Simon ripped the homunculus from his back with a steely grip and held it at arm's length. His other arm pulled back and he slammed a rock-hard fist into the creature's face. Bones crushed beneath the blow. Kate stabbed her dagger in deep at the lower back of the homunculus. It screamed and arched.

Simon picked the horrible body up and heaved it over Kate's head, where it crashed into the chained creature in the corner. The second thing had one eye bulging out farther than the other and its naked torso was covered with surgical cuts stitched together. Internal organs were visible, pulsating and contracting under near-translucent skin. The skull was still covered with the tattered remains of long, flaxen hair. It had once been a woman. She fell upon her weakened brother with incredible savagery. The two creatures screamed at one another, each one clawing at the other. Finally, the terrible woman tore the head off the homunculus with a victorious shriek and threw it across the room to tumble at Malcolm's feet. There was a sizzle as the homunculus melted into a puddle of desiccated ooze. A tangle of mechanical gears and metal rose out of the goo, but the woman fell upon that as well, scattering it like an angry child slapping at toys.

The three humans backed out of the cell. As Malcolm shut the bolt, they heard a high-pitched wail from inside.

"Kill me!" It sounded vaguely human. "I beg you!"

"Oh my God," whispered Kate.

Simon kept a firm hand on her elbow and pulled her down the hall. "We have to move."

"But . . ."

"She's already dead," Malcolm said. "We don't have time to waste. Somebody might have heard that fracas."

The former woman's plea followed after them, picked up and repeated from other cells. Inside the open doors they passed, wretched figures crawled or huddled in thankfully dark corners. Their pace quickened as they turned left into the final hallway, ending at a door with a grated window. Beyond it was one of the great airing grounds, where patients were allowed to enjoy the outdoors.

The last cell before the end of the hall was also open, and Kate glanced inside against her will. She didn't see a horrific patient but rather something else. She stuck her head farther inside. It was a much larger chamber than the patient cells. Massive iron cauldrons sat in the corners and a great table commanded the center of the room. On the table was an alchemical apparatus that put Kate's lab at Hartley Hall to shame. It was a complicated network of beakers and glass tubes, hoses and reservoirs, all ending in a spigot that dripped liquid into a wooden barrel. Several similar barrels were stacked against one wall. The stench of the ghostbloom mushrooms was unmistakable. They smelled of decay and earthy loam.

"Here it is," Kate said.

Simon joined her at the door to the cell. He whistled in admiration for the alchemical factory.

"They reduce the ghostbloom in those vats and process the residue into wulfsyl, which they drip out into barrels. Incredible. It's like a factory."

Malcolm clucked at them from the corridor. He stood by the door at the end of the hall. He pointed through the window grate, which allowed Kate and Simon a view of a large garden surrounded by a high wall, surmounted with cheval de frise, a definite impediment to patients with its spikes.

Even though the hour was very late, there were patients milling about outside. To Kate's surprise, there were even children, at least five young boys playing with a ball and a cherublike young girl with blond hair playing idly with a doll. All of them were dressed in ragged and worn clothes.

Kate's expression changed to one of curiosity. "Why are they outside?"

"They're werewolves," Malcolm said calmly.

"What?" Kate remained focused on the children, trying to ignore the agonies behind her. "All of them?"

Simon crowded the small window. "How do you know?"

"I've seen that girl before. And there's that." Malcolm nodded to the far left, where at least ten hulking werewolves stalked the shadows under the wall. One beast strode right between the children, who hardly blinked, although the girl regarded it a bit cautiously, turning away abruptly to stare at the door. Kate swore they locked eyes before Malcolm shoved her out of the way.

"Blast it!" He pulled his pistols. "Get ready."

Chapter Twenty

NO WEREWOLVES BURST THROUGH THE DOOR. They breathed a sigh of relief. They hadn't been seen.

Malcolm jammed the pistols in the holsters. "Let's get this bloody thing done before we're rooted out."

Simon went back to the processing cell. He waved them inside before closing the door and turning up the gas fixture on the wall. Malcolm stuffed the space under the door with straw to prevent light spilling out.

"Hurry, Kate," Simon urged.

Kate reached into her satchel and pulled out the vials of botanical poison. Her hand hesitated. She said quietly, "I didn't expect there to be children."

"They're not children," was Malcolm's sharp retort. "They're beasts."

Kate turned to the Scotsman. "She was playing with a doll like any other child, like Imogen."

"That child is a werewolf, and she will tear out your heart and eat it given half a chance." Malcolm turned angrily to Simon. "Tell her!"

Simon's hand touched Kate's shoulder. "There's no time for anything else. We have only a small window of opportunity here. We dare not walk away with so much at stake. Your sister's safety, not to mention all of London's."

Kate drew in a deep breath and handed Simon the vials. "I know." Her tone was laced with bitterness.

Simon had tried to warn her, but she hadn't understood then. She had only believed that all werewolves were adults with nothing but murder on their minds. None of what she had seen here changed her focus, only her heart. It broke for what she was about to do. Gripping one of the last vials in her satchel so tight her knuckles turned white, she poisoned the supply of wulfsyl, and may God have mercy on all of their souls.

"It's done," Simon announced. "Let's go." He moved to the door. With quick strokes of ink he used the transparency spell to make sure the way was clear, which it was as far as they could see in the limited lighting out in the hall. Scrubbing out the scribed spell, Simon opened the door and went outside. He nodded, then stopped as his foot hit something. It was a doll. His head jerked up, and Kate's eyes widened.

"Run," he told her.

They heard the airing-grounds door opening. Malcolm pulled his pistols. The sound of people filling the hallway behind them made the center of Kate's shoulders twitch. A howl broke the chilled air, loud and reverberating in the tight confines. Kate thought she caught a glimmer of trepidation in Simon, but she also sensed his determination as he pressed her forward. The iron door was just ahead.

The baying followed them, growing in concert as more voices were lent to the chase. Kate lengthened her stride to keep up with Simon and Malcolm. She slammed against the unyielding iron.

"Hurry," she cried, fighting the panic of being trapped with a pack of werewolves ready to tear them apart. Simon was saying something, but not to her. He was calling the strength to his limbs.

Malcolm stood, feet apart and facing back, his pistols aimed. When the pack rounded the corner, a mass of fur and rage, Malcolm opened fire with a barrage that ripped through the front ranks.

Simon put his strength to the bars and they separated with a groan. Kate went through first, then Simon. "Malcolm! It's done. Come on!"

Pistols spent, Malcolm spun and ran, diving headfirst through the widened bars. Simon quickly grabbed the bars to bend them back into place. The snarling mob rushed him, and Kate knew he wouldn't get the bars closed in time. Her hand came up with a vial that she threw in front of the charging werewolves. It smashed into a thousand glass shards on the floor, throwing up a low mist that quickly settled to the ground. The floor turned to black treacle and the beasts got stuck in the tarry mess, feet holding so firm that several toppled shoulder and chest to the blackened ground. Simon was wrenching the bars together when a second rank of berserk werewolves leapt over their trapped comrades and flung themselves against the iron.

Malcolm grabbed Simon's collar and yanked him out of harm's way as long, hairy arms and savage jaws tore at the spot he had just occupied.

"Thanks, old boy," Simon panted.

Malcolm grunted.

The trio retreated quickly, leaving the snarling beasts raging at the door. As they ran, the hard stone floor became carpeted, and the hall sprouted tables and plants and portraits of squires with prize horses. Once again, they no longer seemed to be in a house of horror. But as they turned the corner for the front entranceway, they spotted figures coming toward them.

Dr. White walked ahead of a bare-breasted female patient. One of the horrid white homunculi held the feeble, drooling woman upright. A step behind the doctor was a gigantic blond woman dressed incredibly in a leather cuirass. Her eyes narrowed, and she pushed past Dr. White. She smiled, and hissed, "MacFarlane."

The doctor's gaze locked on Kate in astonishment. He barked a command to the creature, and the homunculus dropped the woman, who crumpled to the floor. The thing loped forward, jumping onto the wall and propelling itself past Gretta ever faster to its quarry.

Simon grabbed Kate's hand and they fled in the other direction. Kate didn't know where the exit was, but she could only pray Simon did. She stumbled on the carpeted corridor, and Simon pulled her up. Then Malcolm also tripped and nearly went down. The sound of grating metal filled the air. The worn runner sagged in many spots, then it began to rise and tremble with life. White arms appeared from under the edges of the long rug, and shapes that weren't true arms but closer to tendrils or claws emerged. Moaning and wet, sloughing sounds accompanied twisted shoulders and heads pushing their way into the dim lamplight. Mouths gnashed at Kate and she tore her ankle free of grasping fingers.

"He's set them all free." Simon stepped on the back of one figure as Malcolm vaulted a homunculus reaching out for him.

Mutilated bodies rose slowly, fighting to stay aloft on numb and misshapen limbs. Kate drew her short sword and slashed out, tearing through soft flesh and chalky bones. Simon elbowed a horrid thing into the wall. Malcolm slammed the butt of his pistol into a head, dropping a homunculus to the floor. Ever more arms reached out for them. The hallway seemed to be constricting in a crowd of shambling white things. Only the creatures' confused state saved the three as they continued to shove and batter their way through.

In the distance, a monstrous howl pounded through the asylum. Gretta, calling her pack.

"Stay close!" Malcolm shouted as he ducked under a set of long claws. "Don't get separated."

Kate plunged her blade into a dripping figure that reached for Simon. She kicked the thing aside, nearly stumbled, but kept staggering forward. Simon grabbed her and pulled her onward, swiping back with his own sword, drawing a warm spatter of ooze from a white man-thing. Something exploded near her head, and Malcolm appeared, shoving her and Simon past him. The Scotsman fired again to cover as Simon pulled her to the left.

It was a dead end.

She spun around, ready to face the horrors that were coming for them. Malcolm virtually fell around the corner, hitting the wall. He was covered in dribbling whitish excretion. He reloaded and snapped the breeches of his pistols shut. He jumped back out into the junction and opened fire, peppering the corridor with shot. He pulled back around the corner.

"I hate to tell you but there are dozens of the things." He quickly counted the remaining cartridges in his coat pockets. "And more beasties on the way."

Simon hefted a long table in his arms. "I'll try to batter our way back to the main corridor. And we'll fight our way out from there."

Kate didn't bother to think how impossible that was since she could hear the damp shuffling sounds of the homunculi horde approaching. She inspected the vials that she had left—a paltry arsenal to fight an army.

The cell door next to them suddenly opened. Malcolm's pistols jerked up and trained on the dark entrance. It was the girl who had been playing with the doll. She wore no expression of surprise. It was as if she had meant to be there. She gestured for them to follow her inside the empty cell.

Malcolm straightened his arm toward the new arrival, his finger about to squeeze the trigger. Kate placed herself between the hunter and the girl.

"Given our choices," she told Malcolm, "I'd rather go with her. There's nowhere else to go in any case."

Malcolm held his fire with a suspicious grimace. The girl took Kate's hand and tugged her inside the room. Simon followed the two into the cell. Malcolm was fast on his heels. The faintest of light came from a grate in the floor. The young girl smiled at Kate, then shoved Malcolm aside so she could reach the door. She manipulated the lock on the outside and slammed the door shut.

"It's locked now," she said. "It will take them a few minutes to get in."

She fell to her hands and knees and grasped the iron grate. Simon helped her lift it. Beneath was a tunnel of dirt and stone.

The girl said, "Come with me."

Malcolm exclaimed to his colleagues, "She gave us away before."

The girl looked angry. "I did not!" Then she crawled in and disappeared. Kate made to follow her when Malcolm roughly pulled her back.

"Are you mad? She could be leading us straight to slaughter!"

"Do you have another plan?" Kate retorted, her hands on her hips, her cheeks flushing.

Simon knelt next to the hole. "I'll go first."

"You're agreeing to this?" Malcolm stammered with barely restrained fury.

"Yes," was his simple reply. And then he was gone.

Kate pleaded with the hunter. "If I'm wrong, you can boast to me later."

"That victory will do me no good from the grave." He lowered Kate into the dark hole and followed after her.

Kate was on her hands and knees in a tunnel that was only about three feet high. She couldn't make out much in the darkness, barely even Simon's form, but she could hear the sound of shuffling just ahead. She hurried to catch up, afraid to lose them in case the tunnel system was vast. The floor was rough under her hands with sharp stones and debris digging into the soft skin of her palms. Her hair brushed the roof, bringing dirt down around her.

Suddenly she bumped into Simon's feet and let out a soft exclamation.

"Is Malcolm with you?" he asked.

"I think so."

"I'm here," the Scotsman growled.

"We're turning left," Simon whispered. "Stay close."

A few minutes later, she could no longer be sure of their direction as they had veered sharply a few times. Gradually her vision lightened and the walls around her came into view. She wished they hadn't. There were tiny animal bones everywhere. Had the child been eating them or had they just perished in this horrible tunnel? Spiders and beetles crawled over her hands. She tried not to think about them on her clothes and in her hair. She shuddered but kept going, following Simon.

Suddenly he stopped and his frame went upright. His legs disappeared. She hurried forward in case he needed help. When her head popped out into the air, she was surrounded by a grass lawn. Simon reached down and helped her out. Malcolm came up soon after.

Kate saw the towering structure of Bedlam close behind her. They were in one of the other airing grounds. However, it was empty and quiet.

"Child, why would you want to help us?" Simon asked the girl.

She shrugged, almost coyly, but then brightened. "You seem nice. Nicer than everyone in there. They're mean and horrible. And it's getting worse. Gretta has brought in all the little packs from around London and shoved us all in here so she can keep an eye on them."

"Why don't you leave them?"

"I can't. They'll know."

"They'll know you helped us."

She smiled. "No they won't. My scent is all over this place. I come here all the time to be alone."

"What's your name?" Simon asked.

"Charlotte." She pointed at the high wall. "Can you get over that?"

He nodded. "Yes, we can. Thank you for your help, Charlotte."

The girl blushed under Simon's sweet, handsome gaze and she rocked back and forth as if she were at a party. She turned to peer at Kate and seemed distraught. "Your beautiful dress is a mess."

Kate laughed. "Luckily I have others."

"I did too once." Excitement sparked in the girl's eyes and she sighed wistfully.

Malcolm strode between them, heading for the wall. "Stop jabbering and come on."

The child stuck out her tongue at the brusque hunter. "You're welcome."

Kate touched Charlotte on the shoulder, then hugged her. "Thank you. Please be careful." And then Kate stared up at Simon, remembering what they had done to the wulfsyl. Her heart sank. She shook her head at Simon, whose lips were in a grim line. She looked back at the girl. "Don't take the wulfsyl."

The girl looked surprised. "Why?"

"Just don't. It's our secret, all right?"

"Bloody hell!" cursed Malcolm, separating the two of them. "What do you think you are doing?"

"Saving her life." Kate was steadfast.

Malcolm snarled at her, then regarded the child, whose large brown eyes lifted to him. "The wulfsyl is fine, lass. It's delicious. Have as much as you want."

The girl stared hard at him for a moment, then looked at Kate. "I think I'll not."

Simon was already atop the wall and had bent the spikes on the cheval de frise back. He reached a hand down to Kate, who shook her head, afraid of what Malcolm might do. She waited until Malcolm spun on his heel and clambered up the wall with Simon's help. Then the two men reached down for Kate. She rose beside them.

She turned to wave farewell, but the girl was already gone. Kate's stomach knotted at what she had done. The thought of murdering the child who had so innocently helped them, no matter what the girl truly was, seemed too cruel. She couldn't face the judgment for such an act.

They dropped to the ground on George's Street.

"What's done is done, Kate," Simon told her as they ran toward the next street over. "We need to get back to Hartley Hall. Dr. White saw us. I suspect your home is about to have visitors."

Malcolm veered away. Simon stopped and stared after him.

"You're not abandoning us, are you?" Kate asked.

"I bloody well should after that fiasco," Malcolm spat, but he shook his head, making his queue dance in the moonlight. "I'm going to fetch more ordnance. I've had Penny Carter working up some special devices. We're going to need all of it before this is over."

"You'll meet us at Hartley Hall then?"

"Yes."

"Don't be late," Simon instructed.

"Don't be dead."

Simon grinned. Then he grabbed Kate's hand and ran toward the Anstruther coach, which they had left a few blocks away.

"I'm sorry," she told him as she fell into the seat and the carriage kicked into high speed.

"No, you're not." Before she could reply, he waved her off. "I understand why you did it, Kate. As I said, there's no one to judge us except ourselves."

Kate leaned forward and buried her head in her hands. Simon placed a firm hand on her shoulder and left it there to comfort her. She swallowed her dismay, clinging tightly to Simon's resolve.

Chapter Twenty-one

DESPITE THE WEE MORNING HOUR, HEAVY FREIGHT wagons creaked along and merchants pushed carts rattling with pots and cutlery. Malcolm reached the river, shoving through gangs of wanderers. The northern side of the river was a bit less busy and some streets were actually deserted, a rare thing in crowded London.

The Scotsman felt as if chilled fingernails were scraping along the back of his neck. He turned to the bustling bridge. His trained tracker's eye saw several men who slipped in and out of sight, moving through the crowd with more purpose than most of the early-hour street folk. They could have been laborers on the way to work; they could have been thieves seeking unwary victims. All the same, Malcolm walked faster.

He made for the decrepit Devil's Acre, hoping to lose any pursuit in that warren of ratholes. For several blocks, he walked at a normal clip to prevent any shadowers from increasing their pace. Suddenly he spun and bolted into an alley. He dodged piles of refuse and leapt over a wall, where he paused to get his bearings. A tremendous chorus of howls rose, singing his death. Sweat broke out on his brow and he started to run again. A scrabble of claws sounded behind him and his legs pumped all the harder. His arms reached around his chest and pulled his pistols.

A shape loomed on his right and he fired. In the flash of the pistol, Malcolm saw the horrific visage of a were-wolf. The ball struck the creature in the face, shoving it back into the wall. Malcolm continued to run. Another werewolf leapt past its dead comrade and gave chase. It virtually climbed the walls, bounding from side to side and exploding forward, landing just beside Malcolm on a pile of crates. Its cruel jaws shut on the sleeve of the Scotsman's greatcoat, ripping it. Malcolm didn't stumble but aimed and shot it in the chest.

The narrow confines of the alley slowed the pursuing pack and kept them from spreading out to encircle him as true wolves would in the wild. Malcolm made a sharp turn into a cross lane. He gained ground as the pack could not slow their frenzied momentum and the two in the lead were bowled over by a third one running madcap behind. The crumbling buildings shook with the impact of the creatures. One poor soul looked out his third-story window at the commotion and wished he hadn't.

A werewolf landed in front of Malcolm on all fours, claws digging onto the cobblestones to halt its slide. Malcolm drew a long knife with a blade coated in silver, leaping straight for the beast, bearing it backward to the ground. The knife rose and fell into the creature's throat. The werewolf thrashed, a massive clawed hand ripped across Malcolm's back, sending him flying into a brick wall. He scrambled to his feet and ran out into a main street just ahead. He prayed that the pack still craved secrecy and wouldn't emerge into open view, even at night. He risked a glance back and saw the narrow darkness undulating with a horrifying motion as the pack hesitated.

Malcolm paused to break his pistols' breeches and load custom shells. When he glanced up, he spied dark shapes climbing onto the rooftops. He cursed again, this time in Gaelic. Malcolm counted only two in pursuit. Two such creatures were a deadly match, but his guns had four barrels each and silver loads. He wanted to kill them rather than lead them to Penny. The Lancasters required close range, so he needed to lure them to him.

He slowed, stumbled, and limped deliberately into a dark alley. Within seconds, he heard heavy breathing to match his own. A werewolf dropped off the roof, leaping from wall to wall until it reached the ground in a cloud of dust. Its tongue lolled from the slavering jaws. It sniffed the air for him. Malcolm stepped from the shadows and fired. The shot took the beast in the shoulder, spinning it to the ground. Malcolm dropped on it with the silver dagger as if to scalp it. A deep strike into its heart gave it a wound from which it wouldn't recover.

A dark shape appeared farther down the alley and started for him. Before the beast could gain momentum, Malcolm stood and aimed with the utmost calm as if facing a challenger on the field of honor. The werewolf was in midleap when the silver ball struck its heaving chest, and it died in the air. The pistol was spinning its barrels, but hadn't locked back into place. Malcolm couldn't dodge the hurtling mass of the dying creature, and it smashed him to the ground with bone-jarring force.

Malcolm struggled to wrest his half-cocked pistol free from beneath the leaden carcass. Everything was agony as he twisted. A shadow fell over him. Another beast loomed above with a ruined face. Rank saliva and blood dripped. The creature tilted up its muzzle and howled, either in mourning or calling to more of the pack.

Malcolm yanked his pistol free with a hoarse shout. The barrel hissed and fell into place. The gun fired in a flare of light, cutting off the howl. The werewolf grasped its bleeding throat and fell back. Malcolm couldn't see where it dropped, but he heard its death throes.

The Scotsman dragged himself from beneath the burden of the dead monster. He was covered in blood, but at least most of it wasn't his. He staggered to his feet, methodically checking his loads. There were only two silver shells left. He stumbled to the far end of the alley and out into a wide boulevard. A few people watched him pass but left him alone, no doubt seeing the blood on his clothes and the heavy gun in his hand.

Malcolm now truly limped across St. James's Park in the direction of Penny's shop and prayed she was an early riser. Thankfully, he saw no more shadows pursuing him. He removed a flask and poured the liquid out behind him. It smelled horrific and Malcolm placed a sleeve over his lower face to ward off the worst of it. He sprayed as much as he could all about him. The stinking solution would hopefully disrupt the olfactory senses of the werewolves. He didn't count them as skilled scent trackers, but he couldn't take any chances. He purposefully trod through the watery sewer filth that ran like blood in the street. He threw the bottle with all his might.

Malcolm almost missed the turn to Bond Street. Another exhausted glance around him confirmed there was no sign of pursuit. He darted the last few blocks to Penny's shop. The sign in the front window read CLOSED. He pounded on the door, but no one appeared. He had no choice, so he picked the lock.

He nearly toppled inside the darkened shop, but there was no time for a respite. He began to scour the shelves for any shot of the Lancaster's caliber. A large dark shape went past the window and Malcolm ducked behind the counter, yanking out a pistol. He peered around the corner, his heart pounding against his breastbone, hearing the sound of something sniffing just under the door. A huge shape loomed across the shaded glass. Malcolm aimed his weapon. The door smashed open and a large grey werewolf stood snarling in its frame.

Malcolm opened fire, the bullet smacked into its shoulder and it staggered backward. It let out a howl that shook the windows. Malcolm stood up and fired again, aiming for its heart, but the ball shattered the doorframe. His vision and arm wavered with fatigue.

Blast it!

He was about to toss the empty weapon aside, tightening his grip on the dagger when the door to the back room slammed open behind him.

"Get down!" came a sharp order.

Malcolm hit the floor as a thunderous whomp vibrated his ears. A burst of flame lanced over his head. The fiery ball struck the werewolf and blasted the creature into bloody bits. It also took out the rest of the door and the windows.

Malcolm cautiously raised his head, shaking off dust and shards of glass from his hair. He stared at Penny Carter, who stood over him with a long brass tube casually resting on her shoulder, tendrils of smoke slipping from both ends. She was dressed in leather chaps over tweed pants and a heavy leather apron over a white linen shirt. A thick wad of wool protected her shoulder. His breath came in gasps but no words.

Penny raised a soot-streaked eyebrow. "Was that an honest-to-god werewolf I just blew to kingdom come?"

"Aye." Malcolm nodded. He gestured weakly at the device on her shoulder. "Bloody hell."

"You like it?" She patted the weapon. "I call it my Stovepipe Blunderbuss."

"I'm going to call it my best friend."

"Charles is going to have a fit." She set the tube heavily on the floor and regarded her ruined shop. Then she shrugged. "Coffee's on the stove and you look like you need it."

"No time," he wheezed, staggering to his feet.

"You're covered in blood." Penny's face hardened as she pulled him toward a chair.

"You don't understand," He slumped against the wall. "There may be more."

The engineer paused, wide-eyed, then shrugged. She hurried behind the counter and rummaged a bit. "You stink something awful."

Ignoring her comment, Malcolm straightened off the wall but staggered a bit as the room spun. He quickly righted himself with a hand against the wall. "I'll take whatever you've completed of my last order and be on my way. If anything comes through the hole in the wall, kill it."

"Even Mr. Wilhelm, the butter-and-egg man?" Penny hefted a canvas bag that rattled and walked it to him.

"If he's large and hairy." Malcolm looked in the bag at the cache of silver-tipped shells for his Lancasters.

"You're badly hurt!" Penny exclaimed to the Scotsman. Blood stained the wall where he had been leaning.

"Few scratches." Malcolm shook his head. "I'll tend to it once I reach Hartley Hall."

"You won't get to Charing Cross like that, much less Surrey."

"I've lingered too long already." With that he headed for the door.

"Just hang on!" Penny insisted. "I'll take you."

"No," Malcolm snarled.

She wasn't listening to him and her voice vanished with her into the back room. "I'll fetch transport and be back presently."

The hunter waited in the darkness and felt isolated in the thin glow of the gas lamps through the smoking storefront. A curious few were already gathering in the street to gawk. He hoped Penny would find a horse or a buggy. And a fast one.

A roar filled his ears. He turned with both pistols drawn. What emerged from an alley was a one-eyed beast of metal and fire with Penny Carter in the saddle. It resembled a walking machine, a foolish fad used by the indolent to get around garden paths. It had two in-line wheels. The front one was steerable, as Penny was currently demonstrating. The mechanical vehicle glowed with heat and spewed steam from various orifices, including a series of long, extruding pipes in the rear underneath a shimmering grill. It had a heart of flame that flickered when the vehicle shuddered to a halt beside him. The contraption had a strange, wheeled side compartment, perhaps for balance. The Stovepipe Blunderbuss was strapped to its side.

"Get in!" Penny wore a dark leather jacket with goggles over her eyes.

"Get in what?" Malcolm shouted back over the din of the motor. "What in the hell is that thing?"

"My spinebreaker steamcycle will get us to Hartley Hall faster than a horse."

He caught a glimpse of red eyes blazing in the darkness down the street. "Oh damn."

"Get your arse in the sidecarriage!" She pointed to the buggy attached to the side of the two-wheeled vehicle.

Malcolm had barely placed his feet inside the small space when Penny put the machine into a jerking motion, flinging him back against the leather padding. He was trying to wedge his muscular frame down into the strange contraption as they roared off.

Penny wheeled the vehicle in a loop to face south and the machine's heart flared, flames licking through the grill in the rear. The machine shook them like someone standing before the devil himself. They shot forward with an unheard-of speed. Wind whipped Malcolm's long queue. They sailed toward Piccadilly, and the approaching werewolves.

"You do see them there, right?" Malcolm shouted, incredulous, as four hairy bodies drew closer on both sides.

"Keep your head down!" Penny bent low over the controls and throttled the machine even higher.

The werewolves slowed, confused by the smoking terror bearing down on them. The Scotsman attempted to keep his aim steady, and he fired. Hitting a beast in the hip, it tumbled through garbage and slammed into a wall. Penny threw off his next shot by careening the vehicle toward a werewolf on the left. She held out her booted foot and it smashed into the creature's chest, sending it crashing into an iron lamppost.

Malcolm tracked over Penny's lowered head and fired, spinning the stunned werewolf to the pavement. The other two beasts skidded on the street as the vehicle roared between them.

With a smoking squeal of the rubber tires, Penny leaned left onto Piccadilly. Starlight wanderers and after-hours drunkards stared at the passing metal monster. Penny jerked the contraption over the curb and skirted past St. James's churchyard, catching a pair of shadowed lovers by surprise. She skidded into the grass and dirt of St. James's Square, and dodged trees handily. Malcolm gripped the sides of the car, staring back for any sign of pursuing creatures loping on all fours.

Penny made the motor roar. "Sit down and hold on."

"Why?"

"Because there's a drop coming up."

Before she finished the sentence, they were airborne. Malcolm felt himself flying up and out of the vehicle. Penny shouted in elation. And just as suddenly, they slammed to the ground, and Malcolm crashed out onto the front of the sidecarriage. Penny fought to keep the vehicle under control while she used one hand to grab Malcolm's collar, dragging him up to prevent his slipping under the wheels.

The Scotsman struggled his way back toward his compartment and saw two large figures launch themselves into the night air from the top of the uncompleted terrace they had just sailed off. The werewolves landed and charged in pursuit as Penny skirted the edge of the park, driving toward the river.

"Damn it!" Malcolm tumbled headfirst into the side-carriage. "Go! They're still coming."

Penny pointed at a rucksack on the floor of the little car. The hunter scrambled for the bag, his body vibrating as if an earthquake were striking Britain. Cursing, he grabbed the sack and yanked it open.

"The round ones are grenades," she shouted. "I built them for you."

Malcolm's eyes went wide and he bit off a scathing retort. He was surprised none had gone off with the bone-shaking ride. Explosives weren't something you wanted bouncing around, but he should have realized that anything the Carters made was durable and manufactured with the utmost care and deliberation. The grenades were small, dark grey metal globes with a small cylinder protruding from the casing.

"You press that button for a ten-second fuse," Penny instructed. "Oh. And be sure to throw it."

Malcolm timed the beasts' pursuit, then he pressed the switch. He counted to five before lobbing one of the bombs behind them. It bounced and rolled toward the creatures, and exploded in a sharp blast. White slivers glinted in the moonlight. The lead werewolf screamed and fell instantly, but the other veered away from the fight.

Malcolm gaped at Penny.

"Silver shrapnels," she told him. "First test in the field. How did they do?"

"Bloody brilliant!" he exclaimed, pulling another grenade from the bag. "I'll take all that you have!"

"I only made a few and they're all in there. Don't waste them because they're going to cost you a fortune." Penny threw him a pleased grin and caught sight of the last werewolf closing the gap, running like mad. Penny lost speed.

"What the hell are you doing, woman?" Malcolm bellowed. "Are we running out of power?"

"Trust me," she replied. "They don't like fire either, right?"

"Nothing likes fire."

Her grin turned wicked. "Good."

The werewolf howled its victory as its jaw snapped just shy of the rear wheel. Malcolm half stood in the tiny seat and faced backward, pulling reloaded pistols and aiming. The werewolf bit the wheel and the velocipede swerved dangerously. Malcolm felt himself lifted up and realized in alarm his cart was airborne. They were going to flip over. Penny cursed loudly and struggled to right the careening vehicle while Malcolm threw his weight to the opposite side. His sidecarriage slammed back down to earth.

"Whatever you're going to do, do it now!" he shouted.

Penny obliged, slapping at another lever. The rear pipes belched tongues of brilliant white fire. Flames engulfed the werewolf in midleap and it flailed, its fur burning. The motor sputtered and the steamcycle bucked, threatening to stall. Penny shouted. The smoldering beast climbed onto the back of the sidecarriage. The Scotsman didn't flinch but instead grabbed the creature by the throat, much to its surprise, and shoved the muzzle of his pistol under its snout. He pulled the trigger and the creature's face disintegrated. Malcolm threw the hairy thing off and it somersaulted into a dark lane.

Penny gunned the engine back to life and they roared past a few stunned people onto Westminster Bridge. Penny skillfully maneuvered her smoking terror through the flowing chaos of shouting people and rearing horses.

Something caught Malcolm's eye. A shape moved quickly in the spaces between wagons and horses. Then he realized that a werewolf was loping along the bridge railing with uncanny grace.

Malcolm grabbed one of the handles controlling the front wheel and swung the vehicle hard left. The boiling steamcycle nearly crashed against a brace of already skittish horses, which shied with wide, white eyes. The terrified pair dragged their heavy wagon piled high with barrels against the rail. Pedestrians screamed and scattered.

Suddenly the werewolf landed high atop the barrels. The creature snarled down and Penny struggled desperately to keep steady with the runaway cart without being stomped by panicked horses. Malcolm teetered out of the sidecarriage, seizing one of the heavy ropes restraining the mountain of barrels. He brought his large dagger against the cord, and with two swipes, the razor-sharp blade sliced clean through the rough cable.

The wagon shifted as the driver fought his powerful draft horses. The tower of barrels creaked toward Malcolm, threatening to smash Penny and him under a deadly landslide. But when the werewolf tensed to pounce, it kicked the top barrel out behind it. The creature lost its footing and fell flat. Barrels began to roll away.

The werewolf struggled frantically to regain its feet. It clawed at each of the massive hogsheads as they toppled one after another over the railing in a roaring crash. A heavy, iron-shod barrel struck the werewolf on the head, knocking it to the side. Another battered its shoulder. The werewolf screeched and disappeared under the avalanche of wood and iron. A clawed hand reached helplessly and then the werewolf was borne to the dark Thames far below, buried under countless heavy thuds of barrels smashing into the water.

Penny revved the motor and turned the front wheel over hard. Malcolm grabbed hold as the steamcycle bucked away from the catastrophe around the wagon. Ignoring the furious shouts and angry fists, they drove on. They broke out of the bridge congestion and roared south through Lambeth.

Penny watched behind in a mirrored glass set on one of the handles. "Is that all of them finally?"

The Scotsman appraised her. "You don't seem overly shocked by all this."

She smirked. "You're not the first hunter to waltz in my door. Some talk a lot more than you, so I have an idea what you do. You order silver ordnance. I'm not feebleminded. I can make connections as well as contraptions."

"So I see."

Penny glanced over at him briefly before returning her attention to driving. They shuddered over the rough but wide roads. Malcolm noticed the edifice of Bedlam in the distance. It appeared as normal as usual. He stared at it in disgust, fearful that more werewolves might come boiling out of the madhouse. Finally the wretched place was lost from sight and they rolled noisily into the Surrey countryside.

Chapter Twenty-two

THE FOUR-HORSE CHAISE CLATTERED TO A STOP
at the front portico of Hartley Hall. Simon leapt to the
ground and handed Kate down.

"Do not unhitch," she said to the coachman. "Go to
the stables and prepare everything that will roll. Every
carriage and wagon."

"Yes, miss." The coachman looked quite disturbed,
but he shook the reins and rumbled off toward the stables behind the vast house.

Simon raced with Kate to the front door, nearly slamming into Hogarth, who was heading out to meet them.
Despite the clear distress on Kate's face, the servant
remained calm.

"What do you need from me, Miss Kate?"

"Hogarth, good. We must empty Hartley Hall immediately."

"Empty it?"

"The servants. All of them must go now. And particularly Imogen. The staff will return as soon as it's safe.
Go and tell them. No time to pack. I will foot the bill
for whatever they need, but impress on them that it is
very dangerous for them to remain."

"Where shall they go, miss?"

Kate raised her voice in frustration. "It doesn't matter

where they go. Family. Friends. If necessary, I'll pay for any hotels. They just have to go. Now." She squeezed his arm. "Hogarth, please. Believe me as you would my father."

The servant nodded and turned on his heel. He took Barnaby, the butler, who stood nearby looking confused, by his arm and led the older man down the main hall in close consultation.

Kate was already taking the grand staircase two steps at a time. Simon caught up and they saw Imogen crouching on the top stair glaring at Kate. The young woman scrambled to her feet and raced away down the hallway.

"Imogen!" Kate followed until the girl ran into her room and slammed the door. Kate gripped the knob, but the door didn't budge. "Imogen. Unlock this door, please."

"No," came the voice from inside.

"Imogen," Kate demanded more forcefully. "Open this door."

"I can't."

"She seems agitated," Simon said.

Kate put a hand to her forehead. "This is no time for a tantrum."

He indicated the door. "Shall I?"

"Please."

Simon whispered a word and placed his hand against the white-paneled door. It was thick oak, but with a few seconds of pressure, the wood began to crack. He tensed his arm, straining his back, and the door tore away from the jamb, leaving a chunk of wood, complete with knob, suspended in the lock. The door swung open easily to reveal Imogen huddled in the center of her huge bed. Her eyes grew wide with surprise.

"You can't come in!" she shouted. "You don't have permission."

Kate slipped around Simon and approached the bed.

"We are leaving the house now to go on a trip. Come with me."

Imogen dropped onto the floor and quickly crawled under the bed.

"My God!" Kate shouted. She went to her knees and shoved up the lace ruffle, peering into the darkness. "Imogen, stop this. Come out now. Now!"

"I'm not supposed to," Imogen moaned. "You can't take me away."

"Just come out, please. If you don't come out, Mr. Archer will just lift the bed off you and we will carry you out."

"No he won't."

Kate leapt to her feet, her distress growing. She pushed past Simon into the corridor. "Stay here and watch her. I'm going for something in my laboratory."

"All right," he said as her footsteps were lost in the growing noise of servants hustling around the house. Simon leaned against the open door. He felt a presence beside him and saw Nick yawning.

"When did you get back?" Nick asked.

"Just now. Where have you been?"

"I was asleep. It's the middle of the night."

"Actually, it's well on toward noon."

"Oh." Nick shrugged, then saw the broken lock. He also attended the frantic voices coming from around the house with a look of confusion. "What's all the tumult?"

"Long story, but the short version is we're trying to get everyone out of the house before the werewolves appear on our doorstep."

Nick rubbed his unshaven face, seemingly unperturbed. "So your attempt at stealth was a failure?"

"You could say that."

"Why is the young Miss Anstruther under her bed?"

"That's what I'm trying to find out." Simon knelt so he could see the shadowy outline of Imogen's face close to the floor. "Miss Anstruther, you're causing your sister a great deal of trouble."

Silence.

"She wants to take you on a trip now that you're feeling better."

Silence.

"It would be generous of you if you cooperated with her."

"I can't."

"Why?"

"I'm not allowed to leave, not until . . ."

"Not until what?"

Imogen closed her eyes tightly and shook her head.

"Simon!" Kate's voice came from downstairs. It was a cry of alarm.

He leapt up and ran with Nick just behind him. As he spun around the bottom of the railing into the main foyer, he caught sight of Kate in the main hall, waving for him to follow. She was already running for the rear of the house. Soon they caught up and the trio pushed into the servants' dining room, where a group of morose and terrified men and women stood around a table. As Kate approached, they all stepped back to reveal a bloody form on the table. It was a young boy.

The coachman, his face bloody and his clothes ripped, stood over the lad with tears flowing down his cheeks. "They came at us, miss. Two of them. I don't know what they were. Some kind of beasts. They killed Thomas here as he was leading a team. They killed four of the horses, and the others bolted. They wrecked the coach. I couldn't stop them. I'm sorry, miss."

Simon took Kate by the shoulders and turned her away from the dead boy. "There's no escape now, Kate, for any of us. You must get all the women and children into the safest place in the house. Imogen too, but keep her isolated from the rest."

"Do we have time?" Kate asked.

"If they were ready to attack, they would be inside now. They're waiting for something. Let's take advantage."

Nick started for a rear door. "You tend to things here, old boy. I'll have a stroll around."

"Right," Simon replied. "Be careful."

Several of the young maids began to cry and ask frantic questions. Mrs. Tolbert snapped her fingers once and gave a stern look, along with a comforting hand on one panicked girl's arm. The crying quieted to sniffling.

Kate's voice was firm but calm, "Mrs. Tolbert, take all the women and lock yourselves in the scullery until someone comes for you."

Simon pulled a folded linen tablecloth from a shelf. He shook it out and draped it over the dead boy. Blood immediately began to seep through the cloth. "Now, load every weapon in the house. Every musket. Every pistol. Dole them out to any man capable of carrying. Swords as well, if you have them."

Kate shook her head. "My people are no match for these creatures."

"Likely none of us are. So we need every one of them, Kate. We need all the power we can muster. These things can die if we hit them hard enough."

Hogarth said, "They'll serve, miss. The older ones particularly have had some experience under your father. They'll bolster the younger ones."

Kate took a shuddering breath and nodded agreement.

Simon continued, "Lock every door and window. If there are shutters, seal them. If not, nail lumber over the windows. Main floor first, then upstairs."

Kate turned to Hogarth. "Fetch Imogen out from

under her bed and lock her in the wine cellar. And you stay with her."

"Very good, miss." The manservant pulled the coachman away from the bloody boy on the table and the two men departed quickly.

Simon led Kate from the room. "What do you have in your laboratory that might serve?"

"A few things, perhaps. I certainly haven't spent much time designing weapons."

"Put together what you can. I'll be in the library shoring up our defenses." Before she stepped away, he took her hand and looked into her eyes. "Kate, we can survive this. Our resources are extraordinary."

She gave him a tight-lipped smile. "I intend to make these things regret they ever laid eyes on my home."

Simon laughed and sent her on her way, watching her figure move down the hall, first at a quick walk, then breaking into a run. He turned, stepping around a valet carrying a double armload of muskets followed by a young lad with powder horns and shot bags draped off his shoulders. A footman was standing on a chair, wrenching swords off ancestral displays.

As he neared the library, a strange sound made itself known. He stopped to listen, the crease in his brow deepening. There was so much activity in the house he wondered what it could be. It reverberated the dust motes floating in the sunlight that filtered through the windows. Several servants also stopped work in confusion. They watched Simon pass toward the front door, and he gave them a confident smile that he didn't quite feel.

He threw back the front door and stepped out onto the portico. The rumbling grew louder and Simon felt the vibrations in his chest. From the distant forest, birds rose in alarm into the morning sky.

A dust cloud appeared on the yew-lined drive that ran

straight from the house. Then a roaring shape rose into view. It didn't seem to be a living creature. It was squat, much smaller than a carriage, and lower to the ground than a horse. Sunlight glinted off metal. Simon blocked the glare with his hand in an attempt to discern if it was friend or foe.

Then he saw Malcolm. The Scotsman's face bobbed to the side of the main bulk of the thing. Clearly, it was a vehicle of some sort, but nothing Simon had ever seen or heard before. He now thought he recognized Penny Carter hunched low in the center.

Strange, flailing shapes broke through the smoke behind the vehicle. Greyish brown figures rocked forward, then back. Long arms. Fierce snouts.

Werewolves. At least three of them loping in close pursuit and gaining fast.

Simon leapt from the portico and started up the gravel path toward the oncoming chaos. A bright flash of light came from his left and a streak of fire shot toward the rumbling mechanical thing. A blossom of flame hit one of the werewolves, sending it cartwheeling into the distance.

Nick appeared at a run, angling in on Simon and raising a smoking hand. He stopped and wound up his arm like a cricket bowler. He pitched another fireball toward the roaring vehicle. It flared across the lawn and crashed into a second werewolf.

Simon ran harder at the approaching machine. Penny waved him aside, shouting unheard. Malcolm was trying to twist in the small side buggy with a pistol in his fist. Simon caught the Scotsman's eye and prayed the man's wary look showed that he grasped what Simon was intending.

Simon took several more long-legged strides and just as the vehicle reached him, he leapt into the air. Malcolm fell flat against the sloping metal sidecarriage.

Simon drew up his legs and sailed over the Scotsman's head, shouting an ancient word and feeling the runic tattoo spark on his chest.

A werewolf was just ready to strike the bike but looked up in surprise as a figure hurtled at it. Simon caught the creature with an outstretched arm against its throat. It was driven off its feet as if it had collided with a sturdy tree limb. The werewolf toppled back into the gravel, rolling over and over. Simon landed hard and fell into a crouch, sliding onto his knees. He leapt up and brought a fist against the werewolf's head like a blacksmith's hammer. Simon pounced on its back and started smashing the thing's head. When it snapped at him, he seized it by the snout and gave a terrible wrench. He heard the satisfying sound of its jaw cracking.

A figure appeared in front of Simon. He reared up, ready to strike, but saw it was Nick. The older magician's hands were both aflame and he stood facing away, as if challenging someone in the distance. Simon saw the other two werewolves crouching some fifty yards away in the grass, glaring at them. He took a position next to Nick. A rustling sound to his other side heralded the arrival of Malcolm with both massive Lancasters ready.

Nick started toward the creatures. "Let's get them."

"Don't be a fool," Malcolm said. "They're scouts. Mere fodder. And they're luring us."

"There are only two," Nick snarled. "Scared?"

The Scotsman's face was ice. "There are more than two, and bigger ones. You just won't see them until it's too late."

"He's right, Nick." Simon scanned the area to ensure they weren't being flanked. He noticed Penny twenty-five yards behind them, about halfway to the house, with some outrageous brass blunderbuss on her shoulder.

The three men stood, waiting for the werewolves to make their decision. The creatures bobbed with uncertainty, snarling and waving their clawed hands. Then they turned and raced away into the forest.

Malcolm glanced at the dead werewolf on the gravel and up at the blood-spattered Simon. "You needn't have risked yourself."

Simon shook his head in annoyed bemusement. "But I like Penny."

"Well then, come on," Malcolm said, peering all around for safety. "She brought a few things that might be helpful."

"Good. I hoped she needed that steam horse for more than just to ferry you out here." Simon and Nick hurried back to the house, leaving the Scotsman to follow slowly.

Chapter Twenty-three

"SHE'S COMING," SIMON SAID.

"She's already here." Malcolm stood to his left, staring through the glass into the wild woods beyond the well-tended garden. "I can see them moving. They'll attack soon."

Dusk had fallen, but outside the windows of Hartley Hall it appeared as bright as a milky day thanks to the moon rising in the east. Its radiance illuminated the lines in Simon's face as he looked out the French windows in the Blue Room. The scattered clouds glowed with the eerie light, while the high, manicured hedges stretching off to the dark forest looked almost otherworldly in the moonshine.

Simon placed a hand on the wall and closed his eyes, seeking out the power of the runes he had scripted throughout the house and across the grounds. To his relief, they were all as he had placed them, waiting. So he reached out, touching them all, and took control of their power. He could feel the connections through the aether as if he now had a series of outposts along a frontier, but in the face of the threat lurking in the forest, his magic seemed distant and weak. Simon's jaw tightened as Kate entered the parlor in close conversation with Penny. Nick was on their heels.

Kate wore her bandolier of vials, carried a sword in her hand, and sported a pistol in her belt. Simon studied the martial figure with appreciation. Her face showed no fear, only the resolve to protect those in the house. She took a position at his shoulder, peering through the glass. He took strength from her tenacity.

"There's not much time, I assume?" she asked.

"No. They're scurrying around. Is everything prepared?"

"As best we could." She smiled back at Penny. "Miss Carter is a wonder. She prepared a number of swords with silver nitrate and managed to provide some of the men with silver loads for their firearms."

Penny hefted her thunderous stovepipe weapon. "Have you seen the workshop her father has here? If I had a few days, we could hold off an army."

"No doubt," replied Simon. "I wish we had those days, but I'm sure you've worked miracles in the time you had. And I'll remind you, Miss Carter, that this isn't your fight. I would rather you place yourself out of harm's way."

Penny regarded him with a hand on her cocked hip. "Just give us a rousing St. Crispin's Day speech, will you?"

Simon nodded to her and looked around the room from under a downturned brow. His face remained a mask of effort as he gripped the doorframe. His air of authority was all the more powerful as the tattoos on his bare forearms shone with eldritch energy. His voice deepened. "The way to win this battle is to stand together. They will concentrate their attack on the house, most likely at this place because the hedges provide good cover nearly to the door. So Malcolm and I will hold the line here in the Blue Room. Kate, you and Penny take the library in the east wing to cover the entrance to the wine cellar."

Kate gave Penny a glance over her shoulder, and the engineer shot her a lopsided grin.

Simon continued, "Nick, your task is to cover the rear entrance in the west wing to ensure no beasts threaten the servants in the scullery."

"Where's the dog?" Nick huffed a disgusted breath. "I'll stand near him. He always turns out well."

"Good idea," Simon nodded at his friend. "Kate, if you and Penny find your position in the library untenable, fall back to the wine cellar. We can give ground but not people. Those creatures out there have no goal but to kill all of us. We won't let that happen. Our duty is to destroy them. Destroy them utterly. Every one of them you kill is one that can't hurt us in the future."

"Hear hear," Malcolm muttered.

"Very well." Simon stared into Kate's bold green eyes. Part of him was apprehensive for her, but the other part was struck hard by her unabashed fire and valor. "Off you go. Good luck, everyone."

"I'll see you when it's over." Kate hefted her long sword and laid a hand on her pistol. She gave Nick a sharp whistle and jerked her head toward the door. He looked annoyed but followed her and Penny.

"She's quite impressive." Malcolm's eyes lingered on the door.

"She's an Anstruther," Simon said, annoyed by the Scotsman's ill-timed observation.

Malcolm grinned and flipped back his long coat and pulled his sleek Lancaster pistols. He nodded toward a grove. "There."

The darkness abruptly shifted and a lanky form moved just shy of the line of trees. Then others moved on the western side. A howl reverberated through the woods outside. Reflexively it brought the hair standing straight on end along Simon's skin.

"Here they come!" shouted Malcolm in a voice that

boomed through most of the house. A horde of were-wolves broke from the darkness and swarmed through the mazelike hedges like an onrushing wave. Simon's hand slapped the wall beside him and his skin smoldered with wisps of greenish smoke. Within fifty yards of the house, runic symbols flared to life on the ground under the charging beasts. Explosions sounded on all sides of the house as the traps were triggered. The were-wolves were flung up into the air as the runic bombs exploded. The surprised pack retreated and milled together back at the edge of the forest.

"God Almighty," Malcolm whispered with a quick glance of amazement at Simon.

Beads of sweat appeared on Simon's brow as he controlled the magic of the runes outside. His intense stare never left the window. "There's our girl."

From the edge of the woods, a figure stepped forth into the moonlight and Malcolm exhaled sharply. The giant creature's light grey fur shone almost white, as did the enormous battle-axe clenched in her right hand like a banner of war. It stood almost as tall as she. Her howl of rage shook the glass in front of Simon. An exclamation slipped unintentionally from his lips. Simon took in the heavily scarred leather armor that Gretta wore and the huge helmet adorned with a terrifying wolf's head.

"She won't stop till she gets what she wants," Malcolm warned.

"That won't happen," Simon stated, his mouth drawn to a thin line.

Gretta threw back her shaggy head and howled again, loud enough to make Simon wince. Suddenly the were-wolves all darted forward. They crossed the garden quickly, vaulting the torn bodies of their comrades. Simon placed his hand lightly on the doorframe beside him, his demeanor unflinching as five huge, slavering werewolves rushed onto the brick walkway, charging at him with nothing but a pane of thin glass to protect him. His muscles strained as primal aether surged through him.

Malcolm stepped back to raise his weapons but held his fire, his eyes narrowed to determined slits.

The werewolves launched themselves at the two men, but instead impacted something hard. Amidst a bright flash of light they were thrown back violently into the others rushing forward behind them.

Malcolm gave a shout of victory. "Losh!"

"I'm surprised it held." The sheen on Simon's forehead grew more pronounced. "Not my most elegant casting."

Werewolves gathered themselves and rushed the barrier again. The light flashed hot and more of the creatures were bloodied and killed. Still Gretta drove her pack forward.

Another horde of werewolves tore out of the darkness and threw themselves at the barrier. They tore against the runic protections with tooth and claw, screaming in pain but refusing to quit.

Gretta fixed Simon with an icy glare through the glass. She snarled at him with stark hatred, knowing full well who was responsible for the deaths of so many of her soldiers. She lifted her massive axe and threw it tumbling end over end straight at Simon's head.

It crashed directly in front of Simon's face and embedded itself in the wall of magic. It was an attempt to break his concentration. It failed. He shouted defiance in a hoarse roar and the runes held with another flash of bright light. His own body echoed the flare as the tattoos all rewrote themselves furiously over his skin.

Most of her pack was flung back, either dead or quivering hurt. Gretta stood rooted to the ground and roared in anger, bearing the brunt of the blast. Her weapon was heaved back toward her with tremendous force and she caught it in one large, fearsome, clawed hand. Then she sprung straight at Simon.

He tried to reconnect the runes again, but his body was spent. He felt his muscles weakening.

"Let it go!" Malcolm shouted.

Simon knew he was right. His meager protections would be useless now against the fury of this werewolf, and he would need his reserves. At least he had winnowed the pack. He released his hold on the wall, his fingers contorted with rigid stiffness. Malcolm grabbed his waistband and hauled him back into the room.

Gretta crashed through the glass. Four werewolves rushed in behind her. Around the house more crashes could be heard. A sliver of light traced a rune on Simon's forearm and he knelt. The scribe put his hand down and a violent rumble of earth swept the smaller werewolves off their feet.

Malcolm stepped out from behind Simon, both pistols firing rhythmically, all the shells slamming into Gretta, forcing her back with each impact. The silver seemed to have little effect on her, but her scream of pain was so massive that spittle sprayed over both men.

"MacFarlane," she roared. "I'll eviscerate you! What you did to my wulfsyl killed too many of my pack."

Malcolm grinned wickedly in response.

Simon leaned against a chair, breathing roughly, trying to tap into any energy he had left. A werewolf leapt for him. He reached out for his walking stick on the table. Spinning around and pulling out the sword, he stabbed the beast. He said a single word and the blade glowed. The werewolf suddenly went rigid, and its slobbering jaws snapped shut so hard that it bit through its tongue. The werewolf convulsed and lay still.

Malcolm sprang back to Simon's side, and together the two men faced Gretta and two werewolves climbing back to their feet. The third one lay struggling across the jagged teeth of the broken French doors. Glass jutted up through its neck. Bright red blood sprayed the floor. The little silver dust coating the panes worked well enough on the rabble.

"Gretta's mine," Malcolm snarled.

"By all means," was Simon's reply with a weary wave of his hand.

Gretta swung her massive axe toward Malcolm's head. The Scotsman ducked just in time to hear the weapon whistle over him. It was followed by a swipe of claws that Malcolm barely dodged by flinging himself over a couch. The furniture disappeared in a flurry of horse-hair stuffing and oaken splinters. Malcolm rose over the shambles and swung out with a claw of his own. The blade of his knife struck her deep in the shoulder just shy of her chest. Her cry was agonizing since the man's blade was laced with pure silver.

An explosion abruptly rocked the house and dust shook loose from the ceiling. Penny, no doubt. The sound of musketry came from various directions as the men of Hartley Hall laid into the enemy. Simon's heart pounded with pride. That was all the contemplation he was permitted as two more werewolves sprang at him. With a whisper on his lips, he dug into his reserves once more for strength.

Simon stabbed his sword deep into the throat of the first one. It fell into him, but he didn't stagger, his feet rooted to the floor. His hands dug deep into its fur and he threw its limp body into the path of the second one. They collided and crashed in a heap. Another creature entered the room so Simon hefted one of Kate's fine sofas and flung it at the newcomer. Its attention was on Gretta and Malcolm so the hurtling furniture took it full in the face, driving it back on its haunches and out of the room. By then the other werewolf had disentangled itself from its dead brethren and was stalking Simon with a slavering roar.

There was a fire glowing in the fireplace. Simon maneuvered so that he crossed close in front of it. His hand found a symbol he had scrawled previously on the hearth. With a word, he threw himself to the side, just as the jaws of the werewolf closed on the meat of his biceps. The fireplace belched a furnace of flame, engulfing the werewolf. The heat washed over Simon, making his skin prickle. The escaping hiss of the flames caught Gretta also, but Malcolm managed to dart aside at the last moment, separating them momentarily. The stench of burnt hair and flesh filled the room. Gretta's leather harness smoldered. The bottom of Malcolm's coat flickered with flame.

Simon gained his feet unsteadily and staggered at Gretta. Her attention was on Malcolm. The Scotsman was breathing heavily and bleeding from a number of wounds. Simon ran her through with a whispered word.

Gretta screamed and struck out. Her large, clawed hand slammed against Simon. His chest constricted in agony, then he was flying through the air. He impacted against the wall. Simon held on to consciousness by an act of sheer will, nothing more, but his body didn't respond beyond that. His breath was a wheezing attempt. He raised his head with trembling neck muscles to see the massive werewolf stalking toward him. Her leather armor sizzled and her fur was singed black as coal.

Suddenly Malcolm leapt into view with pistols firing another barrage. Gretta staggered, but then surged forward in a berserker rage so fast that Simon couldn't see her. Her massive head snapped at Malcolm and he barely had time to drop his pistols and hold her jaws at bay. She shook her head free and battered Malcolm across the head. He flew back into the unsteady Simon,

and the Scotsman collapsed into unconsciousness. Simon
struggled to raise his sword.

Gretta's clawed hands crunched through plaster behind them. To Simon's amazement, the wall shifted. She
pulled back, creating a shuddering rain of dust and
a deafening creak of timber. Gretta vanished amidst a
deep rumbling sound and an avalanche of bricks and
timber. Simon raised his hands but there was no stopping the side of the house and part of the floor above
from coming down on top of them.

Chapter Twenty-four

THERE WAS A GAPING HOLE IN THE LIBRARY, smoke curled from the edges, and dust was still settling to the ground. Four werewolves lay dead, the silver slivers embedded in their fur glinting in the dim lights still flickering in the wall sconces.

Kate strode with sword in hand to the hole and threw a vial through the entrance. A plume of golden dust billowed, then began to solidify into what appeared to be a large slab of amber. The orange crystal filled the gap in the wall.

"That's a keen thing there, that amber." Penny rose from behind an overturned table, dusting off her breeches. She raised her powerful blunderbuss to her shoulder.

"Just an old alchemy experiment that never came to anything," Kate remarked. "Use another one of those bombs inside and you'll bring the house down on us."

"On your left!"

A werewolf entered the library from the inner door. Penny dodged a savage swipe as Kate stabbed her sword into the exposed chest. Her aim was off, but still the beast curled inward over the pain. She fell back and Penny let fly with the heavy gun. A flash of flame and smoke accompanied the earsplitting boom. The werewolf was pounded into the wall, smashing against portraits and knickknacks. It tumbled awkwardly to the rug and shuddered. Its chest was littered with a collection of silver knives and forks.

"The family silver is finally worth something," Kate said with a measure of pride and exhilaration, nodding toward a pile of silverware on a table. "Fresh batch?"

"No time!"

Another werewolf streaked through the door. Kate and Penny both raised pistols and fired. The silver balls ripped through the werewolf. It stumbled, then flopped hard to the ground.

"My ammunition is almost spent." Penny hastily reloaded her pistol.

"Then let's retreat and hold the line downstairs." Kate hated to think how many of the beasts were already inside and how many humans they could have killed on the way in.

The two women made for the door to the wine cellar, stepping over the numerous carcasses. Behind them, a trio of werewolves snarled their way through the tight doorway into the library, back on their haunches with their hackles on end. Their claws dug deep into the wooden flooring as they inched forward. Kate threw her last amber vial. The three creatures couldn't avoid the golden fumes and immediately became encased in a sticky ocher resin, unable to move, trapped like insects from a bygone age.

Kate and Penny raced down a staircase to a wide landing, where Hogarth waited outside a single door. He carried a massive war hammer in his hands. He moved up a few steps to provide cover. Kate took a set of keys from Hogarth. "Inside!"

She unlocked the door and they rushed into the chamber. Kate swung the thick door shut, throwing the bolt. Hogarth and Penny pushed a heavy rack of oaken barrels in front of it. The wine cellar was huge, easily stretching under half of the house. It had a high-vaulted brick ceiling. The walls were stacked with rack after rack of wine bottles. Flickering lamps created terrifying shadows.

Imogen sat in a simple wooden chair. Her face was blank, but there was a cold terror in her eyes. Her hands were clutched in her lap, wringing with worry. "You have to go."

Kate replied, "Hush, dear. Everything will be fine. We can't go just yet."

"You, Kate. You have to go."

Kate stared at her sister, mystified by the remark. She came forward and embraced her.

The door abruptly shuddered. Hogarth and Penny braced themselves against the desk.

"We're safe here." Kate stroked her sister's arm. "I won't leave you. Ever."

Imogen slowly looked up, directly into Kate's eyes. Her lips quivered. "They're not here for me."

Before Kate could reply there was another earsplitting crack against the door. Hogarth exclaimed, "They're coming through!"

The door broke apart as a massive blade cut through the thick mahogany wood like it was paper. Gretta Aldfather ripped the door to pieces and smashed her way inside, shoving the rack and barrels easily out of the way.

Hogarth swung the great hammer in a wide arc, striking the side of a werewolf's head with a loud crunching sound. Before he could bring his maul to bear again, Gretta swept Hogarth and Penny aside like toys. The werewolf's gaze fell on Kate.

The blood in Kate's face fled. The presence of the werewolf leader here meant she had gotten past Simon and Malcolm. She swallowed back her fear for the two men. She drew her resolve inward and steadied her wildly beating heart.

Kate threw a crystal vial straight at Gretta's face. The werewolf quickly lifted an arm and took most of the acid on her leather bracer. The armor began to bubble and dissolve. The alchemist rushed the monster, sword held tight, stabbing straight. Gretta slipped aside and the hardened cuirass turned the blade. A massive arm swung out and bashed Kate. She went flying into the wreckage of the barrels, her head slamming painfully against the edge. Her vision swam. Nausea and vertigo prevented her from rising. Kate let out a strangled gasp as Gretta seized her neck in a clawed hand.

"Give me the key!" came Gretta's inhuman growl.

Kate wasn't sure what she heard.

"The key." The werewolf shook her in anger. "Your father's key. Where is it?"

"She's wearing it," Imogen called out, still sitting in her chair. "Around her neck."

Gretta ripped the leather bandolier from Kate's shoulder and tossed it aside. Then she tore open the jacket and blouse and scraped sharp nails across Kate's soft skin. With a quick snap, the werewolf tore the chain holding the gold key and held it up in front of her animalistic eyes.

Kate still couldn't grasp why the creature was asking about the key. Or why Imogen was talking to the werewolf. Kate had hardly thought about the key in days. Gretta threw her down hard onto the floor.

The werewolf looked at Imogen. "You know its secret, yes?"

Imogen stared at the hulking monster with amazing clarity, as if she were conversing with a maid. "No. I told the pale man everything I know."

Kate shoved herself up onto unsteady legs, grabbing her sword. The werewolf was starting to turn back just as Kate thrust the sword at Gretta's side, now unprotected, her armor gaping in spots from splashed acid. Kate was still disoriented and so was her aim. Instead of hitting a vital area, the blade dug deep into the werewolf's arm, piercing it all the way through to enter the torso. The point glanced off a rib and lodged tight. A single flex of Gretta's arm snapped the sword in half. The werewolf snarled and Kate knew she wouldn't be able to avoid the coming blow.

Suddenly, Hogarth smashed his hammer into Gretta's spine. The beast crashed against the far wall hard enough to leave an imprint in the wooden beams before crumpling to the floor.

Gretta rose and grabbed a heavy barrel. She swung it with the force of a typhoon to club Hogarth, who tried to break the impact with the length of the hammer. His body went airborne and crashed into a wine rack, smashing bottles and spraying red wine. He dropped to the floor and didn't rise again.

Kate was on one knee, trying to catch her breath. Penny was unconscious, slumped in a corner, blood trickling from her temple. Kate scrambled toward Imogen. Gretta seized her ankle and dragged her back, tossing her across the room. Kate's breath left her in a rush and the world spun so that bile rose forcefully in her throat.

Kate fought one more time to stagger up on limbs that would not hold her. The room swayed sickeningly and finally she succumbed and lost her tenuous hold on consciousness and slumped to the ground. In her subsequent nightmare, she heard a terrible howl in the distance. Dark shapes streamed around her and out into the night, emptying the house, save the moans and wails of the remaining humans.

Then darkness.

Chapter Twenty-five

SIMON STAGGERED INTO THE LIBRARY, TAKING in the smashed furniture and gaping hole in the wall. Dead bodies lay on the floor; all the werewolves had returned to human shape. He stumbled over wreckage and pushed through the door to the wine cellar. His rubbery legs carried him down the stairs, where he saw the shattered door.

He pushed inside to a scene of silent destruction. Splintered barrels. Overturned wine racks. Smashed bottles. Pools of dark liquid seeped across the stone floor. His heart twisted when he saw an object draped over the ruin.

Simon knelt and lifted Kate's bandolier. His hands clenched around it. Blood dripped from the wound in his arm.

"Kate!" he shouted and stood, nearly blacking out. He steadied himself. "Kate, can you hear me? Are you here?"

He climbed over the remnants of crushed barrels, searching for her form amidst the detritus. Then he heard a groan and the tinkling of a rolling bottle. He saw an arm shift from under a pile of wood and straw.

Simon scrambled over and braced himself. He managed to lift heavy oak fixtures and shoved them aside. Hogarth's face showed bloody and swollen.

"Where is Miss Kate?" the manservant asked.

"I don't know." Simon helped the man sit up. "What happened here?"

"It was Gretta, sir. She came, and there was no stopping her. We tried, sir. Miss Kate, Miss Carter, and I fought."

"Where are they, Hogarth? I don't see them here."

"I'm over here," came a voice from across the cellar. A shape moved under more wreckage. A small figure struggled up onto her arms. Penny wiped straw and splinters from her hair and put a hand to her head. "I feel like I was run over by a coach."

Simon left Hogarth and struggled across to Penny. He studied her for grievous wounds. Dried blood caked down her face, but she had suffered no obvious terrible damage. He took her face and stared into her eyes. They were clear, or nearly so.

"What happened to Kate?" he asked. "Where is she?"

Penny looked confused. "I don't know, Simon. She was still fighting when I went down."

"Gretta took her? And Imogen." He looked from Penny to Hogarth for confirmation.

The servant said, "She must've done, sir. The creature disabled me when she entered. I managed to rally, but she made short work of me, I'm ashamed to say."

Simon stood with a groan of pain and started toward the door. "I'm going after them."

Nick appeared in the doorway and put a firm hand against Simon's chest. "Easy, old boy."

He started to push by only to find Malcolm standing in the hallway. The hunter was covered in a mixture of blood and plaster from where the wall had collapsed on them.

"Damn it!" Nick shouted, grabbing Simon by the arm.

"Will you stop and think. We're dead on our feet. All of us, you included. If we go up against Gretta and her crew now, we will die."

Simon pulled his arm free. "I must do something."

"You're smarter than this, Simon." Nick stared intently at his friend. "Don't play her game. You can't win like that."

"He's right, Archer." Malcolm spat blood on the floor. "You can't catch them; they're all well away. But we know where they've gone."

Simon growled in desperation, "We have no idea what they might do to her while we sit here doing nothing."

"We're going after her," Malcolm insisted. "But we must reload and staunch the bleeding at least. There are dead and wounded all over the house."

Simon took a long breath. He nodded as if in understanding. Then he said, "Hogarth, can you find horses?"

"I'll do my best, sir." The manservant pulled himself upright, shedding dust and shards of glass.

"Good man." Simon draped the bandolier over his shoulder. "All of you take one of Kate's vitality elixirs, pack anything you can find that will kill werewolves, and meet me out front in thirty minutes if you're able. I'll be leaving for Bedlam then."

Nick shook his head. "You damned idiot, you're going to kill yourself."

Malcolm watched Simon silently limp up the stairs. He smiled grimly, helped Penny to her feet, and led her out of the wrecked cellar.

Chapter Twenty-six

KATE FELT AS IF SHE WERE BOGGED DOWN IN A mire though she had no memory of how it had happened. She attempted to drag open her eyes, which were gummed with deep sleep residue. The area around her was mostly in shadow. A horrific stench flooded her nose and she gagged. Her coughing started a fierce ache in her skull. As she tried to lift a hand to cover her mouth, she found it wouldn't move. Neither of her arms responded. Through the haze, she saw that her wrists were strapped down to the arms of a chair. There was also a broad strap around her chest, pinning her upright, and her ankles were bound tight. She was in a wooden wheelchair. The stench assaulting her was suddenly all too familiar. Her gut twisted.

She was in Bedlam.

She started violently. Her memory snapped back to Hartley Hall and the werewolves. She struggled wildly at her bindings, but they had no give at all. Fear pushed its way up from her stomach, but she fought to bring it back under control.

Her gaze swept around, squinting at medical equipment. A dull metal examination table sat in the middle of the dim room. Leather straps hung from iron rails

that ran the length of the table. Black blood and desiccated ooze clung to them.

Kate felt sick. Her fingers fluttered, stretching as far
as they could, but the buckles trapping her remained
tantalizingly out of her reach. She glanced about for
anything to cut through the thick leather. A knife or a
scalpel. Then she saw a frail shape on the far side of the
room.

"Imogen!" Kate whispered as loud as she dared.

Her sister stood in the corner, head hanging low on
her chest, her hair a tangled mess obscuring her face.

"Imogen, help me!" Kate pleaded.

Imogen didn't move although Kate could see the shallow rise and fall of her chest. She shouted her sister's
name, trying to shake the girl from her stupor, but to no
avail.

A door creaked open and Dr. White walked inside,
carrying a metal tray. Kate fought to keep her fear under
control, breathing heavily through her nose, and stok-
ing her anger instead.

"Why are you doing this?" she demanded, praying
that perhaps he was also Gretta's prisoner and working
under duress.

The white-haired doctor didn't glance at her. He merely
strolled to a cabinet and set the tray down. He went
about placing instruments upon the cabinet's surface.

Kate's fragile hope was dashed. There was no concern
or compassion in his manner, only a clinical distance. It
was the demeanor of someone who knew full well the
true situation. Her face grew hard and settled. "What
have you done to my sister?"

He continued with his deliberate work of arranging
his instruments. Kate noted with alarm his tray carried
vials of liquid and a syringe, as well as horrific-looking
medical utensils including scalpels of many sizes and
serrations. She swallowed hard. "You were behind her

condition from the start. You were working with Colonel Hibbert."

White regarded her with annoyance as if she had finally said something worth his time. "Please. Colonel Hibbert was merely a tool, and a flawed one. I used him to draw your sister into my hands. When he was no longer useful, I had him killed and I treated Imogen here so I could ensure she would do as I wished. She has been a tremendous help. You should be proud of her."

"What did you do to her?" A horrifying thought occurred to Kate. "Did you perform surgery on her? Did you operate on her brain? Oh, God!"

"Don't be silly," he replied. "A few potions sufficed to turn her. Surgery is only reserved for my final experiments."

"Experiments? You mean the homunculi," Kate repeated weakly. Her wrists twisted cruelly against the restraints. The bindings bit deep into her skin, but she didn't care.

White looked over his shoulder toward a milky white creature lurking in the threshold. Kate's lungs emptied of breath in a sharp exhale. The thing bent its grotesque limbs to scuttle forward. Its protruding dewy eyes swiveled in her direction. It took several minutes before Kate trusted her voice, and even so, it sounded frail and frightened. "You made those creatures."

"Yes."

"Why? Why create something so horrible?"

"Because I can." White smiled, then gave her a more elaborate answer though the first was perhaps the most truthful. "They are my eyes and ears outside this hospital. Over the years, I've become a trifle notorious in some circles as a master of alchemical biology, so I've taken care to occasionally alter my appearance and my name. No one would suspect a kindly gentleman doctor named William White."

"You're a mad dog." Kate fought against her restraints with renewed vigor.

His hand slammed down on the table, making the steel instruments jump about with a clatter. His face darkened in a contortion of rage. Kate sat very still, not daring to move and incite his anger more. Several seconds slipped by as she waited in terror. Finally his age-specked skin slackened and stretched into a sickening smile.

"That's quite rude." White turned again to methodically reorganize his instruments. "I'm surprised at that statement coming from you. You are an alchemist as well. You should fully appreciate a life of scholarly pursuit. Perhaps your outlook is colored by our location. But you see, Bedlam is the perfect place for work such as ours. I am unencumbered and free to do what I wish to advance medical science."

"What possible advancement could that creature offer?"

"Ah, I have made them useful in ways they never imagined. Each subject had a special quality that I could enhance. My science enabled their transformation from simple person to magnificent anthroparion. Through my surgical and alchemical skills, they became a miraculous blending of man and mechanics, embodying and disembodying the very spirit of man. One day such a thing will be the norm, and I will be renowned for ushering in a new era. You shouldn't be alarmed by its appearance. The very act of creation is at once shocking and beautiful. Only through torment can they become something more than what they were. They become that which destroyed them."

Kate paled in absolute dread. If she understood his mad ramblings, then each of the various homunculi were representations of how White had killed them: quills, spears, acid.

"That's horrible," she murmured.

"Birth is horrible from the perspective of the ignorant. Or the maid who must tidy up afterward."

"What do you want with Imogen? Or with me? Surely there is nothing special about us?"

"You are mistaken. You possessed something very extraordinary." He raised his hand to show the gold key dangling on its chain.

"That stupid piece of jewelry?" Kate tried to appear amazed and confused, but she instantly felt there was power in that key that she hadn't been able to understand. "That's what all this is about?"

"Being obtuse won't free you from that chair. I know this isn't a stupid piece of jewelry. We've been looking for this thing for years. Your father and a man named Edward Cavendish developed it decades ago. Cavendish died alone. We tried to run your father to ground but failed. Then we began to suspect he might have hidden the device in his house of wonders or with his living relatives." White walked over to Kate's sister, lifting her chin with a finger. Imogen's eyes remained wide open and vacant. "Lovely Imogen fit my needs perfectly. So eager to escape her domineering sister. So eager to experience that which was forbidden by you. Colonel Hibbert gave her an enticing taste. A glimpse of her father's world."

The doctor stepped to a cabinet along one wall and slid back a panel. He removed a human skull. It had thin metal rods dangling from it, and Kate recognized it as the skull of the homunculus that she and Simon had destroyed at Hartley Hall. White held it up and examined it, fitting his fingers into a space near the jaw and manipulating something inside, as if turning a small wheel. The skull's jaw began to go up and down, over and over, in a mockery of speech.

Kate heard a thin reedy voice emanating from the skull. It sounded familiar. Then she realized, with an incredulous shock, that it was Imogen's voice. The skull was a machine for recording and playing back sounds. As the bare teeth grinned, she heard the skull say as Imogen would, "My sister has a gold key that our father made. It's what you want. My sister has a gold key that our father made. It's what you want. My sister has a gold key that our father made. It's what you want."

"Stop it!" Kate screamed, barely holding back sobs. She couldn't have driven Imogen to this. She couldn't.

White nodded contentedly and placed the skull on a countertop. "Thanks to Imogen, I have the device in my possession. So you will tell me how it works."

"If your scheme was for me to talk, welcome to the end of your plan. I can't tell you something I don't know. If she told you I discovered the secret of how it works, she was wrong."

"Please, Miss Anstruther, you'll need to be a better actress for me to believe that your father would create a device that allows instantaneous translocation and leave it with you but not tell you how it works."

"Instantaneous translocation?" Kate stared at the gold key. Her father, and Simon's, created something so powerful.

"Stop playing stupid. You don't do it well." Dr. White approached the crouching homunculus as if it were a dog and placed a hand on its hairless head. He then walked toward Kate, with the thing shambling after him. She couldn't help but shudder as it came closer and its appalling details became more pronounced, the milky skin, its mouth sewn shut with thick hemp twine.

Kate stammered as bravely as she could, "How do you dare do anything to me without your master here? Gretta wanted me alive obviously."

"Gretta is hardly my master. At best, she is a junior partner. We were in the Bastille together. She's useful, yes, but only for very specific duties. Clawing, biting, and such. I make wulfsyl for her, and she comes when I whistle." The doctor waved the homunculus close.

Kate leaned back in the chair, desperate to get away. Never before had she felt so helpless. The white thing dragged its damp torso onto her legs. A long-fingered hand coated with a thick glistening slime slithered over her face, pulling at her skin, leaving a film. It reeked of decay. She didn't cry out or scream for she had locked that down in her throat, refusing to give the doctor any satisfaction. Still, her terrified exhalations sounded loud and fitful as she tried to twist her face away.

"You're far stronger than your sister. She started sobbing just at the sight of them. No matter." Dr. White leaned over Kate and tapped her mouth with his finger.

Immediately the creature's hand slipped down her cheek to cover her lips and nose. She thrashed wildly, but there was no means to get away. Viscous flesh from the thing's palm pushed its way into her mouth. Her eyes bulged above the creature's hand as her lungs fought. A minute went by, then two. Kate glanced frantically at her sister, who stood completely dispassionate at the traumatic scene being played out. Kate's heart broke. *Imogen!* Kate bucked again, trying desperately to dislodge the creature, but failed. Her vision started to grey and her struggles weakened.

"Release her," White commanded. Immediately, the homunculus slid away.

Kate gasped painfully, drawing in rough breath after rough breath, spitting out slime. Her chest ached. Her head hung as limp as her sister's across the room. In her heart she knew Simon and the others were coming for her. They would! Simon would not leave her to this fate.

"You won't . . . kill me," she spat out. "And I can't tell you anything."

The homunculus crouched on the cold stone floor,

one eye staring dully at her and the other stalk focused intently on Dr. White. It played a rubbery finger along Kate's arm.

"On the contrary," the doctor stated. "You will tell me all I wish to know."

Kate's heart pounded in her chest as he lifted a syringe with a long thick needle.

NICK WAVERED IN HIS SADDLE, ONE FOOT FLAILing, having lost a stirrup again. He reined to a halt. Simon pulled his steed up sharply, his mount bouncing a bit after being given its head for a decent stretch of open ground. Simon's color was pallid and he clenched his teeth in pain, but he said nothing. The rolling downs of Surrey spread out around them, broken only by trees gathered along streams. The cold night wind ruffled the horses' manes and pushed the grass. The shrinking moon was barely bright enough to light their way.

A thunder of hooves followed them and another group of horses drew close. Malcolm was in the lead, riding a black mare, sitting a horse like a centaur, his hair flying out behind him. His horse carried heavy saddlebags and Penny bounced on the horse's rump, clutching the Scotsman's waist for her life. Hogarth brought up the rear, a silent, fearsome presence. A lively night ride in an early frost was not the best tonic for a group of people so injured, but they had no time. Thankfully, Kate's *elixir vitae* had worked miracles in a short time.

Nick held the reins tight on his snorting mount. "Take it easy, Simon. We're not at our best."

"You'll need to be when we reach Bedlam."

"But I don't see why we couldn't have taken my spine-breaker," groused Penny, stretching her aching back. "This horse is intolerable."

Malcolm was quick to answer. "Too noticeable. Besides, I've been a passenger in that infernal machine. Now it's your turn."

"We're running out of time." Simon gave his mount his head again. Nick's colorful curse filled the space he had just left, but they all whipped their mounts into a gallop after him.

The pace he set was so furious, it took them less than three hours to reach the city. It was just past one o'clock in the morning when the spires of London loomed in the starlight ahead. A curse fell from Simon's lips as he maneuvered around a broken-down flower cart. The owner raised a fist and shouted something after his horse bumped into the cart in its excitement, displacing more of his wares.

"Steady." Nick kept his voice even to keep from fueling his friend's fire. "Gretta took Kate for a reason. She won't harm her till she gets what she wants. We'll be in time."

Simon and Nick rode side by side, fighting the flow around them. Nick turned in the saddle to ensure Malcolm and Hogarth were still in sight. Simon's impatient actions agitated his horse, which continued to prance and toss his head at being kept in check. The grand majesty of Lambeth Palace appeared before them. They turned right onto Church Street and slowly fought through the thinning masses, the very people they were trying to protect but who now stood in the way. As they continued up the widening thoroughfare, Malcolm and Hogarth broke free from their entanglements and trotted up behind. Finally the road opened up and Simon reined his horse to a stop across the street from Bedlam sprawling behind its wall.

Simon stared through the forbidding wrought-iron gates at the grey structure. His face contorted with fury.

He spurred his horse forward toward the gates. Nick raced after and grabbed the mount's bridle.

"Simon!"

The horse pulled up sharply, its ears flat against its head. Nick was in danger of being bitten by the horse or receiving a right cross from the rider.

"Let go! Don't try to stop me, Nick!"

"Think, Simon!"

"I am thinking! Of what they must be doing to . . ." Simon couldn't finish his sentence. His hand went to his chest, touching the bandolier beneath his coat.

Nick pulled the horse's head back to him. "We're going in, just not through the front door. Come with me." He wheeled his own horse roughly in the opposite direction.

Chapter Twenty-seven

KATE'S BODY FELT NOT HER OWN. SHE SLUMPED forward in the wheelchair; the only thing holding her upright was the band across her chest. Her hands and legs were numb after being immobile for so long. Her spine should be aching, but she felt nothing. She forced herself to straighten. A flash of white immediately started her chest pounding. She instinctively tried to pull against her restraints, to try to get away, but the white shape didn't move. It coalesced into the homunculus hunched placidly in a corner. Its mechanical eyes rotated, staring at her. It shuffled toward her and she whimpered against her will. The creature reached out a hand to touch her leg and she jerked reflexively.

"Leave me alone, you sodding piece of filth!" Kate raged at it, calling it a stream of unflattering things. Her anger was all that she had left now and she wielded it like any other weapon. "Come near me again and I swear I will bite off your bloody hand!"

It recoiled, then studied her. Her harsh breath was visible in the air of the chilled room.

"Now, now. Miss Anstruther." Dr. White reentered the room. "Such language."

Kate swiveled her head to face him, her fear boiling in her gut.

"And in front of your very impressionable sister." He tsked at her.

Kate tried to hold on to her fury, but in her weakened state it fled all too quickly, leaving her spent and ragged in her bonds. She shouldn't have wasted her energy on the creature. The doctor had something new up his sleeve by the sick way he smiled at her. She would need all her strength to endure it.

Imogen still stood in the corner of the room watching impassively. Kate couldn't fathom how anyone could look on such horrors and not be moved to some sort of action. They were family. Kate still believed there was some part of Imogen that recognized her and felt the slightest remorse.

Dr. White said, "I'm certainly glad you've recovered your stamina. For a time there I thought we might have lost you."

"I don't fade that easily."

"Yes. I see that. I gave you an enormous amount of serum; too much I feared. But I'm willing to stop these harsh actions if only you would tell me how the key works. It's such a simple thing."

"Even if I did, you would still kill us."

"I would never do something so wasteful! You totally misunderstand me, Miss Anstruther. To me, all life is precious. I would no more kill you than I would harm a hair on this creature's head." White stroked the rubbery skin of the homunculus.

"You said you killed them first."

"No. I transformed them. No one mourns the caterpillar after a beautiful butterfly emerges."

"You perhaps need your spectacles repaired. That is not a butterfly."

"Beauty is in the eye of the beholder. I find human life remarkable. Such vitality. So capable of adapting once the brain is altered to accept the coming change. You'll see."

"What?" A cold knot gripped Kate's stomach.

"Well, if you aren't going to be cooperative, perhaps you will be more disposed to talk to me as a homunculus."

"I'll never tell you anything!"

"We can't know that until we try." Dr. White strode behind the wheelchair in which Kate was imprisoned. At the same time, two more homunculi entered the room. One had draping tentacles and the other walked hunched and had long, spindly fingers tipped with needles. They gathered near the operating table as Dr. White wheeled Kate toward it.

"You will make a fine addition to the family."

"No!" Kate shouted.

"Yes!" Dr. White jerked the chair to a halt and spun her to face him. "Or tell me what I want to know!"

"I can't!"

"You won't! You believe you will be rescued. It's foolish fancy. I've made adjustments after your earlier visit to ensure no one can enter Bedlam. My homunculi are patrolling above, and the werewolves hunt below. No one will find you down here. No one is ever found down here."

The thought of being rescued created a surge of energy in Kate. But immediately she recalled the fight at Hartley Hall, and that crushed the light in her. Simon might be dead. Everyone might be dead. Kate ached to believe that he was coming for her, but she wasn't even sure she had the strength to hope any longer.

Then her rage blossomed again. She wouldn't allow the disgusting Dr. White to strip her of her faith. Through clenched teeth, Kate growled, "Even if I knew how to operate the key, I would take it to my grave."

"A pleasant thought, but unlikely." He snapped his fingers and the three homunculi swarmed her chair. The restraints were loosened, and tentacles and claws quickly grabbed Kate's limbs. She screamed and thrashed, but her body was stiff. She was manhandled onto the table. Her wrists and ankles were positioned, and Dr. White took his time securing her with the straps. He added a band of thick leather across her hips and one over her forehead.

Imogen just stood in the corner.

"Help me!" Kate shouted. "Imogen. Help me, please!"

One homunculus retreated from the room and returned, pushing a large container of disgusting red slurry. White helped position it close to the table.

He leaned over so Kate could see his face. "Dear girl. Please tell me and I won't continue."

Kate struggled to remain calm. She couldn't shake her head so she ground out, "I don't know!"

"My, you are a stubborn one."

A hairy, hulking shape appeared in the corner of her eye. Gretta Aldfather, with great axe in hand, straightened to near the full height of the room, her eyes burning coals. "Has she told you how to open the portal?"

"Not yet." White was annoyed at the intrusion. He turned away and one of his homunculi helped him into a stained surgical gown.

Gretta stalked to Kate. The werewolf did not need to bend over the bed for Kate to see her ferocious form and sharp canines. "You. You ruined my wulfsyl. I can smell it on you. You killed some of my best fighters. It took years to gather those beasts together. And you slaughtered them with poison like the coward you are." The creature snorted. "Perhaps if I chopped off your limbs one by one, you'd be more willing to talk."

Kate stifled a gasp and clamped her teeth down hard. She would not be weak. Fear was a thing born of uncertainty, but she was strong in her conviction. "I only wish I'd killed all of you monsters. Do what you want. It won't change anything!"

Dr. White cocked his head and stared at his reflection in a broad scalpel. "You're absolutely right, of course."

Gretta snarled at the physician. "What are you blathering about? Make her confess!"

"No. You see, Kate here is the strong one. I don't think she will break despite my best efforts. There is little we can do to her physically that will change that. And I don't want to kill her by accident. Then we'll never know."

"You said threatening her with the transformation would make her talk."

"So I did. I see now the slight miscalculation I made. But I believe I know where the chink in her armor is." Dr. White walked to the corner and pulled Imogen by the arm to the examination table. "I'm threatening the wrong person, aren't I, my dear?"

"My God! You filthy animal!" Kate hissed.

"Poor Imogen will be my next homunculus."

"No!"

"Remove that Miss Anstruther and strap this Miss Anstruther to the table," White commanded the giant werewolf.

Gretta grinned, exhaling loudly with delicious glee. When the homunculi unstrapped Kate, Gretta shoved aside the pasty things and transferred the woman roughly to the hated wheelchair. Kate struggled, flailing, kicking, biting, but she was no match for the werewolf's strength. Within moments, her fears were realized and she was helplessly tied down once again, watching Imogen lie compliantly on the table. The doctor restrained the girl's arms and legs without any struggle.

Kate sobbed. "Please don't hurt her. I don't know anything about that key."

"I'm not hurting her." White turned to Kate. "You are. All you need do is tell me what I need to know.

Then I will put you and your sister together in a cell and leave you in peace. I will depart, never to be seen again. And eventually your friends will find you and arrange for your release. You will both be back at home in Hartley Hall, a family again, brought closer by adversity."

"I can't tell you." Kate felt paper-thin on the verge of a breakdown.

Gretta's lips curled back in a snarl. "Just do it."

"Your petty honor versus the suffering of your sister. How selfish are you?" Dr. White waited a beat, then sighed and began inserting thick needles into Imogen's chest. Imogen screamed for the first time and thrashed wildly.

"Stop it!" Kate screamed. "All right! I'll tell you. I'll tell you how to use the key. Please don't hurt her!" It was a lie, but she had nothing else left. She had to buy time, if only another minute.

"Excellent. You won't be sorry. Everything will be fine." White stepped closer to Kate with a smile.

Kate's throat convulsed, as if words had to be forced out through her lips. Her head bowed low to her chest. "You have to—"

"Don't . . ."

Kate's head snapped up at the sound of her sister's weak voice. "Imogen!"

"Don't . . . tell . . . him," she rasped.

"Shut up, whelp." Gretta shook the table hard.

Perhaps the pain had shocked Imogen out of her stupor, but somehow she was lucid for the first time in days. "He'll kill us both . . . even so."

Dr. White grabbed Kate's chin. "She's delirious, the shock of the drugs wearing off. I swear to you, I'll not harm either of you if you give me the information."

"Lies," Imogen continued. "Promise me, Kate. Never . . . give them . . . what they want."

The girl cried out as Gretta's massive hand gripped

her throat. Then the sounds were cut off abruptly as Gretta squeezed.

White snarled, "Tell me, Kate. And all this will stop."

Kate drew in a deep, shuddering breath.

"Tell me or Gretta will tear out her throat!"

Gretta salivated over the helpless girl and brushed a long claw over Imogen's placid face. Imogen's head jerked toward Kate. Her eyes locked with her sister from across the room. Imogen wasn't frightened. She looked calm even while she gasped.

"No," Kate whispered.

"No, what?" Dr. White asked in a flat tone.

"No. I won't tell you." Kate's gaze never left her sister's. Did Imogen really believe Kate knew how to operate the key and was refusing to save her life by not confessing? Kate's heart was in shreds at the thought.

"Bah!" shouted Dr. White. "Gretta, stand back."

Gretta snarled, "You said—"

"I lied! Now, release her. I have more interesting plans for our little Imogen. I'm sure Kate will find my procedure quite fascinating to watch, won't you?"

Kate remained stock-still in her chair as Gretta raged, smashing a metal cabinet with a single blow. Her growl was a monstrous echo.

"Enough, Gretta," White rebuked. "You will have ample throats to rip soon enough."

The werewolf gripped her axe, and for a moment it looked like she would behead the doctor. Instead, she stalked out like a gigantic, petulant child.

"Forgive me, Imogen," Kate gasped out. "I don't have what they want. Please forgive me."

"I do forgive you," was her sister's soft reply. "As you have always forgiven me."

And Kate wept.

Chapter Twenty-eight

SIMON AND HIS COMPANIONS FOUND AN EN-
trance to the underground at Kennington. It was a black
maw that reeked of the waste and the garbage that had
fed into it over the many years. The subterranean world
bade them enter, eager for more souls to get lost within
its chambers and tunnels. Simon knew they had no choice
but to obey. A gentle flow of stinking water lapped at
their boots. It was what was left of the River Effra.
They followed its path into the dark hole, sloping down-
ward into the infernal bowels of the city. Rats and insects scurried aside at their intrusion. A filthy cat arched
its back and hissed before darting farther into the tunnel.

The moonlight behind them fled and the darkness
ahead was a stygian blackness. The noise of the city faded.
What remained were sounds like no other that echoed
about the stone walls; from the steady dripping of moisture all around them, to the insistent scratching of rats
in the shadows, to the mournful bellow of wind.

Simon lit a lantern, illuminating grime-covered stone
glistening in the new light. They followed the tunnel
north several hundred yards and soon reached a junction
that opened wide with brick columns and a multitude of
arches leading to new tunnels running off in different di-

rections. They continued north. The surroundings were shapeless and monochrome in the murky gloom. Diminutive, beady eyes reflected in the lanternlight for brief instances, then turned away to flee to safer, less-traveled areas.

"How are we going to find our way down here?" Malcolm asked. "Do you know it runs under Bedlam?"

"I think so," Nick replied. "Some years back, the Bedlam cellars flooded from beneath."

"It's utterly foul," gasped Penny, holding a sleeve over her face.

Simon's footing slipped and he put out a hand against the wall but instantly regretted it. A slick residue coated the bricks, discoloring them from a onetime red to an ocher yellow. Raw sewage most likely. The walls sweated moisture as if in a fever, and the floor reflected back their lights, blinding them if they didn't keep their eyes ahead. Their splashing was a loud and raucous thing, but it couldn't be helped. A slick of scummy water coated the ground. The water had rotted through anything that was not stone or iron. Flotsam practically disintegrated when they stepped through it.

Nick tapped Simon's shoulder and gestured toward a new archway veering east. Simon nodded and turned into the suggested tunnel, keeping a keen ear cocked for anything out of the ordinary. He wasn't worried about the odd criminal or swarm of rats; far more dangerous things might await them in the dark. If they encountered resistance, not a single enemy could escape to raise the alarm. All of them knew the stakes and were prepared to do what they must.

Suddenly there came the faintest of sounds, an insistent scratching as if a bored child dragged a stick along the stones. The noise echoed in the passageway ahead of them. Malcolm crept forward, Simon on his heels. Penny came after with Nick and Hogarth now bringing up the rear. The scratching ceased abruptly as they reached another crossroads.

Simon scanned with a light. Four black-browed arches provided choices of direction, but the tunnel straight across led northeastward. Water seeped from the vaulted walls in a trickle in some places, in others as a torrent. It flowed into a wide dark pool in the center of the arches. He tested the depth with his cane, measuring it about three feet deep. He shrugged. They had little choice but to cross the thirty or so yards of water.

Malcolm signaled for Simon to wait with the lantern. He stepped cautiously into the subterranean lake, his Lancasters firmly in hand. He sank in and the frigid, stagnant water lapped at his thighs. Malcolm waded into the black. Simon waited a moment before he drew the sword from his walking stick and slipped the empty wood into his belt. He eased down into the water. He waved for Nick and the others to hold, and followed in the Scotsman's wake. The hard bottom was slick.

They were halfway across when the water rippled between the two men. Simon caught a glimpse of white flash under the murky surface that veered toward Malcolm. Simon thrust his sword deep as if he were using a spear to fish. He struck true.

The water erupted in a wild torrent as whatever was beneath the surface thrashed about. Something heavy struck Simon across the back of the knees and he fell. The blade pulled free from its victim.

Malcolm spun back to see a monster rear out of the water and loom over Simon. Most noticeable was a great mouth of razor-sharp teeth, much like a shark, but it had muscular arms that lifted it up. The gaping mouth set beneath bulbous eyes snapped as Simon thrashed backward in the vile water. A Lancaster came up and fired off a round. A thick, heavy tail struck Malcolm's chest hard enough for him to lose his breath. The beast flopped back down and disappeared with a twitch of its powerful tail.

"Bloody hell!" Malcolm helped a sputtering Simon to his feet.

"Are you all right?" Nick shouted to them, almost stepping down himself before Simon waved him back.

"What was that?" Nick asked.

"A homunculus," Simon told them. "Part salamander, or maybe part fish."

He slicked back his hair, eyeing the water around him. He and Malcolm were in the center of the junction lake with nowhere to climb for safety. Lantern beams swept the black water.

"I can't see it." Malcolm cast about.

"There!" Nick shouted as something crested to their left.

A white streak leapt for Malcolm, its body coming half out of the water, but it never landed on the Scotsman. Simon grasped the tail with one arm, and his sword stabbed deep into the flesh to provide a better hold. The monster was jerked to a halt. Simon used his new strength to swing the creature and slam it hard against a column. Bricks cracked at the impact and black blood splattered, adding new ichor to the already stained walls.

Malcolm wasted no time and pulled one of Penny's standard grenades. As soon as the great mouth swung to him, gaping wide, he shoved the device inside the toothy maw. "Let it go!"

Simon obeyed, yanking out his sword, and the beast dove again. Both men struggled for the far side as best they could in hip-deep water. There was a muffled whomp. Water and sordid debris blew up, then rained down. A hot breath of putrid exhalation coursed over them all as bits of pale white flesh fell all around them.

"Oi, that's disgusting!" exclaimed Penny. "But bloody effective!"

Simon got his feet on dry ground and pulled Malcolm up beside him. He held his injured arm with a grimace.

"If I get cholera from being down here, I'll be blaming you." Malcolm's thick finger stabbed Simon in the chest.

"Let's not argue in front of the children, dear." Simon pulled out a vial of Kate's rejuvenating elixir and took a swallow. He waved the others across.

Malcolm kept a close eye on the water's surface, while Simon assisted everyone up onto the landing. Luckily there was nothing more hiding in the pool.

Nick warned, "Drink that elixir sparingly."

"Of course," was Simon's quick reply. He couldn't tell his friend just how miserable he felt. Every single one of them was in the same state.

Nick's breath was an exasperated huff as he followed after Simon. They moved quickly, aiming east for a quarter of a mile. The catacomb grew wider and the walls still glistened wetly, but the standing water existed only in small pools in the corners. They reached another arched junction where two more tunnels branched away. There was one just to their left, and another across the intersection some twenty yards away. As they came out into the vaulted chamber, everything grew deathly silent save for their own footsteps.

Low growls brought everyone to a halt. Something shifted in the dark straight ahead in the mouth of the passageway, hiding in the shadows, with breathing loud and throaty. It wasn't trying to be stealthy. It wanted its prey to know it was there, stalking, hunting.

Malcolm raised his weapons at the archway straight ahead but resisted the urge to fire blindly into the darkness. Then the sound of breathing could be heard from the closer tunnel to the left as well. Simon turned in that direction.

Malcolm growled, "Show yourselves, you miserable monsters!"

"Don't encourage them," Simon pointed out, but it was too late.

Something came rushing from the facing tunnel, colossal and covered in rust-mottled fur, with huge claws and teeth. Malcolm fired as the speeding thing filled his vision. The gunfire was an explosion echoing around them. The beast stumbled to the side, losing its momentum. A second creature leapt, landing with a rumbling thud, its long arms coming forward. The werewolf swatted at Malcolm like he was an annoying pest. The Scotsman dodged under the blow just as Simon slapped his hands together in front of him with a deafening clap of thunder. A force wave punched the werewolves back into their brethren crouched in the dim confines of the tunnel. The other creatures shoved their injured comrades aside and rushed out at the intruders.

More creatures also poured from the closer tunnel to the left. Simon and his group spread out and took up positions in an attempt to cover one another's backs as the melee began. Hogarth swung a bone-crushing mace, its pointed tips coated with silver. Each rhythmic swipe connected and drove beasts writhing to the ground.

Malcolm twisted aside and fired the Lancaster at the base of a werewolf's skull as it rushed him. The beast flopped to the ground. Penny was at Malcolm's back and she fired her pistol into the black obsidian orbs that glared up at her, eyes so large that she saw her own diminutive reflection in them.

Nick's hands were in constant motion and a combination of flame and frost flew from them. Fur caught fire and the slimy pools turned to slippery ice beneath clawed feet.

Simon's sword was out and dancing in the flashes of bright light from Nick's frenzied spells. The steel struck out at targets like the flicking tongue of a snake. Its blue runic glow burned hot, drawing howls of pain from each beast it touched.

Then Simon was amazed to catch sight of a familiar face behind the mass of werewolves. It was the girl who had helped them escape Bedlam. Charlotte. She stood inside the tunnel, in human form, her face a conflicted mask. Her large eyes met Simon's and she reacted in shock, and perhaps shame. She was trembling, but then her features hardened with decision and she transformed. It was an agonizing process, the small form growing larger and darker, her flowery print dress shredding. Her flailing limbs grew longer and her face shifted horribly, reshaping its charming pugnacious appearance into the fearsome countenance of a monster.

The beast that had been Charlotte answered the howls reverberating in the chamber, but instead of joining her brethren, she collided against them with her claws and teeth. She took advantage of their surprise, jumping from one target to another, tearing and ripping.

Simon lost sight of her in the chaos, barely dodging a sweep of claws. With a single hand, he grabbed the short, stiff bristles of a nearby werewolf and heaved the creature into the mouth of a tunnel. Then he caught sight of another long snout, filled with row upon row of sharp savage teeth, snapping inches from his head. Charlotte appeared at his side and fell on the werewolf with a tremendous ferocity beyond her smaller stature. She tore at its legs, hamstringing her opponent. Malcolm spun and stabbed the lame werewolf low in the back, twisting his knife. The wounded creature arched with a tremendous howl that made eardrums ache in the narrow confines.

The Lancaster in his other hand leveled at Charlotte, but Simon seized the barrel and shoved it aside. "No! It's Charlotte!"

Another werewolf bowled into the hunter, and he fell prone to the ground. The beast towered over him, a vision of teeth and savagery. Simon slammed his stonelike fist into the side of its head. Blood spurted from its eye and it screamed an unholy sound before backhanding him. The blow hit Simon's chest and sent him flying against a wall. The beast hurtled toward him, claws extended, vicious mouth agape. It crashed against the magician, but Simon spoke a word and brought both fists down atop the werewolf's back and, with a sickening snap, crushed its spine.

Gaining his feet, Malcolm widened his stance and kept fighting, his pistol firing, steam pouring from the barrel. Werewolves fell. He backed up until he was near Penny. She pulled a grenade and pressed the button. Then she sailed it over shaggy heads. The bomb whined shrilly and exploded. Hundreds of argent slivers hissed through the air, tearing into them from behind. Inhuman screams and chaos abounded.

Simon's hand reached for Kate's bandolier across his chest and pulled a canister that Penny had brought from her shop. He checked to ensure Charlotte was clear of his target area, then he threw it with deadly accuracy at the left tunnel. It released a cloud of sparkling dust that rose in the air and coated the walls and everything inside the tunnel with a fine powder of special silver nitrate.

The werewolves that touched it roared in agony, falling to the ground writhing or running blindly, desperate to get away from the silver flakes that seemed to burrow under their skin. The mad creatures stumbled into Malcolm's path and the hunter was quick to deliver their ends.

Penny stood with him, having quickly reloaded her pistol. She fired into one werewolf that slipped past Malcolm. It was blind in one eye, and she efficiently ruined the other. With a scream of agony, one clawed hand struck her hard on the shoulder, near her neck. Her weapon suddenly dangled from nerveless fingers as she went down to her knees.

Malcolm was there, standing over her with both his pistols, firing multiple times until the beast dropped dead. Penny offered up a brave, wry grin at her savior.

"Damn foolish, girl," he scolded her.

Her expression fell. "How do you think I feel? Taken out by a blind werewolf."

"Can you stand?" He offered her his forearm, still holding on to his pistol.

"Of course." Penny struggled to her feet, her face contorted in pain. She cradled her injured limb.

"Is it broken?"

"Afraid so. I'm disarmed."

Malcolm's wild laugh echoed in the chaotic tunnels.

A bolt of heat made them duck their heads as Nick let loose a blast of fire into the tunnel behind them. The tunnel lit up with an orange glow and warmed considerably. A smoke cloud of burning fur and flesh billowed at the ceiling.

"Reinforcements!" he shouted, his hands aflame.

"Coat it!" Simon tossed him a canister. "Charlotte! To me!"

Nick snatched the cylinder out of the air and in one fluid motion flung it into the tunnel as the small grey werewolf darted past him to Simon's side. The canister spewed a thick cloud and gave that tunnel a silvery sheen in the flickering light. Two panicked werewolves fled the contaminated tunnel straight into Hogarth's cruel mace, which slammed into the skull of one, sending it careening into the other. They went down in a tangle of limbs.

The uninjured one, nearly the size of Gretta herself, bellowed its rage. Hogarth was drawing back for another blow, but the huge thing grabbed the manservant in its cruel claws, digging deep into his flesh.

Nick shouted and ran toward Hogarth. He struck twice with hands aflame, once across the arm that held the manservant and another across the beast's throat. It seared the exposed flesh, but the massive werewolf would not loosen its hold. Nick pulled back, aiming for its cold heart, but the werewolf raised its other arm, claws extended.

Simon appeared, blocking the blow aimed for Nick. He drove his sword deep into the creature's stomach. It roared in agony but continued to crush Hogarth's middle. Runic light flared around Simon as he used his free hand to wrench claws from the manservant. He pulled the fingers back with an audible crack.

Growling furiously, the werewolf raised an arm to deal with Simon, but Nick seized it. The monster's broad head swiveled toward him. It would only take a single snap from that mouth to take Nick's head. Simon released the claw to grab the beast's snout. The werewolf shook itself violently, but Simon would not relent. He took hold of the jaws and started hissing an old spell between his lips. A flash of light shone out from under his torn collar, illuminating them all. Simon was slowly wrenching the beast's head away from Nick. The creature growled and released Hogarth, still trying to shake off Simon's death grip. Hogarth slid to the ground, holding his ribs.

The werewolf slashed at Simon, but he ignored it, putting all his concentration into his effort. His own howl echoed the werewolf's. With a final mighty heave, the beast's neck snapped with a sickening crunch. The gigantic werewolf seized in a spasm and fell limp next to Hogarth. The flames on Nick's hands flickered out.

Simon stood panting, the rush of the aether saturating him. A frantic Nick grabbed him, yanking open his tattered coat to check the blood flow from his wounds.

"Just scratches," Simon said.

"I don't think so."

Simon shrugged off his ministrations and turned toward Hogarth. "Are you okay?"

Hogarth nodded, but his arms were wrapped tight about his bleeding chest.

Malcolm emerged from one of the silver-treated tunnels and stood bloody, with steaming guns in hand. Penny leaned unsteadily against the archway and Charlotte crouched across the chamber. Monstrous bodies lay in piles around them. Some of the first killed were already transforming to humans, either naked or covered in rags. Limbs flickered in death throes. Malcolm set about dispatching a few twitching creatures with shots to their hairy heads.

Penny groaned and looked away. Charlotte slipped behind a column and let her beastly form fade. She clutched at the rags that barely covered her sad, naked form.

Malcolm gave a grim nod as he reloaded. "The way looks open now."

Simon breathed heavily with a hand braced against the wall and said to Malcolm with a fevered grin, "That fight was glorious!"

Malcolm grunted. "You have that mad air about you."

"Nonsense!" Simon waved an arm whose sleeve was shredded like lace. "That went much better than the last time, don't you agree?"

The Scotsman rolled his eyes. "Bloody fantastic."

Simon laughed, the echo of which made it sound louder and more manic than it was. He took another swig of the rejuvenation potion. "A bit of Kate's *elixir vitae* and we're right as rain."

Nick grabbed Simon's arm, and said, "You're getting aether drunk. We can't have it."

Simon sobered a bit at his friend's warning and patted Nick's chest in understanding.

"We're down two already," Malcolm noted. "And we haven't even met up with Gretta yet."

Simon whispered to him to keep the others from hearing, "Our core is still intact. We have our most powerful."

Malcolm plucked at Simon's torn coat spattered red. "Do we?"

"Near enough. I won't feel this till tomorrow. And we've winnowed Gretta's forces considerably."

Malcolm turned his suspicious attention to Charlotte. "Still one left."

The girl pressed her back against the putrid wall. Her fear was palpable, but she stood her ground, obviously something more important than her safety was keeping her here. She glanced at Malcolm, then back to Simon, who stepped toward her. When he saw her state of dress, he diverted his eyes and removed his torn coat, handing it to the girl.

"Here, put this on. It's better than what's left of your dress." And once she had, he said, "It seems we must thank you again, Charlotte."

"What do you want here?" Malcolm thundered at her.

Charlotte stood defiantly away from the wall. "They have her. The lady who was nice to me. They're doing terrible things to her. You have to help her!"

That's all Simon needed to hear. "Do you know where she is?"

"Yes! She's in the lower rooms." Charlotte started running up one of the tunnels.

Simon went to follow her when Malcolm grabbed him and spun him about. "It could be leading us into a trap!"

"We've played this scene before. I'll do anything to find Kate." The timbre of Simon's voice deepened unnaturally as he felt the aether rising unbidden in him. The stone of the tunnels seemed to take on a greenish hue.

Malcolm muttered something to himself and backed away from Simon. He turned to Hogarth, who was leaning on Nick. "How bad?"

"It won't stop me from finding Miss Kate or Miss Imogen," the powerful man wheezed through gritted teeth.

Nick shook his head.

Malcolm helped Penny rise. "And you?"

"Never better," Penny piped up, but her face was pinched in pain. Malcolm took hold of her good arm and helped her balance.

Simon hurried forward until he reached Charlotte, who was waiting impatiently at the next juncture. She led them all through the twisting labyrinth for several more minutes. Whatever confidence Simon had had about finding their way without Charlotte's help faded. They would have been lost if not for her. The tunnel went on for hundreds of yards before finally stopping at a heavy iron gate locked with thick chains.

"Bedlam," Charlotte announced.

Simon cracked his knuckles.

Chapter Twenty-nine

KATE WAS WITNESSING THE UNTHINKABLE. DR. White was performing a grotesque surgery on her sister. The smell of the blood and the sound of flesh being mangled would never be wiped from her memory. The doctor had narrated certain portions of the procedure, crowing about how his mastery of alchemy allowed him to achieve techniques that no other surgeon could. The pain of even a simple operation made it unendurable for most patients for more than a few minutes. However, Dr. White had potions that deadened pain so successfully that he could perform extraordinarily lengthy and complex surgeries; he would change the future of medicine. Kate took small comfort that perhaps Imogen felt no pain.

The surgeon labored under flickering gas lamps with the homunculi assisting him, handing him his glittering instruments or reaching into Imogen to hold something aside so he could work better. When he claimed he was preparing to remove her arm so he could replace it with automata, Kate lost consciousness.

When she came to, she saw Dr. White still standing alongside the operating table in a pool of thin yellow light. The homunculi were no longer present. A large glass canister of pale red liquid hung from a rack over the table with a tube ending in a sharp, beveled piece of metal that was inserted in the abdomen of the bleached figure stretched out under the doctor's hand.

Kate moaned.

White glanced at her over his shoulder and smiled. His face was bloodstained. His eyes were wide and frenzied.

"Imogen will be a fine addition to the family," he said in a voice thick with excitement. White held up a tube of filamentous quills. "Since you took my favorite, I will re-create your sister in his likeness. She will be magnificent."

Kate said nothing. Even if she had wanted to, she couldn't. She had a gag over her mouth, which White had placed to stop her cursing and threatening during the surgery. Throughout the operation, she had been steadily flexing her limbs, restoring circulation to them. They burned with fiery needles, but one image kept her focused: White dead at her hands. There was nothing that would stop her, nowhere he could run.

"Nearly done now." White straightened the tube dangling from the canister and studied the filthy trocar that dripped pinkish liquid. He took a large syringe of green substance from a side table and set it on the operating table. "I tried to tell you what would happen. Did you think I was lying? You cannot play games with me, Miss Anstruther."

Kate kept her eyes on him, afraid to catch a fuller glimpse of Imogen.

He walked toward her, wiping red hands on his gown. "I haven't decided what to do with you. The key will take care of itself; it's really none of my concern ultimately. But I asked you quite nicely to tell me about it. And you refused. Now I will make you pay for your arrogance."

The door exploded open and slammed against the wall. Simon stormed into sight, one fist clenched, lines of power sparking over his arms and torso. His sword glowed like lightning in his hand.

The doctor recovered surprisingly fast from the shock. He grabbed the wheelchair and spun Kate around to face the door. She felt a sharp prick of a needle on her neck as White shouted, "Stop or she'll die!"

Simon held out his arm to block Hogarth, who surged in behind him. The manservant was a figure of rusted iron, his chest swathed in red linen and his face bleached marble. His gaze locked on the dreadful table that rose from the floor between the door and the trapped Kate. Hogarth's face fell with devastation. The pile of familiar clothes on the floor told him all he needed to know. The manservant shoved Simon's arm aside and walked toward the table, step by slow step. He stopped, towering over the still, white figure. He looked at the poor thing, unsure what to do. He unstrapped one of the hands, then seemed to freeze in confusion. His fingers tightened on the table edge. It was unclear if he was trying to crush it, or if he merely needed the support to stand. His form quivered and his head rose.

Dr. White pressed the large needle deeper into Kate's throat. She gave a muffled cry of pain. One of the doctor's grotesque homunculi skittered from the far corner to crouch on its weird, misshapen legs near White. One of the thing's eyes locked on the table, while the other swept around the dingy chamber.

"Hogarth!" Simon warned. "Don't do anything to endanger Kate. Do you hear me?"

"Wise advice, Mr. Archer," White said. "Have you come so far just to see her die?" The doctor's eyes tracked Malcolm, who moved into the room behind Simon with pistols in hand. The Scotsman slipped to one side to gain a clear view, but he stopped when White inclined his head toward his restrained prisoner again.

"I must say, Mr. Archer, I am grateful to see you here because now I don't need to seek you out to destroy you."

"You're welcome," Simon said as he flexed his hands. "Now, we'll have Miss Anstruther and her sister."

White chuckled. "You won't have anything, I'm afraid. Frankly, I don't see how any of you will get out of here alive."

"Don't you?" Simon raised a hand and Penny entered the room, brandishing a pistol, bluffing out the extreme pain she felt. Young human Charlotte crept in behind her. Simon glanced quickly back. "Where's Nick?"

A pale-faced Penny said, "He went off to hold the stairs in case reinforcements come."

"Damn it," Simon whispered. He removed a vial from the bandolier, tossing it to Penny. "The door if you please."

Penny calmly poured liquid on the threshold. In a moment, a shimmering amberlike mass started to grow. It expanded, sticking to the wall and swelling until it filled the entire doorway.

"That is impressive work, obviously yours." The doctor eyed Kate. "Very accomplished. I will try to keep you alive so I may pick your brain." He giggled strangely as if an odd thought struck him.

Simon stepped to the operating table. "Now, let's talk about who will and won't survive." For the first time, he saw what had been done to Imogen. Certain lines and curves such as the chin and the cheekbones still spoke of familiar features, but much of the beautiful young girl, her right arm and her skin, were like the horrible homunculi, deathly pale and translucent. Her eyes were stark white and more machine than human, the pupil of the left one contracted with a mechanical whir. Simon's face froze as he worked on suppressing his own wrath.

He laid a hand on Hogarth's trembling shoulder. The manservant studied the tube dangling from the glass canister that throbbed like a vein. Imogen's white abdomen was beginning to distend as fluids continued to pump into it. Pink liquid bubbled from her mouth. Hogarth reached out and yanked the trocar from Imogen's stomach and tossed it aside. The liquid continued to gurgle out onto the floor.

White frowned. "That is unfortunate. I may not be able to salvage her now. You have ruined this experiment. I'm quite cross about that."

Imogen slowly raised her human arm and took Hogarth's wrist. She lifted the manservant's hand and brought it to her throat. The white thing placed his massive fingers around her neck and squeezed them, signaling what she wanted him to do.

Hogarth managed a pained, "I can't, Miss Imogen. I can't."

"No, you can't," the doctor threatened. "Move away from her. Now."

Malcolm took a step forward and murmured to Simon, "I can take him."

Simon shook his head slightly. He laid a hand on the metal table and whispered a word. A shock wave shook the table and carried down to the floor, rippling out across the stained tiles. The wheelchair bucked into the air and the doctor toppled off his feet like a rag doll. The entire group was rocked by the unexpected blast. They fell to the floor or crashed against the wall, except for Simon who was prepared. He vaulted Imogen and the table and bounded toward Dr. White.

A shape dropped from above. A shouted warning from Penny enabled Simon to twist and face his attacker with the rapier-like fingers. Simon managed to bring his sword up, impaling the creature, but the weight still drove him to the floor. The homunculus's stiff fingers thudded into the stone on either side as if it was mere upholstery. The white thing gibbered, with its horrid face a few inches from Simon's. It wrenched one of its hands free and raised it to strike. Simon shifted to the side as spike fingers slashed down, catching the edge of his shoulder. He cried out.

Through the pain, Simon whispered a word and the sword flared. The homunculus squealed as Simon used both hands to force the sword up through the creature's body, spilling ooze. The thing thrashed in agony and fell limp.

Meanwhile, Dr. White had struggled to his feet and grabbed the intact glass syringe from the floor. Shaking his head to clear it, he lumbered toward the wheelchair. Suddenly the chair was pulled away by Hogarth. The manservant swung a gigantic fist at the doctor, but White managed to dodge the blow, falling back as Hogarth lifted Kate and the chair to carry her away from the madman. White recovered his balance on the shoulder of the homunculus, which weaved on mantislike limbs, watching everyone at the same time.

Malcolm rose to his feet, sighting Dr. White down the barrel of a Lancaster pistol. Something quivered down in front of his face. His arm was seized and pulled up. A white creature clutching the dim ceiling draped tentacles down to entangle the hunter.

Malcolm rose off the floor, dragged by pale tendrils. His arms were trapped. Penny ran for him and reached under his coat to yank out his dagger. She swept through the tentacles holding his right arm. Liquid spewed. Malcolm raised his heavy pistol and blasted the ceiling. The automatic barrel rotated, and he fired one shell after another. Viscous black fluid poured down on Malcolm. The tentacles frayed into slime and Malcolm dropped into a growing puddle as the homunculus fell apart.

Hogarth and Charlotte pulled the last buckle away from Kate's ankles and the woman struggled to stand, her legs still on fire. Her hand ripped away the strap from her mouth.

"Thank God, Miss Kate." Hogarth pulled a vial from

his pocket. It was the elixir he had been given but saved for her. "Drink this. It will revive you."

"Bless you, Hogarth." Kate pulled the stopper and took a long swallow. She smiled at Charlotte. Then she turned and stared at Imogen on the table. Kate seemed momentarily frozen, unwilling to go closer to her horribly changed sister, even as Hogarth returned to stand beside Imogen. Kate walked stiff-legged to where Penny and Malcolm were rising to their feet. She pulled the second Lancaster pistol from the gagging Malcolm.

Simon kicked the sizzling cadaver of the clawed homunculus aside, shifting his attention between the approaching Kate, with the heavy pistol dangling from her hand, and the trapped doctor, with his last freakish protector. "Careful, Kate, that last homunculus is likely the most horrific if it's his last defense."

Kate leveled the pistol. She fired and the white thing was blown off its feet to slide dead against the wall. She handed the weapon to Simon and advanced on the doctor.

"Kate, stop!" Simon cried. "We have no idea what he is capable of."

The doctor raised the syringe of green liquid, but Kate slapped it out of his hand. She seized his collar and drove a fist into his face. Then again. And again. His nose flattened into pulp and blood flowed down across his mouth.

Kate shook him. "Now tell me that you can reverse what you did to Imogen. Tell me that."

White gurgled blood. "That thing is your sister now and forever."

Kate put both hands around the doctor's throat. "Then there's no reason for you to live." Her voice was cold and unemotional as she tightened her grip.

He struggled to speak, working his jaw from side to side. He spat a tooth in her face and bit down on something in his mouth. "I would prefer to die by my own intellect, than allow your pathetic hands to finish me."

Kate's fingers squeezed deep into his throat, disappearing into softening flesh. White began to change shape. His face grew flaccid. What had been his head caved in and cascaded over her hands in a slimy rush. The body spilled to the floor with a sickening splash. His empty suit dropped into the puddle that had been Dr. William White.

"Coward," Kate snarled, staring down in anger rather than horror or amazement. She knelt and reached into the slime. After a second, she stood, clutching the key.

Simon spun Kate around and embraced her. The tightness in his chest finally abated, allowing him a natural breath of relief. He held her up and took in the sight of her. He smoothed the hair from her face. With one arm, he removed the bandolier from across his shoulders. "I believe this is yours."

Her eyes filled with warmth that he had carried it into battle. But it was fleeting. She forced her gaze to where Hogarth was holding the limp, pale hand of the figure on the table. The sturdy manservant looked back at Kate with tears streaming down his face.

Simon said, "Kate, forgive us. We failed."

She shook her head emphatically and found herself supporting Simon rather than the other way around. They went to the table, and Kate touched the white thing lying there. Imogen's eyes, one human but pale and one darkly mechanical, rotated toward her. An inhuman hand with grotesquely long fingers gently reached out. Kate grasped it.

"So brave you were," Kate whispered, brushing her other hand over Imogen's smooth, bald head. "Father would have been so proud of you. As I am."

Imogen's already ragged breathing grew rougher. She began to writhe, causing Kate to stiffen in alarm.

"Oh my God," Kate breathed. "She's dying. The transformation process wasn't finished."

"Perhaps it's for the best." Simon stepped to her side. "She isn't Imogen."

Kate stared at the horrific thing that had once been her sister, and she could still see Imogen there. She could hear her sister's old voice in the rasping noises. Kate took the syringe of green liquid from the table and inserted the needle as she had seen Dr. White do with other substances. She pushed the plunger, injecting the green into her sister's body. Imogen went rigid, as if her muscles were stone. Her peculiar eyes stretched wide. Kate slid the needle out and violently threw it aside.

She put a hand against her sister's frozen cheek. "I'm sorry, Imogen. I'm not as brave as you. I couldn't let you go."

"Kate, we must leave," Simon said. The entire group was in tatters. Wounds half-healed and others newly raw and vibrant showed on all of them. Everyone's movements were slow and pained. They were injured and exhausted, fortunate not to be dead. Perhaps it was only the effects of Kate's elixir that kept them upright. "If we don't go now, we may not be able to walk out under our own power."

Hogarth removed his coat and wrapped it around Imogen to protect him from the quills that lay flat along her arm. He gathered the gasping woman against his chest.

There was a deep thumping sound from the door. All heads turned to the amber monolith that blocked the entrance. Through the distorting orange substance, they saw a large shape moving. Something smashed against the amber, shaking the wall. Small lines webbed the crystal. The dark figure struck again and the tiny fissures widened into cracks.

"Oh my God," Charlotte whispered. "It's Gretta."

Chapter Thirty

NO ONE SPOKE. THE ONLY SOUND WAS THE POUND-ing of the werewolf against their fragile protection and the sharp cracking of the amber.

"Is there another way out?" Kate finally asked.

Simon handed his sword to Kate before he went to the far wall. Using his own dripping blood, he runed the stones. Then he did the same to the floor. "We are surrounded by earth. There is only one door."

She looked up. "The ceiling?"

Simon shook his head. "Stone foundation. Too thick."

Hogarth set Imogen down gently. "When she comes through, I will take her. I will buy you time."

Kate waved her hand flat. "No. We take her together. She's alone now."

"This way we don't have to kill her later." Penny smirked through the pain of her cradled broken limb.

Malcolm snorted a laugh as he inspected his pistols, muttering about ferocious women.

Charlotte crouched next to Kate and bumped her head against her much like Aethelred would do when he wanted attention. It was a little disturbing to see the young girl do it. Kate glanced up questioningly at Simon.

"Charlotte led us to you," he said.

Kate dropped to her knees and embraced the young girl with unabashed affection. "Oh child! Thank you!"

Surprised, Charlotte's arms slowly wrapped around Kate and her eyes brimmed with gentle tears.

Simon turned to Malcolm, and said, "Penny is right. Since Gretta is thoughtful enough to be right outside just now, this is the time to take her."

"Good man." Malcolm snapped the breech of his pistol closed.

"And since her presence in the hall means that Nick is likely dead," Simon said quietly, "I believe I shall take the honor of destroying her." Kate started to object, but Simon continued, "I'm the only one of us who could possibly stand up to her."

"Perhaps," Kate argued, "if you were well, but you're exhausted and under the influence of the aether."

"Yes, that's very true," He laughed bitterly and pulled the last three remaining vials of the revitalizing elixir from her bandolier.

"Simon, you can't take three at once. It will kill you."

There was a massive strike at the door and a chunk of amber flew across the room.

"The time for arguing is past, even for you," Simon said softly and took her hand in his.

Kate shook her head defiantly. "Don't play charming. We're so much more powerful together. Whatever you're thinking, there's another way."

"There is indeed, but it ends up with one or more of you dead. That I can't allow." His mouth was a firm grimace. He uncorked the small bottles. "When the doorway is clear, you will all need to move far away. Back into the tunnels. You won't survive what I'm about to do."

"Will you survive?" Kate asked.

"You shouldn't worry, my dear." Simon couldn't look her in the eye.

Kate watched with dread as he drank all three vials.

The rush of the elixir swept over Simon in a dizzying wave, every nerve and muscle coming alive with excess power. He crouched on the floor, swaying, on the verge of passing out. Kate took a step toward him, but he waved her off. After a second, he steadied himself and, using the blood dripping from his hand, inscribed a large rune on the floor. When he completed it, he pressed his hand flat. The rune glowed a brilliant green, then faded.

He stood slowly, breathing labored, his eyes staring unseeing into the distance. He began to speak odd words in a low voice and the tattooed runes on his body glowed, writing and rewriting themselves in chaotic repetition. He strode to the door, his feet crunching in the debris, lost in his own mind and surrounded by the aura of power sparking across his body. Light bled from every inch of him. He braced himself in front of the crumbling amber wall. The dark shape on the other side paused and cocked her head, staring in at the man.

He could feel the terrible tension in the room, so he glanced over his shoulder at Kate and winked. Then he wedged his fingers into the cracks in the amber and began to push. His arms quivered with effort. Fissures in the orange grew deeper. He grunted one last time and the giant crystal shattered into tiny pieces. His hand snaked out immediately and seized the werewolf by her leather armor. "Do come in."

He dragged the surprised Gretta against him. He clamped his arm around hers, then twisted her neck tight against his inner elbow. He dragged her deeper into the room. She snarled in shock.

"Go!" Simon shouted. "All of you."

"Hold her, Simon." Malcolm ran toward the grappling pair and leveled his pistol at Gretta's head. The werewolf, even locked in Simon's clutch, swung her axe at the Scotsman, spoiling his aim. He got off one shot.

The bullet glanced across her skull, creating a deep furrow of silver. Gretta screamed and flailed at him again with her weapon. Her momentum took one of Simon's feet off the ground and she spun with a roar, lifting the magician into the air. With a massive flex of her shoulders, Gretta shrugged Simon off into the wall, where he crashed down to the floor

"Why doesn't anyone listen to me?" Simon muttered dizzily as he struggled to his feet.

A howl sounded from across the chamber. Charlotte twisted in the final throes of an agonizing transformation. The young werewolf tossed her hairy head and growled.

Gretta looked surprised. "Charlotte. So here's where you got to. We'll talk about your punishment later, but help me kill these wretches."

Charlotte growled and leapt on Gretta's back, her jaws clamping on the giant's corded neck. The young werewolf was dwarfed by Gretta. With a furious snarl, Gretta reached around and grasped Charlotte by the scruff of the neck, pulling her off, fur and flesh tearing as she did. She shook the young werewolf angrily.

"What is wrong with you, Charlotte?"

The young werewolf's claws found purchase and gouged deep grooves in Gretta's forearms.

Gretta's eyes narrowed as her lips curled upward into a fearsome snarl. "I should have killed you when you stood up in front of me in Samuel's hovel."

Gretta dredged a growl from deep inside her belly and it turned into a horrific howl of fury that shook the room. She raised Charlotte over her head with one arm and smashed her into the floor. The equipment around the chamber rattled. The massive werewolf raised a foot and brought it down onto Charlotte. There was an audible crunching sound and the girl gave a muffled scream. Gretta pressed her formidable weight down into Charlotte, grunting with the effort to drive the life from the traitor.

A hand grasped Gretta's massive hairy arm and yanked her around. A furious Simon looked up at her. He smashed a fist into her snout. She staggered. He backhanded her and she lurched a few more steps away. Gretta wiped a hand across her dripping mouth. She still clutched the axe in one hand, staring down at Simon with a strange mix of fury and unaccustomed confusion.

As he confronted the werewolf, Simon shouted to the others, his voice reverberating with authority and immense power. "When I say *run,* I don't mean *toward* me. Now get out, the lot of you!"

He heard the sound of feet retreating. Pain from the last blows radiated up his blood-soaked arms, but the bubbling sensation of potent aether still fueled him. However, there was a dreadful numbness collecting in his extremities. He didn't have much time left.

"If you'd care to surrender," Simon gasped to Gretta, "I'd consider it."

The werewolf snarled and threw her axe. It whistled past Simon's ducking head and the blade cleaved deep into the stone floor behind him. He surged forward, smashing another stone fist into her face and knocking her around. Her claws dug into the brick wall to steady herself, but Simon wrapped his arms around her midsection and lifted her into the air. His knees bent but didn't buckle. Gretta heaved about with enough sheer force that it should've shattered Simon's bones, but he held her, grunting with tremendous effort each time she threw her shoulders or kicked out with her massive legs. It was like trying to cradle an enraged tiger while shuffling back slowly toward the rune he had drawn with his blood on the floor.

Gretta must have caught a glimpse of the faint glow of the rune behind her. She snarled viciously and threw herself with renewed vigor against his grip, clawing at Simon. Luckily, she could barely reach him, so she just clipped him with the tips of her sharp fingers. She roared and grasped his hands clasped across her stomach. She ripped at his flesh, trying to tear his hands away. Simon gritted his teeth, screaming through a clenched mouth, continuing to haul the thrashing beast closer to the circle, step by unsteady step.

They passed the axe embedded in the stone floor. The werewolf grabbed the long handle and Simon's progress jerked to a stop. He felt the power of the rune circle wafting up just at his back, but Gretta was still outside it. She used the haft of the steady axe for leverage and his foot slipped as she tugged herself a few inches farther away. Simon braced himself, leaning back, crying out as muscles of stone strained to the edge of cracking. Still the great beast was immovable. His aether was fading and his strength along with it. If he released his hold now, he would be ripped to shreds.

Suddenly Kate appeared in the door and rushed in, her hair flying. Her hand drew back as she approached the struggling werewolf. Gretta continued to pull herself forward with the axe, paying no attention to Kate. The beast was bent forward at the waist, fighting against Simon, who was red-faced with strain. Kate popped the cork off a small vial and threw it in the werewolf's face.

Gretta screamed in pain, and Simon felt the creature jolt, losing her grip on the axe. He tightened her against him with all his remaining strength. They fell back onto the floor and he was smashed against the stone by the massive, crushing weight of the werewolf. He nearly lost consciousness, but he felt the caress of the runic circle all around him.

"Simon!" Kate's voice reached him from a great distance. He paused, hesitant to unleash the power with her nearby, but he couldn't draw enough breath to tell her to get out.

Then he heard Malcolm's voice shouting, "I've got Kate. Do what you must."

"No!" Kate's desperate protests grew fainter as the hunter made good on his promise and took her away.

Simon breathed with relief and gave himself to the aether. The power coalesced from the air around the circle, blasting though whatever strange netherworld it existed in, tearing a hole inside him. The eldritch energy stormed through his body and pounded into Gretta. Waves of magic shook the giant creature as if she were nothing, burning hair and shredding muscle. Simon felt the bulk of the figure in his arms shrink as the aether tore her strength from her. The werewolf screamed as she was changed from beast to woman. And then she went from woman to wizened crone, whimpering in fear because she had never been so frail and helpless before. Simon's arms enveloped the shivering cadaverous form in an almost tender embrace.

The aether flood slowed to a trickle. There was nothing left in the man to channel it. He was an empty shell. His heart shuddered laboriously in his chest, desperate to maintain a rhythm. Simon wished he'd had a chance to say good-bye.

To Nick.

Mostly to Kate.

THEY HAD FELT THE INCREDIBLE RUSH OF RAW aether where they crouched in the catacomb. Malcolm swore in Gaelic with a dark expression full of astonishment. Kate sensed the tremendous power wash around them. Penny crouched with her head covered. Hogarth clutched Imogen close to his chest, but she still reached out with her inhuman hand like she was collecting butterflies from the air as if she could see the power the others only felt. Kate held Imogen's other hand tight against her face, whispering soothing words that she didn't feel. This was power Kate, or any of them, had never experienced before. She knew that Simon was a scribe, but she had never thought him capable of this.

When the onslaught slowed, Kate checked on everyone. Her head jerked from side to side. "Where's Charlotte?"

They all looked around, but the girl was gone. No one had seen her slip away. Kate shook her head sadly and started off toward the lab and Simon, but Malcolm stopped her.

"Wait. Wait until we know it's over." His voice was assured even though it was clear he was as anxious as the rest of them.

So they stood their ground for several aching minutes. They listened for Simon's approaching footsteps, praying he would come looking for them, but there was no sound. Finally, Kate could wait no longer. She raced into the cellar of Bedlam. She slid to the door of the operating room and saw Simon's body lying alone on the floor. She shouted and rushed to his side.

"Simon! Simon!" She struggled to lift him into her arms. His head slipped to the side. His torn limbs were slack. She put a hand on his cold, waxy cheek. "Oh God, no. Simon! Can you hear me? Open your eyes. Please. Open your eyes."

With trembling, unwilling fingers, she searched his neck for a pulse. There was none.

Simon Archer was dead.

Kate bent over him, knowing it was too late to protect him now. "Why did you do it? There had to be another way."

Penny crouched behind her. "Oh, Kate. I'm so sorry."

Malcolm watched the women gathered around the body of Simon. He announced with a creaking voice, "I'm going to search the area for Gretta."

When he reached the door, he bumped into another figure. His pistol flashed up into the face of Nick Barker. Nick raised a hand of flame. The two men took a breath, and backed up.

"Where the hell have you been, Barker?" Malcolm snarled.

"Covering the stairs, like I said." Then Nick looked past him and he saw Simon draped across the lap of a sobbing Kate. His expression of annoyance shifted swiftly to shock. "What happened?"

Malcolm shoved the magician against the doorjamb. "You're a liar. How did Gretta get past you? Why aren't you dead instead of him?"

Nick's face grew dark like a storm cloud. "Take your hands off me, Angus, or I'll hurt you in ways you can't imagine." He shoved Malcolm away and went quickly to Simon.

Kate looked up at Nick with accusing eyes. "He's dead."

"You don't know what you're talking about. He's just drained." Nick put a hand on Simon's forehead. He paused as if listening, then he slumped. "No. This can't be."

"You said you were his friend!" Kate shouted. "If you had been here, he wouldn't have sacrificed himself. We could have defeated her together."

"Shut up! Who are you to talk to me about him? Some doxy he met a few weeks ago. He was meant for better things. He sacrificed himself for *you*."

Kate's eyes welled at the kernel of truth in his words, but she shook her head. She wanted this to be Nick's fault, someone's fault. She wanted to hurt him even though she could see the pain on his face and the way his hand trembled over Simon's arm. "He would have done no less for any one of us. That's who he is. But where were you when he needed you? What kind of friend are you?"

"The kind he needs. Give him to me, damn you, and stand back." Nick grabbed Simon's body by the shoulders and seemed shocked by how limp it was. He gave Kate a vicious stare. "Do you want to see him again? Then get back! You can't help him now. None of you. But I can."

Malcolm settled Kate to her feet, and walked the stunned alchemist away from Simon. Penny waited, crouching by the door. Hogarth stood like a statue, still carrying Imogen.

Nick sat cross-legged on the floor, with Simon's head resting in his lap. He took several deep breaths and dug his fingers into Simon's chest. He began to mutter unintelligible words, then repeated them, then again. The sounds grew into a chant. It was more guttural and harsh than the spells whispered by Simon. There was anger and grime in it. Putrid green wisps swirled around both men, living and dead, old eldritch power that made Kate feel ill. It was the same dread power that she had felt Nick use at the Gillingham party so long ago, only more sickening than before.

Then Kate felt a warm breeze ruffle her hair. It caught her skirt and whipped Malcolm's greatcoat. The wind grew stronger and hotter like it was blasting off a desert. She put a hand above her eyes as if she sensed blowing sand scraping across her face.

Small sparks of lightning circled Nick's body, occasionally shooting out with sharp, cracking arcs. The glow created a halo around him. He slowly bent over and pressed his forehead to Simon's. He began to shake. The lightning traveled from Nick's fingers across Si-

mon's torn chest. Odd, spidery lightning shapes walked
their way down Simon's form.

Then Nick threw his head back and a wrenching howl
tore from his throat. It looked as if his hands plunged
deep into Simon's chest and Simon appeared to be made
of nothing more than light. Nick's scream went silent.
His head was still up and his mouth gaped wide.

The lightning vanished and Nick fell over on his side.

Kate ran to Nick, but when she touched him, he was
white-hot. She shouted and pulled her hand back, confused, watching. Her gaze drifted to Simon. His torn
flesh was whole. To her shock, he moved! His name fell
from her lips.

Simon's eyes cracked open and he saw Kate's stunned
face. He raised a hand and wiped his forehead. "Oh,
hello, Kate. Bit warm. Could you open a window, please?"

She gasped and fell at his side. The heat pouring off
Nick was so enormous that she grabbed Simon and
pulled him off his friend's legs. His head bumped the
stone floor and he exclaimed in pain. She pulled him up
and embraced him. Simon pressed a comforting hand
against her back.

"This is rather nice," he murmured.

"Simon?" came Nick's whisper. "Is that you, old boy?"

Simon stiffened at the sight of his crumpled friend
with an exclamation of alarm. With Kate still supporting him, he reached for the prone man. Despite the sear-
ing heat, he grasped Nick's hand. "Are you all right,
Nick? What have you done?"

The older magician smiled and lowered his head to
rest on the floor. "We're all square now."

Chapter Thirty-one

SIMON PULLED OPEN THE DOOR OF THE DEVIL'S Loom and welcomed the rush of warmth. His bones ached from the cold English air even though it had been a week since the fight at Bedlam. His strength had returned, but there was a gnawing sense of vulnerability inside him. Voices greeted him happily. He had been conspicuously absent from his regular bench over the last week or so. All was well with the crowd, however, when he entered.

"Simon!" A hefty barmaid seized his arm with a great smile on her lips. "How are you, love? We were wondering where you'd gotten to."

"Busy, Rebecca. Just busy."

"I thought as much." She escorted him to the bar past cheerful waves and claps on the back. "Some felt you had to abandon us lot if you were to keep receiving your invitations from viscounts and such."

"Hardly. I'd abandon the viscounts first."

"I knew you would, dear." Rebecca handed him a pint. "Other wags said you were on the run from a jealous husband."

Simon relished the common feel of the glass in his hand. "That's impossible because I'm saving myself for you."

"Wait no longer then!" She slapped her hand on the bar and shouted to the barman. "I quit!"

The barman rolled his eyes at her and gave Simon a pleasant nod as he headed to the front.

Simon laughed. "Have you seen Nick?"

"I have. He's in the corner. Been there a few hours."

Simon patted her plump arm and went toward the hidden booth in the corner. There sat Nick, looking up expectantly. "Mind if I join you?"

The older magician jerked his chin toward the empty seat.

Simon settled in and tried to appear comfortable. Nick seemed relaxed enough, as always, but there was a curtain of distance around him that Simon had never felt before the Bedlam affair. Nick's eyes were furtive. Silence dragged on.

Finally, Simon said something he rarely said to Nick, or needed to, "How have you been?"

"Good. Yourself?"

"Bit melancholy. Just been by Beatrice's grave. Otherwise, though, I feel rather well, thanks to you."

Nick nodded with satisfaction. "Gratified to hear it. I trust Beatrice is pleased now that you've stepped from the shadows to become a hero."

"I don't know about that, but I sleep better at night."

A moment of silence drifted between them like a thick London fog.

Simon coughed. "The newspapers have already lost interest in Dr. White's disappearance and the horrific conditions of the hospital. It's all been shunted over to a parliamentary committee to clean up."

"What about all those deformed atrocities that White created?"

"From what I hear through sources, the homunculi are all dead and gone. I assume without the doctor to maintain them, they just collapsed eventually. A dead man's switch of sorts."

"And the Anstruther sister?"

"Imogen still lives. It seems probable that she was saved, in a terrible sense, because Dr. White never completed her transformation. Kate is working day and night, trying to find a way to undo what White did to the poor girl." Simon tightened his mouth sadly. "We've no idea what will become of her. I don't know how much of her is truly in there. Kate will never abandon her, that much I know."

"Foolish. What good is life to that thing now? And why bother coddling it when it might just turn to a pile of mush any minute?"

"That's an idiotic statement," Simon replied harshly. "We're all going to die. Today. Tomorrow. In ten seconds. That's no excuse to stop trying."

Nick tilted his head and drank.

Simon sighed. "Let me ask you something, from a purely scholarly point of view. Student to teacher."

Nick eyed him sarcastically.

Simon continued, "What did you do to me at Bedlam? How did you bring me back? Kate assures me I was quite dead."

"Kate may not know everything, contrary to her own opinion. You were salvageable by using the necromancy you hate."

Simon paled. "You mean vivimancy?"

Nick shrugged. "Use the polite euphemism if you wish, but the world is too dangerous to be so naïve."

"But I'm relatively certain that I'm not a reanimated corpse. I'm alive. Is it possible you've been the most powerful mage on Earth all this time without telling me?"

"No." Nick took a deep breath. "As you often note, I am a dabbler. Possessor of many skills, master of none.

I mixed a bit of this and a bit of that, necromancy and elementalism."

"I see. And what did it cost you?"

"I have no idea."

"You must. Necromancy drains life from the user. Magic isn't free, as you well know."

"What did you sacrifice, Simon? You gave up your life to stop Gretta, who may or may not have been stopped since we have no idea where she went. That seemed a stupid trade."

"I'd do it again tomorrow to keep everyone safe."

"That doesn't make it any less stupid. You must be proud of yourself. You took out two of the Bastille Bastards. Your days of anonymity are over. Your pointless grandstanding just put you on the map for every crazed mage out there to notice."

Simon rapped the table with his glass. "You may have noticed we were not talking about me. Now, what did you do to yourself in order to save me?"

"Nothing at all. I'm the same lovable Nick."

"You're lying. I can look at you and tell you're lying. I've always been able to tell when you're lying."

"Oh have you?" Nick threw back his head and laughed uproariously. "Simon, your entire problem is that you can't tell when *anyone* is lying, including yourself."

"Then just tell me, for God's sake. Why play games? What did saving me cost you?"

Nick pursed his lips in thought. He looked bemused. "Just a few years."

"A few years? It aged you? You look the same to me. Your magic always allowed you an extraordinarily long life span."

"It did. However, from this day forward, I will grow a little older every year until I finally die just like everyone else in this pub."

Simon sat back, stunned. "I'm sorry. I never wanted that."

"Stop it!" Nick snarled. "It was my choice, not yours. I can be noble, too."

"I'm sorry. I didn't mean to insult you. Why don't we head to Hartley Hall, where we can—"

"No." Nick drained his pint.

"I'm sorry?"

"No. Simon, I'm not staying."

"What do you mean?"

"I'm leaving London. It's lost its luster." Nick leaned forward. "Come with me."

"I can't. Not now. You know that."

Nick rolled his eyes in exasperation. "Simon, there's nothing to hold you here. You've done your Galahad bit. You did what you could for the Anstruthers, which was none of our affair from the beginning. And it nearly cost you everything."

"Kate needed help. She and Imogen would both be dead now if we hadn't intervened."

"Job well done then. White is dead. Gretta is dead or gone. You owe those women nothing more." Nick's voice grew more insistent. "Come on. Come with me, old boy. We'll go to Rome or Constantinople or Mandalay. If you miss England, we'll come back when it's over."

Simon paused, dread rising in him. "When what is over? We destroyed Dr. White and Gretta. Her army is dead or scattered. They were at the root of all the disturbances that have been troubling London. It's done."

Nick rubbed his chin angrily and sat back. "Look, it should just be the two of us again. That worked well, didn't it? Everything was easier then. Don't you want it to be easy again? There's so much more for you to learn."

"What aren't you telling me?"

"Everyone forever doubts my intentions! I'm sick of it!" Nick shouted. Then he grew quiet. "Listen, Simon, you must come with me. The world is about to split open. I'm asking you, I'm begging you, come with me."

Simon frowned. "You know my answer."

"Why, for God's sake!" Nick shook his head and closed his eyes, almost as if suppressing tears. "Simon, the next time you die, it's final. You should do your best to ensure there isn't a next time. So I'm telling you for your own good, because I'm the only one who will, you are not the magician you think you are. You're not the *man* you think you are."

Simon stared angrily at his friend. His fingers clawed at the tabletop. Breath poured heavy from flared nostrils. His voice was strained with pain and hurt. "Thank you. Your confidence is bracing."

Nick stood up and started across the floor. A few steps from the table, he turned back. "Are you coming with me?"

"No, Nick." Simon looked at him as if he were suddenly a stranger.

"Damn it, Simon, you don't understand anything that's going on around you."

"You're certainly right about that."

"Well, I'll not be the one to teach you." Nick looked at Simon for another moment, then he shook his head and left the pub.

SIMON GLANCED UP FROM WHERE HE SAT PON-dering. Kate and Malcolm stood beside his table. The crowd was thinner now in the Devil's Loom. His half-finished ale was still in front of him.

Kate eyed Nick's empty glass on the table and the displaced chair. "You found him?"

"Yes."

She scanned the crowd at the bar. "Where is he?"

"Gone."

"Gone where?" Malcolm asked casually.

Simon shrugged.

"Oh." Kate raised her eyebrows in surprise. "Do you mean he's gone, and not coming back?"

"That's what I mean."

"No loss," the Scotsman said. "From what I could see, the only good he ever did was bringing you back to life. And it's still up for debate whether that was good."

Simon prepared an angry retort but gave an empty laugh instead.

Kate slid onto the bench next to him. She tapped his glass. "How many is this for you?"

"Just the half."

Kate gasped theatrically and placed a cool hand on his forehead. "You don't feel feverish." She allowed her hand to gently run back across his hair. "Malcolm, fetch a round."

"Here?" The Scotsman looked disgusted. "Can't we go somewhere that's been aired out since the Great Fire?"

"I like it here." Kate regarded the warm, jubilant faces reveling in their daily life. "It's homey."

Malcolm went to the bar, muttering.

Kate leaned on her elbow. "I'm sorry about Nick. I know he was your friend, but it's not really a surprise, is it?"

"I suppose not, in hindsight."

She shoved his shoulder. "You're not going to have some romantic poet's collapse while you mourn his departure, are you?"

"I may mourn the death of your sense of tact. Beyond that, I suppose it depends on what happens next." He searched her face and the warmth in her eyes was like being held in her arms again.

"The future is bright, Simon." Kate laid a comforting hand over his.

For a second, Simon saw Beatrice's face staring at him across the table. He then broke into a cynical grin at Kate. "I once thought I had a very bright future. A man of vast potential. Years later, that's still what I have. Potential."

"Nonsense. You've created a remarkable thing."

"Have I?" Simon laughed quietly. "I can't think of it."

"Look at me." Kate gripped his hand. "Me. Malcolm. Penny. You've taken those separate things and made them into something stronger and more resilient than any of us could've imagined. We did an amazing thing. Together. You did that. No one else did. No one else could have." She dipped a finger into her collar and pulled out a chain with the gold key. She looped it off over her head. "And we have this."

Simon laughed. "Ah yes. The key. What did White say it was, a device for instantaneous translocation? That's grand, and there it is. And what does it do? Nothing. I'm suspicious of that thing, Kate. Magic is full of philosopher's stones that turn out to be merely stones."

Kate ignored his bitterness. She dangled the key from her finger, letting it swing back and forth.

His intense eyes tracked the object. "Really, Kate, we have no idea about that key. White was obviously insane; why should we believe anything he said?" However, a glimmer of begrudging interest replaced the anger in his gaze.

Malcolm abruptly returned, carrying three pints. He settled into a seat and slid ales to the others. "So, why did Barker run off? He hated Kate?"

"What?" Kate snapped, dropping the key to the table.

"No," Simon replied casually. "Well yes, but that's not why he left."

She scowled. "Not that I care now, but do tell."

"He was frightened."

Kate and Malcolm exchanged glances. She asked, "Frightened of what?"

"I don't know. He wouldn't tell me." Simon looked at the two with concern. "If there's something that has Nick scared, it's certain to be unpleasant."

Malcolm drank. "That's too bad because what we've seen so far has been delightful." He set the glass down heavily. "I've something to say, and I'd best do it now or it won't happen."

Simon and Kate regarded the Scotsman, whose quiet frown was the only betrayal of his troubled emotions. Finally Malcolm said, "Thank you."

Simon raised a confused eyebrow. "Are you talking to me? It's difficult to know."

"I am talking to you, you ass." The Scotsman stared at the table. "You saved my life at Hartley Hall. Gretta pulled half the house down on me and I would have been crushed to death had you not saved me."

"Hardly half the house. A bit of a wall, part of the upper floor. And recall, I saved myself too."

"Aye, but you could have done so without including me. I'm grateful to you. I can tell you that once I thought little of you, but I was wrong. You are an honorable man, and while there are times I would as soon throw you through that window, I'd stand with you if you need me. And let's say no more about it."

Kate drank and slammed her glass down like a sailor. "Yes, these maudlin scenes are so emasculating."

Simon smiled. "Thank you, Malcolm. I appreciate your words."

The Scotsman grunted and drank.

Simon looked at Kate's fingers. Her knuckles were still raw from the battle. Her usually flawless face was marred by bruises and scratches. He winced at her unconsciously. "Kate, I'm bound to say that you should think about your safety, and that of Imogen. I have no idea what I'll be involved with in the future. There's no reason you should put yourself in danger."

"No reason?" She yanked her hand free. "You're the one always standing in the line of fire, like some stalwart knight of old. I learn from your bloody example. I will do all I can for Imogen, and I damn well need your help for that. I don't care how dangerous you think the world will become, we are connected now. Do I make myself clear?"

"You do," Simon whispered, caught up in Kate's passion. She was extraordinary.

She recovered her demeanor with a slight clearing of her throat. Then she pushed the key across the rough table. "Here. I want you to have this. It was your mother's."

"No. I suspect your father gave it to her to hide it. Anyone who was chasing your father or my father to find this key would've had no idea my mother was connected to them. It doesn't truly belong to either of us."

"Then it belongs to both of us."

Simon touched the key reverently and nodded at her. He then regarded the Scotsman. "Malcolm, will you be staying with us?"

The Scotsman gestured toward the ale. "Well, almost certainly until I finish my drink. Then I'll decide about a second one."

Simon grinned and lifted his pint. "Cheers."

"Cheers," Kate and Malcolm replied.

The glasses clinked together as the key glittered in the candlelight, casting sharp reflections on the three faces.

If you loved *The Shadow Revolution*,
be sure not to miss the next book in the thrilling
Crown & Key trilogy:

The Undying Legion

by

Clay Griffith and Susan Griffith

Here's a special preview.

And stay tuned for the final book
in the Crown & Key trilogy,
The Conquering Dark,
which will follow next month!

Chapter One

MALCOLM MACFARLANE LET THE FRIGID LON-
don night swallow him. A cold hard rain had begun to
fall. His thick, wool coat had soaked up so much water
that it felt like he carried an additional load of ammunition on his broad shoulders. He wiped the excess water
from his face, brushing it back over his coal-black hair,
which was pulled and tied with a strap of leather. Tonight, he would do what he did best. Hunt. He had
spent the last few months tracking down the stragglers
from Gretta Aldfather's werewolf pack and putting silver bullets in their animal brains.

Malcolm had hunted the wild places of the Highlands
and beyond all his life, studying the spore of monsters
until it was his art form. Here in this city, however, he
found it was not so easy. The maze of filthy hovels and
wash of humanity made such skills almost worthless.
So he had created makeshift ways to track quarry here.
He found that the poor and wretched were fonts of information. Like water holes or game trails, he learned
to go where unfortunates huddled to sniff out hints of
monsters.

Malcolm liked to believe it was the prospect of information and not the warm glow and promise of a dry
place that led him to the soup kitchen in St. Giles. He

was surprised to see it open since it was well past midnight. He had made a habit of haunting the poorhouses and soup kitchens because the people of the street heard and saw a great many things. They were the first to know when something was amiss, or a beast was stirring. This place would make the third one this evening. He stepped inside and the frigid cold lifted. Unlike the other hovels that made him despair over the condition of man, this one made him feel safe and contented.

His eyes found, at the far side of the dingy hall, a mouselike woman who was cleaning up after serving late supper to the unfortunates. Her bonneted head and her small hands focused on gathering dirty utensils and used plates. She was dressed in plain clothes and wore small round spectacles. When her gaze lifted briefly to Malcolm, it fell again toward the pile of dishes in front of her. Next to her were baskets of extra clothing and odds and ends for those in need. The woman left her place behind the table and snatched a wool scarf from the basket. She held it out to Malcolm as she approached.

"We have finished serving for the evening," she said with a smile, "but I can find a bowl of soup for you if you'll wait."

"No, thank you. I'm not hungry." Malcolm dripped water from his sleeve to the floor. Drops glistened on his dark hair and thick eyelashes. "And I am not in need of your scarf."

"Please." Her voice had the timbre of a frightened rabbit. "I made it myself, and you will have need of it before this night is through. I can't have you falling into an ague from the damp."

He stared at her homely features. "I've seen worse weather in Scotland, and me in nothing but a kilt." She blushed but still she wrapped the soft grey wool around his neck.

She seemed so unassuming that her sudden boldness

took Malcolm aback. He wasn't one to accept charity, but he wouldn't offend the young woman. Perhaps he looked like a bedraggled vagrant after so many nights on the streets. He would give the scarf to someone more in need than he but let the woman think she had helped his poor soul.

"Tell me then, miss, have you seen anything strange about? Anything out of the ordinary?"

"Aside from yourself?" she asked, obviously judging his accent. "You are far from home, I hear."

"Aye, that's for sure." Malcolm let a little extra lonely brogue pepper his words to stir the tender heart of this woman. "But I'm here to do a job. And it would help me if you could say if you've heard talk of unusual events about."

The woman sized up Malcolm and took on a look of sadness that actually disturbed him a bit. She whispered, "I take your appearance as something of a sign then. Because some of the people here have been sorely frightened."

"Tell me."

"Tonight, a man said he saw figures robed in red with a young woman in white."

Malcolm exhaled in disappointment at the story. Clearly not a sign of Gretta's old pack. "Is that some local haint?"

"Not to my knowledge, sir. He seemed quite disturbed by it. If you're here indeed to help, you might look into it."

"Where was this weird visitation?"

"St. George's Bloomsbury, sir." The young woman swallowed hard as if gulping down her terror now that she had spoken it aloud.

"I thank you for your information."

"Bless you, sir."

Malcolm opened the frightened woman's hand and placed coins into her palm. "For the poor."

She grasped Malcolm's arm tightly and the gratitude in her eyes moved the hunter. "The Devil has great power."

"Well I know it. Perhaps after I take a look, I'll return for some of that soup."

She bowed her bonneted head shyly. "It will be waiting when you need it, along with a friendly word."

Malcolm smiled at her, thinking that her face could have been pleasing if not tightened in some permanent grimace of penance. "One can't have too many friends, eh?"

"No."

"Thank you for the scarf." With that, he went back out into the cold, miserable night, where he was more at home.

THE GREAT WHITE BLOCK OF ST. GEORGE'S BLOOMSbury looked serene in the misty lamp glow. Malcolm could barely make out the odd, pyramid-like steeple around which the haunting dark shapes of lions and unicorns clambered while King George I looked down disdainfully in his pagan Roman attire. The church squatted between two tall neighboring edifices, enhancing its resemblance to a classical temple.

In its shadow, Malcolm saw two dim figures lurking under the massive colonnades by the south doors. Not too surprising. The spiritual presence of the church called vagrants and the poor to its doors whether they were open or not. But when Malcolm went round the side, he saw three more shapes in the narrow space between the buildings. There was a flare of a cigar end as well as a faint trace of spicy smoke. Malcolm came closer.

These were no vagrants. They were well fed and muscular, all with beefy shoulders and ham-sized fists. Guards of some sort, apparently meant to make sure no one disturbed whatever was happening inside the church.

That wouldn't do. Not werewolves, but suspicious enough for Malcolm to work off a bit of frustration on. These men were probably hired in a local pub for a couple hours' work. There was no need for the use of firearms. Malcolm stepped out of the shadows and strode up to the men. They started, as he was sure he looked like a wraith coming out of the mists in his black garb.

"Waiting for services?" he asked them in a friendly manner.

"None of yer business, Angus," snarled the man with the cigar, noting Malcolm's brogue. He was a big man with square shoulders and a noggin to match. "Best you head back where you come from."

"Nothing interesting happening there." Malcolm looked past him to the side door. "Seems like something interesting here though."

The second man pulled a bludgeon from his ragged wool coat. "Does this make you change your mind? You're no match for all of us."

"You're mistaken," was Malcolm's answer, flinging back his own black coat to show the twin Lancaster pistols.

"Hellfire!" said the man as he pointed at the weapons with his measly club. "What are you hunting? Bear?"

The big fellow laughed. "All's quiet here, Angus. Just move along."

"Is it?" Malcolm asked. "Or is there something going on inside that church you don't want me to see?"

"Folks need to stay out for a few hours. Why don't you come back at dawn?" A third man drew a thin, wicked blade.

"Step aside." Malcolm had to give them credit. Just

the sight of his weapons was usually enough to cow most men, even a werewolf once or twice. These men were obviously paid very well for their bravado.

The two men who were armed came at Malcolm quickly, thinking they would catch him off guard before he could pull his weapon. They were wrong. The pistol rose in a blur and he shot one man, shattering his forearm, and the knife dropped with a scream. Twisting about, Malcolm slammed the gun across the face of the man who had raised his cudgel.

Malcolm rammed his shoulder into the big man's chest. So fast did the Scotsman move that the man could do little more than cry out in surprise. They went down in a tumble and he lost his grip on the pistol. Malcolm rolled away as a meaty fist drove into the ground where his neck would have been. He had to be quick and keep his opponents off balance. The big man was dangerous and needed to be disabled fast. Malcolm made it to his feet first.

Two new arrivals came running, and a red-bearded brute jumped into the fray. His chin lifted as he raised a wooden club. Malcolm swung a fast left jab into the man's jaw. Red Beard's head snapped around and Malcolm planted a right cross on the man's temple. He dropped.

As Malcolm whirled back to the big brute, Red Beard's partner grabbed him around the chest from behind. Malcolm used him as a brace and brought a boot into the brute's midsection. The man fell back with a grunt of pain. Then the Scotsman threw his head back and connected with the nose of the man holding him. Restraining arms dropped and Malcolm spun about with a wild look.

His opponent gave a wicked swipe with a razor, but it caught in the folds of Malcolm's grey scarf instead of his jugular. He grabbed the man's arm and shoved his palm under the elbow and pushed up. The arm cracked and the man flopped to the ground with shrieks of pain.

The big thug, shaking himself, rose from the ground. He plunged again at the man in black with fists flailing, and the hunter let him come, slipping under to land a power blow of his own. It crushed the man's lips and sent teeth flying. Malcolm's fist darted out again, but this time it merely glanced off as his opponent shifted his head. Malcolm stumbled a step beyond the big man. The brute took advantage of the off-balance Scotsman and landed a hard blow on Malcolm's ribs. It took the breath out of him.

Malcolm ducked just in time to avoid the thug's next bone-crushing blow. He felt the wind as it passed over his head. He also heard the splintering of the wooden planks along the wall. Spinning on his heel, Malcolm locked both his hands together and brought them down onto the big man's unprotected back. The behemoth shuddered and fell to his hands and knees.

Malcolm turned to face the thug with the cudgel, who had gotten up finally. The man came in swinging madly. Malcolm dodged under the first two swings, then stood up quickly, smashing his elbow under the brute's chin. The man's jaw shut hard and his head jerked back. He staggered and allowed Malcolm to deliver a hard right cross. This time the man went down and didn't move.

Malcolm didn't turn around fast enough before the behemoth struck him hard in the side of the face. The sheer impact rattled his bones to the core. Malcolm fell into the dirt, a cloud of dust rising beneath him, his breath going with it. He struggled to stand and got a boot in his face for the effort. The world went black for a second, and when his vision returned, he found himself in the grip of the huge man. Iron arms were wrapped around his chest so tightly that breathing was no longer a possibility. Malcolm groaned with the agony that spread across his ribs.

He struggled to shake off the darkness and get his feet beneath him, but not before the big man whirled around, slamming the hunter against a wall. His right shoulder took the brunt of it and his arm erupted in agony. He didn't have much time. There was a roar in his ears. His numbing mind tried desperately to find a way out of the bear hold.

Malcolm pulled a pistol from across his hip. He couldn't lift the weapon up, but he could point it down. Praying the leg he was shooting wasn't his, he fired. The bullet blew through the big man's knee. The scream that came almost brought a smile to Malcolm's lips except that he was too busy trying to breathe and stay conscious.

The big man bellowed in agony and dropped Malcolm to clutch his shattered knee. Slumping to the ground, the Scotsman rolled to the side, sucking in a great lungful of sweet air. Letting go of his bleeding leg, the man came unsteadily at Malcolm once more. Malcolm slipped under a clumsy blow and brought his hand up, and with the heel of it caught the brute full in the face. Then a series of strikes forced the man's head side to side. They were short and quick, flicking in so fast they were just a blur of movement. The man's big frame shuddered before momentum carried him past Malcolm, thudding to his knees. He cried out in more agony, clutching his injured leg.

Malcolm's hand brushed across the blood dripping into his eye. His strength was rapidly running out. Amazingly, the lame man strained one more time to rise, fear in his eyes as Malcolm took one step toward him. Using his bloody left fist like a club now, and putting the weight of his whole body behind it, he struck the man on the neck below and behind the ear. It made a sickening, dull sound and the big brute's eyes rolled white. He slumped into the dirt with a groan and did not move again.

The sudden relief of victory swept through Malcolm. He stared down at his lame and bloody attackers. Not one of them was conscious. The hunter was straight and deadly and utterly still, yet every line of him was eager and alive.

"Done, are ya?" he spat out anyway. "Because I can keep going."

There was no answer so he limped back to the steps and shoved open the door of the church. Inside, a faint glow beckoned from the right. All else was cast into deep shadows. He stepped through the pews and saw, in a ring of light on the floor, a distant shape, as pale as the cold tile it lay upon. Malcolm's jaw tightened. The splayed figure was female. Her chest was a bloody mess. She had been flayed open to expose the organs inside.

Malcolm was too late.